Eric Wilder

Primal Creatures

Gondwana Press

Edmond, Oklahoma

Other books by Eric Wilder

Ghost of a Chance
Murder Etouffee
Name of the Game
A Gathering of Diamonds
Over the Rainbow
Big Easy
Just East of Eden
Lily's Little Cajun Cookbook
Morning Mist of Blood
Prairie Sunset – of Love and Magic
Big Billy's Little Texas Cookbook
Simply Southern
Southern Comfort Food Cookbook
City of Spirits
Mama Mulate's Little Creole Cookbook

Gondwana Press LLC
1800 Canyon Park Cir., Ste 401
Edmond, OK 73013
gondwanapress@gmail.com

For information on books by Eric Wilder
www.ericwilder.com
www.gondwanapress.com

Front Cover by Higgins & Ross Photography/Design

ISBN: 978-0-9791165-6-8

Acknowledgments

I wish to thank G. Terry Felts for his many contributions to this book. A close friend, Terry has been an undercover police officer, private detective, petroleum landman, researcher, and death investigator. He owned the crematory where I learned, first hand, about cremation. He and wife Deborah own I Systems where they locate missing persons every day. They also own Private Autopsy Services. Terry, quite literally, has forgotten more about investigation, particularly death investigation, than most people will ever know in a lifetime.

For Marilyn

Primal Creatures

A novel by
Eric Wilder

Prolog

Fingers of lightning laced the cloudy sky as the sounds of lovemaking issued from a patch of tall grass, a woman's throaty voice disturbing the night's stillness. For just a moment, a full yellow moon poked through the clouds.

"Stop it, Rance. You know I don't like it that way."

Laughter followed the woman's words. "That's a first. I didn't think there was any perversion you didn't like."

"Maybe I'm just in the mood for something new."

"Oh? Tell me."

The woman had no time to explain as an ominous howl echoed across the shallow waters of the bay, momentarily interrupting the midnight chorus of frogs and crickets.

"What was that?" she asked, squeezing the man's arm.

"Sounded like a wolf to me."

"Oh shit! Are there wolves on the island?"

"No one ever told me if there are. Maybe we should

find our clothes and go to your cabin."

"Pussy," she said.

She squealed when Rance bit her neck. They both stopped what they were doing when another roar, closer this time, riveted their attention again.

"Whatever that was, I'm not liking it. Let's get the hell out of here."

"Our clothes are down by the water," the woman said. "Whatever's out there is between us and the bay."

"Forget the clothes. Sounds to me like it's circling us. We need to move it."

Confused for a moment, they didn't know which way to go. When a tree limb cracked ten feet away, the woman screamed.

"Oh shit! It's right behind us."

Not waiting for her companion, she sprang to her feet, squealing again as the underbrush resonated with the sound of something extremely large moving toward them. The man tried to follow but fell when he caught his foot on a tree limb.

"Oh shit!" he called. "I twisted my ankle."

Ignoring his cry of pain, she sprinted through the tall grass, the full moon lighting her way. Tripping on a vine, she stumbled face first into moist earth as another howl pierced the night. It was followed by crazed growling and her lover's tortured screams as the creature that was stalking them began its attack.

Fear surged up her spine when she stopped and turned, watching for a moment as the shadow of some creature ripped into his victim. Sensing her presence it wheeled around, red eyes blazing and bloody fangs flashing in the moonlight.

Grabbing her breast, as if her heart might suddenly stop beating, she screamed again. Revived by the sound of her own voice, she ran from the melee, unmindful of briars scratching her bare skin, or broken branches bruising her feet. She didn't stop running until she reached the berm surrounding Goose Island.

Unable to climb over the concrete structure, she sank

to the damp ground and covered her face with her hands, listening to a dying man's last cry for help. Though she waited for the creature to find her, the attack never came. Instead, dark clouds opened, releasing a driving rain.

When the deluge finally ceased, the howls and cries of distress had ended, and moonlight illuminated the footbridge across the berm. Unmindful of her nudity as she climbed over the bridge, she raced toward the distant monastery without looking back.

Chapter One

When a glass of cold water in the face awakened me from a drunken stupor, I sprang up from the bed, staring into the blue eyes of an angry, redheaded woman.

"Is that what it takes to get you out of bed?"

"Chrissie, I. . ."

She didn't let me finish the sentence.

"I felt so sorry for you when you showed up at my door. I understand your ex-wife died of cancer, and your runway model joined a convent. I've heard it over and over. I'm tired of hearing about it."

"Chrissie. . ."

Her finger pointed at her chin when she said, "Up to here. Grow some balls and stop feeling sorry for yourself. I'm sick to death of all your drama, and I can't abide it anymore. Get out of my bed and out of my life!"

"Chrissie. . ."

"Just get your clothes on and go. I'm done with you for the last time, Wyatt Thomas."

The clear anger in her voice left little room for misinterpretation. Stepping on my shoe when I slid off the bed, I rolled an ankle and sank to my knee.

"I'm going," I said, holding up a palm when she took a step toward me.

"Is that all you have to say?"

"What do you want me to say?"

"Maybe something like thank you Chrissie; you're a remarkable woman Chrissie. Just don't say I love you because I don't believe you anymore."

"Thank you, Chrissie. You saved my life."

"Can it! I don't need you or your lies."

Hesitating a moment, I said, "I thought you needed me as much as I need you."

"For what? Someone to bring you more booze? Cry on my shoulder, and then expect me to have sex with you all night? I'm done, now get out."

"I'm going," I said, pulling on my pants. "I can't find my socks."

A cup whistled past my ear, sending shards of glass through the air when it crashed into the wall.

"Screw your damn socks! Get out of here and don't ever come back."

Chrissie's voice had become increasingly louder. Grabbing the shirt from the bedstead, I slipped it over my shoulders, reached down and clutched my shoes, ducking a vase flying over my head. I was out the door and down the stairs before she had time to find something else to throw.

An elderly couple glared at me as I hurried away. They weren't the only ones that had witnessed the incident. A regular from the Irish pub where Chrissie worked was giving me the evil eye as he hurried up the stairway. He seemed to know where he was going and didn't bother stopping to say hello.

❦

Eight in the morning, Bertram's neighborhood bar was all but empty. Bertram wasn't alone, his collie Lady at his feet, my tailless cat Kisses treading on the countertop, rubbing against his arm. He was polishing a glass with a bar rag, dropping it when he saw me. Lady's tail began banging the floor, and Kisses jumped off the counter, into my arms.

"Well look what the cat drug in," he said with a big Cajun grin. "Guess I don't have to say you look like warmed over shit."

Born on a Terrebonne Parish bayou, Bertram was one hundred percent French Acadian. He had a small mustache, and thinning hair, usually topped by a south Louisiana trapper's hat. His costume aside, you only had to hear him speak to know he was the real deal.

"Glad to see you too, Bertram. Thanks for taking care of Kisses while I was out of pocket."

Fishing under the counter for a bottle of Jack Daniel's, he poured whiskey into a glass. When I pulled up a bar stool, he shoved it in front of me.

"You drink it," I said. "I'm off the sauce."

"Oh yeah? Since when?"

"About an hour ago. Since Chrissie kicked me out of her apartment and explained, in no uncertain terms, how the cow eats the cabbage."

"Maybe you better tell me about it."

"You don't want to hear. My ears are still ringing from the dressing down she gave me. In all my years, I never realized what a son-of-a-bitch I am."

"Well now you know, maybe you can start doing something about it," Bertram said without cracking a smile.

"I needed that," I said.

Bertram's bar was on Chartres Street, in the French Quarter. The building had been there for decades, the same wooden floor and ornate counter built by craftsmen from a different era. Panties, bras, and other assorted fragments of personal apparel—testimonies to losses of inhibitions—decorated the rafters above the place where Bertram usually held court. Taking the whiskey, he sipped it with a wink and a sly smile and then replaced it with lemonade in a tall glass of ice.

"You're welcome," he said. "I been wondering what happened to you. Kisses, here, was kinda getting used to me and Miss Lady."

"I can see," I said, rubbing the cat that hadn't left my arms since she'd jumped into them.

"You look fine. Are you okay, I mean about Desire and all?"

Desire was the beautiful woman I'd fallen in love with that had left me and joined a convent after the suicide of her twin sister Dauphine. Bertram rested his elbows on the countertop, staring at me with his dark eyes, waiting for an answer to a question I was still wondering about myself.

"Everything's feeling strange, though my mind's a lot clearer. Chrissie helped a lot."

"I thought you said she kicked you out."

"Sometimes a kick in the head is what it takes. She said I don't need a mother and that she doesn't need a dysfunctional drunk of a son."

"Brutal."

"It's what I needed, not another bottle of Black Jack."

"When did you figure it out?" he asked.

"About halfway through her rant; after I'd ducked the cup and vase she threw at me. I was almost dressed when it crashed against the wall. I just grabbed my shirt and headed for the door."

"I see you ain't got no socks on," he said.

"Hell, I'm lucky to have my pants and shirt."

"You're smiling so it must not be too bad."

"Hey, I finally remembered why I left her in the first place. Remind me not to get serious with a redheaded Scottish lass again, no matter how pretty she is."

"You're right about one thing. She's a good looking woman."

"I'm going to send roses and tell her how much she helped me. Then I'm swearing off relationships for a while."

"Good idea. You look about ten pounds lighter. I doubt you'd have lasted another two weeks. You eat lately?"

"Tell you the truth, my mind's a bit fuzzy right now. Then again, I don't remember much since I liberated the bottle of Jack Daniel's from beneath your bar. Has it been two weeks?"

"Give or take a day or two. I'll whip you up some grits and eggs if you're hungry."

"Bertram, you're a life saver."

I waited at the bar, Bertram whistling a Cajun tune as the aroma of cooking eggs wafted from the kitchen. He quickly placed the steaming plate in front of me, along with a bottle of hot sauce, grinning as I sprinkled a liberal dose on the fried eggs and grits.

"Guess the whiskey didn't hurt your stomach any."

"I'll live. What's happened since I left?"

"Mardi Gras ended, and most of the tourists went home. At least for a while."

"Guess I missed it."

Bertram gave his mustache a twist. "Mama Mulate got her wish."

"Oh, and what wish was that?"

"She was jealous about Father Rafael's job as a rent-a-priest with the cruise line. He got her an interview with them, and they hired her to lead a voodoo trip to Jamaica as a rent-a-mambo."

Mama Mulate was my sometime business partner, Tulane English professor, and full-time voodoo mambo. When I had questions, she always had answers.

"You're kidding."

"She and Rafael left port yesterday, bound for Jamaica with a stop in Haiti along the way."

Rafael Romanov had married my ex-wife Mimsy sometime after we'd divorced. We'd become acquainted following her untimely death, at her wake, and soon became friends. Though defrocked, he was technically still a priest. Cruise line passengers are comforted by having a priest on board, performing weddings, conducting services, and so on. A shipping company specializing in cruises had readily hired him, not caring that he was defrocked.

"They'll be gone a while," Bertram said. "Mama thought she'd died and gone to heaven when they called her with the job offer. Pays pretty decent, too."

"Well I'm happy for her. She deserved a break. I could use one myself."

"Your holiday is over. You got a job waiting for you,"

8

he said.

"Oh?"

"You told me to check the answering machine in your room. A man called to see if you're available. Since I didn't know when you'd be back, I took the liberty to give him a call."

"Oh?"

"Said he needed you for two weeks to a month and wanted to know how much you charge."

"What'd you tell him?"

"I said hell yeah, but a job taking that long would cost him ten grand, plus expenses."

"Did he hang up on you?"

"Why hell no. I said you got clients backed up in the wings, waiting for your services."

"You didn't."

"He said money was no issue if you'd put him first in line, that is."

"No way!" I said.

"Then what's this?" he said, pulling a cashier's check out of his cash drawer and showing it to me.

"Oh my God! Bertram, I'm going to make you my business manager."

"You do that. Meantime, just pay me the rent you're behind on because of your moonin' around."

"You got it," I said, unable to suppress the silly grin growing on my face. "Did he say why he needs me?"

"Only that he wants you to call him soon as possible."

Bertram handed me a piece of paper with a phone number on it. Thanking him again, I grabbed Kisses and headed up to my room at the top of the stairs.

❧

I'd rented the apartment upstairs from Bertram's for going on three years. It was small, a single room with a tiny bathroom. Still, it had its charm, and a covered balcony, complete with draping ferns, overlooking Chartres Street.

When the nights weren't too hot or too cold, I'd sit on the balcony in my old rocking chair, enjoying the sounds of tourists passing on the street below. That's where I was my feet propped up on the iron filigree railing, giving Kisses a few well-deserved caresses when I remembered the message from the person that wanted to hire me. I called him from the phone beside my bed.

"This is Wyatt Thomas. I have a note to call you."

"Quinlan Moore. You know who I am?"

"The movie producer?"

"Bingo. I sent your agent a check. I'm sure you've put it in the bank by now."

"What exactly do you want me to do, Mr. Moore?"

"Nothing I can explain over the phone. We're filming in Jackson Square. Can you come by the set?"

"Sure. When?"

"Tomorrow, first thing, if that's not too soon."

"No problem."

"We've got most of the square blocked off while we're filming. Just show security some I.D. and they'll bring you to me. Can you do it?"

"I'm just around the corner," I said.

"Fine, Mr. Thomas. I hope you're not going to flake out on me."

"I'm not a flake, Mr. Moore and my dance card is open."

"Then I'll see you tomorrow."

Chapter Two

Louisiana, and especially New Orleans, is a Mecca for the motion picture industry. Fueled by valuable tax breaks, movies are more advantageous to shoot in Louisiana than in other states. Many successful productions hit the can there. The movie filming down the street from Bertram's was witness to the trend.

Quinlan Moore's production company was shooting scenes in Jackson Square, seemingly oblivious to the tourists, participating extras, or those there just to watch. The director sat at the center of the action on a tall chair, barking out directions that no one seemed to pay much attention to.

His entourage flanked him, tending to his every whim as if he were a star quarterback in a crucial football game. A flock of pigeons, arguing over which one would get the majority of popcorn some tourist had spilled, didn't seem to care. When a young man wearing a jacket that said security approached me, they flew off in a flurry of beating wings.

I glanced up at the frowning young man with muscular arms and a blond crew cut.

"You got business on the set?" he demanded.

"I'm here to see Quinlan Moore. I have an appointment."

"Then show me some identification," he said, not

impressed. After a peek at my I.D., he said, "Come with me. Mr. Moore's waiting for you."

I caught a backward glimpse of the stars as he led me away from the filming. The crowd watched in rapt silence as they exchanged what was apparently a meaningful kiss. I didn't get a chance to see the outcome, but heard applause and encouraging shouts as we walked to an R.V. parked on the street. I waited as he knocked on the door.

"Mr. Moore, your appointment is here."

The young man didn't stick around once the door opened.

"Mr. Thomas?"

"That's me."

"Come in," he said, holding the door open.

The inside of the R.V. looked like an expensive hotel room, complete with original paintings, Persian rugs, and the pungent smell of pot someone had recently smoked. Moore motioned for me to take a seat in a plush, leather chair.

"Get you something to drink?" he asked.

"No thanks."

I watched as he poured himself a glass of vodka from the well-stocked bar. He seemed young and looked nothing like I'd anticipated. Nerdy, in fact, with a little, black mustache much like Bertram's that shouted inexperience. I was wrong.

"You look surprised, Mr. Thomas. Not all the movers and shakers in the movie biz are over sixty."

"I didn't mean to be so obvious with my expressions. I'm sure you're the person most qualified for the job, or else you wouldn't be here."

"Bravo. I can say the same for you. I didn't just choose your name out of the phone book. You come highly recommended."

"Glad to hear that."

"In a town filled with detectives, you're the only one that seems to possess the esoteric qualities I most desire."

"Such as?"

"Someone with a deep understanding of ghosts,

magic, voodoo, and the paranormal. Am I mistaken, Mr. Thomas?"

"Perhaps you give me too much credit. Every citizen of the Big Easy knows about the things you just mentioned."

Moore smiled and sipped his vodka. "I'm convinced no one knows more than you do."

"I hope I don't disappoint."

"I knew you were the best person available when your agent told me your fee. No one would charge that much unless they were the best there is."

"Thank you Bertram," I said beneath my breath.

"What was that?" he said.

"Just mumbling to myself," I said.

As I gazed into his dark eyes, I saw something that seemed familiar to me. "Do I know you from someplace?"

"Bravo again, Mr. Thomas. You're everything I expected, and a keen observer. The face you remember is that of Dr. Darwin Porter.

"I beg your pardon."

"I'm also an actor and played Dr. Darwin Porter for three years on the T.V. series Central Hospital."

"Of course. I was a fan of the show. Why exactly do you need the services of a private detective?"

I nodded when he said, "You know how many movies are filmed in Louisiana each year?"

"Hundreds, probably. I hear we're in third place, behind only Hollywood and Bollywood."

"You heard correctly. This is a prime venue for us. We move quickly and sometimes film two or three movies in a row, often using much the same cast and crew."

"I could tell by the production going on outside. I'm impressed," I said.

"One of our production offices is right here in the city, and many professional film workers make their homes in the state."

"But."

"But many of our people aren't from Louisiana, and it's not out of line to compare New Orleans, and the state of Louisiana, to a foreign country. You know what I'm saying?"

"I think I do."

"Weeks and months away from home are difficult, even if you're making twenty million dollars doing so. Our production company needed a place to give our players a little rest."

"I'm listening."

"A monastery not far from here was all but destroyed by Hurricane Katrina. Our production company, with help from the industry, rebuilt it, turning it into a world-class resort and spa. Our leading actors and production people often spend time there between movies. They even look forward to it."

"Where is this place?"

"In a remote area of southern St. Bernard Parish, at a place called Goose Island."

"I see."

"Rance Parker was staying there when he was killed."

Rance Parker, recently up for best actor, was one of the most popular movie stars in America. I'd seen him at a Mardi Gras party in the Garden District less than a month before. I was unaware he was dead, and Moore's announcement caught me by surprise.

"I've been out of pocket a while. Rance Parker's dead?"

"You have been out of pocket. Everyone else in the world has heard about Rance's demise."

"Mind telling me how it happened?"

"That's my problem. No one knows. His death certificate says he died of a heart attack."

"And his death occurred at the monastery?"

"Like I said, it doubles as a retreat."

"And you don't believe the stated cause of death?"

Moore didn't answer my question, saying instead, "His body was horribly maimed."

I had to pause a moment. "I'm finding this hard to understand. Was he attacked and horribly maimed, or did he have a heart attack?"

"It seems the former is the most likely scenario," he said.

"If that's the case, then a medical examiner was involved. What did the report say?"

Quinlan Moore cleared his throat, and we waited through an explosion on the set outside the R.V.

"Something I must explain. I have a slight conflict of interest here. The medical examiner wasn't involved. A good thing. If the press had gotten wind of this, there'd have been a feeding frenzy. I couldn't let that happen."

"Now I am confused," I said. "You had something to do with the way the case was handled?"

Moore gave me an icy look.

"I didn't say that."

"Look, Mr. Moore, I'm not trying to be combative. I'm on your side. Just spell out your problem to me. I'm a little slow sometimes."

"Our production company has three of Rance's films in the can. They cost millions to make but should pay out many times over, as long as the wrong stories don't start coming out. You know where I'm coming from?"

"What about the police?" I said, not answering his question because I didn't know the answer.

"That's not our problem."

"Then what is?"

"I have to know if it's okay to continue sending our best people to the spa for rest and relaxation. I want you to visit the monastery and get me some answers."

"And what exactly do you expect me to find?"

"Who or what killed Rance, and is the monastery a safe environment. You think you can do it for me?"

I was still thinking about his phrase, who or what, when I said, "I'm an information junkie, and I'll probably discover more than you'll want to hear. Then what?"

"When we know what we're dealing with, then we'll know what to do," he said.

The movie had continued filming outside Quinlan Moore's fancy trailer, bullets, screeching rubber and blaring police sirens reverberating through the thin walls. I waited a moment for silence.

"Is the monastery we're talking about the one where monks build burial caskets and sell them around the world?"

He nodded. "The monks still do their own thing, including the building of caskets. Legally, they own the monastery and the land it's on. They share in the profits of the spa but don't manage the daily operations."

He nodded again when I said, "You have a staff that handles that."

"Not only our people, but artists, writers, and creative souls from all over the world spend time at the monastery turned spa and resort. It's become a valuable concern."

"I see."

"I know everything I've told you so far must sound a bit cryptic. I'm sorry it has to be that way. Can you help solve my little problem?"

"I'll do my best. You want me to visit the monastery and get some answers for you."

"And be discreet about it. I don't want anyone knowing your true purpose. Are you an actor, Mr. Thomas?"

I smiled. "My late wife thought so."

Moore gave me an appraising look, as if assessing the possibility I could make it in Hollywood as an actor.

"You're good looking enough. When this is over, maybe I'll have you read for a part."

I smiled again. "One job at a time."

"Then your answer is yes?"

With the ten thousand dollars freshly in my bank account, there could be no other answer than yes, even though I was still confused about what he wanted me to do.

"I'm your man."

"Wonderful," he said. "Pack casually. I'll send someone to pick you up and take you there."

"When?"

"After lunch tomorrow. Why, is that too soon?"

"I've been away from home for several days, and I don't have anyone to take care of my cat. She's barely let me out of her sight since I picked her up from the person that was keeping her."

It was Moore's turn to smile. "Take her with you. She'll love the island, and you won't have to find anyone to take care of her."

"You sure?"

"If it makes you happy, it's okay with me. Believe me when I say I'm used to working with demanding people."

"Thanks," I said.

"The person picking you up thinks you're a mystery writer. Everyone there, including the monks, will also think you're a writer."

"So then I'll be undercover."

"Can you handle it, Mr. Thomas?"

"No problem."

"You can use your real name, but your pen name will be Jethro Wolfe."

"Anyone on the Internet can Google a name."

"Yes, well there is a Jethro Wolfe, author of a single mystery novel, *Blood Horror.*"

"What if someone there knows Mr. Wolfe?"

Quinlan Moore smiled. "They won't. I'm Jethro Wolfe, and I wrote *Blood Horror* when I was a freshman at U.C.L.A. You'll use my pen name and no one will be the wiser."

"I'm on it, Mr. Moore."

"Magnificent. Here's my business card, and take this with you," he said, handing me a carrying case.

"What is it?"

"A laptop. You're a writer. Remember? You'll need it to create the appropriate illusion. The card has my personal numbers."

"You want me to call you?"

"I'd prefer you keep me posted by email. Only call if you have something that can't wait, even for an hour. Now, I'm off to Antoine's for lunch."

As I carried the computer out the door, I didn't bother telling him I'd never used one, much less know how to email him. Since I didn't want to give the money back, I decided to worry about it later.

Another car crashed as I exited the trailer. It took a moment to realize it was all part of the movie being filmed, the action framed by the antiquity of the Cabildo, and St. Louis Cathedral behind it. Bertram's eggs were only a memory in my growling stomach. Since Moore hadn't invited me to lunch with him at Antoine's, I made do with a hot dog purchased from a street vendor.

Clouds had begun covering the French Quarter. I hadn't gone far when warm rain began to fall. Tourists crowding Jackson Square didn't seem to mind.

Chapter Three

I was up early the next morning, Kisses kneading dough on my chest to get my attention. The time I'd spent away with Chrissie seemed forgiven, and we'd easily fallen back into our old routine. As she ate from her bowl on the balcony, I finished packing for my trip to Barataria Monastery, not knowing what to expect when I arrived there.

"I'm taking another trip, and you're coming with me this time," I said, putting her in my cat carrier.

I scooted my suitcase and the carrier outside by the stairs, shutting the door behind us. Kisses took everything in stride, not seeming to mind that we were taking a little trip.

"I didn't make you mad, did I?" Bertram said as I descended the stairs, bag and cat carrier in hand. "I thought I did a decent job taking care of Kisses while you was out of pocket."

"The job you got me. Someone from Barataria Monastery is picking me up. My new employer said I could bring Kisses with me."

"Now that's the kind of boss to have," he said.

"By the way, thanks again for negotiating my fee. I'm not sure Moore would have hired me if you hadn't asked for the moon."

"Just the way some people are. They judge the value

of most everything by how much it costs. Good thing I ain't like that."

"That's a fact, Bertram. I can't disagree with you."

"Ain't the Barataria Monastery where they make the coffins?" he asked.

"Yes. What else do you know about it?"

"Nothing much. Just that it's about forty miles south of here, but it might as well be in a whole nother country. What you going there for?"

"There was a suspicious death. My employer wants me to look into it for him."

"You got that right, Cowboy," the man sitting with his back to us at the bar said.

I immediately recognized the voice of homicide detective Tony Nicosia.

"Tony," I said. "You're out early."

"Maybe I didn't go to bed last night."

Tony was sipping Scotch from a tall glass and smiled when he glanced at me. Probably mid-forties, he had the brooding eyes of a longtime, homicide detective. Despite all the murders he'd investigated over the years, he'd somehow managed to keep his sense of humor. At the moment, he didn't look very happy.

"Glad to see you're among the living."

"Barely," I said. "How are you?"

"Making it. Both of my partners are in the hospital, and we're having a little shake up at the precinct."

"Shake up?" Bertram said.

"The Feds have been up our ass ever since Katrina. I've been suspended from duty. Maybe even fired. I'm not sure which."

"What the hell for?" Bertram asked.

"Corruption, excessive force, and brutality."

"You never done none of those things."

"Thanks, Bertram. I wish you had some sway with the Feds."

"Sounds as if they're throwing the baby out with the bath water," I said.

Bertram agreed. "That don't seem fair, long as you've

been on the job."

"Don't seem to matter," Tony said. "You a lawyer, Cowboy. What rights do I have now?"

"Ex-lawyer. It would be beneficial to see who's doing what to whom."

"The Justice Department's monitoring the N.O.P.D. now. Gonna change everything, from what I hear. They think the whole force is corrupt."

"No offense, but well-deserved for some," I said.

"Well try doing my job a day or two and see how easy it is. Got any other pearls of wisdom?"

We both knew someone that could give him all the answers—the Assistant, Federal District Attorney in New Orleans.

"Eddie Toledo can tell you more that I can. Why don't you call him?"

"Fast Eddie and I had a little falling out since I kneed him in the nuts."

"Mama Mulate told me about it. You two ain't kissed and made up yet?" Bertram asked.

"He's too busy saving New Orleans to worry about me. Meanwhile, I'm out of a job."

"You're drinking early."

"Gettin' fired is the least of my problems. Lil kicked me out. I'm staying in Tommy's apartment till she cools down. If she ever does."

"Hope it's nothing permanent," Bertram said.

Tony grinned. "I stepped in it this time. She's pissed, and I can't say I blame her."

"You get rid of that young girlfriend you had?" Bertram asked.

"She's history, just like my job."

"Call Eddie. He may be mad at you, but he knows you're an honest cop. He'll help you. I can't give you any advice about Lil. When it comes to relationships, I've been batting zero lately myself."

"Thanks. Now why are you going to the Barataria Monastery?"

"A P.I. job. Movie star Rance Parker just died there."

"You must know all about it. You read the Picayune every day."

"I've been out of pocket for the past two weeks. What's the deal?"

Tony killed his shot of Scotch and motioned Bertram for another.

"Rance Parker. Up for an Academy Award last year. He was filming a movie in N.O. Took a few days off afterwards and spent time at the monastery."

"And?"

"He was killed."

Bertram said, "I heard he died of a heart attack."

"I have a little insider information that says it isn't so," Tony said.

"Then what is the cause of death?" I asked.

"This is scuttlebutt I heard from my detective friend in St. Bernard Parish and wasn't in the papers. Whoever, or whatever killed him ripped him to shreds. Tore his genitals off. He was naked when they found him."

"Sweet mother of God," Bertram said. "What was he doing at the monastery? I thought they only made coffins there."

"It's a retreat. They got first class accommodations, fabulous food and lots of peace and quiet. Costs a bunch, from what I hear. The movie companies send lots of their people there."

"So Rance Parker was chilling out at the monastery after filming a movie in New Orleans. I just saw him at a Mardi Gras party," I said.

"He loved New Orleans and was trying to buy a place here," Tony said.

"What else did your detective friend say?" I asked.

"That's about it. I could call him and get the straight skinny on it, though."

"You been in the bottom half of St. Bernard Parish recently? Delacroix's at the end of the road. I'll bet the cops don't even patrol that far south," Bertram said.

A horse drawn carriage passed outside on the street, the sound of hooves echoing off the cobbles and buildings.

"I'm starting to get the picture," I said.

"Hey Cowboy, I don't want to horn in on your business, but now that I'm out of a job, I could use some extra money. Let me know if a P.I. case comes along you aren't interested in."

"How much do you charge?"

"Don't have a clue. Why?"

"The person that hired me pays well. You could do a little leg work for me. Interested?"

"Hell, I'll help you out for nothing."

"No way you're doing anything for nothing. I just bet Quinlan Moore wouldn't mind having another pair of legs, especially someone here in the city, working his case."

"Let me negotiate this deal for you," Bertram said.

"Bertram's the best," I said with a grin. "He's going to be my personal manager from now on."

"Your ass," Bertram said. "For ten percent, maybe."

Tony handed us a couple of business cards. "It has my home and cell phone numbers. You won't have any luck catching me there for a while. Don't matter none because I always have my cell phone with me."

"Thanks," I said.

"No problem. I'm going stir crazy hanging around doing nothing."

I stuffed the card into my shirt pocket. "I'll call you soon as I get my bearings, and find a phone to use."

Tony smiled. "I almost forgot, you're not exactly tech savvy."

"Hell," Bertram said. "I don't even think he can drive."

"Knock it off you two," I said.

"I'll talk to my Chalmette buddy and see if he'll give me the straight poop on Rance Parker's murder."

"Thanks," I said as a large man in worn jeans and sleeveless tee shirt appeared in the doorway.

"One of you Wyatt Thomas?"

"That's me. You must be the person from the monastery."

"You look familiar," Tony said. "Do I know you?"

The man shook his shaved head. "Don't believe so."

"What's your name?" Tony asked, not letting the matter drop.

"Dempsey Duplantis."

"I got cousins named Duplantis," Bertram said. "Ayoù tu deviens, bro?"

"Sorry, man. I'm a little hard of hearing sometimes. What'd you say?"

"I was just asking where you from."

"Arkansas. My parents moved there when I was just a kid. I came back to Louisiana after Katrina. These your bags, Mr. Thomas?" When I nodded, he picked them up and headed for the door. "I'll wait outside till you're ready. No hurry."

"He ain't got no Arkansas accent," Bertram said as Duplantis disappeared through the door.

"No, and that's a gang tattoo on his neck. Mr. Duplantis, or whoever he is, has spent time in prison. Looks like you got your first suspect, Cowboy."

"Thanks," I said as I fingered Tony's card in my shirt pocket, hoisted the cat carrier and followed Dempsey Duplantis out the door. "Wish me luck."

"Sounds like you gonna need it. Glad this gig's paying you so well," Bertram said.

"Set up a few more jobs while I'm gone and I'll give you that ten percent."

Duplantis had already stowed my bags in the back of an expensive-looking Land Rover. The tailgate was still open, and I slipped the carrier beside them. The man with the shaved head and gang tattoo on his neck was waiting for me behind the wheel, the city's skyscrapers and bridges spanning the Mississippi rapidly disappearing in our rearview mirror.

As we headed south, out of town, I noticed he'd covered his neck with a red bandana. Unlike the tattoo on his neck, a wolf howling at the moon was in full view on his hairy arm. Like Bertram had said, a few miles south of New Orleans was like being in another world.

"Nice vehicle," I said. "Must have cost a fortune."

"The monastery doesn't have to worry much about money."

"Oh? I know they sell handcrafted coffins. I didn't realize there was that much money in it."

"Not the only thing they do there. The place is a haven, known all over the world. The reason you're headed there."

"My agent booked this little sabbatical for me, and I don't know much about the Barataria facilities. Maybe you can fill me in."

Duplantis hesitated before answering. By now, all vestiges of the city were gone, replaced by the Mississippi River on one side of the road, low-lying islands in an endless marsh on the other. A flock of brown pelicans lifted out of the water and flew across the blacktop in front of us.

"The monastery is on Goose Island. People come from all over to spend time there. Writers, painters, actors."

"Like Rance Parker?"

"He stayed with us quite a bit, usually between movies he was filming in Louisiana. Said the place took his stress away."

"You knew him?"

Dempsey Duplantis glanced at me and frowned. "Everyone there knew who he was. Hell, the man was a movie star."

"What I meant is, did you ever talk to him, one on one?"

"Sure, he was a regular guy. No pretense, you know. We even went drinking together once."

"Oh?"

"A small bar in Delacroix. Parker liked the Cajun dancing and zydeco band there and got along with the locals. Hell, even in Delacroix they knew who he was."

"What about his death?"

Duplantis looked at me again, frowning this time. "If you read the papers, you know as much as me. I was at the airport in New Orleans, picking up an arriving guest."

"Just curious. He supposedly died of a heart attack.

Word on the street is something entirely different."

"There's talk of that. One of the gardeners on the island told me he was torn up pretty bad, like a pack of wild dogs got him, or something. Parts of his legs and arms were chewed off. I don't know if it's true or not."

"You have to be kidding."

"Like I said, it's second-hand information. I do know his widow flew in and got the body. Had it cremated in New Orleans."

"He was married?"

"You wouldn't have known it. Guess he didn't want his female fans to find out he wasn't available."

A smirk spread across Duplantis' face, and he brushed his day-old growth of beard with a calloused hand.

"What?" I asked.

"Hell, that man had the morals of an alley cat. He'd have screwed a snake if he'd got the chance. I'm not throwing stones you understand."

"I'm not exactly a saint myself."

"Rance Parker sure wasn't."

Dempsey Duplantis grew silent as if he were withdrawing into himself, realizing he'd said too much. The highway, if you could call it that, paralleled the Mississippi River. A similar road, only a mile away but impossible to get to from where we were, followed the other side of the river. The shallow water beside the road was alive with birds.

"I'm a mystery writer. You never know. Parker's death might be a theme for my next novel."

"No problem," Duplantis said.

"What's the retreat like?"

"Plush. The guests have their own personal bungalows. Never more than a dozen guests at any given time. Several restaurants with chefs from New Orleans that rotate on a regular basis. Swimming pools, hot tubs, and health facilities. Masseurs and masseuses. Hell, you know how much it costs."

"Like I said, my agent booked this gig for me. How

much does it cost?"

Duplantis grinned. "If you don't know, then I hope you're rich and famous. Ten grand a week."

"Whoa!" I said. "I must be selling more books than I thought."

"You better be. You're booked for two weeks, and open for two more if you decide to stay on."

Dempsey Duplantis grew silent. It didn't matter because I was tired. Less than thirty miles south of New Orleans, we were surrounded by water, stunted trees draped with Spanish moss, and low-lying islands. Leaning back against the Land Rover's headrest, I closed my eyes and took a much needed nap.

Chapter Four

I opened my eyes when we pulled off the blacktop onto a dirt road few people probably knew existed. The road was built on a natural levee with water on both sides. Two colorful wood ducks, with ducklings swimming behind them, weren't startled as we drove past.

"The monastery is on Goose Island. Not much of an island, the water around it only five or six feet deep," Duplantis explained.

"It's beautiful here, and so peaceful."

"Almost too peaceful. Gets monotonous sometimes."

We reached a berm, a tall, concrete wall occupying both sides of the road. A picturesque bridge spanned it, and Duplantis drove across.

"The berm is a six foot levee around the compound. Wouldn't automatically protect the place in a hurricane, but it keeps us dry whenever the water rises."

"Does that happen often?"

Duplantis laughed. "Wait'll you get out of the car and feel the humidity. When it rains down here, it doesn't do it halfway. It usually comes a gully washer."

The scenery changed quickly when we drove over the bridge, acres of manicured St. Augustine grass carpeting the grounds of the expansive estate suddenly appearing. A peacock crossed the road in front of us, stopping briefly to show off his plumage. In the distance, I could see several buildings. The monastery wasn't what I expected.

"I know," Duplantis said. "Everyone here for the first time is surprised by how it looks."

The large monastery appeared to cover several acres and looked more like a futuristic building at a N.A.S.A. facility than something in the Vatican. Someone, it was quite obvious, had spent lots of money on architects.

The only building that seemed out of place was the steep-roofed, plaster and wood cathedral. It's Orthodox architecture, complete with a towering cross on top, seemed like something you'd see in Europe and not south Louisiana. Its walls showed the scars from every storm that had passed over the island, though the circular, stained glass window was still bright and unmarked by time.

"It's beautiful," I said.

"The only building that remains from the original monastery. It somehow managed to survive everything Louisiana's fickle weather has thrown at it for way more than a hundred years."

"The other buildings are so modern in comparison and look so architecturally opposed to the cathedral. What's the story?"

"California architects who had their own ideas about how things should look on Goose Island." When I gave him a glance, he added, "Someone else was paying for it, and the modern buildings do have a way of growing on you."

"They're beautiful, just so. . ."

"Out of place?"

"Exactly. What are they made of?"

"Steel reinforced structural concrete, designed to withstand hurricane-force winds."

"Guess that would be an issue this close to the Gulf of Mexico."

"Ever been in a hurricane, Mr. Thomas? You think Katrina was bad in New Orleans. You should have been here."

"Were you?"

"No, but I've heard about it."

As Duplantis parked in front of the main building, I gazed at the surroundings, amazed at the amenities that included a large swimming pool, several tennis courts and what looked like the first hole of a golf course. The people walking around in Bermuda shorts, sandals, and colorful tee shirts didn't look like monks.

"Father Domenic meets all the incoming guests when they arrive. He's waiting for you through those big doors. Someone will take you to his office."

"Thanks," I said.

"Happy to be of service. I'll drop the bags off at your bungalow. And I'll let your cat out and give her some water."

"I appreciate it, and I'm sure she will too."

The outside of the building had a stucco finish artfully daubed a shade of pinkish-white. The front doors were cypress and beveled glass, a less than subtle hint that the building had cost lots of money to construct. A man in a black robe met me at the door, the blast of air conditioning already beginning to cool the sweat dripping down my forehead.

"You should wear a hat, Mr. Thomas," the man said with a smile. "Or at least a cap. The sun down here can fry a person's brain in a matter of hours. I'm Brother Dunwoody," he said, grasping my hand.

Brother Dunwoody's black, horn-rimmed glasses dominated his face, balding head, and gap-toothed smile. He stood five inches taller than my six feet, and his grip was bone crushing.

"I never wear a hat," I said.

"You may reconsider that decision before you leave here. Father Domenic's rectory is at the top of the stairs."

I followed Brother Dunwoody up the winding staircase to the building's second story. The rectory was through the first doorway, and Brother Dunwoody swung it open without knocking. Another tall man was staring out a floor-to-ceiling picture window his hands clasped behind his back.

30

"Father, Mr. Thomas has arrived."

"Thank you, Brother Dunwoody," the man said. Without turning around, he began to recite:

> Our share of night to bear,
> Our share of morning,
> Our blank in bliss to fill,
> Our blank in scorning.

When Father Domenic finally looked at me, I surprised him when I recited the poem's next stanza:

> Here a star, and there a star,
> Some lose their way,
> Here a mist, and there a mist,
> Afterwards—day!

"I see you're also a fan of Emily Dickenson," he said.

"Not as much as my favorite aunt was. I spent several summers with her, and she saw to it that I could recite the gentlewoman from memory."

"Schoolteacher?"

"How did you guess?" I said, both of us smiling.

Like Brother Dunwoody, Father Domenic's black smock draped the hardwood floor. His brown, curly hair, good looks, and big hands imparted the aura of a film star. He was also much younger than I'd anticipated.

"I see the expression of disbelief on your face. I assure you that I'm older than I appear," he said.

He towered over me as he pumped my hand and smiled when I said, "I was amazed how tall you are. Does your order only recruit ex-basketball players?"

"Something in the water," he said.

"Must be. I've heard lots about this place. From the looks of the grounds, it's everything I expected."

"You're going to like it here, I promise."

"I'm sure I will, your Excellency."

"Please, we are only monastics, and I'm just an Abbott, not a Bishop."

"Sorry. I've always had trouble keeping Catholic titles straight."

"We're not even Catholic. Just a small religious denomination you've probably never heard of."

"I'd love to hear," I said.

"We're Tracists Monks. Sounds similar to Trappists though quite different. Just call me Father Domenic. Would you like a glass of cognac?" he asked.

"No thanks. I'm a teetotaler."

"Do you mind if I partake?"

"Not at all," I said.

There was a wet bar near the door, and Father Domenic poured a glass of cognac. Clasping his hands around the snifter to warm the liquor, he returned to the window. I joined him, curious to see what he was gazing so intently at.

"The closest building is our recreational complex that includes a swimming pool, gym, spa, a couple of restaurants, and a movie theatre."

"I didn't know what to expect. It certainly wasn't this," I said.

The large pool was only a hundred feet from the window, and a few sun worshippers were lying on chaise lounges. A golfer teed off, watching his ball fly high in the air and disappear in the distance.

"Expect the ultimate and you won't be disappointed, I promise," Father Domenic said.

"I'm curious. Your monastery is in the middle of nowhere. How did the order acquire this piece of property?"

"We're called Tracists because our original order helped survey the Natchez Trace, not all that far from here."

"And the Crown rewarded you for your service?"

"Very perceptive, Mr. Thomas. The land here was granted to us when France was still in power. Except for the cathedral, our original monastery was destroyed by Katrina."

"Then it's been rebuilt?"

"With the assistance of a large donor, a Hollywood production company. They helped us raise sufficient funding to complete our task. Are you familiar with the movie industry in Louisiana?"

"A little."

"It's more than big business now. It's part of the culture. They're even thinking of filming a movie on Goose Island."

"How did the island get its name?"

"There are more migratory birds here than perhaps any place on earth. During your stay, you'll see thousands of birds. The masses are quite extraordinary sometimes, especially when they're coming or going."

"So the movie industry contributed to the restoration of the Barataria Monastery?"

"For a price, Mr. Thomas." Father Domenic said. "They wanted something out of the deal."

"Oh?"

"We lost our privacy and seclusion. Some of the people that come here. . . . Well, you'll soon see for yourself."

"I know you get lots of visitors from the film industry. I don't guess they were happy with the death of Rance Parker?"

"That's putting it mildly."

"The newspapers reported he died of a heart attack."

With hands still clasped firmly behind his back, Father Domenic turned around, frowning as he stared at me with his dark eyes.

"He had no heart attack. He was killed by a pack of wild dogs."

"You can't be serious."

"I'm afraid I am."

"But. . ."

"Hollywood coverup," he said with a flick of his hand. "They were afraid the truth would hurt their box office bottom line."

Father Domenic turned away again, staring out the big picture window. We could hear Brother Dunwoody outside the door, chatting with someone that had entered the offices.

"Are there wild dogs on the island?" I asked.

"This is wilderness, Mr. Thomas. Wetlands, to be

politically correct. In times past it was just the swamp. There's every manner of wild animal in the swamp."

"Then it wasn't, perhaps, a murder?"

"You're the writer. No motive, no murder. I can assure you there was no motive to Rance Parker's demise."

He seemed taken aback when I said, "Some murderers don't need much of a motive."

"Guests arrive and leave. What motive could they possibly have?"

"There are those that kill for pleasure, not to mention various other sordid reasons."

"Rance Parker wasn't killed by a serial killer."

I let the subject drop, moving on to a different topic. "How many guests were on the island when the death occurred?"

"Just four. Except for Parker, two of them are still here."

"And how many monks reside at the monastery?"

"Again just four. That includes me."

"Not many for a monastery this size."

"Unfortunately, we are a declining religion. Since we're not Catholic, we have no support from the Vatican. What you see here, we've gleaned for ourselves."

"What about employees? Do you have many besides Dempsey Duplantis?"

Father Domenic didn't immediately respond. "What does it matter?"

"I only write fiction, but all fiction is based on facts. I was just delving."

"You're writing about the monastery?"

"Just considering the possibility. You don't mind, do you?"

"I wouldn't want you to write anything misleading."

"The monastery and my book will never be connected, I assure you. Can you help me on this?"

"I suppose it's okay," he said.

"What about the chefs, entertainers and other employees that don't live here?"

"You are inquisitive."

"As I said, my books aren't anything like real life. I'm just brainstorming for ideas."

"The chefs and entertainers change frequently and certainly don't live here. The spa portion of the monastery is run by a management company in New Orleans. They hire additional workers, during peaks of activity, when they need them. I have no control over anything but the daily operation of the monastery."

"I see. Do the chefs and entertainers live here while they're working?"

"We value our privacy. That is why there are never more than ten guests at a time. Except for guests and monks, there's no one on the island after midnight."

"So they leave every night?"

"The chefs and entertainers are flown in by helicopter for the day. They leave the same way when they complete the meal they are cooking, or finish their performances."

"And the day workers?"

"They all live off the island, many of them in nearby Delacroix, though some commute from as far away as New Orleans. They have electronic devices on their windshields that open the front gate when they arrive."

"So someone knows the actual times and dates when the workers arrive and leave."

"Yes, which would eliminate all of them from the possibility of killing Mr. Parker, assuming someone killed him."

The air conditioning suddenly kicked in, blasting cold air into my face from a vent just above us.

"I'd like to meet your monks and see them at work."

Father Domenic nodded his head. "Of course, you may speak with whomever you like."

"I want to know why they became monks. That would entail knowing a little background information on each of them, including yourself. Can you provide their curriculum Vitae?"

"Not possible."

"Why not?"

35

"Because that information is confidential. Now, let me tell you a little about our retreat."

"Great," I said, not wanting to have him shut the door on my inquiries.

"We have ten bungalows, the people that visit here writers, actors, poets, are rich and famous. They come here, seeking solitude. We give them that, and so much more."

"Is the monastery the only settlement on the island?"

"This elevated tract of land is one of the largest in the marsh. There's a fishing village on the lee side. They are descended from escaped slaves. It's said they still practice voodoo."

"What else?"

"An old man has a house by the water. A retired college professor doing research for the state of Louisiana."

"From what I've already seen, this place is wonderful," I said. "I'm looking forward to the amenities and the peace. Thanks for letting me take so much of your time."

"My pleasure. Please enjoy your stay on the island."

As if on cue, Brother Dunwoody opened the door and poked his head in.

"Are you ready for me to take Mr. Thomas to his bungalow?"

Father Domenic nodded. "Yes, thank you Brother Dunwoody."

"One more question," I said. "You might know I'd forget something. I got away from home without my cell phone. Are there phones in the bungalows?"

"Most of our guests have cell phones," Father Domenic said. "Since you've misplaced yours, you can use the land line in my office anytime you want to. The island has Wi-Fi, and you'll have access to the Internet in your bungalow."

"Anything else I need to know?"

"Just that Brother Dunwoody is my assistant. He will give you a walking tour of the island on your way to your bungalow."

"Thanks so much."

Before I reached the door, Father Domenic spoke again.

"I hope you don't discover all our secrets, Mr. Thomas," he said with a smile.

Chapter Five

I followed Brother Dunwoody out the door of the monastery. Still only April, the island's heat and humidity had yet to become oppressive. The tall monk was soon pointing out things of interest.

"The protective berm around the island was constructed after Hurricane Katrina. It won't stop the onslaught of a full-scale hurricane, but it usually keeps us dry, year round."

"And the buildings?"

"They should withstand a hurricane, though they're as yet untested."

"You didn't stay here during Katrina, did you?"

Brother Dunwoody shook his head. "I wasn't a monk then. Next hurricane, we're all staying."

"Then you must feel confident the buildings are properly designed."

"No, Mr. Thomas, we have faith in God, and we have a secret weapon."

"Oh, and what is that?"

Brother Dunwoody pointed. "See that structure that's shaped like a rocket ship and looks like a metal gazebo?"

"Yes."

"During a hurricane it has a single purpose."

"Such as," I said.

"The building is a security capsule, survival pod if

you will. During a hurricane, the door closes. It is waterproof, airtight, self contained and accommodates thirty people comfortably."

"So you get in, close the door and then don't worry about the force of the hurricane?"

"We stay in the pod until the hurricane passes."

"Supplies?"

"Enough food and water until the flooding subsides."

"But you haven't used it and don't know if it works."

"Not yet, Mr. Thomas. This is south Louisiana. It's inevitable that we will."

Brother Dunwoody continued walking, his long strides hard to keep pace with. A wetlands loon flew overhead, its eerie cry causing me to glance up at it.

"I've spent time in this area over the years. One thing surprises me."

"What's that?"

"I haven't had a single mosquito bite since I've been here. What the heck's going on?"

He laughed. "And you won't feel the bite of a mosquito, at least as long as you stay within the berm. We put mosquito tablets in all the standing water. The tablets are harmless to man and beast, but eliminate the mosquito larvae."

"It's certainly working," I said.

"We also have traps equipped with pheromones that attract female mosquitoes. They are caught when they go there to lay their eggs."

"Sounds as if you're doing a good job of covering all the bases."

"We've effectively broken the mosquito reproductive cycle, and they're no longer a problem at the monastery as you've noted."

"Glad to hear that. I'm not a fan of the little blood suckers. What's that smell?"

"One more safeguard. We use plant oils to repel other bugs. The oils are safe to the environment, but work wonders keeping flies and other nuisance insects away from our guests."

"Like cockroaches?"

Brother Dunwoody grinned. "I'm afraid we still have our share of those particular critters. We haven't found a solution to that problem as yet."

"Being a lifelong resident of Louisiana, I've learned to tolerate most insects. Even cockroaches."

"I wish I could say the same for some of our other guests."

I began to notice the palm trees and other tropical foliage not native to Louisiana. Two snowy egrets fished in a shallow pond decorated with rocks that had probably come from other states. There were fountains in the distance.

"The grounds are beautifully landscaped, though seem more like a park in. . ."

"California?"

"Yes."

"I suppose Father Domenic explained that film money paid for much of the monastery's restoration. Lots of stars stay here between movies filming in Louisiana. The palms and other visual trickery help them feel at home."

"The designers did a great job of it," I said as we passed the swimming pool.

I noticed an attractive woman lying on a chaise. She was completely naked and smiled when she saw me staring in her direction.

"I dare not look when I pass," Brother Dunwoody said. "Many of the female guests like to sun topless, some of them totally nude."

He grinned when I said, "How rude of them."

"To each his own," he said.

A bungalow resided close enough to the swimming pool to be a part of the complex. Like the main buildings, it was constructed of stucco and pink tile.

"Here's where you'll reside during your stay on the island," he said.

The bungalow was more than I'd expected. Much more. Surrounded by a stucco fence, it had a covered patio, sunken spa, landscaped gardens and a view of the marshlands beyond the berm. A flock of squawking pelicans flew overhead as Brother Dunwoody unlocked the door and handed me the key.

"All the amenities of home," he said, trying not to let me see him swat a cockroach crawling up the wall.

Colorful Mexican tile on the floor opened up the spacious room. There was also a king-sized bed, complete with mosquito netting, and a shower large enough for me and my ten closest friends.

"It's gorgeous," I said.

Brother Dunwoody stood with his hands behind his back, smiling as I looked around the beautiful bungalow. With his head almost touching the ceiling, I realized just how tall he actually was.

"You won't need the mosquito net though many of our guests like the ambiance it creates," he said.

"What about you and the other monks? Are your quarters this plush?"

"Our rooms are small but adequate, and not even close to being plush. It doesn't matter because they are all we need and desire."

"What did you do before you became a monk if you don't mind me asking."

"High school teacher," he said.

"I had a feeling you were somehow involved in education."

Brother Dunwoody let the remark drop, continuing his guided tour of the bungalow.

"Fit for a king, of which we've had a couple since I've been here. I'll turn on the air conditioning for you."

"Don't bother. It's comfortable without it. Open windows and the ceiling fans are all the ventilation I need."

"You are from Louisiana."

"Father Domenic seems so young," I said.

"You think he's too young to be the head of the monastery?"

"Not what I said. He must be eminently qualified, or

41

he wouldn't have the position."

"Father Domenic is a wonderful man. He's done many praiseworthy things, not just here at the monastery but throughout the parish."

"I had the feeling that was the case."

"He recruited me and the other monks. All the previous monks had grown old and retired from the order."

"So Father Domenic was the only monk here during Katrina?"

"Yes. Well then, if you have no more questions, I need to get back to the office."

"Thanks for everything, Brother Dunwoody. You've been quite informative."

"Feel free to tell me if you have questions or problems. And dinner begins at six, though many of the guests prefer to dine much later than that."

Before he could leave, I said, "I'd like to know more about Father Domenic and the monks that live here. Do you keep that information on a computer?"

"Father Domenic didn't tell you?"

"Tell me what?"

"That we consider such information confidential, and I'm not at liberty to discuss it with you."

I watched him lumber away toward the main buildings, his long robe, looking hot and uncomfortable, flowing as he walked. He was smiling, though I could see my questions about Father Domenic and the other monks had bothered him.

Once alone in the spacious bungalow, I looked for Kisses and found her in the adjoining kitchen. As curious as I was, she was even more so, nosing around the cracks and crannies. When I opened a can of cat food and placed it on the kitchen floor beside her water bowl, I knew she was going to like the place.

I checked out the little refrigerator stocked with bottles of wine and beer. After changing into more presentable island attire, I headed back out the door to check on the guests at the swimming pool. The nude woman, a large straw hat covering her face, was still lying on the chaise.

"I knew you'd be back," she said without bothering to remove the hat.

"You don't seem to mind. I think you already know I'm staring at you."

"I like it when people look at me."

Removing her hat, she glanced up at me with a perfect smile.

"You look familiar. Do I know you?"

"If you don't, I'll be insulted. I'm Sabine Storm though my friends call me Stormie."

"Of course you are. I've seen most of your movies, and been in love with you for years. You're probably used to hearing people say that."

She smiled without blushing and said, "I never get tired of it."

Stormie was a redhead with the fair complexion that almost always accompanies that natural hair coloring. She also had eyes as green as a Louisiana lily pond and sensuous lips that could make a grown man weak. I couldn't stop staring. The more I looked, the more she seemed to like it.

"What's your name?"

"Wyatt Thomas."

"What do you do, Wyatt?"

"Writer. My pen name is Jethro Wolfe."

A friendly waiter from the poolside bar interrupted us, bringing a fresh drink for Stormie.

"Something for you, sir?" he asked.

"Lemonade if you have it. Iced tea if you don't," I said.

Stormie took the icy glass, puckering her lips around the protruding straw. She had the body of a dedicated exercise fanatic, making it difficult to guess her age.

"Have you written any screenplays? I always like to look at new material."

"I've only written one book so far, and it's a mystery."

"I love mysteries. I'll have to read it. Do you have a copy with you?"

"Sorry, I got away from home without one."

"I'm particularly fond of erotica. All my movies have been commercial, though I've always wanted to make a porn film, just to see what it's like."

"I've seen you in a few steamy scenes that had my heart racing."

She grinned and said, "Maybe because I wasn't acting."

"Lucky co-stars," I said. "I'd be blushing but the sun's too bright."

The young waiter dressed in Bermuda shorts and a Hawaiian shirt smiled as he handed me an icy glass of fresh lemonade. I thanked him and then noticed Stormie was looking at something behind me. When I turned around, I saw the large picture window of Father Domenic's office. A reflection behind the tinted glass told me someone was standing there, looking out at us.

"You're not the only one that likes to look," she said. "Did you see his binoculars when you were in his office for orientation?"

"Father Domenic?"

"He has more kinks than you can count."

I didn't respond to her suggestive comment as a man approached. His balding head was the only part of his body without hair, thick, black hair matting his chest and back. Dressed only in a tiny, blue Speedo, it seemed obvious he was proud of his physique.

"Pietro, this is Wyatt."

Pietro shook my hand with a frown, his grip almost bone crushing.

"Pleased to meet you," I said.

"Pietro is a sculptor. He's doing a statue of me, although we haven't gotten much further than a rough slab of marble."

"Many distractions," Pietro said in an Italian accent. "Will you be available to sit for me later tonight?"

"Maybe," she said. "Unless I can talk Wyatt into a moonlight stroll."

Pietro raised his hand in a haughty wave and walked

away without replying to Stormie's answer.

"He seemed a little miffed. Jealousy?"

"More like inflated ego. He was an Olympic weightlifter before he hurt his back and began sculpting. Now he can't walk in front of a mirror without stopping to admire himself."

"The woman across the pool, sitting beneath that red umbrella, seems interested."

A small woman in a one-piece suit, dark as her eyes and short hair, stared at us over the book she was holding. She smiled when I nodded in her direction.

"Her name's Lilly Bliss, and she's a romance writer. Pietro's had her."

"How do you know?"

"Because I've had them both, at the same time."

"I see."

"You wish," she said, her lips forming a sexy pout when she smiled and winked. "Never know. Might be kind of fun for all of us to get a little wicked one of these nights. Do you go both ways?"

I grinned. "I'm lucky if I can make it one way. What's the story on Brother Dunwoody?" I asked, changing the delicate subject. "He said he was once a teacher."

"Yeah, well they don't allow sex offenders to teach in public schools, at least once they're outed."

"How do you know?"

"I make it a point to check out the people I'm around." What about the other monks?"

"Brothers Bruce and Bruno," she said. "Bruce is a mousey little wimp. Bruno's different."

"How so?" I asked.

"You wouldn't want to meet him in a dark alley. I don't recall ever seeing him smile."

"Father Domenic and Brother Dunwoody were reluctant to provide any background on themselves or the other two monks."

"As I said, Father Domenic is quite strange."

"If this were New Orleans, I could check the Notarial Archives. If I knew their last names."

Why are you so interested in everyone?"

"Never know when something or someone might give me an idea for my next book."

"Are you doing research at the moment?" she asked.

"More like mental masturbation. You're hard not to stare at."

"I hope something else is hard, and not just your imagination," she said, grinning again.

"Now you are making me blush."

"I doubt it. You seem far too confident to me, though I could teach you a few perversions that might surprise you."

She winced when I said, "I'd probably have a heart attack."

"You're getting me too hot and bothered. I think we better change the subject before things get out of hand," she said.

A golf cart tooled by on its way to the first tee, it's passengers waving as they passed. Stormie ignored them.

"You said Brother Dunwoody is a sex offender. How is it he is Father Domenic's closest confidante?"

Stormie cupped her hand over her mouth and answered in a low voice as if someone might be eavesdropping.

"Did you notice how big Brother Dunwoody is?" I nodded. "Well Father Domenic has a small problem."

"Oh?"

"He suffers from a mental condition."

"You're kidding me."

"If I told you what I know, you wouldn't believe it."

"Try me."

Stormie glanced up at the vapor trail of a plane, flying so high above us we couldn't hear the hum of its jet engines.

"I don't want to speak out of turn, but like I said, the Abbott is kinkier that I am, and he's fixated on me."

Chapter Six

Stormie put on a colorful coverup and accompanied me to one of the several restaurants in the nearby complex. An Italian chef presided, his Scampi Fra Diavolo O Caterina as appetizing as anything I'd ever eaten. A bright moon set the clear sky as we walked out the door, Stormie clutching my arm.

"It's not late. Come back to my bungalow with me," she said.

I was tempted. Even more when she pulled me close, stood on her tiptoes and kissed me.

"You have my head spinning, and I didn't even help you drink your champagne. Still, I just got here and have work to finish before tomorrow."

"I can give you something to work on," she said.

"You're one of the most beautiful actresses in Hollywood. I'm an idiot for saying this, but I'd better not."

"Party pooper," she said. "Guess I'll have to call Pietro."

"If he's not already with Lilly Bliss."

Stormie grinned. "Then I'll crash their party. Sure I can't talk you into joining us? A foursome can be fun."

"Sorry. Don't cross me off your party list just yet. I'll be here at least a week."

She grinned again, gave me another peck on the lips, pirouetted down the steps and waved as she disappeared into the night.

Though not quite full, the moon cast shadows off the California palm trees as I walked to my bungalow. An unexpected light shined through the window. I opened the door to find a female, looking barely older than a girl, sitting at the table. The laptop was open and she was keyboarding on it, Kisses asleep in her lap.

"Who are you?" I asked.

"Sierra. Who are you?"

"Wyatt. I thought this was my bungalow. Did I get the wrong place?"

Sierra grinned. She was small, almost tiny and had short, surfer blond hair. She also had eyes the color of south Pacific lagoons, so blue you could almost see yourself in them.

"You're in the right place. Your window was open, and I noticed your computer. I saw you with Stormie and didn't think you'd be back for a while. She has to chase most men off with a stick."

"Well my mom always told me to watch out for loose women."

"Smart mom. Stormie is more than loose. She'd screw a snake if she had the chance."

"Seems I've heard that phrase once already today."

"Then you must have met my stepdad."

She nodded when I said, "Dempsey Duplantis?"

"We're not exactly on speaking terms at the moment."

"No problem. Me casa es su casa. Maybe you can teach me how to use that thing."

She grinned again. "You kidding me? Everyone knows how to use a computer."

"Not everyone."

"You're lying."

"I'm not."

She stared at me an instant, trying to determine if I were being truthful with her.

"I can teach you how to get started in about ten minutes," she finally said.

"I may take you up on that offer. I'm supposed to send

email updates to my new employer, and I don't have the foggiest idea how to go about it."

"You sure you're not making this up?" she said.

"I swear I'm not. I just got this thing before arriving here. Frankly, I was wondering what I was going to do with it."

"You can't be serious. The Internet is the most powerful tool in the universe. There's nothing you can't find online."

"I always go to the Notarial Archives in New Orleans when I need to do research," I said. "There's nothing about New Orleans and its people you can't find there."

"Then you'll love the net. It's the receptacle of all the information on earth. Whatever questions you have, the net has answers."

"Even if you're only half right, it's sounds like something I need to tap into. Where do you live, Sierra?"

"Presently, here in the compound."

"And not with your stepfather?"

"Ex-stepfather. I'm not claiming him right now."

"I won't ask," I said.

"Don't."

She laughed when I said, "You must get your looks from your mother."

"Hey, I love your kitty. Sorry about using your computer. I don't have one, and I was updating my Facebook page for my friends back in California."

"Why are you still on the island? Aren't the people that work here required to leave at night?"

Thunder rumbled in the distance, the sound dying off before Sierra answered.

"Mom and Dempsey split a while back. He emailed her, saying he was working here. When she couldn't come, he sent money to me."

"What happened?"

"He's a prick, and now I know why Mom kicked him out. We had one too many arguments and I left the house, spending the night on a park bench in Delacroix. I hitched a ride in the back of his pickup the next day. I've been here ever since."

"Does he know you're here?"

"No, and please don't tell him, or anyone else for that matter."

"No problem. Where have you been sleeping?"

"This bungalow's been vacant for two weeks. The chaise on the patio is a little lumpy, but not too bad."

"How have you managed to keep from starving?"

"Some of the cooks and waitresses like me. I've been surviving. I do miss my beer, though. That's one thing Dempsey always had plenty of around his house."

"The refrigerator's loaded. Help yourself. I'm a lemonade man myself."

"Thanks," she said, opening the fridge and retrieving a cold bottle of Abita.

More thunder. Wispy clouds floated outside the open window, threatening to cover the moon.

"You'll get used to it. It rains here so often I don't even think about it anymore. So much for sunny California."

"Are you going back there soon?"

"I'm here, and I'm staying."

She didn't answer when I said, "You'll go back to see your mom."

Killing the Abita in one long swallow, she sat the bottle on the kitchen counter.

"Mind if I have another?"

"Knock yourself out. You didn't have to sneak into my room. You can use the computer anytime you want," I said.

"You sure?"

"I said so, didn't I?"

"And you won't report me and have me kicked off the island?"

"No way," I said.

"Thanks. I can't say the same for most of the people on the island."

"Oh? I just arrived. What's your take?"

Sierra glanced at the open window she'd entered

through.

"I don't want to get into trouble."

"You won't get any from me," I said.

"Are you going to make me have sex with you?"

She grinned when I said, "You're just a baby. Do I look like some kind of pervert?"

"I'm twenty, not a baby."

"You could have fooled me."

"I'm so small, most people think I'm a child. I hate it. I'll have sex with you and you won't have to make me if you'll let me stay and don't report me."

"Forget it. We're not having sex."

"Then you're kicking me out?"

"I didn't say that. This bungalow is only designed for one guest at a time."

"I'll sleep on the patio. I swear I won't bother you."

"I'll think about it. You're the only small person on the island. I'm six feet, and almost everyone towers over me."

"Then you understand how I feel," she said. "Not to mention this place is like the set of a porn movie ever since Stormie arrived."

"She is quite candid about her needs. How long has she been here?"

"Two months or so."

"Seems like quite a while," I said.

"She's trying to hustle a role in a movie they're going to shoot in New Orleans. I think she's slept with everyone in the production company."

"She's gorgeous, and a talented actress. Why is she having so much trouble getting the part?"

"She's over forty or haven't you noticed? Most of the movie goers these days are teenaged boys. They like car chases and gunfights and prefer their women to be young and dumb."

"Stormie looks pretty good to me," I said.

"Lots of moms look good. Boys don't fantasize about females as old as their moms."

"What about the monks? Father Domenic and

Brother Dunwoody wouldn't even tell me their last names."

"They're secretive when it comes to personal information," she said. "They won't even tell you what state they're originally from. I've asked."

"You'd think they'd keep records. Do you know if they do?"

Sierra shook her head. "They don't use computers. If they have records, they're kept by hand."

"How do you know so much about the movies?" I asked.

"I'm from southern California. I grew up on this stuff."

Another clap of thunder shook the tiles on the roof. It was followed immediately by lightning flashing over Goose Bay.

"So Stormie was here when Rance Parker died?"

"Oh yeah. She and Rance had a little thing going. Surprise, surprise."

"You knew him?"

"You kidding? Once when he grabbed my ass, I slapped him so hard I didn't believe I'd done it. It just made him try harder."

She grinned when I said, "The proverbial snake in heat."

"I don't know how he could still be horny after all the sex Stormie requires."

"Must have made Pietro jealous."

"He just arrived last week."

"So he wasn't on the island when Parker died?"

"Nope."

She cast me a questioning glance when I said, "Then even if Parker didn't die of a heart attack, Pietro wasn't involved."

"I have no idea what you're talking about," she said.

I'd left the windows open, no air conditioner noise disturbing the frogs, singing between thunder booms. They stopped abruptly as a distant howl punctuated the serenity. Sierra glanced at the open window.

"That sounded like a dog."

"Or a wolf," she said.

"Are there wolves on the island?"

"I haven't seen any, but there are more wild animals around than there are people. The marshlands stretch for miles in every direction. Could be almost anything living out there."

Sierra jumped at another sound, more of a growl and closer this time. Kisses dropped to the floor, stretched, and then crawled up on a kitchen chair and went back to sleep.

"Most guests don't bring their pets. I've never known anyone to travel with their cat."

"Want me to close the window?" I said, ignoring her comment.

"No, but can I have another Abita?"

"Help yourself. I'm not counting."

When she bent to retrieve a bottle from the refrigerator, I could see how small she was. She was wearing khaki shorts and a white tee shirt, her tanned arms and legs doing nothing to change my initial impression of her quintessential, California surfer girl looks.

"Want one?" she asked.

"No thanks. I'm not much of a drinker."

"Then you're the only one around here that's not."

She jumped, almost spilling her beer when a commotion erupted behind the bungalow. Growls, snarls and the crashing of metal trash cans suddenly riveted our attention. Before I reached the door, heavy rain began pummeling the roof. One of the creatures on the back porch sent a trash can clanging across the concrete patio. It fled from the floodlights I'd flipped on before throwing open the door.

A large dog lay on the ground beside an upended can. Sierra rushed outside, kneeling when it whimpered.

"Oh Wyatt, it's hurt," she said, grabbing the dog's head.

"Be careful. It's a Rottweiler. They can be dangerous."

I might as well have been talking to the breeze that had kicked up outside the bungalow, along with the rain.

"Help me get him inside," she said.

The large dog was emaciated, looking as if he hadn't eaten in a week. The marks on his haunch were proof that he'd been in a scuffle with something just as big as he was. Maybe the creature responsible for the howls we'd heard.

"His name is Chuckie," Sierra said, looking at the name plate attached to his faded collar. "His rabies tag is out of date, a year old. Do you have anything to put on his wound?"

I returned from the medicine cabinet with cotton balls, hydrogen peroxide, and iodine.

"This should fix him up," I said.

When Sierra had cleaned the wound and doctored it, she went into the kitchen, returning with several cans of potted meat. The dog named Chuckie ate it out of her hand. When she put the rest in Kisses food bowl, my kitty jumped off the chair and nosed in beside Chuckie, eating her share. Neither seemed to care.

"He's not only hurt, he's exhausted," she said. "We're keeping him."

"Hey, don't I have a say in this?" I asked.

"He won't be any trouble. He can sleep on the couch with me," she said.

"What the hell was out there, anyway?"

'Something bigger than Chuckie. That's for sure."

Seeing the size of the dog, I had to think about what she said in order to get my head around it.

"You're probably right about that."

"Can I stay?"

"Fine," I said. "You can be my assistant and Chuckie our watchdog. You think the two of you can keep out of the way in case Stormie or Brother Dunwoody comes nosing around?"

She stood on her tiptoes and kissed me.

"No problem. Thanks."

Sierra found an extra pillow in the closet, and she and Chuckie were soon snuggling on the couch. They were both soon asleep, and when I covered them with a russet Afghan, neither awakened.

Chapter Seven

Sierra was still asleep on the couch when I awoke the next morning. The big black dog named Chuckie was awake and moving stiffly. He might have wagged his tail when he saw me if he'd had one to wag.

"Hey boy. Want to go outside? I promise I'll walk slowly."

He seemed to know what I'd said, following me with a limp as I went out back. I brought a beef strip I'd found in the refrigerator, and he snatched it out of my hand when I showed it to him. Sierra was awake when we returned.

"He's young, and going to be fine," I said. "I gave him something to eat. You must be hungry yourself."

"I'm starting to get used to it."

"Well get unused to it. I'm going to the restaurant. Want to come with me?"

"I can't. If the monks knew I was squatting on the island, they'd call the police and have me booted."

"Narrow minded of them, if you ask me."

"You're funny. Bring me something back?"

"Happy to. Will you be okay while I'm gone?"

"There's TV, books in the bookshelf, and magazines in the rack. It'll be good just to relax for a while, in a place with a roof over my head."

"I won't be long."

"Take your time. I've got no place to go," she said.

I turned to leave but decided I needed to ask another question first. "You can't stay on Goose Island forever. What are your plans?"

"Guess I'll get a waitress job in New Orleans. I never finished high school. I can't go to college without a diploma, even if I could afford to."

"You can get a G.E.D., you know."

"I don't have a clue how to go about it," she said.

"I do. I'll help."

"Are you sure you're not just angling to have sex with me? If you are, you don't need to go to the trouble."

"Stop it," I said. "We're just friends. I have lots of friends I've never had sex with and never will."

"Sorry," she said. "My opinion of the human race has slipped the past few months."

"Then raise it back up. There are lots of terrific people in the world."

Chuckie and Kisses weren't so worried about their futures, lying on the floor together after licking the last morsels of food we'd placed in their bowl.

"Chuckie is so friendly with Kisses, he must have grown up with a cat," I said.

"What about Kisses?"

"She stayed with my friend and his collie while I was out of pocket. Guess she likes dogs."

"Seems like it."

"Will you do me a favor?"

"Sure. What?"

"The monks belong to an order called the Tracists. See if you can find anything on the Internet about them."

"No problem. What else?"

"When I get back, walk me through the basics of using a computer."

"That's it?"

"Like I said, we're just friends."

She grinned as I started out the door. "You're a strange one, Wyatt Thomas."

One of the restaurants in the entertainment complex was a buffet, and I smelled the spicy aroma of sausage and eggs when I walked through the door. Already late morning, I was the last guest. With lots of food left over, the friendly staff made sure I had a large doggie bag to take back to the bungalow with me. Sierra was sprawling in an oversized leather chair when I returned.

"I found something on the internet about the Tracist Order, she said."

"You did?"

"Yes and it's pretty interesting."

"How so?"

"The French brought lots of criminal types to the colony, offering them amnesty in exchange for helping colonize the New World."

"Go on," I said.

"Some of these criminal types went with the Frenchman that explored the Natchez Trace. You know what I'm talking about?"

"An ancient byway used by very early Indians?"

"Pretty much. Some of the people on the expedition found religion along the way. As compensation for their service to the crown, they were awarded this tract of land on Goose Island. They built the monastery and began calling themselves Tracists. "

"And?"

"They grew their order by recruiting former criminals."

"What else?"

"Something strange that doesn't make a lot of sense. I found an article about the monastery written just before Hurricane Katrina. The story called the Tracist Order a dying sect."

"For what reason?"

"I guess because everyone was so old. They were going to shut the place and give it to the state as a bird sanctuary."

"That is strange," I said. "Father Domenic isn't old. I would think he and Brother Dunwoody are probably only in their thirties. What do you make of it?"

"Beats me. I'm just telling you what the story said."

After eating her ham and cheese omelet, she gave me a basic lesson on computer use. At least she tried. In frustration, I finally called a halt to the session.

"Okay, I give."

"You'll catch on before you know it."

"If you say so. Right now there's something else I have to do. Will you be okay by yourself for a while?"

"You kidding? This place is heaven. I'd like to wash my clothes and take a bath. I have a change in my backpack, but they're dirty too."

"The bungalow has a utility room with a washer and dryer."

"Cool," she said. "Just what I need."

I wanted to check out the rest of the island, perhaps visit the fishing village and the researcher Father Domenic had told me about. I soon reached the distant berm surrounding the monastery. Though I managed to crawl over with difficulty, I tumbled face first to the ground, scraping my knee in the process. Droplets of blood quickly attracted swarms of mosquitoes, making me sorry I didn't have any insect repellent to slather on.

Goose Bay wasn't deep, cypress trees stunted by an occasional influx of salty water growing well out from shore. A pair of herons didn't bother flying off when I reached the water's edge. Not knowing which way to go, I began walking along the bank, a gentle breeze causing water to lap up over stumps, roots, and fallen branches.

Tiring rapidly from my days of inactivity at Chrissie's, I finally sat on the ground, my back propped against a stump. Beneath the shade of a tree, I relaxed as flocks of ducks and geese swam in the bay, feeding on the bounty of plants growing in the shallow water.

I must have dozed off, waking to a horsefly buzzing around my head. Without a watch, I had no idea how long I'd been asleep. From the position of the sun, it was likely an hour or more. I turned back toward the berm, deciding to take a shortcut through the trees.

There were other creatures aloft besides mosquitoes

and other insects. I soon began to see more birds than I knew existed. Watching an eagle soar high above me, I was so mesmerized I failed to watch where I was going. When I stepped on a patch of sticky muck, I lost my footing, hit the ground and began sliding down a muddy slope.

Trying to grab something to halt my progress before landing in the muddy slough proved impossible. Hitting the water with a splash, I sank up to my neck in the foul-smelling pond. When I tried to stand, I found the muddy bottom of the pool too slippery to support my weight.

"Oh shit!" I said.

I fell backwards into the wet hole, murky water dripping down my face as I quickly surfaced. Despite my efforts, I could get no traction against the slimy bottom. Worse, the heavy splash of something sliding into the water riveted my attention. Wheeling around, I saw what it was.

A large alligator, only its eyes peering out of the water was swimming slowly toward me. Forgetting my attempt to walk out of the muddy pond, I dived headfirst and began swimming toward shore. The alligator was in no hurry, watching as I clawed at gobs of sticky mud, trying to get a firm grip on something to help pull me out of the muddy hole.

I yelled at the top of my lungs, not quite believing anyone would hear me and come to my rescue. I was wrong.

"Grab hold and I'll hoist you up," someone called from above me.

The person tossed me a thick rope, knotted at the end. I quickly grabbed it and began pulling myself out of the water. The man helped, and I was soon on the bank beside him, out of breath both from exhaustion and fear. I finally looked up to see who had rescued me.

"Thanks," I said. "I thought I was a goner."

"I keep the rope around for that very purpose. You'd have found it sooner or later."

"Not if that gator had gotten to me first," I said, still out of breath.

"Alligators tend to prefer carcasses with a little age and odor to them. He'd have probably waited until you drowned."

"Glad I didn't have to find out," I said, managing a weak grin. "Thanks again for rescuing me. I'm Wyatt Thomas."

"Glad to meet you, Mr. Thomas. I'm Enos Quinn. You better come with me and let me wash that sticky mud off your clothes before it becomes permanently affixed."

I followed the little man through a thicket of palmetto, saw grass, and pygmy oak trees dripping with Spanish moss. He was short, not more than five eight, weighing in at probably one hundred forty pounds.

Dressed in a long-sleeved, khaki shirt, khaki pants, and big straw hat, he looked like an Amazon explorer. He was an older man, probably in his late seventies or even his eighties, though he moved like a much younger person.

Sweat dripped off my nose as the trail eventually led us to a clearing by the edge of Goose Bay. A wooden house stood high above the bank on stilts, a long and narrow deck extending far out over the water. Below the house was a shed, an old, topless Jeep and an airboat.

"My little slice of heaven, Mr. Thomas," he said. "I have a water hose beneath the house.

Enos Quinn spent the next five minutes spraying me with warm water, washing the mud off my clothes.

"Are you fit enough to climb the stairs?"

"Lead the way," I said, feeling like a wet cocker spaniel as I followed him up the steep stairway to the wooden porch surrounding his stilt house.

"Take your clothes off and hang them on the railing. I'll get you a robe to wear until they dry."

He returned with a towel, robe, and two Dixie beers as I stood dripping on the long deck overlooking the bay.

Once wrapped in the robe, I said, "I'll have to pass on the beer. I don't drink anymore."

I smiled when he said, "One won't hurt you."

"Famous last words. Sorry to make you waste your beer."

"No beer goes to waste around here, Mr. Thomas. Have a seat and I'll get you something else."

He soon returned with a tall glass of iced tea, plopping down in the rocking chair beside the one I was sitting in."

"Thanks. You just saved my life for the second time today."

"Glad to be of service. What brings you to the island, Mr. Thomas?"

"Call me Wyatt. I'm a writer, on retreat at the monastery."

"How many books have you written?"

"Just one."

"Would I know the name of it?"

"Probably not."

"What's it about?"

"A mystery," I said.

"Oh?"

"Nothing remarkable. Just a book."

"Uh huh! I was born, Wyatt, but I wasn't born yesterday. If you'd actually written a book, you'd know every paragraph in it. I'd say you're a liar, or else taking me for a fool."

"But I am a writer."

"You may as well tell me who you actually are. I'm not buying your other story."

"You think I'm lying?"

"I've taught more students than you can count, and I've heard every story in the book. If lying's your game, Wyatt, you better try another profession. You're not adept at it. Your body language belies everything you've told me."

Taken aback by his bluntness and not knowing what to say, I glanced instead at a muskrat swimming in the water, fifteen feet below us.

"How do I know I can trust you?"

"Let me tell you a little about myself and then maybe you'll loosen up."

"Deal," I said.

"I'm a retired professor. I taught geology at the University in Brannerville, Arkansas, though my hobby is birding. What most people call bird watching. There are more birds around here than just about any place on earth, in case you haven't noticed. I got a grant from Louisiana about ten years ago, and I've been coming to this island ever since."

"This house is comfortable and well built. It's so high off the ground, it feels like. . ."

"A tree house? State engineers designed and constructed it for me, to my specifications. It has bathrooms, hot and cold running water, and pretty much all the amenities of home."

"You work for the state?"

"For much of the year, when I'm not traveling around the world. Now tell me what you do, Wyatt."

"I trust you, though I'm breaking one of my own rules by telling you so."

"Go on."

"I'm investigating the murder of Rance Parker, the actor."

Quinn finished the first beer, threw the empty into a barrel on the deck and then popped the top of the second.

"I had you pegged as being in law enforcement. My god daughter Heather was a cop for a while."

"I'm not in law enforcement. Just a gumshoe from New Orleans."

"Whatever. What have you learned so far?"

"Not much. I just arrived yesterday. Rumor has it Parker was killed by a pack of dogs. What's your take?"

Before he could answer, a large cat bounded around the back of the house and jumped into his lap. Quinn stroked the long-haired creature.

"King Tut," he said.

"Hi King Tut," I said, reaching over and stroking the cat.

"He likes you. You must be a cat person."

"I have a tailless kitty named Kisses. I brought her with me, and she's in my bungalow at the monastery."

"You take your cat along on investigations?"

"Long story."

Having received enough affection for a while, King Tut jumped out of Professor Quinn's lap and onto the sill of an open window.

"You asked about dogs. I've seen bobcats, muskrats, nutria, otters, and beavers on the island. There is a fishing village a mile or so from here. They have a few dogs, but I wouldn't call them a pack."

"What about wolves?"

"Killed off years ago. Why do you ask?"

"Because I think I heard one last night. Outside my back window."

"You said you don't drink."

"Or use drugs. I heard what I heard. When I opened the back door, I saw the shadow of something large running away."

"What do you think it was?"

"I didn't get a good look."

"I'm afraid I can't help you much with dogs and wolves. Like I said, I'm a birder."

"You've been on the island off and on for years now. What do you know about the monastery?"

"Not much. They don't bother me, and I don't bother them."

"Did you ever meet any of the monks?"

"I took a tour when I first started coming here," he said.

"Can you tell me about it?"

"The monks were all old and had stopped recruiting new acolytes many years ago. At my behest, they were going to donate the property to the state as a bird sanctuary.

"Why didn't they?"

"Father Domenic, the Abbey of the monastery decided to continue with the order," he said.

"Did you ever meet him?"

"He was unavailable the day I visited. A monk named Brother Degas, one of the few brothers still physically active, gave me the tour. We kept in touch for a while."

"What happened to him?"

"He was from New Orleans and moved back there when he left the monastery."

He nodded when I asked, "Do you have an address for him?"

He went into his house, returning with the corner he'd torn from an old letter.

"This is in the Quarter," I said.

"In a tiny apartment. The monks had little money to distribute among themselves."

"You wouldn't know it to see the place now," I said.

A powerful telescope stood ready at the end of the long deck, binoculars and camera on the stand beside Professor Quinn's chair.

"Sorry I can't tell you more about the monastery."

"That's okay," I said. "I wasn't expecting a break in my investigation this soon anyway. You have an elaborate setup here. Looks interesting."

"Oh, it is. I just wish I had my assistant again this year."

"You have an assistant?"

"Not now, but for the past three years. Mostly grad students from L.S.U. They always graduate, find another job or get married shortly after I have them competently trained. The state promised me a full-time employee, but they can't find anyone to move to the swamp with a crazy old professor."

We both laughed. His second beer finished, he threw the empty into the trash barrel, grabbed my glass and returned to the house.

"You must get lonely here all by yourself with only King Tut to keep you company," I said when he returned.

"It's not so bad. I had a Rottweiler that grew up with Tut. He ran away or got lost a year ago. I do miss him, and so does King Tut."

"His name wouldn't be Chuckie, would it?"

Professor Quinn sat straight up in his chair. "You've seen him?"

"He's at my bungalow. He was fighting with the creature that sounded like a wolf last night. We doctored him up and fed him."

"We?"

"An intelligent young woman named Sierra. She's looking for a job and wants to stay on the island. Do you have any interest in possibly hiring her as your assistant?"

"So far, all my assistants have been males. Still, I'd like to talk to her. Lord knows I could use the help."

"How much does the job pay if you don't mind me asking."

"It's quite adequate, I assure you. Let me speak with your young friend. If I decide she'll work out, I'll discuss the details with her. Meantime, I'd like to see my dog."

"Why don't I go to the monastery and bring him back, along with Sierra?"

"Fine idea. I'll walk along with you and make sure you don't fall in any more mud holes."

Chapter Eight

After beginning the day behind schedule, along with my unplanned nap in the woods, it was late when we left the Professor's cabin. My clothes had long since dried by the time he led me on a circuitous path through the trees to a metal walkway that went up and over the berm.

"Wish I'd known about this earlier," I said.

"Not many people do," Quinn said. "A little road splaying off the main one at the front entrance leads to my house. Anyone that knows about it can get into the compound any time of the day or night."

He grinned when I gave him an assessing look. "You sure I shouldn't be worried about you?"

"Like I said, I was in Nebraska when the actor was killed."

It was my turn to smile. "You don't seem the type that would tear someone limb from limb even if you were younger and lots bigger."

"It's not in my DNA. I'll wait here for you. How long do you think it'll be?"

"Why not just come with me?"

"I have my binoculars and camera, and I've been meaning to check this sector of the island for a while, anyway."

"I won't be long."

"Take your time. There are plenty of birds in the area

67

to keep me occupied. Oh, and Wyatt, it's getting late. If you have no other plans, I'll cook us something when we get back to camp."

"Music to my ears," I said, my growling stomach reminding me I hadn't eaten since breakfast.

I was sweating when I reached the bungalow, Sierra and Chuckie meeting me at the door.

"I was starting to worry about you."

"Hope you're not starving."

"We had something to eat. What about you?"

"Missed out. You're not going to believe it, but I found Chuckie's owner."

"No way," she said.

"You don't look happy."

Sierra knelt and hugged the big dog. "It's not fair. Now I'm attached to him."

"But he's not yours."

"At least I wouldn't have let him starve half to death."

"He's been missing for more than a year. He must have somehow made his way back to the island. That sounds to me as if he missed his owner a bunch."

"Doesn't make me feel any better. Chuckie likes me now."

Seeing I was getting nowhere, I decided to change the subject.

"The person who owns him is a professor that works for the state of Louisiana. He has a stilt house on Goose Bay where he does research. He needs an assistant and said he would consider hiring you. You need a job."

"What would I do?"

"Observe, photograph, and classify bird life," I said, repeating what Professor Quinn had told me.

"No sex?"

"Would you stop it. Professor Quinn is old enough to be your grandfather. What's with this sex thing, anyway?"

"I don't want to talk about it," she said, hugging Chuckie again.

"Look, I'm not a sexual predator, and neither is Professor Quinn. You'll like him, I promise. Come with me to meet him at least."

"I don't want to lose Chuckie."

"You can't take a man's dog. If the job doesn't work out, I'll help you get another pet."

"It won't be the same," she said.

"That's what I thought when I lost my first cat Bob. I still miss him, but now I love Kisses. You'll see."

"Okay, but if I think the person is mean in any way, I'm taking Chuckie and running."

"And I'll come with you."

A disappearing sun had begun casting shadows through the branches of the transplanted oak trees outside the door. A gentle breeze wafted through the limbs, blowing the Spanish moss that affirmed we were indeed in south Louisiana.

"If we go now, we won't cause any attention to ourselves. The monks have prayer service every day at this time in the old cathedral. They'll all be there. Everyone else will be swimming or chilling in their bungalows. I'll get my backpack."

The hottest part of the day, I was wishing for one of the straw hats in the closet by the time we'd reached the berm crossover. Sierra noticed my discomfort and offered me a ball cap from her backpack.

"No thanks. I'm not a cap or hat type. Besides, we're almost there."

Chuckie's ears perked up when we reached the berm. After barking once, he bounded over the walkway to the other side, Sierra and I following. When he saw Professor Quinn, he ran to him, practically jumping into his arms.

Sierra frowned when I said, "Doesn't look like an abused pet to me."

"Shut up," she said.

"Professor Quinn, this is Sierra," I said as we approached the old man, bent at the knees, hugging the dog.

"Pleased to meet you, Sierra. Thanks for saving

Chuckie. You can't imagine how I've missed him. Let's go to my house, and we can get acquainted there."

When we reached the bay's edge, Sierra stood on the bank, gazing out at hundreds of ducks and geese foraging in the shallow water. When she finally noticed Quinn's stilt house her eyes grew even larger.

"Wow!" she said. "You must have quite a view."

"You like birds?" he asked.

"Love them. When I lived in California, Mom would take me to the seashore to watch the gulls and terns. There are lots of birds in California, but not like this."

"You're right about that. Goose Island is like no place on earth," he said.

"I know. I miss Mom and California, but I already love it here."

"I hope you two are hungry. I was beginning to think I'd never see Chuckie again. Now he's back, I feel like celebrating."

We followed him up the steep staircase, Chuckie wagging his short-tailed behind to express how excited he was. Halfway up, he ran around Professor Quinn, hurrying up to the deck to where King Tut waited. After touching noses, Tut purred and rubbed up against him. They soon disappeared around the corner, on the deck encircling the stilt house.

"What say we have an old fashioned crawfish boil," Quinn said. "Make yourselves at home and I'll get it started."

Sierra was still worried about other things. "When's he going to ask me about the job?"

"Don't know. I'm sure he'll get around to it."

Professor Quinn wheeled out a large, metal pot, and a propane burner, proceeding to fill it with water, corn on the cob, crawfish, shrimp, crab, andouille sausage, and plenty of Cajun seasoning. Once the feast was started, he returned from the kitchen with beer for himself and ice tea for me and Sierra.

"As long as we're celebrating, I'd rather have a beer," Sierra said.

"Sorry, young lady, You're underage."

"I'm twenty. Old enough to drink beer."

"Oh, well you could fool me," he said.

"Want to see my driver's license?" she said, pulling a wallet out of her backpack before he could argue. "See?"

"How do I know it's not a fake I.D.?"

Sierra gave me an exasperated look. "It's a California license. There's no one around here you can ask."

"Well then," he said, raising his arms. "That's proof enough for me. When did you graduate from high school?"

"I didn't," she said.

When he frowned, she rolled her eyes, and then walked to the end of the long deck to Quinn's telescope.

"Did she say something wrong?" I asked.

"She's obviously not qualified to fill the position, and she's lying about her age."

Quinn got up to check the boiling pot. When he returned, I said, "Professor, I know you think you have a firm grip on human behavior. Well, so do I. Though you may think you're a human lie detector, we both know there is no such thing. As I see it, you're letting your biases affect your decision."

He wasn't pleased by my opinion of his behavior. I could see from his miffed expression.

"Well exactly what do you think I should do about it, Mr. Thomas?"

"What all good scientists and private investigators do. Keep an open mind."

"I resent your implication, Mr. Thomas."

"Wyatt."

"You're a persuasive talker."

"Every now and then the lawyer in me pops out."

"Lawyer? I should have known."

"Ex lawyer now. I'm just asking you to give Sierra a chance. Unless I miss my guess, someone gave you one once."

Professor Quinn opened his mouth to speak. Sierra's delight as she gazed through the telescope caused him to grow silent.

"Oh my God. I've never seen so many birds in my life. At least three different kinds of ducks and geese are in the water out there."

"That's why they call it Goose Island."

"This is so cool."

"You said you like birds. I didn't realize how much," Quinn said.

"They're part of my reason for liking the island so. Want to see my drawings?"

Sierra ran to her backpack, removing an unlined deck of three by five cards. She handed them to Professor Quinn and he began thumbing through them.

"Quite remarkable. Where did you get these?"

"I drew them," she said.

"These are birds found on the island."

"I started drawing them when I arrived about six months ago."

Quinn handed the pictures to me. "You are a wonderful artist, Sierra," I said. "These remind me of Audubon's drawings. Who taught you?"

"Myself, mostly. I've been drawing for ten years now. Since I was in grade school."

"Well, there's one bird you didn't see around here," Quinn said.

"Which one?" Sierra asked.

Quinn held up a card. "The Limpkin is only found in Florida."

"Would you like me to show you their nest?"

Quinn frowned and glanced up at the sky. "Look here, young lady. I was studying birds long before you were born. Don't you think I'd know if there were Limpkins on the island."

"Apparently not."

"You don't have to be impertinent."

"I said I'd show you."

"Fine! Show me the nest and you've got the job."

"What makes you think I want your job? What does it pay? Minimum wage?"

"You'll be an employee of Louisiana and make

significantly more than minimum wage. Plus, you'll receive benefits, health insurance, and retirement, just to mention a few things."

"But I'd have to work for you, and I can already tell you're an old asshole."

Professor Quinn's mouth dropped. When he glanced at me for help, I just smiled and shook my head.

"I may be an old asshole, but I'm a fair old asshole. What makes you think you can keep up with me, young lady, assuming I give you the job?"

"You kidding me? I'd run your skinny butt into the ground. It's you that would be trying to keep up with me."

"You'll need a high school degree to qualify for the position. That's no problem I can't take care of."

"You'd help me get a G.E.D.? How long will it take?"

"Is tomorrow soon enough?" he asked.

"I'd have my G.E.D. tomorrow? You can do that?"

"Listen, young lady, I've been an educator for three times the years you've been living. All I have to do is sign off on your application, and it's a done deal."

"Tomorrow? You'd do that for me?"

"On one condition," he said. "You'll be on probation for ninety days, and I can fire you for any reason during that time. You screw up, and you're gone. I take no prisoners. I'm an old asshole. Remember?"

Sierra was grinning in disbelief. "When do I start?"

"You can get your things tomorrow."

"Everything I own is in my backpack. I'm ready right now."

"Then consider yourself on the payroll. You'll have a room of your own here in the cabin, with a bed, a shower, and indoor plumbing. I'll request a laptop, camera, binoculars, and Smartphone for you. There's an app I use for cataloging and counting bird species."

"Oh my God! she said. "I've never had my own room."

"Never?" he said.

"We had a little house. Growing up, I always slept on the living room couch."

"No couch for you here. You're going to like your new

quarters."

"Can I go look now?"

"Go for it," he said. "It's down the inside stairway. First door on your right. What?" he said when he saw me smile.

"I thought you were tough. You're nothing but a pushover."

"Bah!" he said, checking the crawfish boil.

When Sierra returned, a mile-wide smile on her face, he handed her a beer.

"You get me busted for contributing to the delinquency of a minor, and I'm going to kill you. We'll fill out the paperwork tomorrow and then drive into Chalmette and get you a bank account and an advance so you'll have some spending money."

"Can I buy some new clothes?"

"You can get anything you want. The money you make is yours."

"What about college?"

"You're interested in going to college?"

"It's been my dream since I was a little girl."

"All right then. I'll help you get enrolled at L.S.U. I'll also see to it that this summer's work counts as six semester hours. You can start with a few courses online when we get your computer."

"Oh Wyatt," she said, hugging me. "I think I'm dreaming."

"Then don't wake up."

The delicious aroma wafting across the deck caused me to remember I hadn't eaten since breakfast. When Quinn's crawfish boil was done, we dined like royalty. The moon was high when we finished eating, Chuckie and King Tut lying on an outdoor couch between Sierra and the professor.

"It's late," I finally said. "I have to return to the monastery."

"Sure you can find your way?"

"It isn't that far, and I've done it twice now already."

"It's not the same after dark," he said. "Things have a

way of getting turned around before you know it."

"I was a boy scout. I'll be fine."

"I'll go with you," Sierra said.

"I'm a big boy. I'll be okay," I said, waving her off.

"At least let me give you my cell phone number, just in case," Quinn said.

"It would do me no good since I don't have a cell phone."

Then you're on your own," he said as I started down the steep stairway, away from the flickering lights on the deck and toward the darkness of Goose Island.

Chapter Nine

Though I sensed my chance meeting with the professor would result in the best thing that had ever happened in Sierra's life, I felt a little guilty about leaving without her. My intuition told me she had nothing to worry about. I might not be so lucky, it soon informed me.

It wasn't far to the footbridge over the berm. It didn't matter because the lights from Professor Quinn's stilt house had long disappeared when I realized I'd somehow gotten off the path leading to it. As I exited the trees and saw moonlight glimmering off Goose Bay, I knew for sure I'd erred in the wrong direction.

The light from the moon didn't last long. A late-spring storm had begun moving up from the Gulf, bringing with it moist clouds and dense ground fog dancing around my ankles. The eerie cry of a bayou loon gashed the night's serenity.

With no compass to guide me, I decided to return to the bay. From there I would follow the shoreline back to Quinn's house. When I arrived, I'd have to swallow my pride and let him lead me to the berm bridge. At least that was my plan.

Twenty minutes of following the shoreline convinced me I'd somehow gotten turned around, walking away from the house instead of toward it. The cry of the loon pierced the night again as I stopped to rest on a log.

The fog hadn't stopped the mosquitoes, and I soon wished I was wearing a long sleeved shirt. The little dive-bombers weren't my only problem. Somewhere on the island, and not that far away, an animal that sounded like a wolf was howling. Even worse, the howls were coming from the direction in which I thought Quinn's house lay.

I made an easy target for the flying blood suckers as I walked away from the shoreline, thinking I would surely reach the berm. If I could manage to traverse a straight line. It was something I'd begun doubting the farther I went. More howls echoed across the island, causing me to wonder if I'd become hopelessly lost. The moon, popping through wispy clouds for just a bit, provided no response to my question.

The clearing by the water soon disappeared, swampy terrain becoming wooded as I reached the top of a gentle rise. It didn't seem to matter. The storm rolling in from the Gulf had blanketed the moon and stars. At least the ground fog was gone. The howling continued, closer this time, when I encountered something that frightened me worse.

Without a better plan, I continued walking, soon reaching a small clearing in the trees. The moon, poking through cottony clouds, illuminated the clearing. As it did, I stopped dead in my tracks. Something was moving in the brush. From the low-throated growls and pawing of the ground, I knew there was a dog right in front of me. A big dog from the sound it made.

And then I saw what it was. From the shadows, two large black men appeared. One of them held a leash with both hands to restrain the two dogs tugging to get at me. A sawed-off, double-barreled shotgun in the arms of the second man was loosely pointed in my direction. The two men looked like twins. Almost.

"Quoi c'est ton nom?" the man with the shotgun asked.

"Wyatt Thomas. Tu parles les deux langues?"

"Come with us," he said in Cajun-flavored English.

"Don't let no grass grow under your feet. And put your hands down. I ain't gonna shoot you."

I wasn't so sure about the dogs, fangs showing as they strained to get loose from their chains. The odd man tightened his grip on the chains and yanked. Turning them away from me, he led us through the brush, his partner with the shotgun behind me.

"Where are we going?" I asked.

He didn't answer, putting a finger to his lips and shaking his head instead. A branch snapped in the bushes beside us. When it did, he turned toward the darkness and opened up with both barrels, the resultant twelve-gauge explosion causing my heart to skip several beats.

Thrashing in the underbrush followed an almost unearthly shriek and a loud crash as buckshot connected with something large and very much alive. Not dead, it soon began moving away from us. The hounds began barking and tugging at their leashes, trying to get loose to pursue whatever it was the man behind me had unloaded his shotgun on.

"Depecher," he said, ejecting the shell casings and inserting two more cartridges into the chambers.

Though not understanding much Cajun-French, I fully understood he wanted us to leave the area, and fast. With the shotgun blast still ringing in my ears, I hurried after the man with the hounds.

The sky opened up, drenching us with rain as we came out of the woods into a clearing by the bay. Wood-framed houses, more than I could count, occupied the clearing, looking like a dream-sequence amid the haze-cloaked moon. The man with the shotgun wasn't taking any chances, walking backwards as he followed us into the village.

When we reached the largest house near the center of the community the man in front released the hounds into a fenced area. Still excited, they ran to the edge of the enclosure, pawing at the fence as they continued to bark and growl at something in the darkness.

The shotgun man opened the door of a tarpaper and unpainted, wood house that was little more than a shack. Fragrance, smelling like sage, permeated the interior. Several candles burned on an altar, dimly lighting the room. A woman, dressed in a yellow, African print dress was kneeling on a rug in front of it.

"Sit beside me," she said.

There wasn't a chair, so I joined her on the rug.

"I'm Wyatt Thomas."

"I know who you are," she said. "Please be quiet until I finish the ceremony."

Distant drumming accompanied the steady tympani of falling rain on the shack's tin roof. The woman was chanting something in a language I didn't recognize as she sprinkled colored powder into the flame of a black candle.

Purple cloth draped a wooden box. On the satiny fabric, in addition to the black candles, there were various items including rosary beads, an offering bowl filled with rice and beans, and a human skull with a noticeable hole between the eye sockets. The last handful of powder she sprinkled into the flame caused it to flash brightly, sending smoke rising slowly to the ceiling. As the last wisp disappeared in the rafters, she turned to face me.

The two men were still standing in the doorway, rain pelting the covered porch behind them. The man with the shotgun was young, probably mid-twenties, with thinning hair but healthy good looks. His ragged tee shirt did little to hide his muscular chest and arms. There was also something about him so peculiar it made me stop and stare; his eyes were as clear and blue as a Stockholm Swede's.

The eyes of the large man with him were just as anomalous—dark, empty and focused on nothing in particular. His arms seemed disjointed, out of sync with his body. The eyes and limbs of someone not quite alive, I thought.

"You can go now, Landry."

When the woman nodded, the two men departed,

shutting the door behind them. Unlike Landry, she spoke excellent English with no discernible accent.

"I am Mama Malaika. Why were you in the woods alone?"

"Trying to find my way back to the monastery. I got turned around in the dark."

I nodded when she said, "You were visiting the bird man."

"You know him?"

"He keeps his distance, and we keep ours," she said.

I see your altar. You practice voodoo?"

"Vodoun is my belief. Some people call it voodoo. Cajuns call it hoodoo. I am the village mambo."

I heard something out there. Do you know what it was?"

"You almost found out."

"Was it a wolf?"

"A human wolf. It's afoot tonight."

"You mean. . . ?"

"A rougarou."

I'd grown up listening to tales of rougarous, the south Louisiana werewolf that supposedly stalks swamps and bayous, and carries away children that are disobedient.

"A man that transforms into a wolf?"

She nodded. "Can you hear it? It's circling the village right now and probably will continue all night long."

"But why?"

"It wants you."

"For what reason? If it does, aren't you afraid it'll come looking for me in the village?"

"Our magic protects us here, and only brave men go out on nights it's stalking."

She shook her head when I asked, "I've heard of rougarous haunting the swamps. Every kid in Louisiana has. I never thought it was real."

"It's real. This rougarou is the spawn of the Devil. The manifestation of pure evil. Only God can kill it."

A clap of thunder outside the shack was followed by a distant, plaintive howl.

"I'm still not understanding."

"Good and evil exists no matter where you live, the swamp no different. I have potions and antidotes for almost everything."

"Even one that will kill a rougarou?"

Bottles and jars containing various items lined one of her walls. She stood on her tiptoes and grabbed a Mason jar filled with some unknown concoction.

"I have something that works temporarily," she said, showing me the jar. "Wolfsbane."

"I've heard of it."

"Landry soaks his buckshot in it before he loads his rounds. It will stop a rougarou, at least for a short time."

"One of the men that found me?"

"Yes."

"How long does your potion work?"

"Long enough to run away to safety," she said.

"Is the rougarou someone from your village?"

The old woman shook her head. "It is true there is evil on this island. It doesn't come from this village."

"Landry and the other man were out there tonight even though they knew the rougarou was afoot."

"Looking for you," she said. "I sent them to bring you here."

"How did you know I was out there?"

"I knew," she said. "The Spirits told me to protect you and bring you here."

Wind had picked up, blowing the canvas drapes covering an otherwise open window. Though damp spray blew against my face, Mama Malaika didn't seem to notice.

"Your village is remote. How long has it been here?"

"Forever."

"How in the world did it survive Katrina?"

"Magic. It protects us."

"You had no damage?"

"We lost a few boats, some chickens and a dog or two."

"Amazing. This whole island must have been under six feet of water."

"We are on the lee side of the island and on a hill."

"A hill?"

She smiled. "A few feet out of the water is a hill in south Louisiana. It was enough. Even our gardens survived the storm and big wind."

She smiled again when I said, "What crops do you raise?"

"A few acres of corn, tomatoes, beans, squash, and okra. We trap and trade with the Cajuns and other people of the swamp. Oh, and there's plenty of shrimp, crawfish, oysters, and redfish. We have learned to survive and flourish."

When one of the candles flickered brightly for a moment, I became aware the drumming had ceased.

"I don't want to create a threat to the village."

"Landry," she said, not answering me. "Take this man. He will stay with you tonight. Tomorrow you will take him to the place of the priests."

The person named Landry must have been waiting on the other side of the door because he quickly appeared, motioning me to follow him. His house wasn't far away, a smaller version of Mama Malaika's. He pointed to a pallet on the floor, several candles the only illumination.

"You sleep there."

I didn't argue. Even the pallet felt comfortable and supportive as I listened to the hypnotic rhythm of rain against the shack's tin roof. Somewhere far away, the creature the old woman called a rougarou was howling at a remnant moon cloaked in cottony clouds.

Chapter Ten

The toe of Landry's boot prodding my ribs awoke me the following morning.

"Allons asteur," he said.

"Is everything okay?"

"Tout va bien. Time to go, mon."

We were soon out the door, Landry stopping at a pen in back and returning with the two dogs from the previous night. For the first time, I got a close look at them. They were big, probably a hundred pounds each. Though buck-skinned colored, their long muzzles were black, almost to their eyes. When they barked at me, I saw their lips and the inside of their mouths were also black. They weren't happy to see me, and I was glad they were restrained by chains.

The village proved much larger than I'd originally thought, twenty or more houses built around a cove in the bay that led out to the Gulf. A dozen pirogues were tied to the wooden decking extending over the water. Two coastal shrimp boats, their nets drying on the masts, were beside them.

Happy children followed after us on our path through the settlement, dogs barking and old men and women sitting in rockers on their front porches. We stopped at an outhouse before continuing our journey down the rise, and were soon into the brushy terrain we'd encountered the previous night.

"Where's your brother?"

Landry laughed, answering my question in his Cajun-flavored English.

"Jomo stay in the shed when Mama Malaika don' need him."

"Must get hot in there," I said.

"Him don' care, no. When he drowned, Mama Malaika zombied him. He stay in the shed 'cept at night cause he scare everybody."

He nodded when I said, "Jomo's a zombie?"

"Mama Malaika a powerful mambo. She can draw rain from a cloudless sky if she like. She protect our village with her magic."

"You keep your dogs on chains. Are they dangerous?"

"They ain't mean. They's black mouth curs and I use them as hog dogs. Lots of wild hogs 'round and they can be mean, though."

"Would they kill a man?"

"My dogs or the wild hogs?"

"Either."

"If the dogs was running in a pack, they might. These two jus' bay somethin' up till me and Jomo get there with the gun."

He grinned when I said, "Two's not a pack?"

"Ain't no way," he said.

"What about the wild hogs."

"They'd kill you all right. And eat you too, if they got the chance."

"I have another question."

"Axe me," he said.

"Were your dogs loose the night the man at the monastery was killed?"

"Mon, my two dogs don' kill nobody. The rougarou got that man down by the bay."

"I'm not sure I believe there is such a thing as a rougarou."

He grinned and said, "Well, you almost found out las' night. He was in the bushes, ten feet away when I unloaded the shotgun on him."

"Mama Malaika said you can't kill a rougarou."

"She wrong about that."

"Is there something I'm missing? You said Mama Malaika practices powerful magic. Now you're changing your mind and disagreeing with her?"

"Don' be pullin' my chain, mon. You can surely kill a rougarou, but only when it take the form of a man. Then you can deal with it for sure if you do it before it changes again."

"And when you shot it last night."

"I ain't did nothin' 'cept knock him down. Wouldn't even have don' that 'cept Mama give me a magic potion to soak my buckshot in."

"What if it hadn't worked?"

"If he'd a kept comin', I'd a let the dogs loose on him. He'd a killed them, but it woulda give us time to get away. He'd a kept comin', I'd have sacrificed Jomo. He'd hold him off, least till we got away."

"Jomo's that strong?"

"Stronger than any man alive, but not as strong as a rougarou."

"The creature is that powerful?"

"You shoot him, he don' die. He kill you for sure. And if he don', you got a livin' hell to pay."

"So Mama Malaika sent you and Jomo out last night to find me? How did she know I was out here?"

"Visioned it."

"Why would she even care?"

"Don' know." He grinned and added, "Hell, if it was up to me I'd a left you skinny ass out here."

"I'm glad you didn't."

The weather was hot and sticky after last night's rain, and everything growing in the marsh was lush. We suddenly smelled something that wasn't. Landry motioned me to stay put as the dogs pulled him through the brush.

Two turkey buzzards circled slowly overhead, and my nose informed me something was dead before I saw the carcass. It was one of Landry's wild hogs, its eyes open but staring at nothing. Claw marks raked its sides, and a sizeable chunk of flesh was missing from its neck. Flies swarmed around the body already infested with maggots and other bugs.

Even the black mouthed curs wouldn't go near the carcass stinking to high heaven as it quickly decomposed in the heat and sun of south Louisiana. Motioning me to back up, he led me on a path around the dead hog as the buzzards seemed to hang like dark kites overhead.

"Look like the rougarou got him somethin' las' night after all," he said.

"Or maybe your dogs."

Landry didn't like my insinuation. "Embrasse moi tchew," he said, Cajun for kiss my ass. "They's plenty of things can kill a man in this swamp. Alligators for one, black bear, bobcats. Hell, I even seen a panther once swimming out in the bay."

"No offense. I'm just saying whatever killed that pig didn't have to be a rougarou. Like you said, lots of animals on this island could have done it."

"Mon, I shot something last night point blank, both barrels with double-ought buckshot. We passed the spot on our way here. I didn't see no dead bear or panther. Did you?"

"No."

"Well nothin' human or animal would be livin' if I'd shot them that close, I can tell you that much right now."

I could feel Landry's anger as a nutria splashed into a watery ditch. Dogs were barking back at the settlement, and they sounded far away.

"Sorry. I'm just grasping at straws because I'm having a hard time believing in rougarous."

"Allons," Landry said, turning his attention back to the trail.

We reached the footbridge over the berm about twenty minutes later.

"Thanks. I owe you one," I said as I started up the steps.

I turned around when I reached the top of the berm. Landry and his dogs were gone, already out of sight. Far off, down by the bay, scores of geese were landing in orchestrated waves, the island alive with their honking.

The door of my bungalow was ajar when I got there. Nothing seemed amiss, but I'd yet to unpack my bags. When I checked, I found them opened, my clothes strewn on the bed. The laptop was open. Someone had just visited, the screen still aglow. I took a quick look around, finding nothing.

Someone had probably checked the computer, probably searching for clues to the real reason I'd asked so many questions about the monastery. Finding nothing because there was nothing there to find, they had rummaged through my suitcase. Pacing back and forth in the kitchen was Kisses. She was noticeably disturbed, so I picked her up and gave her a few strokes.

"You okay, baby?" I said, placing her on the bed.

I wondered about the breach of security as I stripped off my clothes and stood beneath warm water pouring from the shower head. Fresh clothes felt terrific, and my growling stomach reminded me I hadn't eaten since the the crab boil at Professor Quinn's. I had other things on my mind. My appetite would have to wait.

The carpentry shop, where the monks made the coffins, was my first stop. Father Domenic said there were four monks on the island, including himself. Only four. The small group of monks at a place the size of Barataria Monastery intrigued me. Perhaps there was a deeper explanation than the one he'd given.

The sun was again bright when I left the bungalow, all the clouds gone from the previous night's rain. I found Brother Dunwoody at his desk.

"There you are," he said. "I was wondering where you'd gotten off to."

"I took a walking tour of the island."

"After dark?"

"Not intentionally. It just happened that way."

"There's lots of wild animals on the island. They come

out after dark."

"So I've heard. Any wolves around here?"

Brother Dunwoody cocked his head and gave me a look. "The island is the southern tip of a large, wilderness area. You never know what might show up."

I let the cryptic comment drop. "Can you introduce me to the other two monks?"

"Father Domenic said you're researching a book."

"Yes and I'm finding it quite interesting."

"Then come with me. Brothers Bruno and Bruce are working in the carpentry."

The odor of freshly cut pine radiated from the room when Brother Dunwoody opened the door. Two men, stripped to their pants and tee shirts, were sawing, hammering, and putting the finishing touches on a wooden coffin sitting on the work bench in front of them.

"Brothers, this is Mr. Thomas. He's a writer and doing research for his next novel. He'd like to ask a few questions. This is Brother Bruno and Brother Bruce."

Like Dunwoody, Brother Bruno was tall and muscular, black hair protruding from the neck of his tee shirt. And like Dempsey Duplantis, colorful tattoos also marked the man's arms and neck. The tattoos were dotted with red marks, as was his neck.

Brother Bruce was his antithesis—small, with thinning hair, narrow eyes and pointed nose causing him to look instantly untrustworthy. Neither man bothered to acknowledge my presence, or to shake my hand.

"Your work intrigues me. Can you tell me a little about it?"

Brother Bruno got a look from Brother Dunwoody when he frowned, not answering my question. Brother Dunwoody's own frown seemed to rouse his attention, and he answered in a heavy, Eastern European accent.

"The woodwork is not complicated, but it is precise. We use pegs and not nails. Everything must fit perfectly. No mistakes."

"It's beautiful. Too bad it has to be buried."

"A fate everyone must someday face," he said.

"You have an accent. Where are you from?" I said.

"Romania."

"How did you manage to end up at a monastery at the end of the road in Louisiana?"

"Long story," he said.

"I have all day."

His smile was more sinister than friendly. Brother Dunwoody answered for him.

"We are not about individuals here at the monastery. Brother Bruno's past isn't relevant to our work. Please don't violate our wishes."

"I see," I said. "Who taught you to do such intricate woodwork?"

Brother Bruno continued scowling. When he didn't answer, I glanced at Brother Bruce.

"Brother Italo," he said. "He was an old-world craftsman who knew every intricacy of carpentry."

"Was? What happened to him?"

Brother Bruce looked at Brother Dunwoody and then glanced away.

"Brother Italo was a master craftsman and a wayward soul. He, alas, left our order to return to the material world."

Brother Dunwoody shook his head when I asked, "Where is he now?"

"Don't know. We haven't kept in touch."

Seeing I was getting no place fast, I decided to catch Brother Bruce at a time when he was alone. Ask him a few questions I had the feeling he knew the answers to.

"Father Domenic said I could use his phone if I needed one. You think he'd mind?"

"If that's what he told you, I'm sure it is okay. Now is an excellent time because he is meditating in his chambers."

Brother's Bruno and Bruce didn't bother saying bye as we left the carpentry. Brother Dunwoody took me to Father Domenic's office, the room dark, curtains closed. He turned on a desk lamp for me.

"I'll wait outside," he said, shutting the door behind

him.

Fishing through my wallet, I found Tony's business card and quickly dialed his number. He answered on the first ring.

"Homi. . . Tony Nicosia."

"Tony, it's me."

"Hey, Cowboy, you calling from the monastery?"

"Father Domenic's office. Got a few questions."

"Shoot."

"I have some names I was hoping you could run for me."

"I still have a few friends down at the precinct. How many names you want me to run?"

"Only four, and I have a problem."

"Such as?"

"They are the monks here at the monastery, and I don't have any last names."

"Without last names, I have no place to start."

"That's what I was afraid of. Maybe you could ask around. Someone might know something."

"I'm in a New Orleans traffic jam and can't exactly use my pen and pad right now."

"You only have to remember four first names—Bruce, Bruno, Domenic, and Dunwoody."

"Dunwoody doesn't sound like a first name."

"It doesn't, does it?"

"No matter. I'll see what I can do."

"I have another problem. The head of the monastery seems lots younger than he should be. Someone on the island told me there's a former monk that lives in the Quarter. Maybe you can look him up and ask him a few questions."

"You got an address, I'll talk to him," he said.

I read the address from the piece of the letter I still had in my shirt pocket.

"You and Lil patched things up yet?"

"Not exactly. She's visiting her mother up in Shreveport for a while. At least she's letting me stay in our house, and that's a healthy sign. What else have you found out?"

"Seems everyone is a suspect. Plus, there are bobcats, alligators, and maybe even wolves on the island, not to mention a couple of mean-looking black mouth curs."

"I checked out the person that picked you up."

"Dempsey Duplantis?"

"Like he told us, he was born in Louisiana. His parents moved to Arkansas when he was young. He just got out of prison there."

"What was he in for?"

"Robbery. Could he be your man?"

"He doesn't live on the island. Only guests and monks are here after dark. At least according to Father Domenic. Doesn't matter because there's another way into the premises, not to mention it's easily reached by boat."

"Peachy! Sounds like almost anyone could have done the killing."

"It's hard to narrow the field when you don't know how many players you're dealing with."

"I'm having dinner with my detective friend from St. Bernard Parish. He investigated the killing and is bringing me the report. I'll tell you what I find."

"Thanks, Tony."

"Hey, I'm on the payroll. Bertram talked to Moore, and he agreed to pay me five-hundred bucks a day plus expenses. I may never go back to the N.O.P.D."

"It's not always this lucrative, believe me. I think we both owe Bertram a steak dinner when this one's over."

"Dinner, hell! Let's give him that ten percent, and we'll still make out like bandits."

"I'm all in on that. Any changes in your situation with the N.O.P.D.?"

"Half the cops are gone, or on leave. If something unexpected came up right now, the city would be in serious shit."

"Lil is probably right. Maybe it's time to hang up your badge. If you're still not convinced then swallow your pride and call Eddie."

"Maybe. Back to this case. Does anyone stick out as

your favorite suspect?"

"I'm just going on pure intuition here. A big monk named Bruno is setting off my alarms."

"What's cluing you in?"

I told him about Landry shooting something in the brush with his shotgun.

"Bruno has red marks on his arms and neck that could have been caused by a shotgun blast."

"I think you're stretching, Cowboy. A point blank blast from a twelve gauge would kill a grizzly, much less a man."

"I know, but that's as far as I've gotten."

"Stay after it down there, and I'll work on it on my end."

"Thanks, Tony. I'll catch you later."

As I returned the phone to its receiver, I had the sudden feeling Tony wasn't the only person that had been listening to me. Turning around, I stared up into the dark eyes of Father Domenic. He wasn't smiling.

"Father Domenic, you startled me."

"What are you doing here?" he asked.

"You said I could use the phone in your office if I needed it. Brother Dunwoody told me you were meditating. I didn't think I'd disturb you. Sorry I did."

"It's just that you were sitting here in the dark," he said.

"The desk lamp is on. It didn't seem that dark to me."

"Next time, please check with me first. Now, will you please excuse me? I have work to do."

I nodded, backing out of the room, trying not to bump into anything before I got out the door.

Chapter Eleven

At least one positive aspect of Lil leaving him was that Tony had already lost ten pounds. U.S. Marshal James Landry had sent him to his orthopedic surgeon, and he'd had surgery on both knees. Now he was glad he did because he didn't know if he'd have medical coverage much longer. He remembered his last visit with the grumpy, old orthopedic surgeon.

"Doc, am I going to have to use a wheelchair the rest of my life?"

"Quit whining. I don't feel sorry for you. You're going to walk out of this office today without crutches or cane. If you end up in a wheelchair, it won't be because of your knees."

"You can't be serious. They hurt like hell whenever I put the slightest pressure on them."

"And it's not going to get any better. At least any time soon."

"It hurts so bad I can hardly stand up. The pain pills alone will kill me."

"That's why I'm not prescribing you any. The pain is all in your mind. Block it out. You have the power."

"You gotta be kiddin' me."

"Get your butt out of that chair right now, Detective Nicosia. Do it!" Tony stood with some difficulty. "If you rely on crutches, they'll be with you forever. Now get the hell out of my office, and I don't ever want to see you again."

Before the day was over, Tony was walking almost normally. Dull pain bothered him, but he deadened it with ibuprofen instead of pain pills. After a week, he was moving around as he had when he was twenty. He wouldn't have believed it.

After talking with his old friend, St. Bernard Parish chief detective Jean Pierre Saucier, he'd also spoken with Wyatt Thomas. Saucier had investigated the death of movie star Rance Parker at the Barataria Monastery on Goose Island. Tony wanted to talk to him about it, and they were meeting at a seafood restaurant that abutted a body of water called Lost Lagoon. The name fit.

Hurricane Katrina had all but destroyed Chalmette, a town just south of New Orleans. On the Mississippi River, it is the site of the Battle of New Orleans where Andrew Jackson defeated the British during the War of 1812. Tony had visited the battlefield once in the sixth grade, though he didn't remember much about it.

He remembered visiting Chalmette after Katrina. The mental picture hadn't left him, or the stench from the rows of porta-potties left and then forgotten by F.E.M.A. He could see they had finally been removed when he turned on Paris Road, heading for Boudreaux's Claws and Craws Restaurant.

Jean Pierre had given Tony excellent directions. Even without streetlights, he'd navigated directly to the restaurant built on the banks of Lost Lagoon. From the cars and pickups in the parking lot, paved with bleached and broken shells, the place was hopping.

Having a police cruiser at his disposal for the past ten years, Tony hadn't needed a personal vehicle. Lil had taken their Ford to her mother's, so he'd used part of his advance from Quinlan Moore and bought a Chrysler Sebring, albeit three years old. The bright red convertible was starting to grow on him.

Accordion and fiddle music emanated from the wooden building as he entered the crowded bar.

New Orleans is known for its fabulous restaurants. What most tourists don't know is there are hundreds of great eateries in the metro area. Most of them serve meals as delicious as any in the French Quarter and at a tenth the cost.

Cajun music met his ears and the scent of Cajun food his nostrils. With a grin, he licked his lips and took a deep breath. He soon spotted Jean Pierre Saucier, waving to him from the bar.

Jean Pierre brushed dark hair off his forehead, his smile revealing a mouth filled with brilliant teeth as he reached for Tony's hand. Dressed in worn jeans and black Western shirt with pearl buttons, he looked more like a cowboy than a homicide detective. He was even wearing cowboy hat and boots.

"It's noisy in here. Let's go out on the deck. We can talk a lot easier out there."

"I'm game. Long as they have Dixie in this joint."

"You and your Dixie," Jean Pierre said. "When you gonna learn to drink whiskey like a real Cajun?"

"Maybe cause I ain't a Cajun, real or otherwise."

"Hell, if you ain't a Cajun, then you ain't jack shit," Jean Pierre said.

Tony grinned and gave him a hug. "Where you been? I haven't seen you in a coon's age."

"Shut," Jean Pierre said. "You ain't been looking very hard, cause I been right here in Chalmette."

Though they could see the restaurant's raucous customers through the picture windows, the dissonance was muffled when the swinging doors closed. They were the only two people sitting on the wooden deck, frogs and crickets singing to them in the dim light of Japanese lanterns.

A pretty waitress dressed in cutoff jeans and colorful Claws and Craws tee shirt, knotted just below her breasts, appeared almost as soon as they'd sat down at a table. Her dark, Cajun hair was tied in a ponytail. Her equally dark eyes flashed in the dim light reflecting from the Japanese lanterns swaying in the bayou breeze blowing across the deck. After giving them each a menu, she placed her hands on her hips.

"I ain't seen you two in here before."

"I'm Jean Pierre, and this is my friend Tony."

"Pleased to meet you," she said, shaking Jean Pierre's hand.

He didn't let go, pulling her toward him. "Don't be runnin' away so fast, pretty girl. Come sit on Jean Pierre's lap a minute."

"I'm Heather," she said, sprawling in his lap and giving him a hug. "I ain't here to hug, although it's kinda fun. You boys need to order somethin' or my daddy will fire me."

"Your daddy owns this place?"

"Yes he do."

Heather planted a hot kiss on Jean Pierre's mouth and then wrestled from his grasp.

"You about a strong one. Bet you're a whiskey man."

"Wild Turkey. A double, amour."

"Hey, you're pretty cute, but you pinch my tush one more time, and I'm gonna cold cock you upside the head."

She delivered the threat with a clinched fist and sexy smile on her face. "And what about you, Tony?"

"Cold Dixie for me."

"The only way we serve it," she said.

"And bring us two dozen raw oysters to get us started," Jean Pierre said.

Heather smiled again. "Hot date later tonight?"

"Depends on what time you get off."

"Sorry, my boyfriend John Lee's picking me up when I get done here."

"Then maybe I better buy him two dozen oysters."

Grinning, Heather said, "He don't need no oysters. He's only twenty."

Jean Pierre didn't miss a beat with his comeback. "Hey darlin', forty's twice as nice at half the price."

"Forty? You likely to have a heart attack just thinking about it."

"That's okay, Darlin'. Then you'd have to give me

mouth to mouth, and that would make it all the mo' better."

"I'll get your whiskey, sweet talker."

Tony and Jean Pierre watched the young woman walk back into the noisy restaurant. Knowing where their eyes were, she gave her well-turned rear a suggestive shake before disappearing through the swinging doors.

"She's about a hot one," Jean Pierre said.

"And half your age," Tony said. "What would that pretty young wife of yours think about all this? What's her name?"

"Christina. Shut. She done kicked me out. About a year ago now."

"Too bad. She was a real looker. Maybe a little too smart for your wild ass."

"Shut. If I was to give her a call, she'd jump back in my bed in a minute."

A boat passed beneath them, the sound of its small engine momentarily quieting the frog symphony. Busy rolling his eyes, Tony didn't notice. Heather returned with the oysters, giving Jean Pierre a wink as she did.

"John Lee'll be out shrimping next week. Maybe you can drop back then."

"I'll make sure I do," he said, sipping the whiskey.

"Now what you boys want for supper?"

"Besides you, I'll have an oyster po'boy and a bowl of gumbo."

They both grinned at Tony when he said, "I'll have the same."

"Don't give me any more ideas than I already have," Heather said. "That one's more than I can handle."

As the swinging doors closed behind her, Jean Pierre said, "Woo wee! That girl's hot, I mean to tell you."

"Yeah, and apparently, not too damn smart, either," Tony said as he forked one of the oysters onto a cracker and then doused it with hot sauce. "Now tell me what you know about the killing at the monastery south of here."

"Mon, if you got a weak stomach, you don't want me talking about it before we eat."

"My stomach's fine, but we can wait till after our gumbo if yours isn't."

"Touché, Lieutenant. I've worked a few murders, but probably not a tenth as many as you, up in the big town and all."

"Seems I've worked my last," Tony said.

"You retired, mon?"

"Canned is more like it. The Feds have moved to town, and they're cleaning house. I'm on disciplinary leave until further notice, along with half the force."

"Damn, sorry 'bout that. What now?"

"I've had my twenty for five years now. Lil's been nagging me to retire."

"Hell, mon, you too young. Retirement's for old men and you ain't that much older than me."

"Same way I feel. I'm doing a little P.I. work until everything shakes out."

"The killing down on the bay?"

"Gotta start somewhere," Tony said.

"Well you coulda picked an easier one. I'll tell you that right now."

They were finished with the oysters when Heather arrived with their gumbo and po'boys. She also brought them more drinks.

"You boys are lookin' mighty serious out here. Didn't like the oysters?"

"Darlin', they just made me wish it was next week already. At least give me another kiss before you go back inside."

Heather plopped into his lap again. They were soon engaged in a groping, tongue-exchanging scene that made Tony's face redden. After finally breaking free, she dusted imaginary lint off her jean shorts and backed away from their table.

"Now you got me thinkin' way too much."

As she disappeared through the door again, Tony said, "I'd say John Lee's in for one hell of a night tonight."

"Just the way my day's going. Make's me feel like the old horse they use to get the mares all hot and bothered before they bring in the expensive stud that's too valuable to take a chance on lettin' him do the foreplay."

Jean Pierre grinned when Tony said, "Quit whining. I about creamed my pants just watching you two a minute ago."

"Then I'd say Ms. Lil's in for one hell of a night when you get home."

"Afraid not. She's moved out of the house and back with her mother. I'm batching it until she decides to forgive me."

"You dog," Jean Pierre said. "What the hell did you do?"

"A slight case of middle-aged crazy. Lil's always forgiven me when I've messed up in the past. This time she hasn't, at least not yet. Guess that's what I get for telling one lie after another."

"Hell, mon. She'll come back. Meantime, take advantage of your freedom while you got the chance."

Flickering fireflies dueled with the Japanese lanterns as Tony and Jean Pierre finished eating, heat lightning beginning to illuminate the western sky.

"Can you tell me about the killing on Goose Island now?"

Jean Pierre leaned back in the wooden chair. "It wasn't the only time I'd been to the monastery."

"Oh?" Tony said.

"First time I got called out, two of them monks had got in a fight. Guess you could call it domestic violence. One of them was cut up pretty bad."

"You mean with a knife?"

"More like claws and teeth. We wanted to take him to the hospital, but they weren't having none of it."

"Who called you?"

"One of the monks. Brother Bruce was his name. Father Domenic, the head dog, showed up and said they'd handle the problem themselves."

"Do you remember the two men involved?"

"Brother Bruno, one hairy ape of a man that talked with a foreign accent. I can't remember who it was he attacked."

"So when you investigated the killing, it was your second time to visit the monastery."

"Right. Early mornin' ground fog about covered up the scene when my partner and me waded through it, into some brush. I could smell the body before I saw it."

"It had already started to decompose?"

Jean Pierre nodded. "Don't take long in south Louisiana. The corpse was cut up, blood all over the grass as if someone had butchered a hog."

"With a knife?"

"More like some wild animal had attacked him. Whatever it was it wasn't nothing human, I can tell you that. Hell, even the man's privates was gone."

"It ripped his pants off?"

"Didn't have to. He was naked as a jaybird. We found his clothes down by the bay, and not just his."

"Oh?"

"A woman's clothes, bra, red thong, shorts, and blouse."

"So he wasn't alone when he was attacked."

"Nope."

"And the woman was nowhere around?"

"They was two women on the island when the killing occurred. Neither of them admitted to being with the dead man."

"You believe them?"

"Why hell no. One of them was lying out her ass, and I'm pretty sure I know which one it was."

"Tell me."

"Sabine Storm."

"The movie star?"

"One and the same, and she's still on the island."

"How do you know?"

"Cause she calls me almost every day."

Jean Pierre laughed at Tony's next question.

"For sex? You got to be kidding me. She's drop dead gorgeous. Don't tell me you've already done it with her."

"Hell, mon, done it ain't the right words if you know

what I mean."

"What do you mean?"

"Just that she likes doing things I never even thought of before."

Bringing more drinks, Heather pushed through the swinging doors as lightning flashed over the bayou.

"You boys telling ghost stories out here? You lookin' mighty serious again."

"Darlin'," Jean Pierre said. "We just need you to cheer us up."

Heather planted a kiss on his mouth and then placed the bill in front of him.

"John Lee'll be here in ten minutes, so I got to check out. You come see me next week, you hear?"

She blew him a kiss and disappeared through the swinging doors when he said, "With bells on, Miss Heather."

As Cajun music faded behind the closed doors, Tony reached for the ticket.

"I'll get it. I'm on expenses. Now finish your story."

"Hell, that girl caused me to forget what I was telling you. Let's drink up and get the hell outa here. It'll come back around once we're on the road."

"I need to get back to town," Tony said.

"Ain't no one waitin' there for you. Come go with me. I got plans."

"Where to?" Tony asked.

"Ever been to a chicken fight?"

Chapter Twelve

It was after eleven when Tony and Jean Pierre finally left the noisy restaurant and drove down a lonesome, Louisiana backroad in the Cajun cop's red Chevy pickup.

"You know where you're going?" Tony asked.

"Don't you worry none. I'll get us there."

"You remember the rest of the story you were telling me before Miss Heather pulled your chain?"

"I don't forget. We bagged the victim and took him to Chalmette. That's when I got relieved of the case."

"Oh?"

"A woman that said she was the dead man's wife showed up for the body. She had a court order signed by a judge."

"Did your coroner get a chance to look at the body before she took it?"

"It was gone, outa there by noon that day. I heard they had the body cremated in New Orleans, with no autopsy."

"That'll be easy to check. Someone had to sign the death certificate. My P.I. friend is at the monastery now, looking into the matter."

"You talked to him yet?"

"He said he has more suspects than he can count."

"Next time you see him, tell him to watch his ass."

Blacktop had long since melded into dry dirt, Jean

Pierre's pickup kicking up dust as he tooled down the rural road. When a skunk ran in front of them, barely making it to the other side, Jean Pierre tapped his brakes. When they passed another road with a rooster sign posted at the intersection, he backed up and took it.

Tall trees bounded both sides, almost blocking the moonlight. They soon reached a gated fence, a man in jeans and cowboy hat guarding it with a shotgun. Jean Pierre pulled up to him and lowered his window.

"Hey, bro, what's happening?"

"I never seen you here before. Who you with?"

"I'm Clotelle Doucette's cousin from Breaux Bridge. I liked to never found this place. We miss much yet?"

"Couple of fights. Still plenty more to come, though. Head on through."

Jean Pierre drove slowly along the winding road until they reached a clearing where dozens of pickups and cars were parked beneath a flimsy string of lights suspended between two trees.

"Looks as though even the rich like chicken fighting," Tony said, eyeing the expensive vehicles in the lot.

"Lots of money'll change hands tonight. You can bet on that."

Footlights illuminated the dirt path through the trees, and they soon reached a small arena surrounded by bench seats. Fifty or so spectators faced the wire cage surrounding the arena's dirt floor. A fight had just ended. Two trainers were in the ring, one walking out with the victor, the other carrying the loser.

The crowd was loud, men shouting as one woman's shrill voice in particular echoed through the trees. They found two empty spots on the back row of benches, next to the walkway leading down to the door of the cage.

"Blood sport," the woman sitting across the aisle from Jean Pierre said. "Gotta love it."

"We ain't been to one of these before. What's goin' on?"

"Those two guys with the carpenter's aprons walking through the crowd are either paying up or collecting lost bets."

"Musta been a big fight. Looks like their pouches are stuffed."

She laughed. "The house never loses. Did you see that red Ferrari parked up there? It's Clotelle Doucette's. He gotta be the richest man in the Parish."

"Guess so. He the head dog in this operation."

The woman started to say something, but the man beside her gave her a nudge and shook his head. Most of the people in attendance were dressed like the man at the front gate—in jeans, Western shirts, cowboy boots, and hats.

Though Jean Pierre fit right in, Tony looked much out of place. It wasn't long before someone spotted him in the crowd. An oversized bruiser in a sleeveless Western shirt that highlighted his muscular arms and colorful tattoos walked up behind Tony and gave his shoulder a shove.

"I ain't seen you here before. Who invited you?"

"He's with me," Jean Pierre said.

"Ain't seen you, either."

"Clotelle's my cousin. We from Breaux Bridge."

"Your buddy here looks like a cop."

"Well he ain't no cop. I promise you that. Just go ask Clotelle who we are if you don't believe me."

"I'll do that."

The bruiser started down the path to the cage, stopping when a pretty young woman grabbed his arm, whispering something in his ear. After answering her question, he walked away.

The woman was dressed in a red-checked western shirt tied at her belly button. That, along with her white bikini, pink cowboy boots and ten-gallon hat marked her as a ring girl. Smiling at Jean Pierre, she hurried up to him.

"Big Troy said you're Clotelle's cousin."

"That's right, Darlin'. I'm Jean Pierre, and this is Tony. You're mighty pretty. What's your name?"

"Cynthia Sue, but my friends call me Cyn."

She smiled when he said, "Well you could make me commit a few."

"That's c.y.n, not s.i.n.," she said.

"Oh hell, you had me thinkin' all sorts of naughty thoughts."

"You comin' to Clotelle's party after the fights? We all gonna get naked, drink whiskey and have a whole lotta fun in his big ol' hot tub."

"Wouldn't miss it for the world, little darlin'. I can hardly wait to see them pretty little titties of yours."

"Why wait," she said, opening her shirt, bending over and rubbing her breasts in his face.

Most of the noisy crowd didn't even notice as the woman named Cyn pulled her blouse in place, blew Jean Pierre a kiss and then hurried down the aisle toward the cage. At least one person noticed. Frowning, a dark-haired man with a pencil-thin mustache started toward them. Grabbing the front of Jean Pierre's shirt, he pulled a knife from his belt and stuck it to his neck.

"Guess you know who I am." he said.

"Cousin Clotelle?"

"You ain't no damn cousin of mine. Tell me who the hell you are before I cut your damn throat."

"You ain't gonna cut me in front of all these people."

"Think again, pretty boy."

Jean Pierre suddenly produced a revolver from beneath his shirt, poking it into Clotelle's crotch and cocking it. Clotelle froze when he heard the click.

"You got about two seconds to drop that pig sticker before I blow your balls off."

After another prod, Clotelle did just that. As the crowd sensed something was happening, Big Troy and several employees started toward them. Tony was wishing he had his own service revolver. It didn't matter because Jean Pierre didn't need any help.

Pushing Clotelle backwards, he raised the pistol and fired two rounds into the air. Distant sirens immediately sounded on the dirt road behind the cage.

"Police. This is a bust. Everybody on the ground.

Now!"

Cops began pouring into the clearing, quickly cordoning off the area, cuffing people and leading them away to police buses waiting on the main road.

"You son of a bitch!" Tony said. "You brought me on a bust and didn't even tell me about it?"

"Shut, bro. You know you loved every minute of it. Now let's get outta here. Our job's done."

When they were back in the truck, Tony said, "Looks like you're hauling in every chicken fighter in the parish."

"They'll all be bonded out before sunup, find another place to fight their chickens and then keep on keepin' on."

Jean Pierre gave Tony a look when he said, "Maybe you should have shot the asshole when you had the chance."

"That's all right. He'll screw up one of these days. He's got serious prison time in his future, and he ain't gonna have his Ferrari or girlfriend Cyn to enjoy when he gets there."

"Got that right," Tony said. "Now it's late, and I've had about all the excitement I can handle for one night. Better take me back to my car."

"Shut, boss, we just gettin' started. You can't go home yet."

"What now? You busting a meth lab and want me to come along for moral support?"

"Nothin' like that. They's a truck stop up the way I haven't visited in a while."

"Truck stop? You outa gas?"

"Gas ain't the only thing you can get at Bernadine's."

"Should I be afraid to ask?"

"The other two gees—girls and gambling. After Miss Heather and Cyn, I either gotta get laid or shoot somethin'."

"Bernadine's is a whore house?"

"Best in St. Bernard Parish. Wait'll you see."

"I'm in enough trouble already. You better take me back to my car."

"Don't be like that, Lieutenant. It's already too late

for bed. At least for sleepin', that is. When we leave Bernadine's, we'll go to headquarters, and I'll give you a copy of the police report."

"Fine, I'll wait in the truck."

"The girls don't bite. At least not real hard. Come on inside and have a drink."

Though the hour was late, patrons were buying gas for their vehicles at the well-lighted truck stop that included a souvenir shop and all-night diner. Rows of semis sat parked in a lighted lot, their drivers sleeping or taking advantage of the amenities. A semi drove by on the highway, its horn blasting.

Jean Pierre bypassed the diner, walking around to a door in back. When he rang the bell, someone opened a port and gazed out to see who it was. They heard a shriek as the door opened.

"Hey girls, it's Jean Pierre."

Before they were ten feet inside the door, three scantily clad young women were hugging and fawning over him.

"Take me this time," a blond-haired, blue-eyed woman said, tugging on his arm.

Another young woman with eyes as dark as her tiny negligee said, "You told me you were coming back just to see me."

"You both so pretty, I can't choose. Come on, Tony. Lets all go have some fun."

"You go," Tony said. "I've had about all the excitement I can handle tonight."

The two women latched on to Jean Pierre's arms, directing him down a long hallway. Tony could still hear their squeals when he turned to look around the place. He wasn't alone.

A fancy bar covered half the wall, a bartender in a white smock polishing a glass. On one of the stools was an attractive though older woman. Tony joined her.

"We got more girls. They're all busy right now, but someone will be available before long."

"If you don't mind, I'd rather just sit here with you."

107

"Oh I don't mind. I've got no one to talk to most of the time, except Otto, and I have to pay him to listen to me."

Tony smiled and nodded at the pudgy man with thinning hair.

"I'm Tony," he said.

"Bernadine," the woman said.

"Then you must be the owner."

"A thankless job, but it pays well," she said. "This has been a day from hell."

"Tell me about it."

"You don't want to hear. I can't remember the last time I've been so stressed out."

"Stress will put you in the grave. You need to do something about it," Tony said.

"I think I've heard that line before. I'm not a working girl anymore."

"That's not what I meant. Let me see your hand."

When Bernadine held up her hand, Tony took it and began softly massaging her palm with his thumbs and fingers.

"You got a pressure point right here. I know it sounds crazy, but a good hand massage does wonders for relieving stress."

Tony worked on her hand, slowly stretching her fingers and massaging her knuckles. Bernadine's eyes were closed, a smile on her face.

"Oh, that feels good," she said. "Where'd you say you're from?"

"New Orleans. Lived there all my life. You?"

"Grew up in Hattiesburg, though I've been here more years than I can count."

"What brought you to south Louisiana?"

"An abusive husband. Last time he broke my nose, I stabbed him. Did five years in the joint, but I never regretted doing it."

"I hope you killed the bastard," Tony said.

"Hell, he threw me through a plate glass window. I was hurt worse than him when the cops arrived. The judge didn't see it my way."

"Surprise, surprise. How'd you end up with this place?"

"Saved every penny I made. This was a run-down old filling station nobody wanted. I just kept making improvements, put in a few slot machines, and eventually built this place in back for the girls. Now I got more money than I can say grace over and no one to share it with."

"I'd be sending you flowers tomorrow if I weren't a married man."

"You're sweet, baby. Otto, bring Tony anything he wants. What are you drinking?"

"Scotch and water."

"Any particular call?"

"I drink Dalmor when I can get it, but any old Scotch will do."

Bernadine nodded to Otto, and he produced an unopened bottle of Dalmor from beneath the counter, pouring Tony a double.

"Thanks," he said.

"Better bring me another, Otto."

Already on top of it, Otto handed her a martini with two olives.

"The girls here seem to know Jean Pierre," Tony said.

"He's a regular. Hell, that man's insatiable. He looks like a young Elvis, and no one can resist that smile of his."

"Sounds like you got a little crush on him yourself."

"Hell, I'm seventy-two. I might have given him a run thirty years ago. He's not on my radar screen now, though."

"You're seventy-two? You gotta be kiddin' me. You got a body most twenty-year-olds would die for. No one would ever think you're a day over forty."

"Honey, you're a bald-faced liar, but I love it. Jean Pierre is like the son I never had."

"How does he afford coming here so often? I know this place ain't cheap, and I also know what it's like trying to live on cops pay. I was one myself."

Bernadine gave him an assessing look. "The girls and I love him so much, we let him slide most of the time. And you're not paying for anything tonight, either. That hand massage was worth a lot to me."

Otto had a fresh drink ready for Tony the moment he finished his first. Instead of drinking it right away, he took Bernadine's other hand and began massaging it.

"Is this helping any?" he asked.

"You just don't know," she said. "Lots of my girls complain they never had an orgasm. Me, I'm having one right now."

"I'm blushing," Tony said.

"You're a cop?"

"Until a week or so ago. The Feds are cleaning house in N.O. They think we're all corrupt."

"I feel your pain, but I've known lots of dirty cops from up in the city."

"There are dirty cops everywhere, and plenty like me that never took a penny that wasn't his, or shot a man that didn't deserve it."

"Don't get all bent out of shape, honey. I've been on both sides of the law."

"Sorry," Tony said.

"You said you're married. What are you doing out at four in the morning?"

"Lil, my wife left me."

"Why?"

"I had a little fling. Not the first time. This time, she hasn't seen fit to forgive me for it."

"Hell, every man plays around. Just ask me. I got names and numbers."

"I bet you do," Tony said. "You still love them though, don't you?"

It was Bernadine's turn to smile. "Long as I don't have to live with them, though I might make an exception for you. You couldn't pay someone to give a hand massage like you do."

"Hell, maybe I've found my second calling."

"You got a job here anytime you want it. Me and the

110

girls would fight over you."

Another hour passed before Jean Pierre emerged from the long hallway.

"You get you any, mon? These girls so pretty, I hate to leave. How you doing, Ms. Bernadine?" he said, kissing her on the lips.

"Sugar wouldn't melt in your mouth, Jean Pierre," she said.

"Maybe not, but you the sweetest woman in this place," he said, giving her a big hug.

"You can get the hell outa here with your sweet talk," she said with a smile. "Tony, here, is the new love of my life."

"Hell, them Nawlins cops got all the moves. Mr. Tony, we need to blow this place. You ready?"

"I could talk to Ms. Bernadine for hours, but I'm sure she's tired of me by now. I'm ready anytime you are."

"Come back anytime, Tony," she said. "With or without this silver-tongued devil."

⁂

Jean Pierre dropped Tony off at his car, and then drove slowly down Paris Road until he'd caught up. The sun was peeking over the Mississippi River as they parked in the lot behind the police station. They were soon drinking day-old coffee, warmed up in a microwave as Jean Pierre produced a report.

"You sure you only worked one day on this?" Tony asked, hefting it.

"I told you somethin' crazy's going on down there in the swamp, and I ain't quit trying to find out what. Now, since I got the best homicide detective in Nawlins helping me, I'm gonna find out."

Chapter Thirteen

It was after dark when I finally made it back to the bungalow. I didn't remember leaving on the light that was shining through the window. Cracking the door, I peered in to see Sierra, Chuckie and Kisses lying on the bed. She had closed all the windows and turned on the air conditioning, the crisp air feeling good after I'd spent much of the last day and night in the heat and humidity. She opened her eyes when she heard me.

"Quit your job already?" I asked.

"Hardly," she said as she stretched toward the ceiling. "I feel like I've died and gone to heaven."

"That's great. After last night, I was wondering if you'd be able to get along with Professor Quinn."

"He can be an old bear, but I've honestly never met a nicer, more thoughtful person in my life."

"What about me?"

"You're okay. I got something for you."

She handed me a small box with a picture of a cell phone on it.

"What's this?"

"Just what it looks like. A cell phone, silly. Professor Quinn and I spent several hours in town today, and I got it for you while we were there."

"Don't you need a plan for these things?"

"Not this one. It's a pay-as-you-go model. I bought

you a hundred minutes. When you start running low, just go into town and get more."

"I don't need a cell phone. I don't even know how to use one."

"Don't be silly. Even seven-year-olds know what to do. I've already programmed in my number, and Professor Quinn's. Trust me, it might save your life someday."

"I could have used it last night. How much do I owe you?"

"Nothing. You need one and apparently would have never bought it for yourself."

The device fit easily into my hand. "Not particularly heavy.

"That's the idea. You keep it with you all the time. It's also an alarm, calculator, camera, and it even has G.P.S."

"That also would have come in handy last night," I said. "Thanks. You sure I don't owe you anything?"

"Forget it. It's my thanks for helping me get my new job."

"Then thank you, I think," I said, still glancing at the phone.

"Professor Quinn got me signed on with the state, and I'm a full employee now. He even got me an advance to tide me over until I get my first real paycheck."

"And your G.E.D.?"

"You're looking at a brand new high school graduate. And I'm already enrolled in some online college courses. I'm going to get a degree from L.S.U."

"Congratulations. What else?"

"I have a new laptop, a bank account, new clothes, and a room I just love. Oh Wyatt, it's so rad."

"I'm happy for you. Can you program these numbers into my new toy?" I said, handing her, Tony and Quinlan Moore's business cards.

"Easy," she said, taking the phone and showing me how to do it.

Before an hour had passed, Sierra had given me a lesson on using a cell phone. With her help, I'd even managed to email a status report to Quinlan Moore. Chuckie didn't bother moving when Kisses pounced on him. Tiring of her stalking, she curled up beside him and went to sleep.

"So you like Professor Quinn?"

"A lot, but he's a little strange."

"How so?"

"He sings to Chuckie and his cat."

"I thought you were going to tell me he carries an ax around."

"You're funny," she said, laughing. "He has an old Jeep with no top, and he lets me drive it when we go places. He helped me pick out curtains and throw rugs to decorate my room, and he's teaching me how to cook. My room even has air-conditioning and its own bathroom with shower and everything. I'm in heaven."

"Sounds like it. I'm glad you're happy."

"He told me what you're actually doing here on the island."

"He did, did he?"

"You can trust me. I've never killed anybody, and I know everything about this island. I can help you."

"Really? I met Brothers Bruno and Bruce today. What's your take on them?"

"Brother Bruce is nice. Brother Bruno is about as strange as they come. Really weird, and I don't mean like Professor Quinn."

"How so?" I asked.

"I saw him catch a rabbit in his bare hands once, and then kill it with his teeth."

"You're kidding, aren't you?"

"Afraid not. I hid behind some bushes before he saw me. I wouldn't be surprised if he ate the rabbit raw."

"No way," I said.

"When I looked for the rabbit's body I only found a few hunks of fur."

"You're stretching the truth, aren't you?"

"If I'm lying, I'm dying," she said.

Not knowing if she were jiving me, I asked, "Did you

know Brother Italo?"

"He was teaching me carpentry before he left the monastery. It broke my heart to see him go."

"And Brother Bruce?"

"He isn't like the others. Somehow out of place here, though I don't doubt his sincerity."

"Same feeling I got. I'm going to corner him when he's alone and talk to him. See what he knows. I got the impression he was intimidated by Bruno's presence the day I met him."

"I'm sure I'm not the only one that's noticed how strange Brother Bruno is."

"I'm hoping Brother Bruce can tell me more about what's going on around here."

"You won't have much luck. They watch him like a hawk, you know."

"Why?"

"Don't trust him, I guess."

I let the issue of Brother Bruce drop. "I told you I met Sabine Storm."

"I haven't forgotten. Has she gotten you into bed yet?"

"Not for lack of trying. She hinted that Father Domenic has anger management problems and is also sexually active."

"She should know."

"You mean. . . ?"

"I mean she's probably doing him right now, as we speak."

"No way."

She grabbed my wrist and pulled me toward the door. "Lets go see."

Kisses stayed behind as Chuckie went with us out the back door and into the shadows. An owl hooted in the distance, and I could hear Landry's dogs barking down by Goose Bay. Sierra seemed capable of seeing in the dark, and we soon reached the side of Stormie's bungalow. With a finger to her lips, she shushed me.

Dim lights shined from the open window, and we

easily saw into the bedroom. Stormie was naked, sitting on a stool, modeling for Pietro, the man I had met at the pool. The slab of marble he was working on seemed untouched.

"What's he doing?" Sierra asked.

"Sculpting her, though it doesn't look like they've gotten far."

"Doesn't surprise me," she said.

As we watched, Pietro walked toward Stormie and touched her breast. When he did, she slapped him. From the look on his face, he wasn't happy with her response, backhanding, then driving her to the bed and pulling down his pants.

"Oh my God!" Sierra said. "He's going to rape her. Wyatt. We have to do something."

Before I could respond, the door to the bungalow burst open, someone entering. Father Domenic rushed into the room, grabbing Pietro, lifting him bodily off the bed, and then tossing him against the wall. No small task since Pietro wasn't a little man.

After being slammed against the concrete wall, he slumped to the tiled floor. He was barely there a moment when Father Domenic reached him, lifted him bodily over his head, and then dropped him to the floor.

"He's going to kill him," Sierra said.

A low growl issued from deep in Chuckie's throat as Bruno and Dunwoody entered the room, grabbing Father Domenic and pulling him off of Pietro. Chuckie was in a snit, growling and pawing the window.

"Better take him back to the room before he joins them," I said.

"What about you?"

"I want to see what happens. Go."

Sierra had to pull Chuckie away from the window. Somehow she managed, leaving me alone in the darkness.

After forcibly yanking Father Domenic off of Pietro, Dunwoody dragged the senior man of the monastery out the door. Bruno lifted Pietro over his shoulder and followed them. Stormie just fell back on the bed, covering her eyes with her arm. Seeing she was shaken but otherwise okay, I hurried around the building to see where the monks had gone.

Light rain had returned to the island, lightning illuminating the sky out over the Gulf. Ignoring the water dripping down my face and neck, I circled Stormie's bungalow, colliding with someone when I rounded the corner. It was Bruno, and I felt how strong he was when he squeezed my shoulders.

"What are you doing?" he asked in his thick, Romanian accent.

"I heard a disturbance and came out to investigate," I said.

"There's no trouble," he said.

"You sure?"

For a moment, his eyes glinted red. I was backing away when Dunwoody appeared behind him, clutching his shoulder.

"I don't know why you're out here, Mr. Thomas, but there's nothing to see. Please, return to your room."

By now, Bruno's frown was ominous. With little to gain by asking anything further, I returned to the bungalow. Sierra laughed when I finally got there.

"Can you believe it?"

"Wild and crazy stuff," I said.

"How did Father Domenic know what was going on?" she asked.

"Stormie told me he often stared at her from his office. She said he liked to watch her, and that she liked it when he did. Maybe he was watching from the other side of the bungalow."

"Creepy. And Dunwoody and Bruno were keeping an eye on him."

"Yes."

She nodded and said, "I can't believe how violent he became."

"Crazy, all right."

Sierra had already lost interest. She began rummaging through the refrigerator for something to eat and drink.

"All the excitement has made me hungry. Don't you have anything to eat in here?"

"There was a bowl of fruit and chocolates when I arrived. How about an apple or maybe a truffle?"

"Both," she said, reaching for the basket. "I'd rather have a bag of chips."

"I haven't had a chance to do much shopping. You'll have to make do with fruit and truffles."

"Never mind. Professor Quinn keeps plenty of snacks, though I did have to lay in a better selection of beer. I'll get something when I get home."

"Will you be okay?"

"Didn't you see how excited Chuckie got? He's all the protection I need."

She gave me an odd look when I said, "He might not help you much if you encounter a rougarou."

"You're weird," she said. "Professor Quinn has an airboat. He'll give you a tour around the island if it will help in your investigation."

"Fantastic. When?"

"Later tomorrow? You can stay for dinner."

"I'll be there."

Sierra stood on her tiptoes and kissed me on the lips. "Thanks, Wyatt."

"For what? I should be thanking you."

"For helping me get this job. I can't thank you enough."

"You already have," I said.

She and Chuckie started for the door, stopping before exiting into the darkness.

"Professor Quinn says there's a tropical storm in the Caribbean. It could turn into a hurricane and enter the Gulf in a few days."

"Just what we need. I better get busy before we have to evacuate the island."

"You're not afraid, are you?"

"You bet I am. Everyone who lived through Katrina is wary of hurricanes."

"Professor Quinn is. When he heard about the storm, he started hurrying around the house, getting things together in case we have to evacuate."

"Does sound a bit overly cautious," I said.

"When I told him I thought he was overreacting, he wagged his finger at me and gave me a lecture about all the possible dangers."

"You were young and living in California when Katrina came courting. We got hit again by Hurricane Rita before the year was over. I can't even begin to tell you how much damage it did to the people who live here. I'm talking both figuratively and spiritually."

"I know. I lived with Dempsey in Delacroix. Remember? The whole town was destroyed by Katrina."

Light drizzle continued to fall as we talked on the porch, silent lightning flashing out over Goose Bay. It had quieted the birds on the island, and I could no longer hear Landry's dogs.

"If you want to talk to Brother Bruce in private, he'll be at Celebration Fountain tomorrow at noon."

"How do you know that?" I asked.

"Because he's in charge of putting the mosquito stuff in all the open water around here. He does it every day, and he's prompt."

"Where is Celebration Fountain?"

"About a hundred yards from the swimming pool, near the start of the nine-hole golf course. You'll see it."

"Thanks again. You sure you'll be okay?"

"Stop worrying. I'm a big girl."

She waved, then she and Chuckie disappeared into the darkness.

Chapter Fourteen

The song playing in my shirt pocket confused me until I realized it was my new phone's ringtone. Not a fan of country and western, I immediately began wondering if there were a way to change it, almost forgetting to answer the call.

"I didn't think you were going to pick it up," Sierra said.

"I thought someone had slipped a radio in my pocket. I'm used to a phone ringing, not singing to me."

"Don't be such a dork. I'll change it tonight. You're still coming, aren't you?"

"I'll be there. I'm on my way to Celebration Fountain to speak with Brother Bruce."

"Just make sure there's no one else around or I promise he won't talk to you."

"I'm hip," I said.

"In your dreams," she said, hanging up.

Dempsey Duplantis' Range Rover was parked in front of a nearby bungalow as I walked out on my porch. He exited the front door, carrying bags he put into the back of the vehicle. Pietro soon appeared, his face swollen, and both eyes blackened. They drove off, down the winding road leading to the only way in or out of the monastery. Almost noon, I was looking for the Celebration Fountain.

After visiting the marshes and bogs on the other side of the berm, I hadn't appreciated how well manicured the monastery grounds were. As I gazed at the fountain that would have done justice to an upscale Vegas hotel, I could see how much money had been spent on esthetics. Just before noon, I rested on the edge of the fountain, watching concrete cherubs blow water spouts twenty feet into the air. I soon spotted Brother Bruce's flowing robe as he walked toward me.

"Nice to see you," I said.

"Good morning."

The monk was no doubt curious about what I was doing at the fountain. Not wanting him to hurry away, I quickly engaged him in conversation.

"What are you putting in the water?" I asked as he sprinkled the fountain with something he carried in a bag around his neck.

"A substance to arrest the propagation of mosquitos. If there's no place for them to breed, the area remains free of the little pests."

"You do this every day?"

"Sometimes more often, if it rains, and not just here. Everyplace where there's a puddle of water. Short of spraying the area with toxic chemicals, it's the only way to stop them."

"Must work, but isn't it dangerous to put chemicals in the water?"

Brother Bruce shook his head. "All natural. No harmful chemicals. We don't pollute anything."

"I haven't been bitten on this side of the berm since I arrived on the island. You're apparently doing a terrific job."

"And you won't be bitten," he said. "At least not by mosquitoes."

As he finished sprinkling the fountain and started to leave, I wondered if his words had some secret meaning.

"Please, one more question before you go."

Brother Bruce glanced around to see if we were alone. A hundred yards away a golfer was teeing up for a drive, his only companion a lone hawk circling high overhead.

"Of course," he said.

He nodded when I asked, "Were you close friends with Brother Italo?" He hesitated when I said, "Do you know where he went?"

"I am part of the monastery. We have a vow."

"Not of silence. I've heard all of you talk many times."

"We share a vow of secrecy. We're Tracists and don't talk about each other, or our pasts."

"That sounds more like a vow of ex-cons to me."

From his frown, I could see he'd taken offense at my words.

"I assure you, I have nothing remotely criminal in my past."

"What about Brothers Dunwoody and Bruno?"

"I can't speak for them."

"They are both huge men. Are you afraid of them?"

"I have to go now."

"Wait, please. This conversation is just between you and me. I'm just curious."

Brother Bruce glanced around again. "I'm a man of God."

"And they're not?"

"You're trying to put words in my mouth."

"I saw something last night that disturbed me," I said.

Brother Bruce glanced around again. "Like what?"

"I heard a disturbance coming from a neighboring bungalow and went out to investigate. Since it was dark, I could easily see what was happening through an open window."

"If you're talking about the incident with the sculptor, I can't really comment."

"I saw him leave this morning. His face was swollen, and he was walking with a limp."

"I have to go now," he said.

"Two questions before you do." He hesitated, but didn't answer. "Do you know how violent Father Domenic can be, and does Brother's Bruno and Dunwoody always follow him around?"

"Look, talking to you can get me into trouble."

"I have the uneasy feeling you're afraid of them. Have they threatened you? I'm not going to tell anyone that we've talked."

Brother Bruce turned to face me. "Father Domenic has a problem. A psychological problem."

"Like what?"

"He suffers from bouts of extreme agitation. When it happens, he has to be restrained."

"How?"

"You've seen how large Brother's Dunwoody and Bruno are. Sometimes it takes both of them to handle him when he becomes violent. You wouldn't believe what they have to do on occasion."

"Tell me."

"They've had to force him into a straitjacket to keep him from hurting himself, or others. Now I've told you too much, and I must go."

"What about the incident last night? Isn't Father Domenic afraid Pietro will press charges?"

"And be accused of assault and attempted rape on one of the biggest actresses in Hollywood? I don't think so. He'll leave well enough alone, I'm sure."

He started off again, but stopped when I said, "Just one more question. Do you know Brother Italo's last name?"

"Palminero," he said in a voice so muted I barely heard.

He shook his head when I asked, "Do you know where he is?"

"The French Quarter. He has a studio and sells his work there. No more questions, and please don't tell the brothers, or Father Domenic that I told you where to find him."

"You have my word," I said.

He hurried away toward another fountain beneath a patch of oak trees as two peacocks strutted up to me, their plumage alive with color. Ignoring me, they jumped up on the ledge for water. Glancing at my new cell phone, I decided to try my first call. I was about to hang up and try again when Tony finally answered.

"Tony Nicosia."

"Tony, it's Wyatt."

"I didn't recognize the phone number. You gone high tech on me, Cowboy?"

"Just keeping up."

" I've got a hangover from hell, and I just managed to crawl out of bed."

"Hair of the dog," I said. "It's the only thing that helps. Believe me, I know."

"After I throw up, I might give it a try. I had dinner last night with my detective buddy from Chalmette. I'd almost forgot what a wild man he is."

"Did you learn anything interesting?"

"Several things. He'd been on another call to the monastery before the death of Rance Parker."

"Oh?"

"Two of the monks got in a fight. Someone called the cops. When he got there, everyone clammed up, and no charges were filed."

"Which two monks, do you know?"

"Brother Bruno, who Jean Pierre described as an ape of a man, got into it with another brother named Dunwoody. Are there just four monks at the monastery?"

"There were five. One brother left around the time of the fight."

"Any idea where I can find him?"

"He's a master carpenter and has a studio in the French Quarter, though I don't have an address."

"What's his name?"

"Italo Palminero."

"Italo?"

"That's it," I said.

"Sounds familiar."

"He left the monastery for reasons unknown."

"If he's in the Quarter, I'll find him. What else?"

"Were you able to pull up any information on the

monks?"

"With no last names, I didn't have enough information. Sorry."

"No problem. I wasn't expecting much."

"When my head stops throbbing, I'll track Palminero down. Ask him a few questions. What can you tell me about the monastery?"

"I thought they were Catholic. They aren't. They call themselves Tracists. The sect was started by criminal types pardoned from France. Seems they've continued in their old ways."

"How so," Tony asked.

"They visit prisons and recruit ex-cons as both workers and monks."

"That would account for Dempsey Duplantis."

"What else did you find out?" I asked.

"Parker's wife showed up at the station with a judge's order that let her take the body. There was no time for an autopsy. Jean Pierre said the body was chewed up pretty bad. Like I told you, he said it looked as if a pack of dogs had got at him."

"I was hoping you'd get a look at an autopsy report. Too bad there wasn't one."

"She had the body taken to New Orleans and cremated. Without an autopsy. At least that's the official story."

"What about all the wounds? It doesn't seem possible a doctor would have signed the death certificate, much less given the cause of death as a heart attack, without an autopsy."

"Well, one apparently did. Getting a look at the death certificate is on my list of things to do," Tony said. "There aren't that many crematories in the city. I'll find out where they burned him, and maybe get to the bottom of it."

"For all the good it'll do us. If the body's cremated, we have nothing to confirm how he actually died. It could be murder, wild dogs, or even a heart attack for all we know."

"Jean Pierre said you can take it to the bank he didn't die of a heart attack. He also told me something else."

"Oh?"

"He said Parker was naked, his clothes found near the water, a hundred yards from where he died."

"Maybe he'd gone skinny dipping."

"If he had, he wasn't alone. They found a woman's clothes and underwear along with his."

"A woman was with him when he was killed? Interesting."

"According to Jean Pierre there were only two women on the island at the time."

"You know their names?"

"Lilly Bliss and Sabine Storm, the movie star."

"They're both still here."

"Jean Pierre seems to think the woman with him was Storm. You met her yet?"

"Oh yeah and your friend's probably right. She's quite a piece of work."

"Not exactly how Jean Pierre described her. It wouldn't hurt to check both of them out. See what they know."

"It's on my list of things to do. Thanks again for helping me with this."

"Anything else on your end interesting to report?" Tony asked

"I'm starting to get a feel for this place. The monks are strange. Something's going on. I don't have a handle on it yet."

"Seen any wild dogs?"

"Two that are large enough and mean enough to kill a man. They aren't wild, though not quite tame, either. Their owner had them on chains. He said a rougarou killed Parker."

"Rougarou? I haven't heard that one since I was a kid. He was kidding, wasn't he?"

"Serious as hell," I said.

"Sounds like you still got more questions than

answers."

"We'll answer all of them before it's over. Thanks again."

"Hell, you're the one that needs thanks. I was spinning my wheels. Now I'm making more money in a week than I did in a month on the force."

"Good for you," I said. "Call me when you get something. You need my number?"

"I already have it, Cowboy. Next time you call, I'll see your name pop up on my screen."

Before I could ask any more questions, Tony hung up. When I glanced around, the two peacocks were pecking at my shirt pocket, looking for treats. Next time, I'd make sure I had one for them.

Chapter Fifteen

It didn't take long to reach Quinn's stilt house in broad daylight. Neither the Professor nor Sierra was there, so I climbed the steep stairway and plopped down in one of the deck chairs. Chuckie and King Tut quickly found me, the big Rottweiler doing a happy dance at my feet as the orange cat jumped into my lap.

"What's happening?" I said, scratching their heads. "Your daddy off in a boat somewhere?"

I quickly got my answer, the throaty roar of a modified engine approaching from somewhere on the expansive bay. The airboat soon appeared, racing through mangroves toward shore. Sierra and Professor Quinn were arguing as they stepped out of the boat.

"You are gravely mistaken, young lady. There's no way you can operate this thing better than me."

"You don't know what you're talking about. You're the one that drives like a little old woman."

They were at the top of the stairway before finally noticing me.

"Mr. Thomas, I can't believe you talked me into hiring this rebellious young woman. She does nothing but argue, and she's always wrong."

"You're an old asshole. For the life of me, I don't know how you made it before I arrived."

"Stop it," I said. "You sound like an old, married

128

couple. Are you getting along, or not?"

"She's bull-headed," Quinn said.

"And you're not?" Sierra said.

"Stop it! How in the world are you getting any work done?"

"I've never had a more productive day," Quinn said. "We found the breeding area for two species I didn't even know lived on the island."

"And who's taking credit for that?" I asked.

"Me," they both said at once.

"Sounds as if you're developing a winning team. Doesn't matter because if you're going to continue to grumble at one another, I'm going back to my bungalow."

They both laughed. "Let us get a beer and use the bathroom, and then we'll take you for a ride on the airboat."

"I'm driving," Sierra said.

"No you're not, young lady. Driving an airboat is man's work."

"All the more reason to let me do it, little old lady."

"Bah!" Quinn said as they disappeared inside the cabin.

They had smiles on their faces though were still kibbitzing when they returned, their hands clutching cold cans of beer.

"You ready, Mr. Thomas?" Professor Quinn asked.

"Yes, but please, I'm just Wyatt."

We were soon racing away from shore, Sierra at the controls as Professor Quinn and I reclined in elevated passenger chairs.

"She's an excellent pilot, and it leaves me free to act as your tour guide." Quinn said.

"I love it," I said.

The boat's raw speed raised my adrenaline level as we raced between low-lying islands overgrown with groundsel bushes and wax myrtles. Turtles, sitting on fallen branches, splashed into the murky water as we raced along.

"This thing is really fast," I said. "What's it got in it?"

"A modified Chevy 327 powering a carbon fiber propeller. The hull is aluminum, and I've yet to find a place in the marsh it can't go. Oh, and yes this baby flies. Almost sixty when it's flat out."

"Which direction are we headed?"

"South, toward the Gulf of Mexico," Quinn shouted in my ear. "The water here is shallow, probably no more than five feet deep. Doesn't make any difference because Jezebel can run on dry land if she has to."

"Jezebel, huh? How far are we from the Gulf?"

"Just a few miles. The vegetation changes as you approach it because of the steady encroachment of salty water."

"There are huge oak trees on the monastery grounds," I said.

"Planted and cultivated by the landscapers, I assure you. You won't see many large trees this close to the Gulf."

Sierra slowed the boat to a halt when we reached a small island covered with palmetto. A curious raccoon poked his head from a small grove of Tupelo gums as we floated through a carpet of lush, flowering pads.

"There's a nest of brown pelicans on this little island. See it?"

The adult pelicans were off foraging for food, the baby birds opening their mouths when they heard us. A giant, loggerhead turtle nosed out of the bushes and splashed into the water, creating wavelets that rippled against the side of the boat. Sierra didn't wait to see what other wonders existed. After turning back toward the big island, she changed directions.

"Now we're heading west," Quinn shouted. "We'll soon reach the fishing village."

Though I'd recently visited in person, I now saw how extensive the village actually was. Seeing it from the bay, the unpainted shacks and rows of boats suggested a long-established center of habitation influenced by several cultures.

The sun was setting in the west when we finally

headed back to Quinn's stilt house, a flock of ducks banking for a landing. He and Sierra were kibbitzing again after mooring the boat for the night.

"She's young, though she may work out," Quinn said as I stepped from the boat.

"Hah! I've given you more ideas than you've had in twenty years."

"I need a beer," Quinn said.

"Me too," Sierra said. "I'll get them."

Geese began spraying water as they landed on the bay's glassy surface. When Sierra went into the stilt house for beer, Professor Quinn sprawled in a deck chair next to me.

"You okay?" I asked.

"I've never worked with someone smarter than I am," he said. "I'm trying to cope."

"Sounds as if she's the partner you've needed."

"She's good."

"Are you glad you hired her?"

"Of course I am, Mr. Thomas. I'm not some stupid old fuddy duddy."

"Wyatt," I said. "Mr. Thomas was my dad's name."

Chuckie and King Tut joined us on the deck, and we enjoyed a spectacular sunset as Professor Quinn and Sierra grilled shrimp and peppers on the deck outside. As darkness descended on the island, I sat between them, listening to a duet sung by raucous night birds.

"I didn't make it home when I left here the other night," I said.

"Oh! What happened?"

"Got lost. Two men from the fishing village rescued me."

"You didn't tell me." Sierra said.

"I spent the night on the floor in one of their shacks, glad I wasn't in the woods alone. I visited with the village matriarch Mama Malaika."

"Is it true? Do they actually practice voodoo?" Sierra asked.

"That's a yes. Mama Malaika has a shrine in her

house. She told me a rougarou was afoot."

"What's a rougarou?" she asked.

"Local nonsense," Professor Quinn said.

"Tell me," Sierra demanded.

"It's a Cajun werewolf," I said.

"You're kidding," she said. "There's no such creature, is there?"

"I didn't see it, but Landry, one of the men that found me fired both barrels of his shotgun at what he said was a real live, honest-to-God rougarou."

"No way," she said.

She went into the house, returning with cans of Abita Amber for her and Professor Quinn, and a glass of ice tea for me.

"I upgraded our beer," she said.

"Bah! Dixie was just fine with me," Quinn said.

"I haven't noticed that you've turned any down," she said.

"What's the story on the settlement? Do you know?" I asked, changing the subject before they had a chance to get at each other again.

"It's populated by descendants of slaves that escaped into the swamps, Native Americans and displaced Cajuns." Quinn said. "What else did Mama Malaika tell you?"

"She said the rougarou is a creature of the Devil and can only be destroyed by an act of God. Any ideas where this idea came from?"

"Eastern Europe," Quinn said. "There's only one virus transmitted by a bite. Rabies. It was widespread in the middle ages."

"You think the legend of werewolves sprang from a fear of rabies?"

"If you were bitten, you got rabies. The resulting death was horrific. The victims became hyper-sexual before finally succumbing to total madness."

"Is it possible there's a strain of rabies that causes someone to become a werewolf?"

Quinn hesitated before speaking. "I can't begin to tell

you how much my research reveals, almost on a daily basis. There's lots more we don't know than what we do."

"And."

"Just look around, Wyatt. Only fifty miles south of New Orleans, we have a place like no other on earth. Is there a rougarou stalking this island? It's likely just a local myth. Still, who's to say no? Not me, I assure you."

"Sierra says there's a tropical storm blowing into the Gulf. Are we in danger?"

"It hasn't shot the gap between Yucatan and Cuba. Too early to tell."

"Crazy. Hurricane season hasn't even begun."

"There was a category 2 hurricane in 1908 in early March. With climate change and all, who knows what's normal anymore?"

"How long till it threatens us?" I asked.

"A week, maybe. If it ever does."

"Then I still have plenty of time," I said.

"What's the big deal, anyway?" Sierra said. "We had lots of earthquakes in California."

"You wouldn't be so nonchalant if you'd been here during Katrina."

"You stayed on the island?"

"Like a fool. Being from the Midwest, I'm used to storms that pass quickly. Hurricanes, especially the bad ones, tend to stick around a while."

"You haven't told me what happened," Sierra said.

The Professor's smile disappeared. "Like you, I was in an earthquake once. When the building I was in began to shake, I didn't know what to do. My terror didn't go away until the shaking ceased."

"And during Katrina?"

"The horror I felt during the thirty seconds of that earthquake didn't abate for more than twenty-four hours. Constant wind and rain attacks your soul. I thought I was going to die, and my fear never left until the hurricane had passed."

Quinn's heartfelt words trailed off into the darkness. The night was glorious, the sky aglow with stars undimmed by street or headlight. Spanish moss hanging from the branches of the stunted cypress trees wafted in a gentle breeze blowing off the bay. Night birds continued to sing in dissonant harmony.

Stoked by beer, good food, and a tough day, Professor Quinn began nodding off. When his eyes closed, chin dropping to his chest, he released his grip on the empty beer can. Sierra grinned as it bounced across the deck, King Tut chasing after it.

"Did Brother Italo leave the island because he fought with Brother Bruno?"

"Who knows? Even my stepfather got into it with Bruno once."

A snort from Professor Quinn caused us both to laugh, and remind me how late it had gotten.

"I better get back to the bungalow."

"I'll rouse the professor. Then I'll show you the way to the stairway across the berm."

"You don't need to do that. I can find it."

"Like you did the other night? Professor, you better go to bed," she said, nudging his shoulder. "I'm going with Wyatt to make sure he finds his way to the berm."

"Good idea," he said. "Take Chuckie with you."

The old man went into the cabin, returning with a shotgun that looked much like Landry's.

"Maybe you should take this."

"Is it loaded?"

"Of course it is. You think I'd give you an unloaded gun?"

"It's not far to the bridge over the berm. We don't need it."

"Suit yourself."

Sierra was grinning, Professor Quinn still grumbling as he disappeared into the cabin.

"I'll lead the way," she said.

Instead of Sierra, it was Chuckie who led us into the woods surrounding the stilt house. Soon, only dim starlight filtering through the growth of stunted trees illuminated our path. When Chuckie planted his feet, bared his fangs and began to growl, Sierra and I stepped backwards. Something rustled the brush directly in front of us. Something big.

Chuckie grew even more agitated, moving side to side, blocking the path. My heart was racing, the big dog's anxiety scaring me. Sierra found a flashlight in her backpack and shined it into the thicket. A pair of red eyes glowed back at us.

By now, Chuckie was in a frenzy. So was the beast in the brush, pawing and snorting. When it stuck its head out, I saw its long snout and sharp tusks. It was a hog, even larger than the one Landry and I had seen on our walk from his village to the berm. This one was alive.

The beast was preparing to charge us when the baying of Landry's black mouth curs caused it to stop and glance around. Bounding through the brush, the two dogs attacked the hog. The huge boar was fierce. So were the dogs. They quickly latched on to its ears and took him down, keeping him there until Landry and Jomo showed up. The two dogs held the big hog at bay until Landry had it hog-tied. It was then they noticed Chuckie.

They would have attacked, perhaps killing the equally large Rottweiler. Landry and Jomo gave them no chance, quickly attaching their chain leashes. Jomo, it seemed, was inhumanly strong, and it took all his strength to restrain the two black mouth curs. We soon heard something else coming up the path.

Several men with a cart appeared through the growth of bushes. With some difficulty, they hoisted the hog into the cart, and then pulled it off, back into the dark forest from where they'd come. It was only then that Landry noticed Sierra. Jomo stayed in the shadows, hanging on to the two dogs as Landry approached.

"Quoi c'est ton nom?"

"Her name is Sierra, and she doesn't speak Cajun," I said. "Sierra, this is Landry."

Landry looked confused when Sierra reached to shake his hand.

"Happy to meet you," she said. "Especially since you

saved our lives."

"Been chasin' that pig since sundown. He almost got away. You lucky he didn't eat you and your dog," he said, looking at Sierra.

"What are you going to do with it?"

"Tomorrow our village celebrate Le Festival de Recommencement. We cook the pig, feast and celebrate the blessings of our island."

"The spring equinox," I said. "They're celebrating the new beginning with a festival as old as time."

"Oh Landry, I'd like to attend. Can I?"

Landry smiled, took her hand and kissed it. "You will make every village woman so jealous, and I will love it. Please come as my guest."

"And Wyatt?" she asked.

Landry glanced at me and said, "He don' like my dogs, him, but he can come anyway. And your daddy too, if he want."

"I don't have a daddy. Professor Quinn is the man I work for."

"No problème. Too much danger out here for a pretty lady. Me and Jomo take you back to your habitation."

"Wyatt has to go back to the monastery."

Landry glanced at me with a frown. "He grown, him. He don' need no help."

"Then neither do I," Sierra said.

Duly chastised, Landry motioned us to follow him. Ten minutes later, we reached the stairs. Standing at the top, I looked down at Sierra, Landry, Jomo, and the three nervous dogs. The moon was full and yellow over Goose Bay.

"Are you sure you'll be okay?"

Sierra grinned, bathing in all the attention. "I'll be fine. I'll call you when I'm safe in my room."

Chapter Sixteen

After his night out with Jean Pierre, Tony woke up feeling like hell. At one, he took Wyatt's advice and had a little hair of the dog. A straight shot of Dalmor Scotch from the bottle he kept hidden in a kitchen cabinet. By two, he'd had his second and third shots. By three, he felt almost good. Almost.

Time had passed since Lil had gone to visit her mother, and he'd yet to receive a call from any of his five kids to find out the problem. This worried him. Lil had threatened to leave him if he didn't quit the force. Now she was still angry, though he was no longer on the force.

There was also a little something about a much younger girlfriend that had stuck in her craw. Even Mama Mulate's love potion hadn't worked this time. Reaching for the phone, he decided it was time to call her. Lil's mom answered on the third ring.

"Ruth, it's Tony. Is Lil there?"

"She doesn't want to talk to you."

"Come on, Ruth. It's been a while now. Put her on the phone. We need to talk."

Tony waited, trying to catch Lil's muted response when Ruth conveyed his request.

"Sorry, Tony. She doesn't want to talk to you."

"Tell her it concerns Janice."

Janice was their youngest daughter, working in

Baton Rouge after dropping out of L.S.U. Though it was a lie he had concocted, he knew she would respond to it."

Lil had brown hair and green eyes. Pretty though not beautiful, she still managed to catch men's eyes in a crowd. An inch or so taller than Tony, she'd never had a weight problem, retaining her perfect size eight figure even after the birth of their five children. Already married more than twenty-five years, Tony wondered how many more were in his future.

"What's wrong with Janice?" Lil said, taking the phone from her mother.

"Lil, I'm happy to hear your voice. You okay?"

"No I'm not okay, Tony. Now what's the matter with Janice?"

"Nothing. I just made it up to get you on the line. Please don't hang up."

She tore into him. "That's your problem, Tony. Your deceit. It's never going to change."

Tony wasn't pleased to hear her accusatory tone. At least she was talking. Now all he had to do was make her listen to him.

"When are you coming home? I miss you."

"You weren't missing me a month ago when you were running around with that little tramp of yours."

"Lil, I said I'm sorry. Can't you forgive me?"

"You can't imagine how much you embarrassed and humiliated me in front of my family, our children, and friends. A simple sorry won't work this time."

"I'm not on the force any longer. That's what you wanted."

Tony waited through a short pause until Lil continued her tirade.

"They had to kick you out screaming and yelling, or you'd have never left. You didn't do it for me."

"The result's the same. I'm done with the N.O.P.D. Can't you come home now so we can work on everything else?"

"Sorry, Tony. It's not so easy this time," she said as she slammed down the receiver.

Despite her words, he'd heard a hint of possible compromise in her voice. Calling the neighborhood florist, he ordered two dozen roses sent to her mother's house. Tomorrow he'd send more. Deciding he wasn't going to feel better anytime soon, he backed his Sebring out of the garage. His headache wasn't going away, so he decided to try and forget about it.

Already late afternoon before he'd finally gotten up and around, he wanted to put the top down on the convertible for the first time. Dark clouds and a light mist of rain precluded him from doing so as he tooled toward the French Quarter.

Tony had three items on his agenda. He needed to locate the person named Italo Palminero. Then he wanted to talk with Brother Degas, the retired monk. Lastly, he intended to pay a visit to the place that had cremated the body of actor Rance Parker. These three things, he decided, could wait as he headed instead to the hospital to see his two injured partners. He arrived as Tommy was being released.

"Well look what the cat drug in," Tommy said as Donna Founteneau helped him out of his wheelchair and into the front seat of her baby blue Toyota.

Tommy was a thickset man, his shirt bought off the shelf bulging at the buttons. His flame red hair was so unruly it seemed to have a mind of its own. Donna was a pretty blond whose hair was a little longer than most female cops. Tommy and Donna were an item, at least on occasion, and they'd been close since Tommy had gotten stabbed during a Mardi Gras parade.

"They finally springing you? I was just coming by to say hi to you and Marlon."

"Marlon's out too. His mom came and got him yesterday. He's rehabbing up in Monroe."

"Sorry I missed him. Happy to see they finally cut you loose."

"Cut ain't a word I like hearing anymore. Me and Donna's on our way to Carlucci's. I been craving a cold Dixie for days. Join us?"

Donna hadn't been happy with him since his dalliance. Still, she was smiling at him, her blue eyes filled with forgiveness.

"Okay with you, Donna?" he asked.

Donna did more than say yes, hugging him and starting to cry.

"Oh Tony, I'm so sorry."

"It's okay," he said, patting her shoulder. "I'll live. The Feds haven't zeroed in on you, have they?"

"They did a ten year cutoff," Tommy said. "Donna and me made it in under the wire."

"It's like a bloodbath at the precinct," Donna said. "Ernie's gone, and Jon's beside himself."

"Meet us at Carlucci's," Tommy said. "I got a bone to pick with you."

Tony hadn't been to Carlucci's since being removed from the force. It seemed like forever as he parked beside the nondescript bar near his old precinct. Mike the bartender, an ex-beat cop, came around the counter and hugged him when he entered the dark pub.

"You okay, Lieutenant?"

Tony nodded and patted Mike's shoulder. "I'm good. Hope I didn't put you out of business by not showing up for a while."

Mike, Tommy's cousin and a smaller version of the big man grinned. "Dixies on me tonight. Glad to see you back."

Someone was playing pool in back. An errant shot sent the cue ball bouncing across the floor. The jukebox was loud, Aaron Neville's falsetto voice weaving a tale of love and deception as Tony headed toward the table of regulars.

"Lookie here. It's Lieutenant Nicosia," Jon Do said as Tony pulled up a chair.

Jon was a first generation Vietnamese resident of New Orleans, his parents refugees from the war. Except for their eyes, he and recently fired cop Ernie Martinez looked a lot alike. Ernie wasn't present. Doc Warner was. A man so small his friends called him Bilbo behind his back, he stood alone, frowning as he threw darts. Tony joined him.

"You okay, Doc?" Tony got no response, the little man continuing to toss darts.

"He's been acting like this for a week now," Donna said.

Tony touched the man's shoulder. "We're drinking Dixie. You gonna join us?"

Though Doc Warner didn't answer, he threw the last dart at the board and then took a seat beside Jon Do. Like old times, Tony started to call for beer. Mike had already beaten him to the punch.

"As a tribute to Lieutenant Nicosia, Doc Warner, Ernie, and all the sacrifices they've made for our city, Dixie's free tonight."

"Thanks, Mike," Doc Warner said. "Things are pretty tight since some of us don't have paychecks to fall back on."

"I still have a job," Donna said. "Mike, bring us a round of tequila shots. And put it on my tab."

Mike had a smile on his face when he arrived with the tequila shooters.

"Thanks, Donna," Jon Do said.

"Keep them coming. At least until my credit card melts."

Donna slammed her shooter and so did Jon Do. Tony, Doc Warner, and Tommy left theirs sitting on the table. Donna held up a hand to get Mike's attention.

"Better hold up on those shots. It's more like a funeral in here than a celebration of Tommy getting out of the hospital."

"You sure you're doing okay, Tommy?" Tony asked.

"I'm gonna make it. I wasn't so positive for awhile. I guess now is as good a time as any to tell you how grateful I am you were there for me. I wouldn't be alive today otherwise."

Tony looked at him, his mouth open. After a moment, he patted his shoulder, almost hugging him. Tommy had no such inhibitions. He and Donna were both in tears when he finally released his bear hug.

"Hey, don't break my ribs," Tony said, trying for levity but achieving none. "You must be okay. You're as strong as ever."

"It just ain't right," Tommy said, still sniffling.

"What ain't right?" Tony asked.

"Damn Feds, nosing in where they don't belong. It just ain't right."

"I'm fine. Same ol' Tony. Nothing's changed."

"Except we ain't partners no more."

"Hey, you'll always be my partner. That's never gonna change. I'm glad you're alive and kicking, and I wish I could have seen Marlon."

"He walked out of the hospital before Tommy," Donna said. "I have to take back all the nasty things I said about your little ex-squeeze."

"Venus?"

Donna nodded. "After you dumped her, she fell in with Marlon. She was there at the hospital every hour she wasn't working and was with him when he walked out."

"How that happened, I just don't understand," Tommy said."

"Voodoo," Tony said with a grin. "At least a few things never fail."

"You may be joking, but I don't know any other way to explain it," Donna said.

As she spoke, Paul Portie joined them at the table, Ernie Martinez with him. Paul was of mixed racial heritage, looking much like an aristocratic Creole in his pressed uniform. Ernie and Jon were brothers from different mothers, and there was no mistaking the resemblance, even though they had different cultural backgrounds. Ernie slammed one of the remaining tequila shooters.

"What are we gonna do, Tony?" he asked.

"Yeah, Tony. Surely you've thought about it," Doc Warner said.

Tommy raked meaty fingers through his unruly red hair and answered for him.

142

"Hell, I think you should sue the bastards for wrongful dismissal."

"What do you think, Tony?" Doc Warner asked.

Everyone had stopped drinking, staring at him as Dr. John wailed on the jukebox in the background.

"Don't know what chance we'd have. It wouldn't hurt to talk to a lawyer and find out."

"Hell yeah!" Ernie said.

"You really think so?" Doc Warner asked.

"We got nothing to lose. Why not call a meeting of everyone dismissed and talk about it?"

"That's the spirit," Donna said, motioning Mike to bring a second round of shots.

When they arrived, everyone at the table slammed theirs this time. Everyone except Tony.

"I'm not trying to be a party pooper, but there's something I have to take care of first."

"You gonna take the lead on this lawsuit thing?" Doc Warner asked.

"Can't do it. Someone else is gonna have to take up the sword," he said as he got out of his chair.

"Don't be that way," Ernie said. "We need you on this."

"I'm doing a little P.I. work now, and I'm starting to think getting canned is the best thing that ever happened to me."

"You don't mean that," Doc Warner said.

"I'm not sure what I mean. I'll help you guys out, even if I don't participate."

"At least tell us how to get started," Ernie said.

"Easy. Ask around for the baddest lawyer in N.O. I'll be back in touch."

Tony walked out of the smoky bar and into an even more dismal day, wondering what bone Tommy had to pick with him.

Chapter Seventeen

Though only late March, it was already hot as Tony walked down Bienville to Bourbon Street. He didn't know where to find Italo Palminero, though he knew where to start looking.

New Orleans encompasses a large area. The French Quarter doesn't. Less than a square mile in size, the Quarter is little, and everyone that lives there likely knows everyone else. The mournful horn of a barge, passing on the river, echoed down the corridor of ancient buildings as he turned the corner onto Bourbon Street.

Because of persistent rain, the fabled street was mostly deserted. An old man stood in a doorway, near the entrance to an alleyway leading to tee shirt and tourist shops. The man nodded as he passed on the street. Tony soon reached the open door of a strip joint where a French Quarter barker waited, unmindful of the drizzle as he held open the door.

"Lieutenant Tony," the man said. "Never seen you down here this early. What up?"

Like his hair, the man's grin was also oily, dark, and thin. Dragon tattoos decorated his muscular shoulders, exposed by a sleeveless tee shirt, his little mustache posting an exclamation point on his face.

"How you doing, Felix?"

"Passable. You, Lieutenant?"

"Like a pig wallowing in slop. Where is everybody?"

"Sleeping, eating, or screwing. With this rain, won't be anyone around till nine or ten."

"Then what are you doing out here?"

Felix grinned. "Gotta keep the bosses happy. Every now and then some dumb Okie slides by. I drag 'em in and sell them a twenty dollar cocktail. Hell, the girls ain't even here yet. What are you doing out?"

"Looking for someone. Know where I can find them?"

"Probably so, but I don't like getting my bros into trouble."

"No trouble. Just answers. The person I'm looking for has them. Can you help me?"

"I got no beef with the N.O.P.D."

"Keep it that way," Tony said. "I'm looking for Italo Palminero."

"What's he done?" Felix asked.

"Not a damn thing. Like I said, I just want to talk."

A group of college students, already drunk and not waiting for darkness or worrying about the light drizzle, passed them, walking in the middle of the street devoid of traffic. Felix watched as they passed, not bothering to call out to them.

"Down the street to Toulouse and turn left. He has a studio in the first alleyway you come to."

"You know him?"

"Hell yeah. He's in here almost every night, half drunk, sitting at the pussy bar and throwing dollar bills at the girls."

"Loser, huh?"

Felix grinned again. "Good customer," he said.

"Thanks," Tony said, giving a backwards wave. "I owe you one."

"And I ain't forgetting about it, Lieutenant," Felix said as Tony walked down Bourbon Street.

The rain was evaporating almost as fast as it fell. Having other things on his mind, it didn't trouble Tony. Since there's little available real estate in the French Quarter, Palminero's studio was a hole in the wall, accessed by an alley used mainly for trash cans. Still, there was an impressive sign on the sidewalk pointing to it and even a couple of appreciative tourists inside the shop, smiling as they touched and fondled the beautiful wooden pieces Palminero had created.

Palminero was a large man, his meaty shoulders, like Felix the barker, revealed by a sleeveless tee shirt. His round head was totally bald, a bushy mustache his only facial hair. His ears had the shape of cauliflowers, likely caused by too many rounds in a boxing ring. When Tony got his attention, the man's sad smile highlighted a missing front tooth.

"You Italo Palminero?" Tony asked.

"Who wants to know?" he said.

"Someone recommended your work to me. I'm here to take a look."

Tony glanced around at the wooden objects—chairs, cabinets, chests of drawers, perfectly fitting puzzles of all shapes and sizes. A gray-haired woman that resembled Palminero was wrapping a puzzle in crepe paper for a happy couple.

"Everything's for sale," Palminero said.

"Really nice," Tony said, rubbing the sparkling surface of a hand-glazed jewelry box. "How much is this?"

"He quickly jerked his hand away when Palminero said, "A thousand dollars."

"My friend said you were a monk."

"Oh yeah?"

"You're not a monk anymore?"

"My objects are for sale. My life is private."

"Sorry," Tony said. "Didn't mean to pry."

More customers came through the door, and Palminero looked at Tony.

"You want to buy something, my mother over there will help you. I got these other customers to see to."

Seeing he was getting nowhere, Tony strolled over to the old woman resting against the wall, fanning herself with a yellow pad.

She smiled and nodded when he asked, "You Ms.

146

Palminero? Your son does beautiful work."

"He just like his papa. Sawdust run in his veins though it took him a while to realize it."

When she spoke, Tony noticed she, like her son, also had a missing front tooth. Hers was replaced with one that was gold.

"Why did he leave the monastery?"

"You know my boy?" she asked.

"I heard about his work and wanted to take a look."

"That one, he don't tell his mama nothing. We have a good life since he come back."

Tony wished he were still a cop. He'd strong-armed many a potential witness to obtain information he needed to drive a case forward. Though he thought seriously about running a bluff, he finally decided against it.

"Thanks, Ms. Palminero. My wife would love that beautiful jewelry box, but it costs way more than my budget will allow."

Ms. Palminero crossed her arms tightly across her chest and stared into his eyes a moment with her own dark orbs.

"What's your wife's name?"

"Lil."

"And you?"

"Tony. Tony Nicosia."

"Okay Tony. How long you and Lil been married?"

"Would have been twenty-eight years next month."

"Would have been?"

"I screwed up. Had a little indiscretion. She's forgiven me before. This time I don't know."

"You wait here," she said, touching his shoulder.

She returned to the checkout counter with the jewelry box and started wrapping it.

"What are you doing?" he asked.

"You give Lil this jewelry box. Tell her it's from you and Mama Palminero. Maybe she'll reconsider."

"Thank you so much but I can't take something so expensive."

"Why not?"

"I haven't done anything to deserve it."

"You a good man. I see it in your eyes and hear it in your voice. You deserve a second chance. I'm gonna give you one."

"But. . ."

"Me and Italo, we don't miss many meals. We got a nice place to live. Nice car. You need this more than us."

When the jewelry box was wrapped, Tony reached over the counter and hugged the woman.

"You a beautiful lady, Ms. Palminero. I thank you from the bottom of my heart."

"It's okay," she said. "Someday maybe you can do me and my Italo a favor."

"I look forward to that day," Tony said as he walked out into the alleyway and back to Bourbon Street.

The rain had halted for the moment, foot traffic picking up. He hadn't eaten all day, and his stomach was letting him know it. Too late for lunch and a little too early for dinner, he decided to tough it out. Open a can of beans when he got back home. Before he got there, he had more places to visit.

Wyatt had given him the address of an old monk he wanted him to speak with. The man lived in a little French Quarter apartment near the intersection of St. Louis and Dauphine. He wasn't far from there when he left Palminero's studio.

Palm trees peeked over the high walls of the apartment complex. It was dark, steady rain continuing again as Tony used his little flashlight to see the names on the door. Finding the one he wanted, he pushed the buzzer and waited.

"Is that you, Sara?" someone's voice said through the tinny speaker.

"It's Tony," he said.

"I don't know anyone named Tony," the voice said.

"I'm a friend of Sara's," Tony said.

There was a buzz and a flash of light. Tony quickly pushed open the door, entered the courtyard, raindrops creating radiating waves on the tranquil surface of the center fountain. He started up the steep stairs, knocking on the first door he came to.

"It's open. Come in," someone inside said.

Tony entered the room. A single candle illuminated the surroundings, the odor of burning wax hanging heavy in the humid air. The place was tiny, probably no more than ten by twelve. Seeing no bed, he guessd one probably came out from the wall. There was a sink and a small refrigerator but no oven. A door in the back led to the bathroom, probably also tiny. An old man in a chair smiled up at him.

"Who are you?" he asked.

"I'm Tony."

"I don't know you," the man said.

"A friend of Sara's," Tony said. "You Brother Degas?"

The man had a blanket pulled up around his neck, but Tony could see he was very old, his youthful eyes a hushed shade of blue.

"A distant cousin," he said.

"Pardon me?" Tony said.

"Degas, the painter was a distant cousin of mine. He had relatives in New Orleans and spent time here."

"Yeah, I suppose he did. You a painter too?"

"A talent that somehow managed to evade me," he said with a grin.

"Me too," Tony said. "How you doing, Brother Degas?"

"I'm alive," he said. "More than most people my age can say."

"That's a fact. How old are you?"

"Ninety-five my next birthday."

"You look good," Tony said. "You live here by yourself?"

"Since I left the monastery. Who did you say you are?"

"Tony. Who brings your food?"

"Sara comes every day."

"You only eat one meal a day?"

Brother Degas smiled, opening his mouth largely

149

devoid of teeth. "I don't require much. As you can see I'm not terribly active. Who did you say you are?"

"Sara's friend Tony," he said.

"Why are you here?"

"Sara told me you were a monk at Barataria Monastery."

"Yes," Brother Degas said.

"You lived there long?"

"Sixty years."

"Why did you leave?"

"If you're to understand why I left, I first need to tell you a bit about the monastery."

"Shoot, Brother. I'm all ears."

Thunder shook the door Tony had left ajar. A cool breeze carrying a spray of rain blew through the room. Brother Degas didn't seem to notice.

"Goose Island is so secluded most people have never heard of the monastery," he said. "Since we aren't Catholic, we had to do our own recruiting. We usually managed to find a few willing souls whenever we visited a jail or prison."

"You recruited prisoners? Weren't you afraid they'd rob or kill you?"

As Brother Degas smiled again, Tony noticed how warm it was in the apartment. Though it was far from cold, the old monk had the space heater at his feet cranked full blast. Tony loosened his tie and rubbed his arm across his damp forehead.

"I'm a felon myself. Seven years for breaking and entering. The brothers got me out of jail. I entered the monastery with an open mind and never regretted it. It turned my life around."

"Maybe you're the exception to the rule," Tony said.

"Maybe not. Sometimes the ugliest dog makes the best pet," Brother Degas said.

"You're probably right about that. What does all that have to do with deciding to deactivate the monastery?"

"As we all got older, our recruiting fell by the wayside. A dying order, we decided to mothball the monastery and go our separate ways."

"And Father Domenic stayed behind?"

"We were going to donate the land and buildings to the state. They were going to create a bird sanctuary."

"Father Domenic changed his mind?"

"He was much younger than the rest of us monks and had more energy left than we did."

"How much younger?"

"A spring chicken compared to the rest of us; probably seventy something."

Brother Degas nodded when Tony said, "Then he's pushing eighty by now. Do you have a picture of him by any chance?"

The old man shook his head. "Cameras weren't allowed at the monastery. You can understand why, can't you?"

"Yes, but it's too bad though. There would be lots of good memories there."

"Believe me, I have lots of pleasant memories locked firmly in my mind."

The old man had told him what he'd come to hear. After shaking his hand, he backed toward the door.

"Thanks for the information, Brother Degas. I have to go now."

"Don't leave so soon. I don't get many visitors, and it gets kind of lonely sometimes. Who did you say you are?"

"Tony, Sara's friend. I'll tell her I stopped by."

Tony hurried down the steep stairs, ready to get out of the hot apartment. Ferns hung in baskets from the second floor walkway. Oleanders were in bloom, their red flowers growing lushly against the old stone masonry. Tony tossed a quarter into the center fountain and made a wish before exiting through the heavy wooden door.

It wasn't far from Bourbon Street to the Central Business District. CBD to the locals. The crematory that had cremated the body of Rance Parker was among the dismal warehouses, tiny eateries, and many ordinary businesses located there.

It was also the area where most of the city's homeless

people lived. It was damp and dreary, and Tony didn't look forward to dealing with the walking zombies that came alive after dark.

When he found the back entrance to the crematory, he locked the jewelry chest in the car's trunk. As he touched the canvas top of the convertible, he suddenly rued his decision to buy it. It would be a miracle if it survived his visit to the crematory. Locking the doors anyway, he knocked on the alleyway door.

"Who is it?" someone said.

"N.O.P.D.," Tony said.

"What is it you want?"

"A few answers. Please let me in."

A little man with spectacles and thinning hair he hadn't bothered combing cracked the door and peeked out. Tony smiled at him, trying not to look like a serial killer or wino. He must have succeeded because the man opened the door and let him in.

"I'm Tony Nicosia. Can I ask a few questions?"

"You're here. Why not?"

After Tony followed him inside, the man locked the heavy door with two deadbolts.

"Lot of crime in this neighborhood?" Tony asked.

"You want something stolen or vandalized, just leave it in our parking lot overnight. I'm getting ready to burn one. You're not queasy, are you?"

Tony shook his head, and the man opened a door near the one he'd just entered, cold air and the smell of refrigerated death accosting his senses as he did. The man wheeled out a gurney with the body of an old man on it. It had apparently been there a while as bare bones protruded through its thin and discolored skin. The old man's cold eyes, locked in the grotesque mask of his face, gaped at him.

The man wheeled the gurney to a room with two chambers for incinerating bodies. After cranking up the gurney, he pushed the old man's body into one of the metal cylinders, gas flames already glowing. Shutting the door and locking it, he raised the temperature in the chamber to full blast.

"How long does it take?" Tony asked.

"Longer than you'd think. About an hour. You got questions for me?"

"You cremated a body a while back."

"That's my job."

"This one was different. The body of Rance Parker."

The man smiled. "I've been doing this a long time. Parker's not the only famous person I've burned."

"Yeah, well I'm not interested in others. Tell me about his body."

"The people that brought it said it was contaminated and warned me not to touch it. They delivered it in a plastic bag."

"Contaminated? By what?"

"They didn't say."

The man smiled when Tony said, "You looked at the body anyway, didn't you?"

"I wouldn't be doing my job if I hadn't."

"Was it Rance Parker?"

"What was left of it. Whatever killed him did a real number. The autopsy made an even worse mess of everything."

"An autopsy? The police have no record of one being performed."

"Guess you haven't heard. We got a place here in town now that does them for a fee."

"I didn't know. Why?"

"Loved ones don't always agree with the official cause of death. Sometimes they just need more information and quite a few people are willing to pay for it."

"What's the name of this place?"

"Confidential Autopsy. Not far from here in the CBD."

"Did you get a look at the results?"

"Nope, it's private."

"But you saw the body."

"Yep."

"And?"

153

"Like I said, it was badly mutilated."

"Reports identify the cause of death as a heart attack."

"Could be," the man said. "Some people's hearts give out when confronted with traumatic situations."

He smiled when Tony said, "You don't sound convinced."

"Lots of things are left after we burn a body: metal used to strengthen broken bones, partials, even bullets. Let me show you something I pulled out of Parker's body."

Opening a drawer, he began rummaging through it. Tony's mouth gaped when he opened his hand and showed him what was in it.

"What the hell!

The object in the man's hand was about an inch and a half long, curved and black. The point that wasn't broken off was dagger sharp.

"I think it's a claw."

"An animal claw?" Tony asked.

"What other kind is there?"

Tony didn't bother answering his question. "Did you generate the death certificate?"

The man shook his head. "No, but the autopsy service provided me with a copy."

Who signed it?"

"Let me look," he said, opening a file cabinet and producing a document from a manila folder. "Dr. Darwin Porter."

"Ever hear of him?"

"Nope," the man said.

He nodded when Tony asked, "You got a copy machine in this place?"

"I'll make you one," he said. "Always happy to oblige the N.O.P.D."

Tony left the crematory with the claw, and a copy of Parker's death certificate, trying to hold his breath until he reached his car to avoid smelling anymore of the place's less than subtle scent of death. Three winos were pawing his Sebring as he walked to the parking lot of the crematory. By now after dark, the wind was still damp with rain.

"Hey! N.O.P.D. Get away from that car."

Despite his lack of a badge, Tony still had a positive tone in his voice that commanded respect. The three men, afraid of the police, immediately dispersed into the darkness.

Thankful to find nothing amiss, he cranked the engine and started down Camp Street, back toward the French Quarter.

Chapter Eighteen

The N.O.P.D. had taken Tony's badge and his dignity. What they hadn't taken was his twenty-five years of accumulated experience investigating homicides, or his detective's intuition. Italo Palminero had information relevant to the murder of Rance Parker. Information, Tony knew, you don't always get on your first interview. After leaving the crematory, he headed back toward the lights of Bourbon Street for answers he hadn't gotten earlier.

Already dark, Palminero's shop would be closed for the night, the pug-ugly man somewhere else. Tony had an idea where to find him. When he did, he had a feeling he'd get the answers he sought.

The all-day rain hadn't hurt the tourist trade on Bourbon Street. It was rocking when Tony found a place to park. Except for police cars, vehicles aren't allowed on the street at night. Now it overflowed with pedestrian traffic, people trying to decide which side of the street to see next in the brightly lit, noisy, adult Disneyland. No one ever left disappointed.

Tony wasn't interested in tee shirt shops, oyster bars, or exotic cocktails as he wound his way through the throng of tourists to the exterior of the strip bar he'd passed earlier in the day. Felix the barker was still there, standing in the same location, yelling at a couple of drunk

Okies that shot him the finger and kept walking. Their rejection of his invitation didn't seem to bother him.

"You back, Lieutenant?"

He laughed when Tony said, "I couldn't resist your lovely girls, twenty dollar drinks, or your homely face."

"You still looking for Italo?"

"Yeah. He in there?"

"He's here. Sitting at the pussy bar all by himself."

"What's the story on his ears? Looks as if he's been in a fight or two."

"Why hell Lieutenant, you a fight fan. He fought for the heavyweight belt ten years ago. The champ made mincemeat out of him. Cut him up bad but he still wouldn't go down. He went the distance, though it was his last fight."

"My old brain's not connecting."

"You gotta remember Bruiser Palminero."

"Oh yeah. Bruiser Palminero. I watched him fight on TV a dozen times. I thought he looked familiar. At least his brains aren't scrambled."

"Pickled is more like it," Felix said. Tony reached for his wallet. "Keep your cash," Felix said with a wave. "Drinks are always on the house for the N.O.P.D."

"Guess you haven't heard. The Feds are cleaning house on the force. Better take the money cause I pretty much been canned."

"I heard. Don't matter. We appreciate you here. You're still drinking free and always will in this place."

"Thanks, Felix," Tony said as he walked through the door held open by the man with the oily smile.

The odor of stale smoke and spilled beer accosted his senses the moment he entered the dank bar, a pretty blond woman with unfocused eyes making love to a chrome pole on center stage. All the tables were crowded with horny men and even a few enthusiastic females. Most of the regulars were sitting around a circular stage they called the pussy bar. Tony could see why.

Two young women, both naked, danced on stage as the men gathered around it clapped, whooped, and threw dollar bills at them. Tony spotted Palminero sitting alone, bathed in wafting smoke and the moving glow of a red and green strobe light.

He turned when Tony said, "This seat taken, Bruiser?"

"It's open."

From his drooping eyelids and slurred words, it was apparent Palminero had already been there a while. Not a bad thing. The ex-boxer didn't recognize him from earlier in the day. A waitress found Tony through the thick cloud of cigarette smoke and the bar's inherent dimness, placing a Scotch and water in front of him.

"Drinks are on the house for you tonight." Tony smiled when she said, "Did you have to suck the boss's dick?"

"Thanks for the drink," he said, not commenting on her remark.

When she bent down to dump an ashtray, he stuffed a ten dollar bill in her ample cleavage. Smiling for the first time, she put her arms around him, grinding her breasts against his face.

"Thanks, baby. I'm Wilda. What's your name?"

"Thank you, Wilda. I'm Tony," he said as she blew him a kiss and strutted off.

One of the young women dancing on the bar noticed. "What about us, big tipper?"

They both squatted on the counter, giving him some love when he handed them each a five.

"Good thing my drinks are free cause I'm still gonna be broke when I leave this place."

Palminero smiled for the first time. "The girls like to kiss and hug, especially if you tip them big. Mama said she's gonna have me locked up if I don't stop coming in here and spending all our money."

He nodded when Tony said, "I met her today. She's a wonderful woman."

"Salt of the earth."

"She Italian?"

"Mama and Papa came over from Italy thirty years

ago. I was ten."

"Was it your dad that taught you how to make those beautiful pieces in your shop?"

Palminero nodded again. "All my life, all he wanted was for me to be a craftsman like him. He was a master carpenter. No one in the world better."

"I don't know about that. From what I saw, you're pretty good yourself."

"Born to it, but it was never what I wanted. That was always boxing. Be champion of the world. Ali was my hero."

"I watched you fight on TV, and once in person at a motor hotel in Metairie. Quite a crowd that night."

Palminero smiled. "I remember. It was supposed to be an exhibition, but the drunk Indian I was fighting musta thought it was for the belt or something. I finally had to deck him to keep from getting hurt."

"Your last fight, when you fought for the belt," Tony said. "The ref should have called it. You were a bloody mess, but you never went down."

"I went the distance. My eyes were swollen so bad I couldn't see the next day. I didn't get out of bed for two days, and then pissed blood for a week."

"That when you decided to join the monastery?"

Palminero poured himself another glass of beer from the pitcher on the bar.

"I thought I'd found my calling. Turns out I like women and beer too much."

"That's not why you left though, is it?"

"No," he said.

"Can you tell me?"

"You wouldn't believe it."

"Not much I haven't seen or heard."

When the Bob Segar song on the jukebox ended, the two girls dancing on stage scooped up the loose cash and hurried off to their dressing room. Soon, another slow rocker began cranking from the jukebox, the blond dancer from center stage replacing the two women. Tony didn't notice, and neither did Bruiser Palminero.

159

"Been a while ago now. We had a carpenter shop where we built the coffins. There was five of us monks at the monastery, including Father Domenic. I'd forgotten something in the shop one night and went back to get it. It was late, and I didn't expect to see anyone there. I got quite a surprise."

The buxom blond with a butterfly tattoo on her calf made eye contact with Palminero. She stopped dancing, stepped down on the bar, squatted and gave him a hug. She wasn't done, taking a swig of beer straight from the pitcher. He stuffed a dollar bill into her sequined G-string before she climbed back up on stage.

"Pretty woman," Tony said.

"She kinda likes me, but I can't get her to go out with me."

"Hey, she'll come around."

"You think?" Palminero asked.

His sad smile returned when Tony said, "Bruiser, I can see you got a way with women. She'll come around."

When someone tapped his shoulder, Tony turned bumping into Wilda's bare stomach. Grabbing his head, she massaged it with her enormous breasts. With a wicked grin, she tongued his forehead. Tony responded by giving her another ten.

"Wilda, you're giving me ideas."

"Those lips of yours have already given me a few."

She winked, gave her ass a hard slap and then strutted away through the smoky darkness. The Scotch and Wilda had given him a buzz, and he tried shaking the cobwebs beginning to form in his brain before returning his attention to Palminero.

"Hey, Champ, you were telling me about the monastery when we were so rudely interrupted. Can you finish the story?"

"First, I need more beer," Palminero said.

"I'll get you some," Tony said, raising his hand to get the attention of a passing waitress. "Bring this man another pitcher. I'm buying."

Wilda returned with the pitcher. After yet another

sultry embrace, he gave her a twenty this time.

"Hell, no wonder I'm always broke," he said. "Good thing I got a new gig."

"Hard to turn down a pretty face," Palminero said.

"I hear that. So someone was in the carpentry shop when you got there?"

Not bothering with his glass, Palminero lifted the pitcher and swilled cold beer straight from its chilled lip. Some of it poured down the front of his tee shirt, and he wiped his mouth with his tattooed arm.

"I heard something before I saw them. It was two of the other monks, Brothers Bruno and Dunwoody."

"Go on," Tony said.

"They were arguing. I was behind some boxes. They didn't know I was there."

"What were they arguing about?" Tony asked.

"I don't know, but as I watched, I got the shock of my life."

"What happened?"

As if not wanting to relive the unpleasant memory, Palminero took another swig from the pitcher before answering.

"Brother Bruno began to transform."

"What the hell are you talking about?"

"He started to change."

"I'm kinda slow. Maybe you better explain."

"Something horrible. Thick, black hair began sprouting from his face, neck, and arms. I know this sounds crazy, but he got taller, bigger, and hairier as I watched. His face contorted into a wolf's muzzle, complete with fangs. It was like one of those old horror movies I used to watch when I was a kid."

"You shitting me," Tony said.

Palminero wasn't smiling. "Bruno and Dunwoody are big men, both bigger than me, and I'm not small."

"No you're not."

"Like I said, Bruno grew even larger as he transformed."

"What did Dunwoody do?"

"Just stood there, his eyes and mouth wide open, as if he couldn't believe what was happening but was too scared to run away."

"What did happen?"

"I was scared shitless myself and wanted to get the hell out of there. I couldn't. I was hypnotized, locked in place. Hell, there was no place to go without him seeing me."

"Bruno attacked Brother Dunwoody?"

"He got after him, roughing him up pretty bad. Brother Dunwoody had bites and scratches all over him. I'd never seen anything like it and was too stunned to do anything but watch. I was surprised Bruno didn't kill him."

"And?"

"Father Domenic showed up. By this time, it was already over, and the wolfman was changing back into Brother Bruno."

"Was Father Domenic shocked and surprised?"

"That's the part that still confuses me. It was as if he'd seen it all before."

"Was it Father Domenic that called the police?"

"Like me, someone else was in the carpentry. He'd rushed out and called the cops before Father Domenic arrived."

"Who?" Tony asked.

"Brother Bruce. When Father Domenic found out, he severely reprimanded him."

"Because?"

"The Tracist code. Father Domenic said what happens at the monastery is nobodies business except ours."

"What do you know about Father Domenic?"

"Nothing much. He and Brother Dunwoody got me out of the drunk tank here in the city. He was the one that talked me into trying life as a monk."

"So you left the monastery after witnessing the attack?"

The music ended, the dancer leaving the stage,

another taking her place. Palminero killed the pitcher of beer and stuck his hand up for another.

"I was ready to leave before that. I probably would have gone anyway. Witnessing the attack just hurried my decision along."

Bruiser Palminero hung his head when Tony said, "You might not be alive now if you hadn't. You okay with all this?"

"I have a friend at the monastery. I told him what I saw."

"Who?"

"A man that works there. Dempsey Duplantis. An ex-con but a righteous man. I should have kept the matter to myself."

"What difference does it make?"

"Maybe nothing."

Tony fished the claw from his pocket and showed it to Palminero.

"He probably didn't believe you. If I hadn't seen this with my own eyes, I probably wouldn't believe you either," Tony said.

"Dempsey laughed at my story," Italo said, touching the black object in Tony's hand. "He said he'd met people like Brother Bruno in prison. He thinks Bruno killed the actor. As a human and not as a wolfman. He told me he'd decided to talk to Father Domenic about it."

"That don't sound good. When?"

"Tonight."

Chapter Nineteen

Feeling good I'd made it back to the monastery grounds without another island misadventure, I glanced up at the starless sky. Thunder rumbled over the bay, and Sierra called as I opened the door of my bungalow.

"Oh Wyatt, Landry has such dreamy eyes. I think I'm in love."

"Then I guess you made it home okay."

"Ten minutes after we left you at the berm bridge. I woke Professor Quinn and told him about the celebration in Landry's village tomorrow."

"Bet that was a trip. What did he say?"

"He thinks it's a wonderful idea and wants to go. He said it was the chance of a lifetime to study a group of people that have hardly changed in nearly two centuries."

"Wow, I'd never have thought of it like that."

"Me either. We're going, sometime after lunch tomorrow. You're coming with us, aren't you?"

"Can't make it that early. I have a few things to do first."

"What time then?"

"How about seven?"

"Kind of late but we'll make it work. Landry and I will meet you at the berm bridge."

When I finally stepped inside the bungalow, Kisses bounded toward me. I'd left the patio door ajar for her, and I knew she had plenty of food and water. I still felt guilty, being gone so long and leaving her alone in a strange place. The way she was rubbing against my leg, I realized she'd missed me too, and all was forgiven.

Kisses awoke me early the next morning, pawing my chest to make sure I didn't ignore her. After feeding and paying attention to her for a requisite amount of time, I was ready to look into a few things that still bothered me about the case. Satiated for the moment by my attention, Kisses didn't seem to mind when I left the bungalow.

Lilly Bliss and Stormie were the only two women on the island when the killing occurred. According to Tony's report, one of them had likely been skinny dipping with Rance Parker shortly before it had happened. I'd talked with Stormie already, but not Lilly Bliss. I hoped she could give me some answers.

Stormie was strange, but neither she nor Lilly Bliss struck me as killers. Both seemed deeply into kinky sexual experiences, as least from what Stormie had told me. I set out to talk with Miss Bliss and find out what she knew, if anything, about the killing.

She wasn't at the pool or in any of the restaurants. No one had seen her that morning. A gardener pointed me to her bungalow as a flock of geese circled overhead.

"Come in. I'm not getting up," she said when I knocked on her door.

I opened it to see the woman sitting behind a laptop computer, the air conditioning blasting. Dressed in green flannel pajamas, she looked more suited for a winter night in Maine than a late spring morning in south Louisiana. When she glanced up from her keyboard, I got my first close look at her.

Her hair was short and black, the same color as the frames of the thick glasses she'd pushed to the top of her head like a tiara. She had expressive, Gulf green eyes and a pixie face, anything but beautiful, though far from ugly. She smiled when she glanced up at me.

"Sorry. I needed one more paragraph to get my five

thousand words for the day. I've been so far behind on my book, I decided to stay awake last night and catch up."

"I'm Wyatt," I said.

"I know who you are," she said, framing my face with her hands. "Take your shirt off."

"And the reason is?"

"I want to see your chest."

"Why not," I said, unbuttoning my khaki work shirt and slipping out of it.

I stood there, feeling the fool as she eyed me from head to toe.

"You're perfect. Will you pose for the cover of my next book?"

"You're kidding, right?"

"Serious as a heart attack."

"I'm sure you'd have bigger sales if you got a younger man to pose for you."

"I don't know how old you are, but with your chiseled chest, you could be the lead dancer for the Chippendales far as I'm concerned."

"Thanks," I said, not knowing what else to say.

"Do you like archaeology?" she asked.

"Don't know anything about it. Why?"

"Have you heard of the Magnolia Mound?"

"No. What is it?"

"Quite possibly the most significant archaeological site in the state. There were Indians in this area eighteen hundred years ago and three mounds not far from here. I want to visit but can't get anyone to go with me."

"Is it outside the berm?"

She didn't answer my question, asking one of her own.

"Have you been outside the berm?"

"A time or two. It's pretty wild out there."

"I can imagine. This place is like a Hollywood resort, and the management frowns on its guests leaving the premises. Doesn't matter because the site is on an undeveloped tract of the island on this side of the berm."

"Undeveloped? You mean bushes, brush, vines, and

undergrowth?"

"You got it."

"Then how would we ever find it?"

"I have the coordinates, and G.P.S. on my phone."

"I'm game," I said. "When do we go?"

"Soon as I change clothes. I'm having a little trouble seeing, since I seemed to have misplaced my glasses."

"They're on top of your head," I said.

"Oh!" she said, grabbing them. "I'll be right back."

She soon returned wearing dark shorts, a Bourbon Street tee shirt emblazoned with a purple and gold fleur de lis, and high-top hiking boots. Her backpack reminded me of the one Sierra always carried.

Clouds had covered the sun, the bathers by the pool packing up and heading for the lounge. Lilly didn't seem to care. Neither did the two peacocks, vying for birdseed one of the monks had spread on the ground for them earlier that morning.

"Which way?" I said.

"West of here, beyond the Celebration Fountain," Lilly said.

"Then lead the way."

The peacocks followed us, patrolling the fountain when we passed it. Both came running when I threw them a handful of unshelled peanuts I'd gotten at the commissary that morning.

"Looks as if you have a way with birds," Lilly said.

"Babies and old ladies like me too."

Grinning, she said, "How old are you?"

"Forty something."

It was my turn to smile when she said, "Yeah, I'm thirty-nine something myself."

The day had become even cloudier, likely due to the tropical storm brewing in the Gulf. It didn't matter because we were both sweating when we finally reached the archaeological site. A clump of bushes standing up much higher than the usual flat marshlands was our first clue. We scared a covey of quail hiding in the tall grass, their disturbed chatter surprising us when they raced skyward in an explosion of beating wings.

"This is it," she said.

"You mean those bumps over there?"

"Well there's not going to be a road sign out here, sweetie."

Three hillocks rose up from the flat, marshy ground. They were bigger than bumps, each about fifty feet in diameter. One of the hillocks had a metal structure situated on top of it.

"What's that?"

"Archeologists did some excavating several years ago. That tin roof protected the diggers and the excavation from rainwater."

"Now what?" I asked.

She raised her arms, glanced at the sky, and then did a twirling three-sixty.

"Can't you feel it? We're standing near a piece of prehistory not included in a single textbook. I feel like Lewis and Clark."

"Now what?"

Lilly slipped the backpack off her shoulders, pulling something out of it.

"My new book is a time travel romance. The heroine comes to the swamp after being jilted by her lover. When she stands on the mound, the spirit of a powerful chief appears. I need you to help me act this out."

"You're not getting weird on me, are you?"

"You'd love it if I did. Now please just humor me."

She handed me a bundle of clothes.

"What's this?"

"Loin cloth. Put it on. You're going to portray the Indian spirit."

"You aren't kidding about this, are you?"

Her frown and hands on her hips told me she was serious.

"Just do it," she said.

"Fine, I'll go behind those bushes."

"Don't be such a prude. Take your clothes off. I've seen lots of naked men."

"My underwear too?"

"Don't be a dork. Indians didn't wear underwear."

As she watched, I doffed my clothes and put on the loin cloth and feathered headdress.

"Lillie, I feel like an idiot."

"Then stop acting like one and stand still while I apply your war paint."

When she finished painting my face, she quickly got out of her clothes, unmindful of her nudity as she put on her own loin cloth, beads and ceremonial headdress.

"What about your blouse?"

"You think Indian maidens wore blouses eighteen hundred years ago?"

"We have our regular shoes on."

"I didn't bring moccasins. I couldn't think of everything. Now paint me."

"You said your heroine is from modern times."

"Quit grousing. I don't have to explain every little nuance of my story to you, do I?"

"I guess not," I said.

"Good, because I don't intend to."

She remained stoic as I decorated her face, but giggled when I painted her neck and chest.

"I think I'm getting hot," she said.

"Me too. Maybe we should do something about it."

Lilly was having none of it, frowning at my suggestion.

"Stay on point. We have work to do."

If you can't give me a script to go by, at least fill me in on the basic premise."

"I already did that. Now, just close your eyes a moment and fantasize that you're a powerful chief of the Magnolia Tribe. Can you do that?"

I gave her a snappy salute as she climbed to the top of one of the mounds, frowning though otherwise choosing to ignore my levity. The sky had further darkened, gentle rain falling on us as she gazed at the distant bay.

"Great Spirit, this is the place where you appeared in my dream. I've come, willing to accept your promise."

Deciding I'd heard my cue, I hurried to the base of the mound, feeling more like a porn version of an American Indian than the fulfillment of Lillie's character's desire.

"Oh beautiful woman. I've waited a millennia for you."

"Not so melodramatic, Romeo," she said, holding up a hand. "This has to be believable, you know."

"It would be lots easier if I had a script."

"If I had this already written, we wouldn't need to be here, would we? Now come up and join me."

"Yes, Mistress Lilly," I said.

"And act like you mean it."

Standing atop the twelve foot mound, even in the rain, I could see for miles, and saw just how flat everything else around us was.

"Even though it's man made, you're standing on the highest point of elevation in the entire parish," she said.

"Why did they build here?"

"It's hallowed ground, and also because this is the lee side of Goose Island, the spot most protected from storms and hurricanes."

"You sure about that?"

"The mounds are still here, aren't they?"

I couldn't disagree with her logic. "The vantage is gorgeous. Look at the thousands of birds out there on the bay. I've never seen anything like this."

"Wyatt, you're playing a role here."

"Sorry. This view is breath-taking, and so are you," I said.

"That doesn't sound like something a first century Indian would say."

"Your perfume caused me to get out of character. I'm speaking for myself."

"You think I'm breath-taking?"

"Better than that. Erotic, exotic, and oh so hot."

"Keep talking like that, Chingachgook, and we'll be humping in the rain, right here on the mound. Come to think of it, that might work."

"Huh?"

"The book, ding dong," she said. "Now get back into character. We still have work to do."

We traded inane dialogue until the ancient mound, primal rain, and sexual tension took control of the situation. We were rolling in soft grass atop the mound when someone near us pulled both triggers on a double-barreled shotgun, the explosion rendering our ardor immediately and totally gone. We popped up to see who'd fired the rounds. It was Sierra and Landry, standing at the base of the mound, laughing uncontrollably.

"I'm not laughing," I said. "That wasn't funny."

"Oh yeah?" Sierra said. "You should see yourself in a mirror."

"No one was supposed to be here except us, and that includes you."

"We're sorry," she said.

"Good, otherwise I was going to tell Professor Quinn to fire you."

"I said we're sorry. Get your panties out of a wad." They started laughing again when she added, "If you were wearing any panties, that is."

It was still raining when Lilly and I straightened our loin cloths and slid down to join Sierra and Landry. Lilly didn't bother trying to hide her bare breasts from Landry. He noticed, and so did Sierra, giving both of them the evil eye.

"Sierra and Landry, this is Lilly Bliss."

"We've met," Sierra said.

"What a lovely specimen of a man," Lilly said, eyeing Landry. "I think I'd like you better than Wyatt on the cover of my new book. Where did you get those beautiful blue eyes?"

"Daddy was Cajun and Mama black. I got Indian blood from both sides, probably straight from the people that built this mound."

"I think I just got an inspiration for a new book. You live on the island, Landry?"

"In the village beside the bay."

Sierra frowned and crossed her arms because of the attention Lilly was paying Landry. Sensitive to her surroundings, Lilly grasped her shoulders.

"I'm not making a pass at your beau, honey. Wyatt's my guy. At least he was a moment ago."

Sierra's frown turned into a smile. "I'm not jealous."

"And why would you be? You're young and beautiful."

"Then why am I always wrestling with my lack of self esteem?"

Lilly embraced Sierra and gave her a big hug. "Baby, I'm probably old enough to be your mother, and I haven't figured that one out myself."

Sierra responded, her mood mellowing as gentle rain stopped falling, replaced by ground fog rising up around our ankles. Still, she gave Landry dirty looks every time she caught him glancing at Lillie's tits.

"What time is it?" I asked.

"Don't know," Sierra said. "Landry was showing me around the island before we came to get you. I never knew this part of the monastery grounds existed."

"Neither did I until Lilly told me about it."

"I'm a writer and always doing research," Lilly said. "Is there a chance I can visit Landry's village sometime? I swear I'll put some clothes on."

Landry glanced at Sierra for approval. When she nodded, he said, "Le Festival de Recommencement is underway in our village till tomorrow's sunrise. You are welcome to attend."

Chapter Twenty

When I grabbed Lillie's backpack and pulled her behind a clump of bushes, it wasn't the only thing I grabbed.

"Watch it, Wyatt Thomas," she said, finally pushing away from my embrace. "Even if we're hot and horny, there's nothing we can do about it now."

"You sure?"

"Positive. Now get dressed, unless you want to go to the village looking like that."

"All right," I said. "But it's just not fair."

"We can talk about what's fair later. Right now, let go of my ass or I'm going to kick you in the nuts."

"Party pooper," I said as I pulled on my pants.

"Shut up and don't make me hurt you," she said, pinching my rear as she did.

We'd soon crossed the berm and were on our way to Landry's village, Sierra noticeably more comfortable without Lilly's breasts on public display. Though the dark and drizzly conditions continued, heavy rain had ceased, leaving only lightning, continuing to sizzle out over the bay.

"Got weather comin' in," Landry said as he led us through the bushes and tall grass.

Lilly and I had been at the mounds longer than I'd realized. As late afternoon drew into evening, we saw the flickering lights of the village long before we reached it.

The usual sights and sounds of the island seemed momentarily muted as if nature was relinquishing the spotlight to the humans for the night.

We found the village awash in music and activity, flaming torches illuminating a group of children down by the docks, watching fishermen unload crabs, shrimp and redfish. The wonderful aroma of a Cajun shrimp boil wafted on humid air, reminding me I'd once again missed lunch.

Children followed after us, and African drums echoed against the many wooden structures as we followed Landry and Sierra through the village. Lilly was in heaven, snapping pictures with the camera on her cell phone, and making notes in her spiral notebook.

Landry led us to an outdoor arena where villagers were gathered, watching two men playing Cajun tunes on fiddle and accordion. Beyond the circle, more people were seated on wooden benches, eating, chatting, and drinking. We joined Professor Quinn, seemingly having the time of his life as he talked with a group of smiling villagers. He had a Mason jar filled with amber liquid in one hand, a fried chicken leg in the other.

"About time you got back, young lady. I was starting to worry."

"It's barely dark yet. What's that you're drinking?"

"Choc beer. Native Indians taught the early settlers how to brew it. Try it."

Quinn handed the jar to Sierra and she smiled after taking a sip. "That's good. Where did you get it?"

"You sit. I'll get us all one," Landry said. "Meanwhile, they's all the food you can eat on them tables over there."

"I'll help with the beer," I said.

He pointed to an old man guarding a ceramic vat at the edge of the crowd. Electric flashes lighted the hazy sky over Goose Bay as we ambled in his direction, fiddle and Cajun accordion music playing behind us melding with the steady beat of African drums. Landry must have noticed the questioning look on my face.

"Ain' nobody here hundred percent nothin'. Like I

174

say before, I part black, a smidgeon Cajun, and mean as an Indian, 'cept I don' have no warpaint on like you," he added with a grin.

When I wiped my face, red paint came off on my hand. Landry was still grinning when he handed me his handkerchief.

"Seems like I forgot something," I said.

"So did Miss Lilly, but let's don' tell her jus' yet."

"Good idea. What about Mama Malaika?"

"She took me an' Jomo in when our real mama die."

"Sorry about your mother," I said.

"We was so young, I hardly remember," he said.

We reached the big vat sitting on a bench. A toothless, old man removed the cheesecloth and produced two empty Mason jars.

He smiled when Landry said, "Need more than jus' them two, Gaston. Maybe you can help me carry this whole damn thing over to the peristyle."

"Hell, Landry, you don' need no choc. You jus' natural drunk."

Landry tapped his shoulder. "I bet they ain' none left if you watchin' the brew. Thas like a fox guardin' the hen house."

"I done took a nip or two," Gaston said.

He smiled again when Landry said, "Or three, or four."

"Sounds like you have the run of the place," I said as we rejoined the others.

"Gaston's my uncle. They also got a vat of shine around here someplace," he said.

"Not for me. I don't drink hard liquor anymore. Can't handle it."

"We got the best fresh water well in the parish. I show you, once we deliver the choc."

Everyone had adjourned to the benches, already eating when we returned. They had paper plates for both Landry and me. Landry sat his beside Sierra and then got me a Mason jar of water from the nearby well.

Lilly and Professor Quinn were conversing like old

friends. He'd apparently not said anything about her face paint, though he grinned and winked at me.

"This village is so unique," she said. "It's almost like. . ."

"An African village?" Quinn said.

"Exactly, except not quite."

"People living here are descendants of Africans that escaped into the swamps and marshlands shortly after arriving in the new world. Many had never actually been slaves."

"Fascinating," Lilly said. "They transcended their harrowing journey from Africa into a fresh start here in south Louisiana."

"Got an uncle thas a fur trader over in Delacroix," Landry said.

"Have you ever been to New Orleans?" Sierra asked.

Landry took a long sip of his choc beer before answering. "Sure."

"And?" she prompted.

"Got lots of pretty women in the French Quarter," he said with a grin.

"And?"

"Not a damn one as pretty as you."

Sierra was smiling when she said, "You're a liar. How many of those pretty New Orleans women did you have sex with?"

"No matter what I tol' you, you'd think I was lyin'," he said.

"Sounds like someone's asked you that question before. You'll probably be trying to tell God a lie when you're knocking on heaven's door," she said.

"Hell yes," he said. "I'm Cajun, ain' I?"

"Cajun and Creole cuisine is really a mixture of the three cultures we see in this village," Quinn said, ignoring their banter.

"This is the best gumbo I've ever eaten," Lilly said.

"Wait'll you try the roast pig," Landry said. "They's digging it up from the hole right now. I promise, you ain' lived till you eat pit roasted pig."

"It'll have to be more than wonderful to be as good as the gumbo," Lilly said.

We feasted on corn on the cob, fresh okra, shrimp, crawfish, and a slice of the best pork imaginable. I even had two slices of sweet potato pie. After many Mason jars of home-brewed beer, the others could have been eating water moccasin and wouldn't have cared.

"With all this beer, someone's going to have to point me to the bathroom pretty soon," Lilly finally said.

Sierra grabbed her arm and pulled her up. "The village only has outhouses. I'll go with you and even help you clean off the face paint the boys have been laughing at."

"You could have reminded me about the paint," Lilly said when they returned.

"And you could have done the same for me."

She was smiling when she said, "It's okay. I'll get even with you."

The storm over Goose Bay remained abated as the festival continued. After everyone had eaten, we moved as a group to the nearby circular arena. As midnight approached, it seemed I was the only sober person in the village, the Cajun fiddle and accordion player replaced by drummers whose beat transcended all other sounds of the night.

Professor Quinn, Sierra, and Lilly had transitioned from choc beer to moonshine, Quinn still lecturing like a college professor, though his words were slurred. It didn't matter because everyone was drunk, and no one listening. All talk ended when an explosion of gray smoke in the center of the arena focused our attention.

"What was that?" Sierra asked.

"The rite begins," Landry said.

Most of the torches burning in the village were extinguished as a bare breasted young woman entered the peristyle, dancing to the frenzied beat of native drums. Though it wasn't hot, beads of sweat dripped down her chest as she whirled around the stage in a costume smaller than the loin cloths Lilly and I had worn earlier.

"She's beautiful," Sierra said.

"What are we watching?" Lilly asked.

"Voodoo," Professor Quinn said. "As old as this island."

"Vodoun," Landry said. "The one true religion."

Another burst of smoke, bright yellow this time, filled the peristyle. When it vanished, so had the bare-breasted girl. Drumming intensified, my heart racing on south Louisiana well water as another explosion accompanied multi-colored smoke near the backside of the ring. When it finally dissipated, Mama Malaika appeared.

The woman had to be at least seventy, maybe eighty. It didn't seem to matter. She was bare-breasted as the girl that had appeared before her, yellow body paint and long strands of beads only partially cloaking her upper body. As we watched, she began creating a colorful design, using sand, in the circle in front of us.

"What's she doing?" Sierra asked.

"Drawing a vever," Landry said

"What's that?" she asked.

"An image made with somethin' like sand, clay, or crushed brick. She invokin' a loa, a spirit."

As she continued drawing the complex symbol near the center of the circle, the drums ceased beating. The people watching her were also silent, their attention rapt.

"What does it mean?" Lilly asked.

"Only she know," Landry said.

When Mama Malaika finished the drawing, she stood and raised her hands high above her head. As she turned, she seemed to look straight at me, and the bonfire behind us flamed up in a sudden burst. As if something had hit her right between the eyes, she fell backwards to the damp earth.

"Oh my God," Sierra said. "She's having a seizure."

Sierra's words seemed real enough. As we watched, Mama Malaika began writhing like a woman possessed. When Sierra stood to help, Landry grabbed her arm and shook his head.

"She possessed. Don' need no help."

Drumming continued as the mambo, possessed by some Vodoun loa, thrashed in the dirt. As the drums became more muted, three Serviteurs, assistants all dressed in white, joined her in the peristyle. Following another explosion, yellow smoke again encompassed the circle. The smoke quickly wafted away revealing Mama Malaika standing alone.

She began an ancient dance, perhaps the Wild Bamboula as drums began beating with a passion we'd not yet experienced. As she danced, she began circling the peristyle, looking for something and finally finding it hiding in the shadows.

It was the young woman whose dance had preceded Mama Malaika's. Now she was totally naked, her face and chest smeared with chicken blood. The two women moved in a ritual dance to the center of the peristyle, the younger woman dropping to the ground where she also became possessed. When her paroxysms ceased, Mama Malaika mounted her.

Lilly's hand was at her mouth. "What. . . ?"

She stared at Professor Quinn in disbelief when he said, "Performing a ritual humping."

"It's so violent," Sierra said.

"Just a dance," I said. "Not real."

"The Spirit Agwe has possessed Mama," Landry said. "Agwé est le maître des flots de la mer."

"The master of the sea," I said, translating for him.

"He protect boats, fisherman, their villages, animals and crops," he said.

"How do you know which spirit it is?" Sierra asked.

"I jus' know," he said.

When the ceremonial humping was completed, the three Serviteurs joined Mama Malaika, bringing her a bottle of champagne which she doused the young woman with. Grabbing her arms, the Serviteurs lifted her, directing her out of the peristyle and into the darkness. With the attention of everyone in the village focused on Mama Malaika, she began speaking in what sounded to me like an African dialect.

Landry held up a hand and didn't answer when Lilly asked, "What's she saying?"

When she finished speaking, thunder shook the crowd of people. It was followed by gentle rain that began dissolving the paint on Mama Malaika's chest, and the intricate symbol she'd drawn in the center of the ring. In hushed tones, Landry finally spoke.

"She say big storm comin'. Tomorrow, we must leave the village."

Chapter Twenty One

It was after midnight when Lilly and I made it back to our bungalows. Landry, after accompanying Sierra and Professor Quinn to the stilt house, had walked with us to the berm bridge to make sure we reached it safely.

The last twelve hours had passed so quickly, I'd forgotten the reason I'd visited Lilly in the first place. When we reached her patio, I remembered and decided to ask her a few questions.

"What's your take on Father Domenic and the monks?"

"I'm drunk on my ass and have to take these contacts out before I bleed to death through my eyeballs. Come in for a minute." I waited for her to stumble out of the bathroom. "I hate those things," she said, slurring her words. "Now, what were you asking?"

"Father Domenic and the monks. The only thing I know is Brother Dunwoody is a possible child molester, and Bruno from Romania."

"Probably Transylvania," she said.

"Huh?"

"The Romanian region famous for vampires. Brother Bruno is super creepy if you haven't noticed yet."

"You think he's a vampire?"

"Have you seen the way he looks? I don't ever want to run into him after dark," she said.

"Stormie's sentiments. There's not much about the monastery on the Internet and nothing concerning Father Domenic. Where would I go to find out more about them?"

"Doing research?"

She smiled when I said, "A dirty job, but someone has to do it."

"Dunwoody's office on the first floor of the administration building. He keeps the historical records of the monastery. At least that's what Brother Bruce told me. I doubt he'll let you see them."

"Have you?"

"I'd like to. Right now I'm drunk and tired. If I don't lie down soon, I'm going to throw up. I may anyway."

Lilly gave me a weak peck on the cheek and then pointed me toward the door. Though Kisses still had plenty of food and water, she was happy to see me. Exhausted, I spent the better part of an hour sitting on the couch in the dimly lit bungalow with Kisses on my lap. I never made it to bed, falling asleep on the couch, the cat beside me.

Kisses was chasing a ball across the floor the next morning when the sounds of a siren blaring outside the bungalow door awoke me. Slow rain had continued throughout the night, and I peeked out the window at a dark sky still filled with angry clouds. When I finally made it outside to check on the commotion, ghostly fingers of ground fog wrapped around my ankles.

Workers, monks, and guests stood gawking at the blue, rotating lights of a police car. Parish cops were cordoning an area near the Celebration Fountain as the slow motion wings of a single crane parted blue cotton clouds above us. A fat deputy in a St. Bernard Parish uniform was talking to someone on his walkie-talkie, not smiling when I approached him.

"I'm Wyatt Thomas, an investigator. Is Jean Pierre Saucier one of the cops working the crime scene?" When he nodded, I said, "Can you clear me to join them?"

After speaking on the walkie-talkie again, he said,

"Go ahead on. He's waiting for you."

As I neared the yellow crime tape, another cop ran toward me, gesturing for me to go to my right. I immediately saw why. A trail of blood painted the path along which something or someone had dragged its victim. A man in a ten-gallon hat met me with a firm handshake and a friendly smile.

"You must be Wyatt. Tony tol' me all about you. I'm Jean Pierre."

"Glad to meet you, Jean Pierre. What do we have here?"

"A brutal killing, just like the last, except this one had on all his clothes when we found him."

"Got an I.D. on him yet?"

Jean Pierre nodded. "A monk named Brother Bruce reported the killing. He was pretty upset but identified the victim as Dempsey Duplantis."

"Oh my God! I knew him. He works for the monastery and was the man that brought me to the island."

"What do you make of all this?"

I glanced at the body on the ground, taking Jean Pierre's word it was that of Dempsey Duplantis. It was so cut up, and bloody, it was impossible for me to tell. I had to take a deep breath before answering his question.

"Mama Malaika, the voodoo woman in the village down by Goose Bay says it's a rougarou."

"Looking at the body, I believe her," he said.

"The blood I saw walking up here. . ."

"Duplantis was killed someplace else, then drug on up here. Why would the killer do that?"

"Brother Bruce. He adds chemicals that kills mosquito larvae to this fountain. Same time every day. I have a feeling whoever killed Duplantis was trying to send him a message."

"If that's the case, he's in danger. I'll take him in for questioning and make up some excuse to keep him awhile."

"I'm having a hard time getting my head around this rougarou thing," I said.

"Hell, mon, crazy things happen down here in the swamp. I been hearin' about rougarous since I was knee-high to an alligator."

"Me too, but I never believed there was such a thing," I said.

We both had a chuckle when he said, "When you was parkin' down some lonesome oil lease road, it was a good story to tell your girlfriend. Hell, you'd have to fight 'em out of your arms."

"We must have gone to the same high school," I said. "What now?"

"I'd like to talk about this case some more. Not now. Can you meet me someplace later?"

"Sure. Where?"

"They's a little bar in Delacroix called Trapper's. It ain't far from here."

"If I can catch a ride. I don't have a car."

"I'd take you, but I don't want people around here seeing us together. Can I pick you up somewhere else?"

"Just beyond the main entrance, a dirt road leads to Goose Bay and a research professor's stilt house. It goes past a footbridge that crosses the berm. I could meet you there."

"I'll be waitin', about eight. Now I need to get the body outa here."

"I'm interested in hearing what the autopsy reveals."

"Me too," he said. "It ain't gettin' away from the St. Bernard Parish morgue till we get one this time.

Slapping my shoulder, he headed off to continue his investigation. I was watching the death investigators load the body into the back of an awaiting van when it hit me that Dempsey Deplantis was Sierra's step-father.

From what she'd told me, she didn't think much of the man. Still, it would be a shock, and I needed to tell her about it in person. I punched in her number on my cell phone, and then listened to a country song until she answered.

"Sierra, it's Wyatt. Are you and Professor Quinn near the cabin?"

"Last night's heavy rain ruined our work plans for the day. Thank goodness because I have a hangover from hell, and so does the professor."

"The choc beer you were drinking last night was probably ten percent alcohol. The way you two were putting it away, you're lucky to be alive."

"It wasn't the choc that got us. Moonshine," she said.

"You know what they say. If you can't take the heat. . ."

"Thanks for the sympathy," she said, not letting me finish.

She moaned, and I could imagine her holding her head when I said. "You'll be okay. Drink a couple of shots of Professor Quinn's whiskey. Hair of the dog, you know."

"I have no idea what you're talking about. I might throw up just thinking about a shot of whiskey."

"I was hoping to stop by if you're going to be there a while."

"We scrambled some eggs, and are working on our second pot of coffee. We're not going anyplace except maybe back to bed."

"Good. There's something I have to tell you."

"Can't you just say it over the phone?"

"Afraid not. I'm on my way there now," I said.

Before heading to the Professor and Sierra's, I decided to check on Lilly. Her door was shut, and no one answered when I knocked. It was unlocked, and opened easily when I turned the knob.

"Hello," I said. "Anyone here?"

"Who is it?" someone called from the bedroom.

"Wyatt. Are you okay?"

"I feel like pure hell," I heard her say.

Pushing open her bedroom door, I peeked in. "I was just checking on you."

"Get a gun. Put it to my head and blow my brains out," she said. "It's not humane to let someone suffer like this."

"Hair of the dog," I said.'

"What?"

"The only way to cure a hangover is to start drinking

again. You have some alcohol in this place?"

"Like what?"

"Vodka and tomato juice? Guaranteed to go down easy and start you on the road to recovery."

"Why not? Vodka's in the kitchen cabinet, tomato juice in the fridge."

"Great, I'll whip you up a bloody Mary."

I quickly created the concoction, at least from the ingredients I had. I held the glass to her lips as she took a sip.

"Are you going to be okay?"

"How long does it take for this to work?" she asked.

"You may have to finish this drink, and then have another."

"Maybe you should just shoot me."

"Trust me. This will work."

"I still feel like hell," she said, handing me the empty glass.

"I left a pitcher of bloody Mary's on your kitchen table. Have another, and you'll start feeling better before you know it. I have to go."

Lilly was still moaning as I walked out the door. The day had gotten no drier, light drizzle continuing to fall, my shoes and socks soaked as I climbed the stairs to Quinn's stilt house. Sierra met me at the door with a cup of coffee.

"I hate you," she said when I started laughing.

"Please don't. I know exactly how your head and your stomach feel. I'm an alcoholic, remember?"

"Then take some of my pain and share it with me."

"I would if I could," I said.

The house was small but cozy, the interior reminding me of a hunting lodge with azure blue Navaho rugs on the polished wood floor. Covered with his old Afghan, Professor Quinn was sunk into a recliner, sipping a steaming cup of coffee.

"Take off your shoes and socks," he said. "You can catch all sorts of nasty fungi and molds out here in the swamp if you don't keep your feet dry."

I took his advice, drying my socks by the potbelly stove they probably rarely used. It felt good. Chuckie came up the inside stairway, wagging his stump of a tail when he saw me.

"How you doing, big guy?" I said, scratching behind his ears.

King Tut got into the act, jumping into my lap and demanding a few full body strokes. I was happy to oblige.

"Now what's so important you had to come all the way out here in the rain to tell me?" Sierra said.

I'd never found an easy way to tell a person that someone they knew and perhaps loved had died. The best way, it seemed to me, was just say it. That's what I did.

"I have some terrible news. There was another death last night on the monastery grounds, the victim your step-father Dempsey Duplantis."

I didn't know what reaction to expect. At first she just sat there. Then, a single tear appeared in the corner of her eye, and she began sobbing. Professor Quinn and I both rushed to comfort her. While she was hugging Quinn and dampening his shoulder, I got her another cup of coffee. She quickly calmed down, and we waited for her to say something.

"Dempsey was never much of a dad, but he was the only one I ever had. He got into trouble after Mom kicked him out. Went to prison in Arkansas. I'm sorry I'm such a wreck."

She started crying again, and Professor Quinn handed her a tissue from the box beside his chair.

"It's okay."

"When he got paroled last fall, he started calling Mom. By this time, her cancer had spread, and she was so sick, she could hardly speak. Dempsey kept calling every day to check on her."

I picked her cup up and held it to her trembling lips until she took a sip.

She nodded when I said, "Your mom had cancer?"

"I barely had enough money to bury her when she died. Mama and me had no relatives, and we'd moved to

California when I was twelve. She worked as a waitress at a restaurant on the pier in Long Beach. That's where she met Dempsey. He was in and out of our lives as long as I can remember."

"Doesn't sound like he was all that bad," Professor Quinn said.

"He wasn't. He wired me a hundred dollars and a bus ticket to New Orleans after Mom passed. He'd gotten a job at the monastery and had a place of his own in Delacroix. He said I could live with him until I found a job and got on my feet."

She smiled through her tears when I said, "But it didn't work out."

"We just couldn't get along. I didn't have much anyway, except what was in my backpack. I was hanging around the island, and had decided to stay. At least until they kicked me off. That's where I was when we met."

"Well you have a home, and a job now," Professor Quinn said. "We'll go to your step-dad's funeral, put some flowers on his grave and thank God he was there for you when you needed him, even if it didn't ultimately work out for the two of you."

She smiled and hugged him, and then began crying again. "Oh Wyatt, this has been a day from hell."

"Your hangover?"

"More than that," she said.

"What else?"

"The people in the village began moving this morning to an area about ten miles from here. Mama Malaika says they'll be safe from the hurricane there."

"Then they'll be fine. They've survived out here for hundreds of years, and through many storms."

"Hogwash!" Quinn said. "The weather forecasters say the storm in the Caribbean is going to continue westward and make landfall on the Yucatan Peninsula. There's no hurricane, or storm, heading in our direction. If there were, don't you think I'd know about it?"

"Landry said Mama Malaika is never mistaken when she makes a prophecy."

"They'll be fine, I promise you," I said, Ignoring Professor Quinn's frown.

"Landry's overseeing the relocation. She's staying in the village alone."

"Why?"

"Don't know, but I'm worried about her," she said.

"She must have a reason, and a plan for survival if a storm is actually on its way."

"Oh Wyatt, I hope you're right," she said, beginning to cry again.

Chapter Twenty Two

With dry feet and several cups of coffee to warm me, I headed back to the monastery. The rain had stopped for the moment. Gloom remained. Fumbling for the cell phone, I decided to check in with Tony.

"What's up, Cowboy?"

"I was about to ask you the same thing."

"I found the crematory last night and talked with the person that burned the remains of Rance Parker."

"And?"

"He had an unauthorized look at the body before cremating it. He confirmed Parker didn't die of a heart attack. He also dropped another bombshell."

"Hit me."

"He told me there was a private autopsy performed on the body before it got to him."

"That sounds just too crazy. Did you see the death certificate?"

"I did. It was signed by Dr. Darwin Porter. The name sounds familiar, but I can't place him."

"Central Hospital," I said.

"Pardon me?"

"Dr. Darwin Porter was the lead character on the daytime soap Central Hospital."

"Oh yeah. One of Lil's favorites. She never missed it."

"The actor that played the role is Quinlan Moore, the

man that hired both of us for this job."

"You shitting me? What's the link?"

"He was trying to cover up the true cause of death."

"But why?"

"To avoid negative publicity, and to protect the investment in the monastery. Still, you'd think he'd have told me he had an autopsy performed on Parker."

"I'd love to see the results on that one," he said.

"Looks like we have another bite at the apple."

"What are you talking about?"

"There was another murder here last night. The victim was horribly mutilated, just as Jean Pierre said happened to Parker. He has the body, and I don't think he's going to give it up this time. You met the victim."

"Me? When?"

"Dempsey Duplantis, the person that picked me up at Bertram's and brought me here."

"You shitting me!"

"I'm not. What's the problem?"

"I told you earlier I connected with Brother Italo last night. He claims he saw one of the monks, Brother Bruno, transform into a wolfman and attack Brother Dunwoody. You still there?"

"I'm here. I'm just getting a sick feeling in the pit of my gut."

"When I tell you what else he said it'll feel even worse."

"I'm listening."

"Dempsey Duplantis was his friend, and he told him about the transformation. Though he didn't buy the story, he did believe Brother Bruno was a possible psychopath. He was on his way last night to talk to Father Domenic about it."

"Then that puts the good father and Brother Bruno at the top of our list of suspects."

"I also tracked down Brother Degas."

"Oh yeah? What'd you find out?"

"The real Father Domenic would be pushing eighty if he was still alive. You think the person you know as

Father Domenic killed the real Abbey and took his identity?"

"That's what it's starting to sound like."

"You have a picture of him? I can get Tommy to run it against some mug shots."

"No, but I'll try to take one."

"While you're at it, a group picture would be nice. At least one of Domenic and Bruno," he said.

"Who knows how many rougarous there are if that's what we're dealing with. Jean Pierre didn't want to discuss the case with me here on the island. He's picking me up tonight, and we're going to a bar in Delacroix called Trapper's."

"I'll meet you there. I got something that'll blow your mind."

"More than what you've already told me?"

"You won't believe it, I guarantee."

"Okay, I'll see you later tonight, Lieutenant."

When I returned to my bungalow, I found the door ajar, Stormie, dressed in a revealing black negligee, lying on my bed, smiling at me with a come hither look.

"I've been waiting for you," she said.

"I see that."

She was in my arms before I had a chance to think about it, her warm body raising my temperature in an instant. It didn't help she'd also put her tongue halfway down my throat.

"I missed you," she said, licking my ears and neck.

Stormie was beautiful. Many of her male movie fans had probably fantasized about being in a similar situation. The fantasy, in my case, was reality, my body heat rapidly rising to its boiling point.

"Oh, baby I need you to get in my pants," she said as her negligee dropped off her shoulders and onto the floor.

She didn't have to say anything. I was already under her spell, her exotic perfume anesthetizing me. At least until my hand brushed against a patch of bristly hair on the soft curve of her spine. Pushing her away, I gazed into her eyes.

"Did you get enough sleep last night?"

"Why do you ask?" she said.

"Your eyes are red."

"Stop talking nonsense, Don't you need me as much as I need you?"

"I'm so hot you can't imagine, and I've never wanted or needed a woman more," I said.

"Then take me."

The room was dim, but I could still see many errant tufts of hair on her arms. As she smiled at me, even her teeth seemed just a little too long. Considering the fire in my belly, her physical anomalies probably wouldn't have made any difference. I didn't find out because Lilly saved me, barging through the door without knocking.

"Oh my God! Sorry!"

"You're just in time," Stormie said. "Wyatt and I are about to have a little fun in bed. Join us?"

I waited for her to say yes. She didn't.

"Sounds inviting. I can't. I'm almost finished with my new book. I just stopped by to say hi to Wyatt."

"You can work on your book tomorrow," Stormie said, her eyes again flashing momentarily red.

When she grazed my face and neck with her fingernails, I noticed they were black, and not from the color of her polish. Her cell phone was lying on my bed and it suddenly began playing the theme from the movie Picnic. When the song continued, she gave it an annoyed glance.

"Sweetie, can you answer that damn thing for me? Tell whoever it is I'm busy."

"Hello," Lilly said, quickly answering the phone. We watched as she stood there, listening to a one-sided conversation. "It's your agent." she finally said. "He says it's urgent. He needs to talk to you."

"Shit!" Stormie said, taking the phone.

She was soon the recipient of a one-sided conversation. From the frown on her face, she wasn't liking what she'd heard. Picking up her black negligee between two fingers, she threw it over her shoulder and marched out of the bungalow, giving us a behind the back wave as she departed. Two landscape workers, their eyes open wide, watched as she marched past them.

"Must have been a disturbing phone call," I said.

"The film director of the role she's up for wants to hire a younger actress instead of her. She's pissed."

"I can see that. Hey, and thanks for saving me."

"From what? Having wild sex with one of the most beautiful movie stars in Hollywood. Most men, and lots of women would kill for the chance."

"I'm more into sexy, female authors that enjoy wearing loin cloths."

She was grinning when she said, "Then you're an idiot, Wyatt Thomas."

"I've been told that a time or two."

"I think what you like is the illusion I created and not me."

"Maybe. Want to find out?"

"Sorry, dear. I'm too hung over from all that home-made beer and jars of moonshine I drank last night. Even with the pitcher of bloody Mary's, I still feel like hell."

"Then what are you doing here? Why aren't you still in bed?"

"I needed something to eat besides potato chips and thought you might want to get something with me."

"It's the time of day all the monks are in the chapel praying."

"So?"

"So it's a chance to get a look at the monastery records in Dunwoody's office," I said.

"You mean break in?"

"No, just jimmy the door and walk in. I can meet you somewhere later, and we can get something to eat."

"No way," she said. "I'm going with you."

"What if we get caught?"

"I want to know about the monks as much as you. We can take turns standing guard in the hall."

"Then let's hurry," I said.

We passed the old cathedral on our way to the administration building, the atonal sounds of an ancient chant indicating the monks were in the midst of their ceremony. Lilly watched as I picked the lock to Brother Dunwoody's office.

"Are you sure you're a writer?" she said.

"A man of many talents," I said as I peeked into the office. "Wait at the front door and keep watch for me."

"No way, buddy. You watch. I'm going in."

"This was my idea, not yours."

"Then we'll both go," she said. "And let's hurry before the prayer meeting ends."

The curtains were closed, lighting in the room dim. Lilly stumbled into me. Turning on the small flashlight I always carried, I found a file cabinet behind the desk. It opened with a metallic thud, and I immediately began thumbing through the manila folders.

"Here's the staff information. The last two folders are for Brother's Bruce and Italo."

"Let me look," she said. "I'm faster."

Lilly quickly sorted through the entire stack. "Father Domenic has been around since the seventies. I can't find a file on Brother Bruno."

"The seventies? That would make him. . ."

"Much older than he is," she said.

"Tony may be right."

"Who is Tony, and what is he right about?"

"I'll explain later."

"What's that in the corner?" she asked.

A large book sat atop a wooden stand. Lilly stumbled on the carpet when she started toward it.

"Wait on me," I said, shining the light so she could see.

"It's a scrapbook history of the monastery," she said, opening it.

I watched as she turned the pages of yellowed newsprint heralding the history of the monastery from at least before the Civil War.

"See what's on the last page," I said.

It was a picture of a half dozen smiling monks flanking a little man with graying hair. The caption identified him as Father Domenic.

"This picture was taken just before Katrina," Lilly said.

"And that doesn't look anything like the Father Domenic we know. Take the picture and let's get the hell out of here."

"What about the files on Bruce and Dunwoody?" she asked.

"Just check the dates they started. That's all we need to know. And hurry because I think I hear someone down the hall."

"They both arrived a few years ago, but certainly after Katrina."

"Good. Lets get out of here."

Lilly tore the picture out of the book, and we were out the door, walking toward the recreational complex when we saw the four monks leaving the cathedral.

"That was close," she said. "What do you think it means?"

"That the person we know as Father Domenic is an imposter. Who knows who Brother Bruno is?"

"What'll we do?"

"Too bad there are no photos of the monks. They could help us determine who they really are."

"I'll get us one," she said.

Father Domenic and the three monks walked toward us, away from the old cathedral and toward the administration building.

"Enjoying the first sun we've had in a while, Miss Bliss?" Brother Dunwoody asked.

"Yes and it's incredible. Can I get a picture to remember the four of you when I go home to Virginia?"

"We don't take pictures on the island," Brother Dunwoody said.

"This will only go in my scrapbook, I promise."

Lilly handed her cell phone to me and joined the four men before they had a chance to protest.

"How does it work?" I asked.

"Just line us up and push the image on the screen."

Father Domenic and Brother Bruno weren't smiling when I took the picture.

"Hope it worked," I said.

"I also want your picture with them," she said.

She took more pictures, just to make sure, Father Domenic and Brother Bruno squirming. When she smiled and waved, they hurried off.

"Now what?" I asked.

"Dinner. I haven't eaten since last night. I hope Sierra and Professor Quinn didn't feel as miserable as me."

"Maybe even worse. Makes me glad I'm a teetotaler," I said.

"Don't rub it in," she said.

"I'm not, but I've been there, done that."

"I barely managed to get out of bed."

"You're up now, and you look pretty good to me."

"Makeup," she said. "We have the pictures. What now?"

"Can you print them?"

"Print them, email them, anything you want. I heard about the death last night. How awful."

"It must have happened while we were at the festival."

"My God!" she said.

"I've never talked to you about this. You knew Rance Parker?"

"Rance made a point of knowing everyone, especially the ladies."

"Did you. . . ?"

"Have sex with him? I did. He was a hunk, and too much of a celebrity to pass up."

I decided to let the subject drop. "Where to?" I asked.

"A little café called the Purple Cow. It's small, intimate, and you'll love it,"

"Moo," I said.

The Purple Cow turned out to be a café in the main

complex that served hamburgers, French fries, and malts. There were only a few tables in the middle of the single room surrounded by booths covered in red imitation leather. The place had two main features: the black and white tile floor, and photos on the walls of movie stars, dignitaries, and famous writers who had visited. Lilly chose a particular booth, and I soon learned why.

She smiled and cocked her head toward the wall until I noticed the picture of her and Stormie. Between them was Quinlan Moore, leering because he had his hands on their breasts. Both were grinning and neither seemed to care. Beside them, also grinning, was Rance Parker.

"Know who he is?" she asked.

"Who are you talking about?"

"Everyone knows who Rance Parker is. I'm talking about the man sitting between us."

"Paul Newman?"

She took a mock jab at my face. "Quinlan Moore, silly. Probably the most powerful producer in Hollywood."

"Was the picture taken in this booth?"

"Can't you see? He was here, at this table, a few weeks ago."

"You mean right before Rance Parker died?"

"They arrived in the same limo."

Lilly ate only a few bites of her Theta burger. I was hungry and ate all of my chili cheese Coney, and the rest of her's. My questions, or else lack of positive response to her knowing Rance Parker and Quinlan Moore, must have dampened her mood because she barely spoke during the meal.

"You okay?" I finally asked.

"You're not jealous, are you?"

"I hardly know you."

"My first husband was the jealous type and made our marriage miserable for the last three years. I got even with him, though."

"Oh?"

"If you'd read my second novel, you'd see. Everyone

in both of our families did."

"You made him the villain?"

"He wasn't smart enough to be a credible villain. He was the town fool in my novel. He still hates me."

"Good for you," I said. "What will I be in your next book?"

"You don't even qualify yet," she said. "Why are you asking so many questions about Rance Parker?"

"Research. There's a rumor floating around that he didn't die of a heart attack."

"Why are you being so mysterious? What was the supposed cause of death if he didn't die of a heart attack?"

"Something else."

Lilly banged my shoulder with her fist. "Like what, Wyatt Thomas?"

"Too early to speculate, though it's the primary reason I wanted a look at the files in Dunwoody's office."

"And the pictures we took?"

"I have a friend in the police department that can check them against mug shots."

Lilly's frown disappeared as she uncrossed her arms. "You're a trip. I may have my fantasies, but you're out there in orbit, buddy."

"What about us?" I said, deciding to change the subject.

"You're a gorgeous man, Wyatt. I'll bet a thousand women have fallen for your dreamy eyes, not to mention your great ass. Doesn't matter because you also have a small problem telling the truth."

"You're the first woman that's ever told me that."

"Yeah, yeah," she said. "I'll bring the pictures to your room when I finish printing them."

An hour passed. I was about to leave to meet Jean Pierre when Lilly bounded through the door, handing me three pictures she'd printed.

"You're not going to believe this," she said.

Chapter Twenty Three

Lilly departed after giving me the pictures, heavy rain returning as she hurried away to her bungalow. Kisses and I cuddled up in bed until it was time to meet Jean Pierre at the berm bridge. She didn't stir when I left her sleeping against my pillow.

Distant thunder and incessant rain accompanied me on my trip across the monastery grounds. I found Jean Pierre waiting on the other side of the berm.

"Hope you don't mind me getting your truck wet," I said as I climbed into the passenger seat. "It's getting ugly out there."

"It's a truck, not a Cadillac. Don't worry about it."

"I talked to Tony earlier. He's meeting us."

"Good deal. You ever been to Delacroix?"

"Can't say that I have."

"It's the end of the road. Last town before you hit the Gulf. Hope you don't expect too much. Katrina pretty much wiped it out, and it's just now comin' back."

"No problem," I said. "I know about the horrors of Katrina all too well."

The road from the monastery to Delacroix was dark, unpaved and bumpy, a route made no easier by the weather. It soon began raining so hard, the wipers couldn't keep the windshield clear.

"Looks like we're in for it."

"Don't worry none. I been drivin' in this kinda weather all my life," Jean Pierre said.

"Glad to hear it. If it were me, we'd already be in the ditch."

"Sure don't wanna do that around here. All the ditches are full of water. With all this weather comin' in, we might end up in the Gulf of Mexico."

"How do people make a living this far down in the marshland?"

"Trappin', shrimpin', and fishin'. Delacroix is on a quarter-moon shaped island, so narrow it hardly has room for the road running through it. It's just high enough outa the water that most storms don't affect it. Katrina wasn't your usual storm."

"Amen to that," I said.

We soon reached Delacroix, houses and water, as Jean Pierre had said, on both sides of a narrow road. Docks jutted out into the water where skiffs and shrimp boats were moored for the night. Many of the houses and buildings, like Professor Quinn's, were on stilts, some ten feet or more off the ground. Trapper's was such a structure.

Jean Pierre found a place to park beneath the rustic restaurant. A good thing as the rain had quickly grown into a deluge. A stairway led us up to the main dining room, most of the lights dimmed. Everyone else it seemed had stayed home for the night. We were the only patrons except for Tony. Sitting alone at a table, he waved when he saw us.

"You a brave man, Cowboy," he said when I grabbed a chair.

"How's that?"

"Last time I was out with Jean Pierre, I helped him bust a chicken fight, and then ended up going with him to a whore house."

"And lovin' every minute of it," Jean Pierre said.

"Let's just say I survived. I figured you boys were on the way, so I ordered drinks for you."

The owner must have let most of his staff go home

early because the only other person in the spacious room was the bartender. Tony was already drinking a cold Dixie. The man brought drinks for Jean Pierre and me.

"A double Wild Turkey and glass of lemonade. Anything else?" he said.

"If your kitchen's open, I'll have an oyster po'boy, dressed," Jean Pierre said.

"Me and the cook's here," the man said.

"Then I'll have the same," I said.

"Can I get half a po'boy and a cup of gumbo? Tony asked.

"You got it," he said.

"And you may as well bring me another Dixie," Tony said as the man started to walk away

The lights were low, the rain still falling on the tin-roofed building making it difficult to hear the jukebox. When the bartender brought our food and Tony's beer it was as Bertram would have said, coming down in Louisiana bucket loads. Thinking ahead, he also brought more whiskey and lemonade. Thunder shook the elevated building as he returned to the bar.

"Did you take Brother Bruce in?" I asked.

"He took off. We couldn't find him," Jean Pierre said. "Guess he's on his own."

"Hope he'll be okay."

"Nothing we can do about it now. How you doin', Lieutenant Tony. Wyatt said you got somethin' to show us we won't believe," Jean Pierre said.

Tony reached in his pocket and tossed something on the table.

"Hope this doesn't mess up your dinner," he said.

"Looks kinda like a bear claw," Jean Pierre said as he fingered the mysterious object. "What is it?"

"Like you said, looks like a claw."

"What's so strange about it?" I asked.

"Where it came from," Tony said. "The man at the crematory dug it out of Rance Parker's body before cremating him."

Jean Pierre handed it to me. "No wonder he looked

like he'd got in a fight with a wild animal and lost."

"Did Wyatt tell you I talked with Brother Italo?"

Jean Pierre nodded as he bit into his oyster po'boy.

"He told me. What'd you find out?"

"Turns out Italo is Bruiser Palminero. You heard of him?"

"Everybody round these parts heard of the Bruiser," Jean Pierre said. "Was wonderin' what happened to him."

"He was at the monastery a while, apparently trying to get his life together. He left because of something he'd witnessed."

"Like what?"

"He claims to have seen Brother Bruno transform into a wolfman, and then back again. Just one of the reasons he left the monastery."

"Mama used to scare my brother and me with rougarou tales. Tell us one of them creatures was gonna get us if we didn't act better."

"There's probably not a kid in Louisiana that hasn't been threatened with that one. Still, what about this thing," Tony said, fingering the claw.

"Could be a bear claw," Jean Pierre said. "Every now and then someone spots a black bear down in the swamp. Maybe even a cougar or two."

"I don't think any of us believe in werewolves or rougarous either one. Whether we believe it or not, it's the simplest explanation of what killed Parker and Duplantis," I said.

"Brother Italo believes it," Tony said. "Oh, and I got something else."

"Stranger than the claw?" I asked.

"Maybe not as strange but just as interesting. Rance Parker's autopsy report."

"There's no record of an autopsy," Jean Pierre said.

"Because it wasn't official. Someone hired a private service called Confidential Autopsy to do it. I have a copy."

"How the hell'd you do that?" Jean Pierre asked.

"A friend of mine at the water department played

games with the service at Confidential Autopsy until they called them. He sent someone to take a look."

Tony smiled when Jean Pierre said, "It was you that showed up?"

"The after hours watchman finally left me alone long enough to locate the Parker autopsy."

"You just took it?" I asked.

"I told the guy I needed an extra tool, and that I'd be right back. I found a print shop down the street. I refiled the report while the watchman was in the bathroom."

"Good job, Lieutenant," Jean Pierre said. "Now tell us what it says."

"Just what you already thought. That something big, mean, and inhuman killed him. They had tests run on all the bodily fluids, including saliva from the thing that did the killing."

"And?" I said.

"It showed traces of a virus they didn't recognize, but that looked similar to one they did."

"Well don't keep us in suspense," Jean Pierre said. "Spit it out."

A clap of thunder that shook the roof preceded his answer.

"Rabies."

Another clap rattled the building on stilts, followed closely by a burst of lightning that momentarily illuminated the portion of Delacroix we could see out the windows. Unnerved by the dramatic electrical display, the bartender brought us more drinks and collected our dirty plates.

"You boys may as well stay awhile," he said. "Won't get no calmer out there tonight. It's dry in here, and we ain't gonna float away."

Jean Pierre said, "You sure about that, bro?"

The bartender grinned. "We got no control over the weather. That's a fact. Don't matter none cause it ain't no better anywhere else in south Louisiana."

"Then keep them comin'." After the bartender had left the table, Jean Pierre said, "I seen mad animals in St.

Bernard Parish—skunks, a coon or two, and even a mad dog. I never seen it cause a one of them to turn into a wolf."

"Maybe because what we're dealing with isn't rabies. Just a similar virus. A researcher wrote a paper on it back in the seventies. The autopsy report cites the man, but says his theory was scoffed at by other scientists."

"I'd still like to hear what he has to say about it," I said. "Did they give his name?"

"Kelton Frenette. From what I found on the web, his theory pretty much cost him his credibility as a researcher."

"I can see why," I said.

"What if Brother Bruno is a rougarou? Ain't much we can do about it. And if I tell the Chief a rougarou killed Parker and Duplantis he'll laugh me off the force."

"According to Mama Malaika, the voodoo woman on the island, you can't kill one anyway, though she did have a potion she says will disable them for a while."

"What kind of potion?" Tony asked.

"Wolfsbane. Heard of it?"

"I didn't think it was real," he said.

"Her son Landry soaks his buckshot in it before loading his shell casings. He swears it works, at least until you can get the hell away. That's not our only problem."

"What is?" Tony asked.

I pulled the pictures that Lilly had given me out of my shirt pocket and put them on the table. Brother Bruno's face was burned off in both photos, as if by a bright flash of light.

"What happened?" Jean Pierre asked. "You get a little crazy with the flash?"

"The sun was shining. We weren't using a flash. The monk with the obliterated face is Brother Bruno. I also got a look at the monastery records. Father Domenic is clearly an imposter, the real Father Domenic probably dead. There's no evidence of where our man and Bruno came from."

I gave the pictures to Tony, and he put them in his coat pocket.

"Surely Father Domenic wasn't the only monk there. Did they kill everyone?" Jean Pierre asked.

"According to Brother Degas, all the monks were old, no recent members. They'd intended to give the monastery to the state and retire to wherever they'd come from. Father Domenic stayed on and was apparently there when Katrina struck."

"What else?" Jean Pierre said.

"I saw Father Domenic, or whoever he is, attack a guest the other night," I said.

"You mean with bad intent?" Jean Pierre asked.

"The worst. I know he's big, but he picked up a two-hundred pound man and threw him against a wall. Brother's Bruno and Dunwoody had to restrain him, or I think he would have killed the man."

"He didn't transform, did he?" Tony asked.

"Not into a wild animal. He just acted like one."

Jean Pierre gave me a quizzical look. "Domenic and Bruno make two. Who else?"

"The actress Sabine Storm was in my room tonight, practically demanding I have sex with her."

"Hot damn! Maybe I need to visit the monastery again. What'd you do?"

"Nothing. She was naked, and had more body hair than most women, or most men for that matter. I got a close look at her body."

"I bet you did," Jean Pierre said with a grin.

Tony glanced at me, and then Jean Pierre. "J.P. and the actress had a little meeting of the minds, so to speak. She didn't bite you, did she?"

"Shut. Bite ain't the half of it. Next morning I was so scratched up, I felt like I'd been in a fight with an alley cat. You think she's a rougarou too?"

"If she's not already, she's heading in that direction."

"Don't sound good," Jean Pierre said.

"You better think about getting a rabies shot," Tony said.

"He's probably not the only one."

"There's more?" Tony asked.

"Quinlan Moore, the person that hired us. Lilly Bliss showed me a picture. He was with her, Rance Parker, and Stormie before Parker's death."

"You think they all had sex?"

"Count on it," I said.

Another clap of thunder shook the roof, followed by rain falling so hard, we all glanced at each other. The window we were sitting beside began heaving as if it were about to burst out of the frame.

"One hell of a storm brewin' up out there," Jean Pierre said.

"It's coming from the Gulf," Tony said. "According to weather forecasters, it could become a hurricane anytime during the next twenty four hours and come ashore in the next two days. Oil companies are starting to evacuate the offshore rigs in its path."

"Any idea where it's heading?" I asked.

"Too soon to tell."

"Kind of early for a hurricane," Jean Pierre said.

"The forecasters are calling it a freak of nature," Tony said.

"Like what we're dealing with at the monastery," I said. "Too bad we can't talk with Kelton Frenette."

"Maybe we can. He's alive and lives in New Orleans. I've got his address and I'm gonna try to see him tomorrow."

"If we don't get washed away by a hurricane," I said. "We may have to postpone this investigation and head for higher ground.

"Where did you say Lil went to?" Jean Pierre asked.

"Her mother's house, in Shreveport."

"Hell, Tony, maybe you better join her there."

"If she was willing, I'd already be with her. Like you said, this storm is too early in the year to develop into a hurricane. I'm betting it'll fizzle out before it gets too bad."

"It better hurry," Jean Pierre said.

Chapter Twenty Four

With the sky still awash in rain, Jean Pierre and Tony kept drinking. Tony, realizing the weather was getting no better, finally decided to beg off.

"Enough of this happy horse shit! I'm heading back to N.O. before the roads start flooding."

"You may already be too late," Jean Pierre said."

"If I run in the ditch, I'll call you to pull me out."

"You jokin', I'm not," Jean Pierre said.

"The road seemed well drained enough on my way down here. I'll be okay."

"I'm not so sure about Wyatt."

"What?" I said.

"I can't drive into the monastery cause it's closed for the night. If you run for it, you're likely to drown before you reach your room."

"You can come with me," Tony said. "I got two empty bedrooms."

"Chalmette's closer," Jean Pierre said. "I only got a couch, but it's comfortable."

"Thanks. You both have things to do tomorrow, and so do I. You could take me to Professor Quinn's. It's down a graveled road from the berm bridge, and I need to talk to him anyway. I'm sure they'll let me stay the night."

"If that's what fits your pistol," Jean Pierre said.

"Let me call first to make sure it's okay."

Sierra answered on the first ring. "Wyatt, why are you calling so late?"

"I'm in Delacroix. With the heavy rain and all, I doubt I can make it back to the bungalow. Would you and Professor Quinn mind if I sleep on your couch for the night, assuming I can get there from here?"

"That's where Chuckie sleeps."

"I don't take up much space," I said.

She laughed. "Of course you can stay here. Chuckie would rather stay in my room with me anyway. The big baby's scared of thunder and lightning. He's outside my door now, whining for me to let him in."

"Great. If you leave the front door open, you won't have to wait on me."

Tony glanced at his watch. "Guess I have time for one more. No one's waiting for me at the house."

"If Lil's in Shreveport at least she's safe from the storm," I said.

"Hope all my kids are. They're scattered from Baton Rouge to Timbuktu."

"Least you got a family to worry about," Jean Pierre said.

Tony nodded. "Don't know if it's a blessing or curse."

"I'm like you, Jean Pierre. The only family I have is my kitty. Right now I'll bet she's curled up on the bed with a full belly, listening to rain pounding the roof. She's not worrying about me or anything else."

"You might be surprised," Jean Pierre said. "My chocolate Lab Lucky waits at the door for me. He's there no matter what time I get home. Hell, he makes me feel so guilty, it's worse than havin' an ol' lady."

"This weather almost makes me wish I was drinking again," I said.

"Then have one," Jean Pierre said. "I'll buy."

"I've only been sober a few days now. Thanks anyway, but I'm not going back anytime soon."

When we'd finally paid our bill, the bartender wasn't smiling.

"If you boys leave, I might as well shut the place

down for the night. Sure you won't have a couple more?"

"If we have a couple more we're liable to be spendin' the night here with you," Jean Pierre said as we started down the stairs to the parking lot.

Wind had picked up, whistling through the pilings as we climbed into Jean Pierre's truck. With his wipers keeping rhythm on the windshield, he pulled out of the parking lot and started back to Goose Island.

The noise and falling water made it seem as though we were going through a car wash. It impeded the headlights, making it difficult to drive more than twenty miles-per-hour. It felt much faster as I gripped the arm rest, my foot planted against the floorboard on an imaginary brake.

Water flowed over the road from the ditches on both sides. Fishes and frogs, caught in our flickering headlights, floated across in front of us. When we reached the road to Quinn's cabin, Jean Pierre shifted into four-wheel drive. We were okay until we hit a patch stripped of gravel and began slipping on the road that had suddenly turned into thick goo. Despite Jean Pierre's best efforts, the rear wheels were soon up to the axles in mud.

"Sorry, Pardner. Don't look like we're gettin' out of this one any time soon."

"I'm the one that should apologize," I said. "I suspect there's room at the inn for both of us. Professor Quinn has a Jeep, and he can pull you out tomorrow. Too bad you can't phone and tell Lucky."

Jean Pierre grinned. "He's got plenty of food and water and a doggie door when he needs to go outside for a potty break. Won't be the first time I didn't make it home till morning."

"I didn't bring a raincoat," I said.

"We ain't gonna melt. Let's do it."

Opening the doors, we ran down the slippery road the short distance to the cabin. A light glimmered at the top of the stairs. When we reached the door, we didn't bother knocking. Sierra, dressed in a pink, terry cloth robe, opened it before we had a chance, and Jean Pierre's expression quickly changed from a frown to a smile.

"We got stuck in the mud up the road. Hope you don't mind I brought someone with me. Sierra, this is Jean Pierre."

"I apologize, ma'am. First time I run in a ditch since I was a teenager."

Jean Pierre's boyish good looks made her smile.

"We have plenty of room, though one of you may have to sleep in Professor Quinn's recliner. Go in the bathroom and take off those wet clothes. I'll get some robes."

"You sure?" Jean Pierre said. "I don't want to be no trouble."

"I wouldn't put my worst enemy out tonight."

"You a real angel," he said.

Ignoring him, she said, "Hand your clothes through the door and I'll put them in the dryer. When you come out, Wyatt, I have something to tell you."

We were all soon sitting on the couch in our robes, our clothes tumbling in the dryer. Sierra and I were sipping hot chocolate, Jean Pierre a shot of Professor Quinn's whiskey.

"Now what is it you have to tell me?" I asked.

"The professor is in a frenzy. He's in his room, packing to leave."

"But why?"

"The storm in the Gulf is already a hurricane and projected to reach shore in about two days."

"Hell," Jean Pierre said. "Anything can happen before then. It could veer off and head to Florida or Texas. Who knows yet?"

"Don't be so sure about that, young man," Quinn said, leaving his bedroom with two packed suitcases.

"Professor Quinn, this is Jean Pierre Saucier. We got caught in the storm in Delacroix. J.P.'s truck is in the ditch up the road and Sierra said we could bunk here for the night."

"Absolutely. Glad to meet you," Quinn said, shaking Jean Pierre's hand when he stood to greet him.

"What's the word on the hurricane?" I asked.

"Hurricane Aguirre. Earliest ever of this magnitude. It's expected to be a Cat 3 by the time it hits the coast, wind velocities reaching 125 miles per hour."

"Jesus," I said.

"That's who we'll need if it hits us as a Cat 3 hurricane," Professor Quinn said.

"Where's it headed?" Jean Pierre asked.

"Looks as if it'll make landfall at the mouth of the Mississippi. It's taking dead aim at New Orleans. You know what that means?"

"That it's gonna hit us first," Jean Pierre said. "Shut, that's action we don't need none of."

"Jean Pierre is with the St. Bernard Parish police department. He's investigating the two killings."

Tears formed in Sierra's eyes. "Dempsey Duplantis was my stepfather."

"Oh ma'am, I'm so sorry," Jean Pierre said.

"It's okay. I never realized how much it would affect me."

"I lost my pop ten years ago, my mama two years before that. I still think about them every day. Ain't easy losin' people you deeply care for."

Sierra wiped her tears away and then patted Jean Pierre's hand.

"You're a truly understanding person."

Jean Pierre held up his glass. "Miss Sierra poured me a shot of your whiskey, sir. I hope you don't mind."

"Excellent idea," he said. Grabbing a glass for himself, and the bottle of whiskey, he topped up Jean Pierre's after filling his own. "Not much else I can do tonight so I'll join you. Sierra's a beer hound, but she can't tolerate my whiskey."

"Not after the moonshine we drank," she said. "Never again."

"Smart woman," Jean Pierre said. "If I hadn't started drinkin' when I was fifteen, I'd probably be rich by now."

"You didn't really start drinking at fifteen, did you?" Sierra asked.

"When you go gator huntin' the first time with the big

212

boys, it's kind of expected. Rite of passage."

"You shot an alligator when you were fifteen?"

We all laughed when he said, "Why hell no. I spent the night face down in the bottom of the boat, throwin' up into the bayou till I was too weak to lift my head."

Jean Pierre continued to regale us with Cajun stories until even Professor Quinn was smiling. When lightning struck nearby, and thunder shook the stilt house, his expression became serious.

"Sierra's the only one of us that hasn't lived through a hurricane," he said.

"What's going to happen?" she asked.

"Two things: wind you can only imagine and that can persist for days, and a storm surge ten or fifteen feet high that can flood inland for miles. There's a fair chance this house won't be standing a week from now."

Sierra's hand went to her mouth, tears again appearing in her eyes.

"Oh my God, no! What about all our work?"

"If it hits us, we'll have to rebuild and persevere. I don't want to get trapped here so we'll need to leave no later than tomorrow."

Chuckie was eating doggie treats out of Jean Pierre's hand, and King Tut was asleep in my lap. We all relaxed when the rain finally subsided to a slow patter on the roof. It didn't stay that way long, rain pelting the house and wind rocking it on its stilts.

"Most of my people left Chalmette after Katrina," Jean Pierre said. "They just now startin' to trickle back in. We damn sure don't need another one like that."

"They'll be okay, my boy," Quinn said. "The state has made significant improvements to the levees and drainage systems."

"Yeah but where does that leave the people and animals on the other side of the levees?" Jean Pierre asked.

"In deep trouble," Professor Quinn said. "Will you come with us tomorrow, Wyatt?"

"Guess there's not much I can do on the island until

the hurricane moves past."

"Then your answer is yes?"

"If you'll wait until I get my cat."

"Of course we'll wait. You can't stay on Goose Island. It'll be under water in a few days. The water and strong winds could destroy the monastery."

"Maybe not. There's a six-foot berm around it. The buildings were designed to withstand a Cat 3 hurricane, and they have an emergency capsule that'll hold thirty people."

"What the hell's an emergency capsule?" Jean Pierre asked.

A waterproof building shaped like a silo and designed to protect it from wind and rain. It has supplies for several days."

"Brother Bruce told me it's never been tested. They have no idea if it'll work or not," Sierra said.

Lightning flashed through the window as I said, "Maybe not, but the monks are sworn to stay. Looks as if they're going to get their chance."

Chapter Twenty Five

Tony's phone was ringing when he finally made it home from Delacroix. Already late, he didn't bother checking the caller I.D. before answering it.

"Tony, it's Lil," the caller said.

"Lil. Are you coming home?"

"That's not why I called. There's a hurricane in the Gulf, and it's headed for New Orleans. You need to board up the house and then come to Shreveport."

There was only silence on the line when he said, "Are you done being mad at me?"

"I'm not thinking about that right now," she finally said.

It's raining like crazy down here, but I thought it was just a bad storm. We've never had a hurricane this early in the year."

"Well it's a hurricane, Tony, and you need to get the hell out of there."

"What about the kids? Are they okay?"

"They will be. They're packing now and leaving tomorrow."

"When's this hurricane supposed to hit?"

"Two days at the latest. Tony, I'm so worried."

"It'll be okay. I'll start boarding up the windows tomorrow."

"I didn't think I'd ever say this, but my mother has a

spare room for you."

"That's not gonna work, and you know it. We need to figure this out and not just let it keep festering," he said.

"You know I love you, Tony. I just don't think I can handle any more stress in our marriage. I've had it."

"Then I'm not coming to Shreveport if that's the way you feel."

"Crazy talk, Tony."

"I'll board the house, but I'm not going anyplace where I'm not wanted."

"I didn't say you aren't wanted. I just can't take any more stress. I think we need a divorce."

"You don't even want to talk about it?" he said.

"We are talking about it. My mother has an extra bedroom. I told you that, Tony."

"I think I'll just stay here," he said.

By now, he could tell Lil was crying. "You're so damn stubborn. You've always been that way. Why can't you ever give in?"

"I didn't know how much I'd miss you when you left. Now my heart's aching. Can't you see fit to give me just one more chance?"

"You'll never change."

"I've left the force, and I'm not going back."

"Only because they don't want you."

"I wouldn't go back now if they begged me."

"Yes you would. You love the N.O.P.D. more than anything on earth."

"Not more than you. I miss you and hate living by myself. You take me back, I'll be a perfect husband."

"Don't go telling lies, Tony. God will punish you for that."

"I'm telling the truth, I promise."

Thunder struck close to the house, shaking the walls as rain began pelting the windows.

"You got a way to get here?"

"I bought a car," he said. "I'm not coming unless I'm sleeping in the same room as you."

"You bought a car and didn't tell me?"

"We ain't exactly been talking. I needed a way to get around since I don't have a squad car any more. Hey, and I got a gig as a private detective. I'm paying for the car with the money I'm making from my P.I. job."

"Tony, I don't know what you're talking about, and I don't think I want to hear about it right now. Just board up the windows and come to Shreveport."

"In the same room as you?"

"You're a bastard, you know it?"

"Your mama's not gonna kill me, is she?"

"She'd have done that years ago if she was going to. She's weak like me and loves you too. I have to go now. Please don't get hurt in the storm."

"I love you, Lil, and I'll call you tomorrow."

Heavy rain continued throughout the night, and Tony kept waking up, thinking about what he should do. He had a job that someone was paying him good money to complete. Before falling asleep, he'd decided to talk with Kelton Frenette. After that, he'd board up the house, leave New Orleans and then join Lil in Shreveport.

Tony awoke the next morning feeling better than he had in weeks. The rain had momentarily abated to just a sprinkle falling from a dark and cloudy sky. Just a brief respite, he knew. His neighbor was boarding his windows as he went out to the car. The man shouted across the driveway.

"You hear about the hurricane?"

"I heard. I got something to do first. I'll be back to board up the windows a little later."

"Need some help, just let me know."

"Thanks, Joe," he said as he cranked the engine on his Sebring.

Though still early, traffic was heavy, people scurrying around, preparing for the approaching hurricane. The storm was in the back of Tony's mind as he splashed through puddles of water on his way down St. Charles Avenue.

Kelton Frenette still lived in the Garden District.

Tony had his address and was on his way there. He hadn't called first because sometimes the best tactic was just show up at someone's doorstep. Give them no time to concoct a story, if that's what they were inclined to do.

Steady rain poured down his windshield as Tony parked on the street in front of Frenette's home. He knew a person's house spoke volumes of the people living in them. As he gazed at the old two story mansion, he'd already formed an opinion of the man before ever seeing him.

The Garden District is known for its eclectic architecture. Frenette's house might have been Greek Revival, Victorian, or plantation style. Tony didn't care. What he saw was a house desperately in need of a fresh coat of paint, trees that had gone untrimmed for years if not decades, broken boards on the porch, and cracked panes of glass in the windows.

The iron gate was unlatched, swung open toward the front door of the house as if there was no one inside that cared if anyone came or went. Pulling his collar up around his neck, he closed and latched the gate behind him.

The doorbell didn't work. After knocking several times, he began wondering if the house was deserted. Before he turned to leave, someone opened the door a crack.

"Help you?"

The large, black woman peeking through the door sounded pleasant enough.

"Is Dr. Frenette in?"

"He's in, but he doesn't see anybody these days. What is it you needed?"

"Dr. Frenette did some research years ago. I'd like to talk to him about it."

"As I said, he doesn't get around much anymore."

A booming voice sounded behind the woman. "Who is it, Latrice?"

"Some person that wants to talk to you about your research."

"Well let him in."

The woman named Latrice opened the door for Tony, and he entered the spacious alcove lined with large pots where ornamental plants probably once grew. Sitting in an antique, wooden wheelchair was the man with the booming voice.

"I'm Kelton Frenette," he said. "How can I help you?"

"I'm Tony Nicosia. You did research on a rabies-like virus. I'd like to talk to you about it."

"Are you a reporter?"

"No sir, I'm not. Just a guy with some questions I hope you have answers for."

"Then come with me," he said as he wheeled into a cavernous room that was clearly the main living area.

Like the paint on the outside of the house, the off-pink walls had the look and feel of faded antiquity. The couch, settee, and chairs were antiques. Probably valuable. Everything was spotless, no dust anywhere in the room. Only the shiny patina of age and continuous use tarnished the furniture.

"Take a seat, please," Latrice said. "Can I get you something to drink? Tea or lemonade?"

"Forget the tea and lemonade, Latrice. Bring Mr. Nicosia a brandy, and one for me too, please."

Latrice didn't argue, soon returning with three snifters filled with expensive brandy.

"I'll be in the kitchen if you need me," she said.

"Is Latrice your help?" Tony asked when she was gone.

"Latrice is my wife," he said.

"I apologize."

"Don't worry about it. A more tolerant age is what Latrice and I needed."

"You haven't been out much lately. Things are better now. Whatever, I can see you made a wise choice."

Frenette smiled for the first time. Like his voice, he was a portly man, probably pushing three hundred pounds. His khaki pants and canvas shirt were pressed and clean but as timeworn as the paint on the wall.

"There was a time when mixed marriages were

frowned upon by people in the Garden District," he said.

"Then you should have moved to the Quarter. They always been a little more tolerant across Canal Street."

"Ain't that the truth," Frenette said in an affected southern accent.

"This is wonderful brandy," Tony said.

"Pierre Ferrand, 1972. I only serve it to my favorite guests. Since you are the only guest we've had in a while, you got lucky. If you like brandy, that is."

"Love it, though it sounds like I probably can't afford the finest stuff."

"None of us can, Mr. Nicosia, but then again none of us can afford not to."

"I like your philosophy."

"Now tell me what you need to know about my research."

Frenette nodded when Tony asked, "You know what a rougarou is?"

"I do."

You think they exist?"

Frenette nodded again. "If you're a journalist, it's too late to discredit me. That was done years ago."

"Tell me about it, please," Tony said.

"When I published my findings in a small medical journal, my colleagues called me mad. My research funds dried up, and I was widely shunned."

"I'm not a journalist, Dr. Frenette, I'm a detective investigating two recent deaths that are baffling, to say the least."

"And you think a rougarou is responsible?"

Tony dropped the claw into Frenette's hand. "You seen anything like this before?"

"Where did you get it?"

"From the horribly mutilated body of a person possibly killed by one of those creatures we aren't supposed to know exists."

Frenette fingered the claw, then tilted his oversized head, rubbing his chin with thick fingers.

"Interesting," he said. "Latrice, we need more

220

brandy."

Latrice must have been within hearing distance because she quickly appeared with the bottle.

"Thanks, ma'am," Tony said as she replenished his snifter.

"We're going into the basement," he said.

"You sure, Honey?" Latrice said.

"We'll be fine," he said.

Latrice pushed him to a hallway near the center of the large house. With some difficulty, she lifted the heavy, metal bar across the door. Using a ring of keys hanging on the wall, she unlocked three padlocks.

Opening the door of an oversized dumbwaiter, she wheeled Frenette in and pushed a button. An old electric motor made grating sounds as the cab of the dumbwaiter began descending into the basement.

Latrice pointed Tony to a door leading to the cellar, removing the metal bar and unlocking three more padlocks as she had on the dumbwaiter door. When he entered, she switched on a bare, overhead bulb that dimly illuminated the musty stairs.

The stairway was steep, Tony thankful for his recently repaired knees. Another dim light greeted him when he reached the concrete floor of the basement. Dr. Frenette waited in a large room that felt twenty degrees colder than at the top of the stairs.

"I haven't been here in ten years," he said. "I know this place looks like something out of Dr. Frankenstein's laboratory. I assure you, my endeavors weren't so manic."

The room was filled with beakers, test tubes and medical paraphernalia, everything coated with dust. There was also a dissection table that reminded Tony of the autopsy room he'd recently visited. The large, open cellar reeked of must, and maybe something else. The subtle, but distinctive odor of death, like he'd smelled in the autopsy office, permeated everything.

"You haven't come here in ten years?" Tony asked.

"That's right."

"Because?"

"There's something here that haunts me to my very core. Are you a religious man, Mr. Nicosia?"

"I go to church on Easter and Christmas. My priest doesn't remember my name because I haven't taken confession in years."

Frenette grinned for the first time since they'd been in the basement. Tony still had the empty snifter in his hand. Frenette motioned him over and refilled it.

"Sometimes brandy is more comforting than a priest," he said. "Since there's no priest to comfort us, let's have another drink."

"Amen to that. What's going on down here?"

"I want to show you something. Do you have a strong stomach, Mr. Nicosia?"

Frenette grinned when Tony said, "I've lost my cookies a time or two. What you got, Doc?"

Dr. Frenette pointed to a large, horizontal freezer against the wall. Like the dumb waiter and the cellar door, it was secured by several locks.

"It's in there," he said. "You might want to take a deep breath before you open it."

Chapter Twenty Six

Frenette tossed Tony a set of keys, and he quickly slipped the padlocks. The lid had long since frozen to the top of the freezer, and he had to give it an extra hard pull. When he did, it popped open with a whoosh, stale, refrigerated air blasting his face. After glancing a moment at the contents of the refrigerator, he took a step backwards.

"Jesus! What the hell is it?"

"Your rougarou, Mr. Nicosia."

Tony stared at the frozen body of something that wasn't quite a man. Dark eyes glinting red in the overhead lighting stared back at him. Tufts of thick, brown hair splotched the creature's face and neck. Long fangs protruded from the half-opened mouth. Black claws, like the one he had in his pocket, extended from his hairy fingers. White frost encased the frozen body.

"Is it. . . ?"

"Dead? It's been frozen for more than forty years, though I fear it's still very much alive."

"It's enormous. How did you get it in there?"

"I had help."

"Where did it come from?"

"Close the lid, lock it tight, and then I'll tell you the story. After we go back upstairs."

Tony closed and relocked the freezer, then wheeled Dr. Frenette to the dumbwaiter. After situating him inside it and pushing the button, he switched off the lights and hurried up the steep stairway toward the dim light shining at the top. Latrice was waiting for them.

She quickly padlocked the doors and returned the metal bars to their catches before giving her husband a hug that dragged on for several anxious moments.

"It's okay, Baby. It's still frozen."

The rain, buffeted by the wind that hadn't been present when Tony arrived, had intensified as they returned to the pink living room. Latrice quickly handed him and Dr. Frenette a new snifter of brandy, and then covered her husband's legs with a tattered blanket. After placing the fancy bottle of brandy on the coffee table in front of Tony, she joined him on the couch.

"Hon, I was so worried."

"It's okay. The freezer's working, and there's nothing to worry about."

Frenette smiled when Tony said, "I didn't toss my cookies, but I almost did. That creature in the freezer. Was it really a rougarou?"

"You already know the answer to your question."

"You haven't told me where it came from."

"The creature is a person and has a name—Calvin Couvillion. His relatives brought him here. Like I said, more than forty years ago."

"And you've had it frozen in your basement since then? Maybe you'd better explain," Tony said.

"It's not like you think," Latrice said.

Frenette waved his hand and shook his head, shushing her.

"Covillion came from the Atchafalaya Swamp, over near Thibodaux. His family brought him here."

"A live rougarou?"

"Let me finish the story, and then you'll see. Most of Couvillion's family was at a fais do-do."

"I know," Tony said when he hesitated. "A Cajun celebration."

"The family had already become concerned about Couvillion's erratic behavior. When a storm came up

224

during the party, he began to transform."

"The storm caused him to transform?"

Frenette nodded. "Perhaps hurried along by a rapid change in barometric pressure. That's the only explanation I can come up with."

"And everyone at the party saw him?"

"They believe in such things out there on the bayou. He might have killed someone, but was struck by lightning, the impact rendering him immobile, at least temporarily. They packed him in dry ice and brought him to me."

"Why?"

"I was doing research on Lycanthropy and rumors had started to spread."

"Lycanthropy?"

"The study of human transformation into a wolf-like creature," he explained, seeing the puzzled look on Tony's face.

"What about his family? They just left him here with you and never said nothing about it, even after all these years?"

"They were afraid. They helped me put him into the freezer, and then left me with their problem."

"He was struck by lightning and didn't die?" Tony said.

"You apparently know little about rougarous, loup garous, werewolves, or whatever you want to call them."

"Tell me."

"The virus that causes Lycanthropy is similar to the rabies virus. Rabies can take months or even years to develop. Before a cure was discovered, people contracting it often became hyper-sexual and then eventually quite mad."

"But we aren't talking about rabies here," Tony said.

"No, but the two diseases are similar in many ways."

"How so?"

"Rabies is the only virus contracted by a bite, the person bitten guaranteed to contract the virus and die, unless they undergo a painful treatment."

"If you shoot a mad dog, it dies. If the disease you're talking about is like rabies, how could someone that has it survive a lightning strike?"

"Because, Mr. Nicosia, the disease makes them immortal."

"I don't believe that. Nothing's immortal."

"Oh, but you're wrong. Cancer cells are immortal. That's why we have no cure. Succeed in knocking out one cell with radiation or chemotherapy, and it usually only results in the propagation of many more."

"We're not talking about cancer here," Tony said.

"The rabies-like virus that causes Lycanthropy mutates the cells in a person's body. Like cancer, the mutated individual becomes, quite literally, immortal. I'm sorry if the concept is difficult to reconcile, but it is what it is."

"Don't get me wrong, Doc. I don't want you to cut me off this great brandy, but I don't quite buy your story. Like I said, nothing is immortal."

"Au contraire, Mr. Nicosia. The creature you saw frozen in the basement is very much alive. Of that, I can assure you."

"Then why didn't you report it to the authorities years ago?"

"Because I was already a discredited researcher when the family brought me Calvin Couvillion. I thought I could show everyone I wasn't crazy by curing the man."

"Why didn't you?"

"A little problem," Frenette said.

"Then didn't it occur to you to get it the hell out of here?"

"More than once," Latrice said. "We even thought about burning the house down."

"Just call the authorities. Let them deal with it. You should have done it forty years ago."

Latrice's hands went to her face to hide her tears. "You just don't know how it was back then. People protesting at our front door, calling Kelton Dr. Frankenstein."

226

Tony grabbed the bottle of brandy, topped up her snifter and then gave her shoulder a reassuring pat.

"Ma'am, I'm not here to point fingers or cause distress. I'm just looking for answers. Maybe I can help get rid of that creature in your basement if that's what it actually is."

Tony's words and the brandy calmed her. Cupping the snifter in her palms, she held it to her nose as if the pungent aroma might somehow drive away her unpleasant memories. Tony topped up his own glass and that of Dr. Frenette's.

"Our paranoia kept us from revealing the creature to the authorities. Not to mention we feared letting loose such a beast on an unsuspecting city," Frenette said.

"I was afraid they'd put Kelton in prison," Latrice said.

"No one's going to jail. If you have a serum that cures the disease, why don't you just use it?"

"The little problem I mentioned. You can't inject serum into a frozen body, and we can't unthaw him because he would kill us."

"Jesus! I can't believe you've lived forty years with that thing in your basement. I take it you stayed here during Katrina."

When Latrice began to cry again, Frenette wheeled over to her, and they hugged again.

"We were afraid to stay and even more afraid to leave," Latrice said when her tears abated.

"It was terrible with the wind and rain. Not knowing if the house would survive, much less ourselves," Frenette said.

"Yeah, well it's not getting much better out there right now. Didn't you lose power? How did you keep that thing in the freezer from thawing out?"

"We had a large generator installed years ago. We've never had to use it," Frenette said.

"I think I'd have carried it out to the swamp and dumped it in the bayou," Tony said.

"Believe me, we thought about it. In the end, it just

wasn't possible. If there were just a way to disable it until the serum had a chance to take effect," he said.

Frenette and Latrice both looked at Tony when he said, "Maybe there is."

"You know something you're not telling us?" he asked.

It was Tony's turn to hold up a palm. "Like I said, I'm investigating two deaths down in St. Bernard Parish, near the Gulf. Both may have been killed by a rougarou. Hell, I don't even think we're talking about a single rougarou. There may be several."

"An outbreak. What I've feared all these years," Frenette said. "I have a possible cure, but no way to administer it, except in the early stages of the disease. What were you talking about when you said maybe there is?"

"My partner's working the case on Goose Island. There's a fishing village with a voodoo woman that lives there. Her son coats his buckshot with something she gives him. He claims it'll knock down a rougarou."

"For how long?" Frenette asked.

"At least until the person doing the shooting can escape."

"Well for God's sake, tell me what it is!"

"Wolfsbane," Tony said, waiting for Frenette to scoff at his suggestion.

He didn't. Turning to Latrice, he said, "Baby, can you get me the Martinsdale?"

"Sure, Hon," she said.

Latrice apparently knew what he wanted because she went to the bookcase lining the wall and pulled a large book from the many volumes. Frenette began leafing through it immediately. Apparently locating what he was looking for, he stared at the page.

"Find something?" Tony asked.

"Aconite," he finally said.

"Pardon me?"

"Aconite, the active ingredient found in the Aconitum species."

"You mean Wolfsbane?"

"That's one of the flowers. The substance has been used in Chinese and Ayervedic medicine for centuries. In small doses, it can be helpful. Its highly toxic in large doses and can paralyze, stop a person's heart, and even kill."

"But will it stop a rougarou?"

"You're the one that said it does."

"Yeah, but I'm not speaking from experience here."

"The Ainu, Japanese indigenous people, used it on their arrows when they hunted bear. It's extremely powerful. It just might work."

"Fine," Tony said. "Now what?"

"We have to thaw him out."

"You're shitting me! You have Aconite?"

"Yes, more than enough to do what we need."

"You sure about that? What if it don't work?"

"Then at least we won't have to worry about it anymore."

Tony glanced at his watch. "Sounds like you're gonna need help moving him. I'm ready if you are."

"You're a brave man, Mr. Nicosia," Frenette said.

"Hell, I don't hold a candle to you and Latrice. Let's do it before I change my mind."

Dr. Frenette smiled for the first time since leaving the basement.

"Baby, you better open us another bottle of Pierre Ferrand, and then join us in the laboratory."

Tony and Frenette were at the basement door when a clap of thunder shook the roof. When it did, all the lights went out.

"Oh hell, there goes the power," Frenette said.

"What happened to the generator?" Tony asked.

"It hasn't been tested since the time it was installed. Who knows? We'll have to make do without it."

Flickering light soon lit the hallway as Latrice joined them, the bottle of brandy in one hand, a hurricane lamp in the other. Frenette took both.

"Go get more candles, Baby. We're going to need

229

them."

Tony and Frenette were soon back in the dank laboratory lighted only by glimmering candle light. Latrice quickly joined them. After steeling themselves with more brandy, Frenette pointed to an operating table, its legs lowered so he could reach it without standing.

"You ready?" Tony asked.

When Frenette nodded, Latrice unlocked the freezer and opened it, her face revealing more than words could express.

"What is it, Baby?" Frenette asked.

"Oh my God, Hon! It's fully transformed. No longer even partially human."

Her words caused Tony to become more nervous than he already was.

"Help me up," Frenette said. "I need to see."

Latrice and Tony helped him out of the wheelchair, supporting him as he gazed into the freezer.

"My God! Even encased in melting ice, he's somehow managed to transform entirely from human to wolf. It must be the storm."

"How is that possible? The electricity hasn't even been off for ten minutes yet." Tony said.

"Then we must hurry. We don't have much time left."

Tony nodded when Latrice said, "Can you help me get him out of there?"

As Frenette watched, Latrice and Tony lifted the large body out of the freezer.

"This thing must weigh three hundred pounds," Tony said, struggling with the weight. "You okay, Latrice?"

"I got him. Just hurry."

Frenette had rigged up a mechanical drip and filled it with Aconite. The creature's body was totally naked, its wolf/human genitals only partially blotched by thick tufts of hair. Latrice covered most of the body with a blanket to accelerate the thawing.

"Now we wait," Frenette said. "Soon as I can penetrate his skin with the needle, I'll start the drip. I don't need you two for that. Go upstairs and lock the door.

I'll call when I'm done."

"I'm not going anywhere," Latrice said.

"In for a penny, in for a pound. I'm staying," Tony said."

Twenty minutes passed. Though he'd tried several times, Dr. Frenette was unsuccessful in inserting the needle into the rougarou's vein. After an hour, the creature's eyes moved in their sockets. For a moment, Tony was sure they were looking straight at him.

"It's now or never," Frenette said. "The beast is almost cognizant."

Latrice clutched Tony's arm as Dr. Frenette began working the needle. The creature was fully thawed and beginning to move. Tony reached for his service revolver before remembering he didn't have it anymore.

"Bingo!" Frenette finally said. "Thank God this instrument has a battery pack or it wouldn't do us any good without electricity."

"Yeah, when was the last time you checked the batteries?"

Frenette didn't answer. Latrice just closed her eyes, crossed her fingers and began praying out loud. Reaching for the I.V.'s control panel, Frenette flipped the switch. The display turned green and the screen began recording drips of Aconite into the creature's arm.

"Shit, that's a relief. Now what?" Tony asked.

"It'll work, or else in an hour or so we'll all be in hell," Frenette said.

The three held their collective breaths, the room silent except for the steady, electronic drip of Aconite into the creature's vein. Finally, it's eyes began to flutter, then close. Its muscles that had been twitching drew still. Frenette exhaled, looking first at Latrice and then at Tony.

"It's working. He's regressing."

"Thank God!" Latrice said.

Another hour passed, the three of them watching as thick hair began disappearing from Calvin Couvillion's face, his fangs slowly becoming human teeth.

"It is working," Frenette said. "Get me the serum, Latrice."

Frenette was soon injecting the serum into Couvillion's stomach with a huge needle.

"I'm not sure how much we need. I'm going to use the same dosage protocol as if he were a rabies patient, and then hope for the best."

"Will it work?" Tony asked.

"It has to work. You said there's a possible outbreak of Lycanthropy in St. Bernard Parish."

"That's right," Tony said.

"Latrice, pack up the pneumatic syringe for Mr. Nicosia. Load six number ten cartridges with Aconite. Make sure it has fresh batteries and a new CO_2 cartridge installed."

Latrice returned with a carrying case and shoulder strap. Frenette opened it, showing Tony what looked like a pistol straight from a science fiction movie.

"What the hell is it?" Tony asked.

"A pneumatic syringe for giving multiple injections at a high rate of speed. The cartridges rotate like in a standard revolver. Designed it myself."

"How does it work?"

"That's the beauty of it. You just flip the switch, push it against bare skin and pull the trigger. The gun does the rest."

"What if we need more than six doses?"

"Then you're in big trouble. Baby, you better prepare a second rotator for Mr. Nicosia. Just in case."

"Are you going to stay here and ride out the hurricane?" Tony asked.

"If Katrina didn't get us, then this one won't either. We're staying."

"How long will it take before you know if the serum is working?"

"A few days," he said.

Tony had purchased some business cards printed with his phone number on it. They'd been cheap and looked it when he handed one to Dr. Frenette. Suddenly

232

feeling as cheap as the cards, he made a mental note to purchase more expensive ones next time.

"Will you and Latrice be okay?"

"I've waited to try this serum for forty years. I had faith back then that it would work. I still have faith, and my researcher's savvy tells me it's a go."

Tony gave the carrying case a tap. "Anything else I need to know?"

"Yes. Make sure whoever you inject with this thing is a rougarou."

"Or?"

"It'll kill them deader than hell," Frenette said.

"Call me when you know something. Good luck and God bless," he said as he started up the dark stairway.

"Thank you, Mr. Nicosia. You're our angel. Latrice and I waited forty years for your visit."

Chapter Twenty Seven

It was dark when Tony finally left the Frenette's house in the Garden District. He'd forgotten his cell phone lying on the Sebring's console. When he checked it, he found he had three missed calls. Two were from Chief Wexler, his former boss in the N.O.P.D. It rang again as he held it in his hand. It was Wexler again.

"Tony here," he said.

"Where are you?"

"Driving through the Garden District."

"I was beginning to think you'd already left town."

"Not yet. I'm going home to board up my windows and then head for Shreveport."

"Hurricane Aguirre has taken aim at the city. The Governor and Mayor have declared a state of emergency and called for evacuation."

"Everyone must have taken their advice. I'm out in it, and my car's the only one on the road."

"Most everyone. You know there are always those who choose to stay," Wexler said.

"Sometimes it's a false alarm. People get tired of packing up and driving to Houston every time the Mayor says boo."

"It's no false alarm this time. This one looks as powerful as Katrina, and it's heading straight toward us."

"Shit! Just what we need. I know you boys got it

handled," Tony said.

"No we don't. We let so many of our people go we don't even have enough warm bodies to evacuate the prisoners in jail."

For a moment, Tony didn't respond. Then he said, "Why are you telling me?"

"Because the city needs you."

"You're offering me my job back if I'll stay and help?"

"I didn't say that. I've already cashed in all my chits, cajoled everyone in power I know. No luck! The Feds are calling the shots here. You're fired. That's not going to change. Tony, I still need your help."

"Can I think about it?"

"Tommy's waiting at your house. If you can't help, tell him," Wexler said before hanging up.

"What a crock of shit!" Tony said as his car sloshed through rain rapidly puddling in the streets.

He found a patrol car parked in front of his house when he arrived. He opened the automatic door of his garage and drove in. With the door still open, he motioned the person in the police car to pull into the driveway.

Tommy Blackburn followed his directions, jumping out of the car and rushing into the garage.

"Tony, did the Chief get hold of you?"

"Oh yeah."

"You're gonna help, aren't you?"

"Come inside and let's talk about it."

The garage door creaked into action when he pushed the button to lower it. The house was quiet except for the sound of rain on the roof and the wind gusting outside. Tommy glanced at the pile of dishes in the sink.

"I can't remember the last time I came in this kitchen and didn't smell something good to eat."

"Yeah, well I got a half-eaten can of pork and beans in the fridge. I can heat it up for you."

"No thanks. I ain't that hungry."

"You sick?" Tony asked.

"It just seems strange, Lil not here and you not on the force anymore."

"Tell me about it."

"You gonna help us out, Tony?"

"I don't have a good taste in my mouth right now for the N.O.P.D."

"I'm the one that needs your help, and I never done you wrong."

Tony slapped his shoulder. "You're the best partner a cop ever had. I can't tell you how much I miss working with you."

"Then let's do it one more time. If you don't, I'm gonna be out on the streets all by myself."

"You don't have a new partner yet?"

"Pickin's are kinda slim around the department these days."

"You're a piece of shit, you know it?"

"Then you're gonna help me?"

"Okay," Tony said. "But just remember I'm doing it for you and not the N.O.P.D."

Ten minutes later they were cruising the wet streets of New Orleans. The neighborhood was dark, electrical power lost to the storm, and not a single car in sight except for a few junkers on the sides of the road.

"What now?" Tony asked.

"We stop and walk. You check the houses on this side of the street, I'll check the ones on the other side."

"We gonna look like drowned rats here in a minute, even with these police-issue ponchos and rain hats."

"Quit your bitchin' Tony. You know you love it."

"Yeah, well I'd love it better if my windows were boarded up and I was halfway to Shreveport."

Ignoring the rant, Tommy crossed the street in the pouring rain. Tony ran to the porch of an old clapboard house. Banging on the door, he called out.

"Police. Anybody home?"

When no one answered, he circled the house, shining his flashlight through the open windows. He jumped the fence, trying the back door to see if it were locked. Satisfied no one was there, he moved to the next house. At the third house, he saw a candle burning through the window.

"Anyone home?" he said, banging on the door.

An elderly black woman peered out. "Help me, please," she said.

Tony followed the gray-haired woman into the house, and she led him to a bedroom where a gaunt old man was lying in bed, a grimace on his face.

"I can't get him to take his medicine," she said. "Will you help me?"

"What's your name, old timer?" he asked the man.

"Jericho," the old woman said, answering for him.

She handed Tony two pills and a glass of water. The old man opened his eyes when Tony shook his shoulder.

"Jericho, you awake?"

Tony gently placed a finger in the corner of his mouth, prying it open enough to give him the pills. After swallowing reflexively, Tony gave him a drink of water to wash them down.

"Thank you," the old woman said.

"Ma'am, you need to pack a few things. I gotta get you out of here. There's a bus waiting on us that'll take you to a shelter with food, water, and medical assistance."

"Cain't go," she said. "I cain't get Jericho out of bed."

Tony glanced around the little room, quickly spotting a wheelchair. Without asking, he rolled it over to the bed and lifted Jericho into it. The old man felt light as a feather. Pulling the blanket off the bed, he covered him with it.

"Ma'am, you're gonna need a jacket. It's chilly out there. And a raincoat, if you have one."

The little old woman returned from the other room in a light jacket. She was carrying a bag of clothes, a large box, and a parasol.

"This is all I need," she said.

"What's in the box?"

"Family pictures."

"Ma'am, you can't take all those pictures. We only got enough room for a few clothes."

The old woman began to cry. "This is my family. It's

all I got."

"Okay, look, choose five pictures. And please, hurry."

Opening the box, she started sorting through them. "This my son, Denard. He got killed in Vietnam. This the Bronze Star he won."

"All right. That counts as one. Four more."

Tony watched and listened as she carefully chose four more pictures. When she finished, she began crying again.

"I cain't go without Sparky."

"Who's Sparky?" Tony asked.

"Sparky, my parakeet. He been with me ten years now."

"Okay, get Sparky. Anyone else?"

The old woman stopped crying and shook her head. She followed Tony as he wheeled Jericho out on the porch with one hand while holding the bird cage in the other. Tommy was crossing the street with a young, black woman and her three children—two sons and a daughter.

They were all soon in the back seat of the squad car, Jericho without his wheelchair. They waited until Tony and Tommy had checked every house on both sides of the street. Tony was running back to the car when Tommy called from the front porch of a house.

"Tony, I need you."

"What's up?" he said, joining him.

Tommy was talking with an old man sitting in a rocking chair, trying to convince him to join them in the squad car.

"I ain't goin' without Mousie."

"Who is Mousie?" Tony asked.

"My dog. He scared of thunder and won't come out from behind the couch."

"You go with Tommy. I'll get Mousie. I promise," he added when the old man gave him a defeated look.

The house was dark and smelled like wet cardboard. The couch looked as if it had come from the city dump. Pulling it back, he shined his flashlight, looking for the dog. The little rat terrier was shaking with fear. Finding a bath towel, he wrapped him in it and picked him up.

"It's okay, Mousie. I'm taking you to Papa. He won't let this bad old thunder hurt you."

A half-dozen, double-decker buses were lined up, waiting in a row about a mile away. Tommy and Tony delivered their passengers to an awaiting team that included medical people. By midnight, they'd canvassed most of the neighborhood, returning to the buses on several occasions, each time with another load of passengers.

"One more street," Tommy said. "You gonna make it, Tony?"

"I'm not as young as you are, but I ain't dead yet. Drive on, bro."

The street proved deserted, except for a big, black Hummer parked at the very end of it. A lone man was standing in the doorway, on the porch, a sawed-off shotgun in his hand.

"What the hell!" Tommy said, not waiting for Tony as he rushed out of the car.

The young man was drenched, his bad mullet clinging to the back of his neck. He raised a hand when Tony and Tommy joined him on the porch. Tattoos covered his muscular arms. His sleeveless tee shirt had Bounty Hunter stenciled on both sides.

"What's going on?" Tommy demanded.

"Got an escaped murderer in there. I can't go in cause I'm alone, and he'll just go out the back."

"Let him go. We ain't got no place to put him."

"No way. He's got a forty thousand dollar bounty on his head. I ain't goin' no place without him. You the police? One of you cover the back for me. I'll go in and get him. Just stop him if he gets by me."

"I'll go," Tony said.

"I'll give you five to get back there, and then I'm goin' in," the man said.

Tony climbed the fence and was positioned at the back door when he remembered he wasn't carrying his service revolver. Too late to worry about it, he waited. In a minute, the bounty hunter kicked in the door and rushed inside shouting at the top of his lungs.

An enormous black man came running out the back door. Not knowing what else to do, Tony tripped him. When he rolled to the ground, he piled on, reaching for his handcuffs that he quickly remembered he also no longer had. The man smacked him hard across the face, pushed him off and started to rise off the ground when the mullet-haired bounty hunter arrived and kicked him in the chest with his boot. He stuck the shotgun in his face.

"On your stomach. Now!" he commanded. When the escaped con rolled over, the man cuffed him. "Thanks. What's your name, anyway?"

"Tony Nicosia."

"You got a card, Tony. I'm gonna call your boss and tell him you're a real hand."

Tony fished in his shirt pocket, handing the man a damp business card.

"I'm my own boss right now."

"You ain't a cop?"

"Until a week ago. You might say I took early retirement. I'm doing a little P.I. work for now."

Still pointing the shotgun, he put the card in his shirt pocket, and then shook Tony's hand.

"I'm Bax Wingate. Proud to meet you. This is Dr. Death. The sorry sack of shit likes to torture his victims before he kills them. He ain't worth living. If I didn't want the bounty, he wouldn't be around for much longer. I can tell you that right now."

"Can you get him by yourself? I doubt there's any place around here that can handle a prisoner."

"Going to Shreveport with him. Thanks again and I'll take it from here."

Wingate marched the man around to his black Hummer. It was the last house on the street and Tony decided to take a look inside. He'd found nothing when he heard an animal's tortured whine coming from the side of the house. A young dog was wired so tightly to a post he wasn't able to lie down or stand fully upright. From the feces scattered around him, he'd been there a while. The wet dog managed to wag his tail when Tony put his hand on his head.

"Tony, where you at?" Tommy called from the back porch.

"Around here. You got wire cutters in the car?"

"You know I do."

"Get them. I need help."

Five minutes later, the rain still falling steadily, Tommy returned with the wire cutters.

"Wingate said Dr. Death likes to torture his victims. Looks as though he practiced on helpless animals too."

Tony cut the dog loose, handed the cutters back to Tommy, and then cradled him to his chest. As Tommy drove to the next block, he dried the shivering animal with his handkerchief. The dog was short-haired and mostly white, though had a black spot that formed a perfect circle around his right eye.

The car was swaying, the wind increasing and starting to uproot trees. Branches tumbled through the air, one striking the hood of the car. Because of debris and fallen trees, Tommy had to keep adjusting his course, sometimes driving through people's front yards. Tony raised his arm in front of his face when a limb struck the windshield.

"I think he's a pit bull," Tommy said. "You better be careful. He might attack you."

"He ain't a pit bull. Just a mutt like me," Tony said.

"I'm telling you, he could be real mean."

"Yeah, well I'm gonna sic him on your big Irish butt if you don't shut up about it."

"Whatever, that's about the ugliest dog I ever seen," Tommy said.

"Shut up, Tommy. You ain't exactly Robert Redford yourself."

Hearing the irritation in his ex-partner's voice, Tommy wisely decided to change the subject.

"I had two dogs when I was growing up. What about you?"

"Always wanted one. Mama said if any of us kids had a pet, all six would. Since we couldn't afford six pets, none of us ever got one."

"You've never had a pet since I've known you. If you wanted one so much, why didn't you just get one?"

"Lil's allergic to dogs. At least she says she is."

"None of your kids ever had a dog?"

"Nope," Tony said. "This neighborhood's cleared. There's someone up in the Quarter we need to go get."

The wind whistled down the narrow street in front of the apartments where Brother Degas lived. Tommy parked the car beside the curb.

"You wait here and watch the dog. I'll be right back."

The tinny voice sounded through the speaker when Tony pushed the buzzer.

"Who is it?"

"Tony. A friend of Sara's."

The door buzzed and Tony pushed it open, entering the courtyard. Rain splashed off the slate flagstones as he hurried up the narrow stairs. As before, the door was cracked and he entered the small room without knocking. Brother Degas was still sitting in the same chair.

"Can you walk?" he asked.

"Not very fast," the old monk said.

Tony smiled. "You got an umbrella?"

"In the corner," Brother Degas said, pointing. "Where we going?"

"A hurricane's coming. I'm taking you to a shelter. You okay with that?"

"Sara's supposed to be here."

"She's not coming tonight. I'll get you something to eat when we get to the shelter."

"Okay," Brother Degas said.

They descended the stairs slowly, Brother Degas holding onto the umbrella, Tony grasping his arm with one hand and the bannister with the other. Halfway down, the wind caught the umbrella, wrenching it from Brother Degas' grasp.

"It's all right. The car's waiting for us on the street." Tony helped the old man into the back seat. "Tommy, say hello to Brother Degas."

"How you doing?"

"Wet," the old man said. "First time I've been down those stairs in a while."

"They may not be there when we come back," Tony said.

"That your dog?" Brother Degas asked.

"Let's just say I rescued him."

"Better keep him," Brother Degas said. "He'll make a great pet."

"How do you know that?" Tommy asked.

"Don't ask," Tony said.

The buses were all gone, so Tony and Tommy took the monk directly to the shelter, not far away in the French Quarter.

The ringtone of Tony's phone pealed before Tommy had a chance to quiz him about the old man. The conversation lasted only a few minutes.

"Who was it?" Tommy asked after he'd hung up.

"Jean Pierre Saucier. A cop I know down in Chalmette. When we catch a breather, we're going to meet him."

Chapter Twenty Eight

After spending a sleepless night on Professor Quinn's couch, I set out to get Kisses and return her to the stilt house. The rain, if anything, had grown harder during the night. Professor Quinn had lent me a slicker. It was so hot I finally took it off and threw it over my shoulder. Better to be wetter from rain than from sweat, I thought.

The monastery campus was deserted. Most of the guests and crew, I suspected, had already evacuated to higher ground. Worried about Lilly, I decided to check on her. See if she had evacuated. Wind howled through her covered patio, hanging chimes performing an atonal symphony in the key of loud. I found her at the computer, seemingly unmindful of the storm exploding around her. She glanced up when I burst through the door.

"Lilly, why are you still here?"

"I'm not going anywhere."

"But the hurricane."

"Riding one out is the chance of a lifetime. I can't let this pass. It'll give me incredible material for a future book."

"If you survive. This isn't going to be your run-of-the-mill storm."

"We're not talking about Katrina," she said.

"Or a simple thunderstorm. If you stay, it'll be the most dangerous thing you've ever done."

"Nonsense. Have you forgotten the capsule? All the monks are staying."

"It's untested. It may not work."

"You go if you're so frightened. I'd never forgive myself if I left now."

When lightning flashed through the window, I thought I saw a glimmer of red in her eyes and took a step toward her for a closer look.

"What are you doing?"

"Gazing at your eyes."

"More like an optometrist's examination," she said.

She had her fingers on the keyboard. I tried to get a closer look at her nails, but the lighting was too dim.

"What is your problem?" she demanded. "Do you have some sort of hand fetish, or something?"

"Just looking at your fingernails," I said.

Lilly stopped typing, pushed the horn rims to the top of her head and stared at me with a silly grin.

"Are you coming on to me? Because if you are, I might be interested. Research, you know."

"Into what?"

"The sensuality of making erotic love in the brunt of a terrible storm."

I had to smile. "You're really into this fantasy thing, aren't you?"

Apparently disliking the tone of my voice, she shut her laptop with the palm of her hand.

"That's it, Wyatt Thomas. Forget making love. I'm never speaking to you again."

"I'm sorry, I was just. . ."

"Just what? You've been acting strangely ever since I met you. Do you know something I don't? If so, then you better tell me now."

"Why not? I've known you long enough to know you're not a rougarou."

"What in holy hell is a rougarou?"

"A Cajun werewolf."

"I'm starting to think you're nuttier than a fruit cake," Lilly said, frowning.

"Rance Parker didn't die of a heart attack. Something killed him, the creature that did possibly a rougarou."

"You're making this up, aren't you?"

"I'm not making anything up. It's another reason you should leave the island."

"And who do you think this rougarou is?"

"Father Domenic, Brother Bruno, and maybe Brother Dunwoody."

"All the monks are werewolves? You are nuts!"

"I thought you might be infected. You did have sex with Parker, and Stormie."

"You think Stormie is a werewolf?"

"She had red eyes, black fingernails and tufts of coarse hair on her back when she came on to me the other night."

"I think it's you that's fantasizing now, Wyatt Thomas. Not me."

"Just doing my job."

"I see, and you thought you could get into my pants and have a little fun at my expense while you did it. Am I playing the right notes here?"

"Lilly, it's not that way."

"Then what way is it?"

A clap of thunder sounded so loud and so close it shook the bungalow. We both jumped, and Lilly grabbed me in a purely reflexive action. The crash had scared her, and I could feel her trembling.

"It's okay. A little thunder isn't going to hurt these bungalows." When she continued holding me, I said, "Lilly, can we start over?"

"You tell me an absolutely crazy story and then have the nerve to ask if we can start over?"

"I didn't have to tell you at all."

"Okay, then. Say I believe your little story. Who else is involved?"

"Quinlan Moore. Does anyone else know he was on the island when Parker died?"

"You mean other than me and fifty thousand of my fans?"

"Huh?"

"I scanned the picture and put it on my fan blog."

"Your what?"

"My blog. You know what a blog is, don't you?"

"Not really."

"My site on the Internet I use for publicity. Surely, you know what I'm talking about. Whatever, the picture is all over the web."

"Then If Moore were trying to cover up his activities on the island, he's too late."

"This is all too much," she said, pushing away from me. "Are you staying or leaving?"

"Leaving, soon as I get Kisses my cat. Come with me. You can check everything out after the hurricane."

"I'm not passing on this opportunity. I'll be safe from the storm in the pod."

"But not from Father Domenic and Brother Bruno if they start to transform."

"You have a line of bullshit a mile long. I don't believe a word you say about werewolves, Cajun or otherwise. I'm staying, and that's that."

Throwing my hands in the air, I left her bungalow. Hopefully the capsule would work, and she'd be okay. It didn't seem to matter because it wasn't just the hurricane I was worried about. I blocked the idea from my mind as I ran through the rain to my own bungalow where I found Quinlan Moore waiting at my door.

"It's about time you showed up," he said.

"What are you doing here?"

"I could ask you the same. You're obviously not investigating the case for me."

"I updated you by email, just like you asked," I said. "But since you signed his death certificate and had a private autopsy performed, you already know how Rance Parker died."

"How do you know about that?"

"I'm good at what I do. I also know you were on the

island when Parker was killed."

"No one knows I was here." he said.

"There's a picture of you, Parker, Sabine Storm, and a romance author named Lilly Bliss on the wall in the Purple Cow."

"Purple Cow?"

"The hamburger joint with photos of all the celebrities on the wall. It's even dated."

"I have to have that photo," he said.

"Too late. Lilly posted it on her blog. She told me at least fifty thousand of her fans have already seen it."

Quinlan Moore closed his eyes and began rubbing his forehead. He was dressed in a short-sleeved, Polo shirt, and I could see the tufts of thick hair on his forearms.

"My career is shot to hell," he said. "What'll I do?"

"Get in your limo. Get the hell out of Dodge. You can worry about everything else after the hurricane passes."

Grabbing the collar of my shirt, he began shaking me.

"Am I becoming a werewolf?"

I pushed him away.

"Get a grip. Tony's located a doctor in New Orleans who has a possible cure. If you don't leave the island now, you may not survive to worry about it."

Moore pushed past me and ran out into the rain. "I've got to talk to Father Domenic," he said as he sprinted toward the administration building.

The storm that had begun in earnest the previous night now showed no signs of abating. As Professor Quinn had said, the hurricane in the Gulf would probably bring with it damaging winds and a torrent of flooding water when it hit the island. Remembering why I'd returned to the bungalow, I went inside to get Kisses and the rest of my things.

Seeing the condition of the room when I entered, I quickly realized someone, or something, had been there before me. The bungalow was a wreck, broken glass all over the floor, the bed covers pulled off the bed, and the mattress ripped to shreds. I tried not to panic as I looked for Kisses, hoping I wouldn't find her body among the piles of destruction I was stepping through. When someone called my name, I turned to see who it was.

"Did you throw yourself a little snitty fit?"

It was Stormie, her red hair, tank top, and short shorts soaked. By the silly grin on her face, she was oblivious to the weather.

"Someone trashed my room."

Though I expected a show of compassion, all I got from her was a wicked grin. I also noticed the same red gleam in her eyes as before, only this time more pronounced. I also saw something else. Her canines were a little too long, and I had a feeling her expensive Hollywood orthodontist wouldn't be able to fix them. She didn't give me a chance to get a closer look.

"You do have a problem," she said.

"Stormie, aren't you leaving the island? It's going to get very dangerous here."

"Leave?" she said, looking at me as if I were a complete idiot. "Why would I leave?"

"Because a hurricane is barreling down on us."

From her wild look, she seemed unmindful of the storm's dangers and totally separated from reality.

"Gotta go," she said. "This storm is exhilarating me. I haven't felt this excited in years."

With outstretched arms, she ran off into the rain, oblivious to the storm.

With Stormie gone, I became even more frenzied as I tore through the rubble on the floor, looking for my cat. She wasn't in the closet, under anything, or anywhere in the bungalow. The patio door was ajar as I'd left it, and I could only hope she'd somehow managed to escape whoever had ransacked the room.

Professor Quinn and Sierra were waiting for me to return to the stilt house. With Kisses gone missing, I knew I couldn't leave until I'd found her. I dialed Sierra's number.

"Wyatt, where are you?"

"I can't make it. You two go without me."

"What happened?"

"Someone wrecked my bungalow. I can't find Kisses."

I could almost imagine Sierra's hand going to her mouth. "Oh Wyatt, I hope she's okay. I'm coming right now to help you find her."

"No you're not. You need to go with Professor Quinn."

"I don't want to go. Landry and his people will need me after the hurricane."

"You won't be much help to them if it blows you away," I said.

"What are you going to do?"

"Hopefully, Kisses and I will be protected in the capsule before the wind and storm surge hits. I've got to keep looking for her."

"Wyatt, Jean Pierre wants to talk to you."

"What the hell's going on, bro?"

"Weird things. I've seen three people since I got back to my bungalow. I think two of them are in the process of transforming."

"Maybe it's the storm. My ex used to get crazy, and not in a good way, every time a front popped up."

"If that's the case, I wouldn't want to see Father Domenic and Brother Bruno."

"I'm followin' Sierra and the Professor as far as Chalmette. Come go with us. It'll give us time to make a few plans."

"I can't. My bungalow was ransacked, my cat missing. I have to find her."

"Leave the doors open. If she's alive and hasn't strayed too far, she'll come back and will be waiting when you return."

"What if she's. . . ?"

"We all love our pets like family. But Wyatt, if she dead, ain't nothin' you can do about it now. Come go to Chalmette with me and we'll make a plan on the way."

Chapter Twenty Nine

Professor Quinn had put the soft top up on his Jeep, loaded it with clothes, research material, Sierra, Chuckie, and King Tut. He was pulling his airboat on a trailer behind the vehicle, Jean Pierre and I following in the truck as he pulled out on the blacktop.

"The rain damn sure ain't lettin' up," Jean Pierre said.

"It'll get worse before it gets better," I said.

"Sierra don't wanna leave the island, but she don't know how to tell Professor Quinn."

"How do you know?"

"She told me while the professor was packing."

"Even if she has mixed emotions, she's better off leaving the island. You've been in a hurricane. It's too dangerous for her to stay."

"Don't do much good tellin' her that since you're staying," Jean Pierre said."

"I have a reason. She doesn't."

"Try telling her that. She don't believe either one of us. You heard from Tony lately?"

"No. You?"

"Nope. Maybe we ought to give him a call."

Not waiting for me to do the honors, he grabbed his cell phone from the console and punched in Tony's number. Tony answered on the first ring.

"What's up, Cajun? You ain't washed away yet?"

"They ain't a hurricane powerful enough yet to blow away this Cajun. What's up with you, Lieutenant?"

"Interesting stuff," he said.

"You got my attention. Like what?"

"I met with the researcher cited in Rance Parker's autopsy report."

"And?"

"What I found out was interesting. You probably won't believe it."

"When you speak, Lieutenant, I listen," Jean Pierre said. "Everybody knows you're the best homicide detective in the Big Easy. Maybe the whole world."

Tony ignored the smoke Jean Pierre was blowing up his butt.

"Doc Frenette had a frozen rougarou locked in a freezer, in his basement. We lost power in the storm while I was there, and it started thawing."

"I enjoy a good story as much as the next person, Lieutenant. Are you makin' this one up as you go along, or lay awake last night thinkin' about it."

"True story," Tony said. "It all worked out. He used a chemical to paralyze the creature until he could start injecting his treatment."

"Shut! You can cure a rougarou?"

"Don't know for sure yet, but it's a definite maybe. He gave me a little something that might help you boys a bunch, just in case you have a close encounter of the rougarou kind."

"What other kind is there?" Jean Pierre asked.

"The worst kind," Tony said.

"You funny, Lieutenant. If my ol' rear wasn't already puckered, I'd be laughin' out loud."

"Sounds like a personal problem to me," Tony said. "Maybe you better talk to your priest."

"You make an appointment, and I'll tag along. I doubt mine would recognize me. What else you got?"

"Frenette gave me a six-shooter that'll stop a rougarou in its tracks. Problem is you have to be close enough to touch him."

"Sounds too damn close if you ask me." Jean Pierre said. "Where you supposed to shoot 'em, anyway?"

"In their neck or stomach. Whatever's the softest."

"Don't want to get that close."

"You may have no choice. If you do, this pop gun might save your ass."

"The voodoo woman's son has shotgun shells that'll stop a rougarou, at least a while. We just need to get hold of a few."

"You think you can?"

"Don't know."

"Where you at, anyway?"

"Headin' north to Chalmette. Wyatt and me are escorting the Professor and that pretty young assistant of his. They're evacuating."

"Yeah, them and half the city already. Problem is gettin' the other half to budge."

"Hell, I'm surprised you ain't in Shreveport. What's up?"

"I got recruited."

"To do what?"

"Play nursemaid to a city I don't work for anymore."

"You confusin' me Lieutenant. Wyatt and me are goin' back to the island soon as we accompany Professor Quinn and Sierra to Chalmette. Where can we meet up and get that rougarou pistol from you?"

"I'm kinda busy right now. We can probably take a break in an hour or so. You know where Elysian Fields and St. Claude intersect?"

"I got more memories from around there than you can imagine," Jean Pierre said.

"Oh I can imagine, knowing you. Meet me there in about an hour. If we're running late, wait on us. We'll get there quick as we can."

❧

When the two vehicles reached Chalmette, Professor Quinn pulled into a shopping center that had a covered parking lot. The garage, like the rest of the town, was deserted. We exited Jean Pierre's truck to say our adieus. Sierra and the professor were arguing as they got out of the Jeep. When Jean Pierre started toward them to mediate, I grabbed his arm.

"They'll work it out."

The wind had increased since we'd left Goose Island. As the two continued their animated argument, it gusted through the openings in the garage.

"I've decided to stay," she said.

"And what do you mean by that, young lady?"

"The island is my home now. I can't go."

Quinn raked stubby fingers through his thinning hair, looking at me for support.

"Help me on this, Wyatt. She listens to you."

"The Professor is right, Sierra. Goose Island will still be there after the storm. No good will come of staying behind."

"You're staying," she said.

"I have a reason."

"Well so do I. I need to be there for Landry, Mama Malaika, and their people."

"You just met Landry. Your relationship can't be that important."

I said the wrong thing, and Sierra began to cry. "Who are you to make that decision for me? Landry is an important part of my life. With Mom and Dempsey gone, I can't afford to lose anyone else."

Despite looking like a wrestling bear, Professor Quinn also had a tear in his eye.

"Well, you're important to me. You're the best assistant I've ever had. Chuckie and King Tut both adore you. I know it's selfish, but I don't think I can handle losing you."

Sierra put her arms around his neck. "I have to do this and I need your support."

"Sierra. . ."

"Please?"

Professor Quinn pushed her away, turning his back to her. "Okay," he said. "But if you get yourself killed, I'm never going to speak to you again."

Thunder pealed through the deserted parking garage as she and the Professor embraced, Sierra sobbing and the old man trying hard not to. Jean Pierre and I watched, mesmerized by the scene.

"Are you two finished yet?" I asked.

"Even though I don't like it one little bit, I'm not the kind of person that always has to impose his will on everyone else," Quinn said.

Though Sierra's arms were locked across her chest, she was smiling when she said, "Like hell!"

"Which way you goin', Professor," Jean Pierre asked.

"North to Jackson, Mississippi. I have friends there, and we should be protected from the weather by then."

Sierra followed him to the Jeep, hugging Chuckie and petting King Tut before shutting the door.

"Be safe you old coot. I'd die if anything ever happened to you, Chuckie, or King Tut."

Quinn gave her another hug.

"You protect her, Wyatt."

"I'll do my best," I said as he drove away, into the storm.

Sierra grabbed Jean Pierre's hand. "Can I go to the island with you?"

"To Hell and back if you ask me," he said.

She grinned. "Let's hope that's not where we're heading."

"We got to go to the city and pick something up first. You okay with that?"

"I'm just one of the boys," she said. "Wish I had a beer."

"They's an ice chest behind you. Reach back and get us both one. You, Wyatt?"

"Not unless you have lemonade," I said.

"Sorry, bro. Guess you gonna have to go thirsty."

We were soon heading north, through the Lower 9th Ward, a part of New Orleans devastated by Katrina. There were no lights anywhere. Not even at the newly built, all night convenience store. Jean Pierre and Sierra were drinking beer as the truck sloshed through rising water. We passed house after shuttered house, making it seem as if everyone had boarded up and headed north. I decided to call Bertram.

"Bertram, it's me, Wyatt."

"You got a cell phone now? The world must be comin' to an end. Where you at?"

"St. Claude, on our way into town. What about you?"

"I boarded up the bar. Me and Miss Lady are on our way to Houston."

"Oh my God! It is the big one. You never left town, even during Katrina. What's come over you?"

"Got a cousin that lives just outside of Katy, Texas. She thought this might be a good time to have a family reunion. My brother's, and all my relatives are headin' that way. What about you and Miss Kisses?"

"Too much to tell you over the phone. Be safe, my friend."

"You ain't staying, are you?"

"I'll be fine," I said as I signed off.

We soon reached the intersection of Elysian Fields and St. Claude. Tony wasn't there, so we parked the car on the side of the road and waited. An hour passed before a New Orleans police car, blue light flashing, came to a halt in front of us. Tony and Tommy Blackburn quickly exited and rushed to the truck, joining Sierra in the back seat of the extended cab. Tony was carrying a dog. Sierra quickly grabbed it, cuddling it to her chest.

"He's so cute. What's his name?"

The young dog wagged his tail and buried his nose into her chest.

"Don't have a name just yet," Tony said.

"What kind is he?"

Tony gave Tommy a dirty look when he said, "Pit bull."

"Don't worry. He's a mix, not pure blood anything. The little fella hasn't done anything except wag his tail and lick my face since we found him."

"He's precious," she said. "I'm Sierra."

"Tony, and this is my partner Tommy."

"How you doing?" Tommy said. "Tony rescued the dog, and they ain't been ten feet apart since."

"You're looking good, Tommy. How are you doing?" I asked.

"Except for the ugly zigzag on my belly, about as good as I ever was."

"Tommy, this is Jean Pierre. Sierra, this is my new business partner Tony."

"Glad to meet you, Sierra," Tony said. "You need to stay in the back seat, away from the one driving. He'd come on to an alligator."

Everyone laughed when Jean Pierre said, "Hey, don't talk about my ex-girlfriend that way."

Tony handed a black bag to Jean Pierre, and he unzipped it to take a look.

"It's a rougarou pistol. Just press it against bare skin, if you can find any, and pull the trigger."

"What the hell's it got in it?"

"Some chemical synthesized from Wolfsbane. I seen it work, and it's powerful. Just don't poke yourself with it."

"What if I do?"

"You won't have time to stick your head between your legs and kiss your ass goodbye. You'll be long gone before then."

"Don't seem like much." Jean Pierre said.

"The drug will knock out an elephant, or a rougarou, for about twenty four hours. You got my personal guarantee. After that, you need to get them to Dr. Frenette's house in the Garden District so he can start the cure."

"What if it takes longer than twenty four hours?" I asked.

"There's another loaded rotator in the bag. Good for a second round of shots. If it takes more than that, you are on your own."

"Now tell us why you aren't on your way to Shreveport," Jean Pierre said.

"Tommy here waylaid me. We're out rescuing kids, dogs, and little old ladies."

"What's Lil think about it?" I asked.

"I was hoping our marriage was on the mend. Now I'm sure it's back to where it was last week. Thanks, Tommy."

"If we survive this, I'll go talk to her for you. She makes the best meatloaf, and red beans and rice in New Orleans. I don't want you to lose her either."

"Wish I could help you boys with the rougarous, but me and Tommy got doors to knock on, and more people to rescue. We better get back to it."

"When will you be finished?" Sierra asked.

"When we drop," Tommy said.

"Good luck," Sierra said, handing Tony the dog.

"To all of us," he replied as they rushed into the rain.

Chapter Thirty

The storm had intensified as Jean Pierre, Sierra, and I turned south, toward Chalmette. The northern edge of the hurricane had reached the southern coast of Louisiana. Professor Quinn's prediction of a storm surge had begun, water already standing six inches deep in the streets. Jean Pierre slowed when we reached Chalmette.

"I gotta stop at the station and talk with the Chief."

We found the station nearly deserted, electricity non-existent, like much of the southern part of the state. A few dim lights, powered by an auxiliary generator greeted us when we entered. A man in a police uniform, cell phone to his ear was the only person there.

"Chief Comier, this is Wyatt and Sierra. What's up?"

Comier's black hair was thin. He had a little mustache and a frown that looked affixed to his face with a marker.

"You know damn well what's up," Comier said. "You got me some answers yet about the killings on Goose Island?"

"Murder, Chief."

"Got a suspect yet?"

"Better than that. We pretty much know what did it."

"Not what, who." Comier said.

"I don't think you want to hear this."

"No, but tell me anyway."

"The killer's a rougarou."

Comier's expression remained unchanged. "You flipped your lid, or what?"

"Wyatt here's a private investigator who's been workin' the case. Tell him, Wyatt."

"I didn't believe it either, Chief Comier. Doesn't matter because it's a fact. There are at least two rougarous on Goose Island."

"Soon to be more if we don't do somethin' about it P.D.Q." Jean Pierre added.

"Now look, you two. I didn't just fall off a turnip truck, and I'm not exactly in the mood right now to have my leg pulled."

"You're gonna have to trust me on this one, Chief. If you can free me up from evacuation duty, I think I can take care of this."

"Except for a few skeleton crews at the refineries, everyone else has left town. I got Samson and Pratt still scouring the neighborhoods, but their jobs are pretty much done. Everything else is buttoned down. I'm stickin' around. I'm not asking my men to stay. More power to you if you wanna leave town."

"Got no place to go," Jean Pierre said. "I'm here for you. Tell me what to do."

"If you're hell bent on gettin' back down to Goose Island, I'm not gonna stop you. Just be careful."

"That's what I wanted to hear. I'm gonna need a shotgun and one of the police boats."

Sheriff Comier threw him the keys to the gun room, and Jean Pierre quickly returned with a shotgun.

"Don't get yourself killed, Jean Pierre. You're the best detective I got," Comier said as we walked out the door.

Jean Pierre drove the truck to the back of the station. When he punched a button on the truck's visor, the gate to the chain link fence began to open. He backed beneath a covering to a boat on a trailer.

"Just take a minute to hook to my bumper. One person can do it. No need all of us gettin' drenched."

Broken limbs banged against the truck as we left the station, pulling the boat behind us on our way to Jean Pierre's. He parked on the empty street in front of a little wood-framed house.

"Need help?" I asked.

"Come on, if you don't mind gettin' a little wet. In case Chalmette floods again, and it looks as if it's gonna, I'm bringin' my dog with us."

We followed him out of the truck, onto the small covered porch. His chocolate Lab was waiting at the door, apparently happy to see him.

"I gotta get him somethin' to eat," he said.

Finding a can of dog food beneath a kitchen cabinet, he dumped it in a food bowl. The big dog ate it quickly, his wagging tail never stopping. Jean Pierre spent a few quality moments giving his head and ears a rub.

"Anyone need to use the bathroom?" he said. "We might not get another chance for a while."

Jean Pierre's house was small but neat. There was only one picture on the wall.

"My mama," he said when Sierra asked. "If everyone's ready, we need to get on the road."

He smiled when I said, "Or in the water, whatever the case may be."

We made a run for Jean Pierre's truck and were soon heading south toward Goose Island.

"What a beautiful dog," Sierra said when he leaped over the console and joined her on the rear seat.

Jean Pierre threw her a large towel." Sorry, Miss Sierra. Hope he don't lick you to death."

Sierra was busy hugging the big dog who was obviously happy to be with people for a change.

"What's your name?"

"He's Lucky, a blockhead Labrador retriever. More of the English variety than the hunting dogs you usually see around here. He weighs well over a hundred pounds and isn't much of a hunter."

"Lucky, you're gorgeous," she said, her arms never leaving his thick neck. "I think you're even bigger than

Chuckie."

"He's an intimidating dog," Jean Pierre said.

"Now what?" I asked.

"Head back to Goose Island. Go as far as we can until the flooding stops us. We'll have to take the boat from there. It's fast, though mainly built for water at least five feet deep. Might get kinda shallow so we'll have to keep our fingers crossed on that one."

We finally made it to Delacroix. All the lights in town were off, not even our elevated restaurant open as we drove slowly through the narrow town. The road dipped toward the Gulf of Mexico. It was soon covered with so much water we couldn't continue in the truck. Jean Pierre pulled to the side of the road.

"Water's too deep to go any farther, but too shallow to launch the boat, at least here."

"What then?" I asked.

"They's a boat ramp close by. Even if it's underwater, we should still be able to launch from there."

Heavy wind whipped the front end of the Chevy truck as Jean Pierre backed down the boat ramp.

"I'll guide you," I said.

Pouring rain quickly drenched me, but not before I was able to direct Jean Pierre and the police boat into the water. The hull of the boat was eighteen feet in length. Powered by a big Yamaha motor, it had a top that Jean Pierre quickly raised.

"You and Lucky gonna get wet, Miss Sierra," he said. "They ain't no other way of doin' it. You game?"

Sierra didn't answer, racing out of the truck with Lucky and quickly climbing into the covered part of the boat. Grabbing our bags and the shotgun, we ran to join them. Sheltered by plastic from the downpour, Jean Pierre cranked the engine and then piloted us away from the road.

"This thing has a G.P.S. and a depth finder. Don't matter none cause it won't stop us from runnin' into a tree," he said.

"No hurry," I said. "The island's not going anyplace.

We have all night."

"You wrong about that, bro. The hurricane's almost on us. If we don't make it to dry land in the next hour or two, our butts won't be worth mincemeat out here in the storm."

Jean Pierre sat in the elevated driver's seat, navigating by the dim, green light of the dash and the G.P.S. I was sitting beside him, Sierra and Lucky on a bench in front of the outboard motor. Driving rain pounded the plastic roof above us.

Jean Pierre followed a narrow path through the trees and brush, high winds and flying debris rendering the boat's running lights of little assistance. A tree falling in our path almost halted our progress.

"We're never going to get there," Sierra said, her arms still around Lucky's neck. "Can't we go faster?"

"We got some protection from the wind here in the trees. We'll capsize if we try to run out there in open water," Jean Pierre said. "Hell, it's gettin' kinda iffy even here."

By now, the wind had picked up, batting the boat like a cork. The noise of the storm had grown so loud, we had to shout to hear each other. When a branch came hurtling through the air, Jean Pierre raised his arm, just in case the projectile penetrated the thin plastic cover protecting us.

"We must be near the frontal edge of the hurricane. Those gusts have to be over a hundred miles an hour."

As I spoke, another blast of air slammed us into a large tree, killing the motor. We whirled in circles as Jean Pierre made his way to the rear of the boat, pivoting the motor out of the water to take a look as I shined the flashlight for him.

"Prop's broke. We screwed," he said.

"What'll we do?" Sierra asked.

"Gotta get to shore. We sittin' ducks out here in this thing."

Finding a couple of paddles under the seats, I tossed him one. Rain pelted us as we tried to paddle the boat to the place where we'd hit the tree. Instead, the wind continued blowing us precariously close to the clearing. Without the motor, we were powerless against the wrath of the approaching hurricane.

"We gonna have to jump out," Jean Pierre shouted. "Swim to that little spot stickin' up outa the water. If we don't, we gonna get turned over in this wind."

Caught in a violent gust, the plastic roof broke loose from its connections and blew away. Trapped in a wind-generated eddy, the boat began rotating, slowly at first and then faster. When Jean Pierre tried to catch a branch to slow us, it nailed him, knocking him into the water. Lucky jumped in after him.

Sierra and I were holding on as the spinning boat finally popped out of the eddy, breaking free of the trees, into the clearing where the wind was even stronger. Propelled by high winds in front of the hurricane, we began racing forward at a rapid pace. When the bow came out of the water, the wind lifted it like a wing.

For a long moment, the boat twirled through the air like a plane in free fall. When the front end slammed into the water, it jarred my grip loose. It was the last thing I remembered for a while.

ᏩᏌᎠᏍᏦ

After losing sight of Wyatt, Sierra had no idea what had happened to him. Having grown up in California, she was a strong swimmer. It mattered little as she swam for her life amid the ferocity of a major hurricane. Whenever she thought she was making progress, gusting wind would blow her back into open water.

Animals, caught in the same situation, began floating past her—an alligator, a deer, and a feral hog. When the dense body of a snake bounced off her arm, she almost panicked. She needn't have worried, the serpent more concerned with finding shelter than biting her.

By staying afloat and riding the current, she finally felt solid ground beneath her feet. Slipping on the wet shore, she fell face first into the mud before clawing her way to a broken tree lying prone across her path. As she sprawled in the mire, she saw something. The flickering light coming from Landry's deserted village beckoned in the distance.

"Wyatt," she called.

When no one answered, she called again, and then again. Not knowing what else to do, she finally pulled herself out of the mire and started toward the light flickering in the distance.

She followed a tree line toward the village. It helped her stay out of the water, at least above her ankles. It didn't matter because she was drenched, her soaked clothes feeling like leaden weights on her body as she bent against the strong wind blowing in from the Gulf.

The rain, by now, was falling in nonstop sheets. Driven by the wind, it pelted her face as she slogged toward the single light shining in the village. An extra strong gust blew her off her feet, and she struggled to regain her footing in the mud.

As she neared Mama Malaika's shack, the plaintive howl of a wolf, audible even over the screaming wind, stopped her dead in her tracks.

Chapter Thirty One

Jean Pierre was out of it when Lucky jumped from the boat and latched on to the sleeve of his shirt. The big, chocolate dog dragged him to high ground, near the tree they'd hit. Lucky was licking his face when he opened his eyes.

"Hey, big boy. What the hell happened?"

Jean Pierre glanced around. Sheltered by the branches of a large tree, he wasn't aware of the rain that continued to fall, or the wind contorting the tree trunks around them. Lucky was the first to hear something approaching through the underbrush. Crouching, he bared his fangs and began to growl.

"What's up, big un? Something out there?"

Jean Pierre soon saw what it was. Landry and Jomo appeared through the gloom, their two black-mouthed curs tugging on their chains.

"That you, Landry?" Jean Pierre asked.

"How you know my name?" Landry said.

"Sierra told me about you, and I recognize the shotgun. We were together in a boat, on our way to your camp when we had a little accident. I got knocked out of the boat, and Lucky here jumped in and rescued me. I hope they ain't in the Gulf."

Lucky was touching noses with one of Landry's dogs. They were large, but he was bigger. One of the black mouth curs began wagging its tail.

"Sierra is with Mama Malaika."

As his conversation with Landry progressed, Jean Pierre's Cajun accent became more pronounced than ever.

"How you know that?" he demanded.

"I got the touch," Landry said.

Landry grinned when Jean Pierre said, "Touch my ass. What about Wyatt, if you know so much?"

"He ain't okay, but he not dead yet, either."

"Guess that's a good thing. And your village? Your people okay?"

Landry nodded. "Mama Malaika sent us to higher ground."

"That's good. You got rougarou rounds for that shotgun under your arm?"

"What you know about rougarous?"

"I know we got at least one on Goose Island."

"My shells can stop a rougarou," Landry said. "But not for long."

"What are you doin' out here?"

"Told you, I got the touch," Landry said. "I come lookin' for you. We gonna need your help, and somethin' tol' me you needed mine."

"Somethin' told you right," Jean Pierre said. "Can you take me to the monastery?"

"If you got somethin' to kill rougarous with."

"Can't kill them, but I got somethin' that'll slow them down for more than a few minutes."

Jean Pierre patted the black case attached to his belt to assure himself it was still there. He pulled the instrument out and showed Landry.

"What is it?" Landry asked.

"A rougarou pistol."

"My ass!"

"I ain't kiddin'."

"It work?"

"Never tried it, but a friend I trust say it do."

"And if it don't?" Landry asked.

Jean Pierre grinned and said, "How fast can you

267

run?"

"Not fast enough," Landry said. "Who you are, anyway?"

"Jean Pierre Saucier. What's your last name, Landry?"

"Don' know my last name."

"How old are you?"

"Twenty," Landry said.

"Hell, you probably my son. Who's your mama?"

"Don' know. Mama Malaika raised me and Jomo. What I do know is you ain't my daddy."

"And how you know that?"

"Cause you ain't old enough."

"I'm almost forty. Old enough and then some. I been around these swamps a long time now."

"Maybe, but you still ain't my daddy."

"Don't be too sure," Jean Pierre said. "We got the same blue eyes. Ain't many Cajuns with blue eyes."

"You look way too soft to be my daddy. He was tough as nails."

"Watch out, now! I can whip your ass any ol' day."

Landry laughed. "Yeah, and probably have a heart attack doin' it."

Jean Pierre grinned and let the remark drop. "What's the story on Jomo? He seem like he lookin' at two places at the same time."

"Jomo a zombie."

Landry grinned when Jean Pierre said, "Get outa here. Ain't no damn zombies."

"Shut, you don' know much as you tink you do."

"Don't matter none anyway. You look like you can handle that shotgun and that's all that matters tonight. I had a shotgun. I lost it when I fell overboard."

"You mean this one?" Landry said, grabbing something from the shadows and tossing it to him.

"Hey, where'd you find it?"

"Bout ten feet from where you sittin' right now. Mighty fancy gun. Won't do you much good less you got some of my special shells."

"You got extras?"

Landry had a bulging bag strapped under his arm. Grabbing a handful from inside it, he began tossing Jean Pierre shells, one by one.

"Automatic," Jean Pierre said. "Just keeps shootin' every time you pull the trigger."

"Mine ain't that fancy. It still work jus' fine."

"Ain't the gun anyway. It's the man pulling the trigger," Jean Pierre said.

Landry grinned. "Got that right. Hope you don' freeze up when you see them rougarous."

"Don't be worryin' about me, bro. How many rougarous we talkin' about here?"

"Don' know. You game to find out?"

"Hey, I'm ready when you are," Jean Pierre said.

"You the one still got your butt in the dirt. If you ain' scared shitless, then let's get it on."

"If you're waitin' on me, you're backin' up."

Landry grinned and shook his head. "Mon, you a talker, that for sure."

"Jomo don't say much, do he?"

"I done tol' you he a zombie. They don' talk, mon."

"You know the way to the monastery?" Jean Pierre said, following after them.

"Hell man, I'm part Indian, half Cajun, with a big dose of African warrior. I can see in the dark and listen on the run. I'm one dangerous mofo."

Jean Pierre laughed. "Hell, they ain't no doubt now. You gotta be my son. Not another swingin' dick in the parish, except me, can brag like you just did."

"Well if you my daddy, get up here with us and quit draggin' you ass like some little ol' lady."

Jean Pierre was grinning when he bounded off the ground. Once out from under the broad branches of the tree, he realized the storm had only increased in intensity. Rain was moving at an oblique angle to the water, the wind strong enough to make walking difficult.

Snakes, fish, and small animals swam past their legs as they slogged through water almost up to their knees. A mocassin, thick as his thigh, bumped against his leg and then swam away. Having other things on his mind, Jean Pierre just kept wading. Their bantering continued until they reached the berm. Landry held a finger to his lips for silence.

"Once we cross over, no more talk unless it real important."

"You the boss, Mr. Landry. Least till we face off with a real live rougarou," Jean Pierre said.

Jomo led the dogs up the stairs that crossed the berm. Lucky was big but usually friendly. He'd taken up with the two dogs on chain leashes, leading the way to the monastery side of the berm. Bringing up the rear, Jean Pierre stopped to take a look around.

A cylindrical cloud filled the southern sky, looking both odd and sinister in the muted flashes of lightning that had become almost constant. Thunder, now, was little more than background noise as Jean Pierre's mind filtered it from his psyche.

Landry and Jomo waited for him on the monastery side of the berm, dense fog snaking around their ankles, even as rain continued to fall. Though there were neither moon nor stars in the sky, dim light radiated from the strange cloud, illuminating the monastery grounds with an eerie glow.

Before climbing down from the berm, Jean Pierre gazed at the distant buildings of the monastery, looking for a light in a window, or some other evidence of life. As he started down the ladder, he saw none.

"Where to now?" he asked.

Landry shook his head. "Never been on this side of the berm. Least not this part."

"Then lets spread out and head for the first bungalow. We'll check 'em out as we go. Strange they ain't no lights."

"Every ting about tonight strange," Landry said as he motioned Jomo to spread out.

Though their ankles were covered with thick ground fog, their feet, unlike on the other side of the berm, were out of the water. Even the dogs sensed the strangeness of the situation and moved forward reluctantly.

Like he'd done so many times as a First Lieutenant during his tour of Iraq, he led Jomo, Landry and the dogs on a controlled sweep across the monastery grounds. Landry, a natural foot-soldier, responded instinctively to his hand signals. He and Jomo covered the back of the first bungalow as Jean Pierre pushed open the front door.

He stared at the rubble strewn across the premises as Landry entered through the back. Broken lamps, dishes, and bed sheets littered the room. Someone or something had smashed everything inside it. A strong clap of thunder shook the bungalow as Jean Pierre signaled Landry to go back out the way he'd come so they could continue their sweep.

Every bungalow they visited was the same, and the dog's had grown anxious as they neared Celebration Fountain. Something was hiding in the darkness. They all knew it when Lucky suddenly went on point. As he advanced toward a wavering shadow behind the fountain, Jean Pierre motioned Landry and Jomo to hold their positions.

"Come out or I'll shoot," Jean Pierre said.

He only had to wait a bit until the minuscule monk, Brother Bruce, appeared from the shadows, his hands over his head.

"It's me, Sheriff. Brother Bruce."

Jean Pierre wasn't the sheriff, but he didn't bother correcting him.

"What the hell you doin' out here?" he demanded.

"You're not one of them, are you?"

"One of who?"

"Those creatures," Brother Bruce said.

Jean Pierre motioned Landry and Jomo to join them.

"We ain't creatures. We creature hunters. We're here to help. You the only one left on the island?"

Rain pelted them, the noise level high. Jean Pierre grabbed Brother Bruce's arm, leading him under the covered pavilion.

"There's about a dozen of us. We need to occupy the

271

capsule, but we can't," Brother Bruce said.

"Why not?" Jean Pierre asked, not bothering to introduce Landry and Jomo.

"The approaching storm. It's caused Father Domenic, Brother Dunwoody, and Brother Bruno to transform. Some of the guests are also affected."

Brother Bruce nodded when Jean Pierre asked, "You know what a rougarou is?"

"Those creatures are horrible, whatever you call them."

"Like I said before, what you doin' out here?"

"Everyone else was too frightened. I came out hoping to find someone to help us."

"Well, here we are," Jean Pierre said. "Now take us to your people and we'll make a plan."

"Thank you," Brother Bruce said, grasping his wrist. "I knew someone would come." When he released his hold, he said, "Follow me."

Brother Bruce led them on a straight path to the back of the monastery and then down a short flight of stairs to a basement door. He knocked, his face close to a peephole.

"I've brought help. Let us in."

The door opened a crack and a little man with a Gallic nose stared out at them. After assuring himself who it was, he let them in.

The room was lit by candles, acrid smoke replacing the cooler air outside the door, though at least the rain and thunder was behind them. Jean Pierre glanced around the dim room at frightened faces staring back at him.

"This is Sheriff Saucier," Brother Bruce said. "He's here to help us."

A woman joined them.

"Sheriff, I'm Lilly Bloom. Everyone's scared to death. So am I, but I'll do everything I can to help."

Jean Pierre smiled when Lilly squeezed his hand. "Ma'am, what can you tell me about those creatures out there?"

"When the storm started moving in, everything got crazy."

"How so?"

Lilly closed her eyes. "Some of the monks and two friends of mine grew fangs and hair."

"Werewolves?" Jean Pierre prompted.

Lilly nodded. "What are we going to do?"

"Is everyone here okay?"

"One of the cooks got mauled, but managed to escape. The creatures don't know where we are."

"They got a sickness," Jean Pierre said. "I got a cure."

Lilly grabbed his wrist. "Then let me help."

Chapter Thirty Two

Sierra's clothes and hair were drenched when she reached the village. One of her shoes was missing, sucked off her foot when she'd stepped in a mud hole. Mama Malaika hugged her as she came sprawling through the door.

"Goodness, child, you look half-drowned. Are you okay?"

"I'm shaking."

Mama Malaika pulled her into the house, stripping off her clothes without asking and then covering her with a blanket. The hurricane was already on shore, the walls and roof heaving like a bellows.

"What happened?" Mama Malaika asked.

"Boat accident. We were trying to reach the monastery." Sierra put her arms around the old woman. "I'm so frightened."

Mama Malaika pushed her toward the fire burning near the center of the room. As Sierra sat in front of the flame, the old woman brought her a cup of herbal tea.

"Drink this. It's Mama's special brew."

Sierra inhaled the fragrant aroma of the hot liquid before taking a sip.

"This is saving my life," she said.

"You're all alone. Were there others with you?"

"Wyatt and Jean Pierre, a parish deputy. We were trying to reach the monastery. Jean Pierre was thrown from the boat before it capsized. I called for Wyatt, but couldn't find him."

Mama Malaika hugged her again, drying her tears with the long sleeve of her dress.

"It's okay. Nothing else you could do. Put this on."

The voodoo woman handed Sierra a colorful, print dress, and she pulled it over her head.

When her tears dried, she said, "I hope they're not dead. Why are you the only one in the village?"

"Spirits. They instructed me to send my people to another place."

"You didn't go with them." Sierra said.

"I'm waiting for something. Perhaps it was you."

Wind whistled through the room, rattling all the objects on the walls and strips of tin covering the roof. A heavy limb banged against the window, followed quickly by another.

"I'm here now. Maybe we should try to reach the monastery, or Landry and your people."

Mama Malaika squeezed Sierra's wrist. "You may be right. Come my child. Let's pray at the altar. Pray to whichever god you believe in, but help me."

Mama Malaika and Sierra knelt in front of the Vodoun altar, candles burning atop the gaping skull. Mama prostrated herself and began speaking in an African dialect, Sierra just praying beneath her breath like her mother had taught her as a child.

Even without electricity, the room had seemed vibrant and filled with light. As they knelt, the candle dimmed, and then flickered out. Mama's hand went to her mouth when the wax dripping from the candle changed to the color of blood.

"What does it mean?" Sierra asked.

"Not good. Agwe has forsaken us. We are powerless against the storm.

"But why?"

"I don't know," Mama Malaika said. "We must find another way."

The old woman turned from the altar, retrieving a

cloth bag from her shelf from which she extracted a handful of animal bones. After tossing them on the floor, she studied them a moment before scooping them up and tossing them again. Finally, she returned them to the bag.

"The bones are giving me no answers tonight. Child, you must help me."

"Tell me what to do," Sierra said, grasping Mama Malaika's wrist."

Another heavy branch crashed into the side of the house, followed by a wind gust that momentarily lifted the tin roof. The single candle flickered, but did not die.

"Get me the jar of ocher powder on the shelf," Mama Malaika said.

"This one?" Sierra said, standing on her tiptoes.

"Yes. Bring it to me, and hurry."

By the fire's dying embers, the old woman began drawing a voodoo vever on the floor, chanting in an African dialect as she did. When the vever was drawn, she closed her eyes.

"I have no answer. We may be doomed."

There has to be something else," Sierra said.

"Sometimes there is no answer," Mama Malaika said, touching her cheek.

"I don't believe it and neither do you."

"There is one more thing."

The old woman went to her medicine bottles, returning with a handful of grayish powder. She held a candle to the powder until a golden flame burned in her palm. When she snuffed it, thin smoke rose up from her cupped hands, and she began blowing it into Sierra's nostrils.

When she clapped her hands, an explosion rocked the room. Sierra's eyes changed from blue to red, then rolled to the back of her head. When Mama Malaika tapped her forehead, she fell backwards to the floor, lying there, her eyes closed and arms outstretched. Quite suddenly, she began speaking in a throaty voice.

"Agwe will soon destroy the village. You must not

stay here," she said.

"We have no way to leave." Mama Malaika said.

"Damballa has sent someone, but he won't appear until the Devil visits. You must prepare."

Sierra was groaning and holding her head when she finally opened her eyes.

Mama smiled when she said, "Did someone kick me in the head?"

"You told me what we need to know."

"I did?" Sierra said, rubbing her head. "I don't remember anything."

"Damballa, the supreme being is sending someone to take us to safety," Mama Malaika said.

"Who?"

"I don't know. I do know we have another problem. The rougarou is out there, and will visit us before we are able to leave. I have something that might protect us."

As Sierra watched, the old woman pulled a dagger from a shelf and handed it to her.

"Why do I need this?"

"It's coated with Wolfsbane. When the rougarou comes near, you must stab him in the heart. It's important, child. In the heart, or you won't kill him. Understand?"

"You're scaring me."

"You can't kill the demon, but you can kill his earthly body if you pierce his heart with the dagger."

Mama Malaika's words brought Sierra once again to tears. "Now I'm really afraid."

"Be brave, girl. Damballa is with us. He doesn't protect cowards."

"I'm not a coward, but I'm frightened."

Sierra screamed when someone pushed through the door. The being spoke in a voice that sounded straight from hell.

"You should be frightened because you are about to die a horrible death."

A hideous creature stood at the door, its mouth open and saliva dripping from its fangs. Sierra clutched Mama

Malaika's arm, and they backed away until they touched the wall.

"Oh Mama, what is that thing?"

"It's the rougarou."

Having begun its transformation, the creature was no longer a person, or quite yet a beast. Still, it had the eyes of a demon that flashed in the light of the muted candle.

"Who are you?" Sierra demanded, regaining her courage.

The creature answered in a voice as deep and hollow as an empty grave.

"You know me. I'm Brother Bruno."

"Then why are you here and not at the monastery?"

"You ask too many questions for someone about to die."

Bruno's face was half transformed. Long canine teeth protruded from his mouth. Coarse hair had begun sprouting from his face. His eyes were blood red. He turned when thunder shook the roof and Wyatt stumbled through the door. Not noticing the creature behind him, he smiled when he saw Sierra and Mama Malaika.

"Wyatt, behind you!" Sierra called out.

As Wyatt wheeled around, the beast's transformation accelerated. The creature that had been a large man grew even larger, causing his clothes to tear from his body as his chest, shoulders and hips expanded at an eye popping rate, his human facial features morphing into the long snout and sharp fangs of a wolf creature. With claws like knives, he serrated the African-print curtain covering the entrance.

"Wyatt!" Sierra called, tossing him the dagger. "His heart. Stab him through the heart."

Wyatt grabbed the dagger, pivoting as the creature's claws raked nasty cuts across his back. As he smelled its foul breath wafting in the damp air, he didn't hesitate, plunging the dagger into its chest. Though he'd missed the heart, the Wolfsbane dropped him to his knees.

"Hurry," Wyatt said, motioning Sierra and Mama

Malaika to follow him out the door.

The wind howled as they burst through the opening, driving rain drenching them in an instant. Wyatt followed the two women, none of them looking back.

Grabbing the knife, the fully transformed rougarou ripped it from his chest, his face contorted into an ugly snarl. Rising to his feet, he followed them into the storm.

Wyatt pushed Sierra and Mama Malaika around the house. "He only wants me. Hide and don't come out."

When the rougarou exited the door, Wyatt already had a head start. Not wanting him to discover Sierra and Mama Malaika's hiding place, he stopped and called to him.

"Hey you sorry sack of shit! I'm here. Come get me."

Waiting until he was sure the creature was following him, he sloshed through water above his ankles, the plaintive howl of the unearthly creature behind him the only motivation he needed.

❧

Sierra and Mama Malaika crouched in the darkness behind her house, both afraid to move.

"That monster's going to kill Wyatt," Sierra finally said.

"Nothing we can do about it. His fate is ordained."

"I feel so helpless."

Shingles, boxes, and objects of every ilk flew through the air, sounding like gunshots when they struck the house.

The noise was deafening when Mama Malaika said, "I hear something."

Sierra would have laughed if she weren't already crying. "The hurricane."

"No, something else. Can't you hear it?"

For a moment, Sierra heard nothing but the howling of the wind. Then something else. The throaty roar of a five-hundred horsepower airboat. Breaking free from Mama Malaika's grasp, she peered around the corner of the house.

"Oh my God, it's Professor Quinn!"

Grabbing Mama Malaika's arm, she pulled her into the clearing in front of the house. Quinn saw them as they waded toward him. Jumping from the boat, he helped them in.

"What are you doing here?" Sierra shouted above the wind.

"No time. The surge is coming ashore. We have to get to the monastery before it reaches us."

With Sierra and Mama Malaika lying prone on the floor of the boat, Professor Quinn performed a turn under full power, and then raced ahead toward the distant monastery.

The airboat's engine was powerful enough to propel it across dry land. In six inches of water, it was capable of speeds up to sixty miles per hour. The professor had the engine at its limit as he powered toward the monastery near the center of the island. Halfway there, they saw the rougarou. It wasn't far behind Wyatt.

"Hold on to your hats," he said, turning the boat and powering straight toward the beast.

Hitting him full speed, though a glancing blow, the contact sent the creature plummeting backwards, into a spray of mud and water.

"Stop for Wyatt," Sierra yelled as they raced past him.

"Too much weight already, and we're filling with water from the rain. If he tipped us getting in, we'd sink. I'll come back for him. No time to find the berm bridge. You'll have to crawl over."

They reached the berm at almost the same time as the frontal edge of the hurricane, the boat's hull banging against the concrete wall as Quinn helped Sierra and Mama Malaika climb to the top.

"Please be careful!" Sierra screamed before dropping to the other side.

An ephemeral glow lighted the manicured expanse of the monastery. A man in a robe was hurrying toward them. It was Brother Bruce.

"Hurry," he said. "We were just getting ready to close

the capsule doors."

"No," Sierra said. "Wyatt and the Professor are still out there."

"We can't wait," he said, hurrying them toward the pod.

Chapter Thirty Three

Most of the people hiding in the darkened basement continued cowering in the corners, Jomo and the dogs providing little solace for their fear. Jean Pierre's uniform was drenched, his Stetson probably on its way to the Gulf by now. The small group still seemed relieved when he stopped to shake their hands.

"Hey, I know this ain't where you folks would rather spend your Friday night. Don't worry none. The St. Bernard Sheriff's department is on it. We'll have you all safe in the hurricane pod before you know it."

A mousy woman on the verge of tears touched Jean Pierre's wrist.

"What about the werewolves?"

The little dark-eyed chef also had questions. "We gonna make it outa here alive?"

"You gotta help us, Sheriff," a maintenance man, still in his work clothes said.

"You got my word on it," Jean Pierre said.

He turned when Landry grabbed his arm. "We ain't got much time."

"Then let's do it. Where was the last place you saw a rougarou?" he asked Brother Bruce.

"The carpentry. I will take you there."

"You don't have a weapon," Jean Pierre said.

"I have God, and he's all I need," he said. "I'm ready."

282

Lilly Bloom came bustling up behind them. "Don't forget me," she said.

"Ma'am, with all due respect. . ."

"Don't you dare try to go without me."

"Ain't nothing but danger out there."

"And I wouldn't miss it for the world," she said.

"But you're. . ."

"Just a woman?" she said, finishing the sentence for him.

"Not what I was gonna say."

"Look, I won't hold you up or get in the way," she said.

Glancing at the pair of cheap flip flops on her feet, he said, "You ain't even got real shoes on. You can't go out like that."

"I had Sunday brunch at Brennan's in these flip flops. If they're good enough for one of the most famous restaurants in the whole damn world, they'll get me anyplace I need to go."

Realizing the futility of arguing with her, he said, "Then let's go."

The little chef locked the door behind them as they went back out into the storm. They moved forward slowly, having trouble walking up the stairs, the rain strong, and wind blistering their faces. Brother Bruce walked point, staying close to the buildings as he led the way to the carpentry. When they reached it, they found it quiet, cut off from the sounds of the storm.

Unfinished coffins lay strewn around the open room lighted only by Jean Pierre's flashlight. The smell of oak and cypress sawdust permeated the humid air. When Lucky growled, Landry stared up into the rafters where boards were stored. Not asking for permission, he suddenly unloaded both barrels of his shotgun at a shadow moving above them.

The blast echoed through the open room as a body tumbled to the ground, hitting the concrete floor with a dull thud. Jean Pierre was on it in a minute, putting Frenette's pistol to the creature's neck and quickly pulling the trigger.

"One down," he said. "Good eyes, Landry. Musta got those from your daddy."

Landry didn't bother smiling as he followed Jomo through the darkness. As they watched, the creature began transforming, soon becoming a naked man curled in the fetal position.

"Who is it?" Jean Pierre asked.

"Quinlan Moore," Lilly said. "Is he dead?"

"Alive, but he'll need the serum to cure his infection."

When Lucky growled again, and something appeared from the shadows, Lilly said, "Don't shoot, it's Stormie."

Though not quite Stormie, it wasn't a rougarou either. At least as yet. As the half woman, half wolf approached them, Jean Pierre didn't wait for confirmation, popping her in the neck with his pistol.

"Why did you do that?" Lilly said. "It's just Stormie. She wouldn't hurt anyone."

"Bull shit! She's infected," he said. "My pistol's just an injection system, and not meant to kill or injure. She'll be okay after she takes the cure."

As they stared at her, Stormie transformed back into a woman, naked as Quinlan Moore.

"Too bad she's knocked out," Lilly said. "If she knew everyone was looking at her right now, she'd be in exhibitionist heaven."

"She got a body on her, all right," Jean Pierre said. "Now what are we gonna do with them? They'll drown if the flood gets over the berm. At least if they can die."

"Put them in coffins," Brother Bruce said.

Jean Pierre gave him a look. "Do what?"

"Help me," he said, grabbing her arms. "I'll show you."

They lifted Stormie's lifeless body into a coffin. With nails in his mouth, Brother Bruce put a cover on it and began pounding it shut.

"Is this thing gonna float?" Jean Pierre asked.

"Trust me," Brother Bruce said. "It'll float, but I need to drill a small hole in the top so she can breathe. Our coffins are airtight."

They quickly lifted Quinlan Moore into a coffin and nailed the top shut. With brace and bit, Brother Bruce drilled an air hole.

"What if it floods and the water gets too high in here?" Jean Pierre asked.

"It won't," Brother Bruce said. "This building has a twenty foot ceiling.

"And if the hurricane blows it down?"

"Then they're in the hands of God," Brother Bruce said.

Until sure there were no more rougarous hiding in the stacks of aromatic lumber they searched the rest of the carpentry.

"What do you think?" Jean Pierre asked.

"Father Domenic's quarters," Brother Bruce said.

They exited the carpentry to a world of eerie silence. The rain and wind were gone, replaced by ground fog that snaked around their ankles as they walked. It's sound muffled by excessive humidity, the cathedral bell sounded far away when it clanged in an errant gust of wind.

Lilly had latched on to Jean Pierre's arm. "What the hell's going on?"

"We're in the eye. Much as I love being near you, pretty woman, you better let me go in case I have to use this thing," he said, glancing at his shotgun.

Lilly released her grip. Jean Pierre motioned Landry and Jomo to spread out. They were both good soldiers. The same could not be said of Brother Bruce. When they reached the passage between two buildings, he rushed into the darkness.

"I think I hear something," he said.

"No, wait!" Jean Pierre called.

Signaling Landry and Jomo, Jean Pierre advanced toward the alley."

"What's the matter?" Lilly asked.

"Could be an ambush. Ain't no exit on the other end, or else we could see through to the other side."

"What are you going to do?"

"Go in after him before he gets killed," he said, motioning Landry and Jomo to hang back.

Jean Pierre moved slowly into the alleyway, his flashlight providing scant illumination. When he reached the dead end, he spotted Brother Bruce picking himself up from the ground. Seeing the light, the little monk raised his arm.

"Go back, it's a trap!"

Jean Pierre spun around, ready to shoot. When the blast of his shotgun echoed from the narrow passage, Landry motioned to Jomo.

"Loose the dogs," he said.

Lucky was already barreling between the buildings, the black mouth curs right behind him. The creature was working over Jean Pierre when the Lab struck it squarely in the back. The two other dogs had joined the fight when Landry and Jomo came up behind.

Jean Pierre was on the ground amid the dogs and the suddenly animated rougarou. The flashlight, along with the shotgun, had flown from his grasp when the creature attacked.

Landry searched for an opening, not firing his weapon for fear of killing Jean Pierre and the dogs.

"Jomo," he called, nodding his head toward the fracas.

Jomo lumbered forward, grabbing the rougarou around the neck. He was powerful, but even with the added strength, he and the dogs were no match for the monstrous rougarou.

When Jean Pierre glanced from under the scrum and caught a glimmer of Landry's blue eyes, the young man slid him the shotgun, hoping it wouldn't get knocked away before it reached him. It skidded across the grass, toward Jean Pierre's outstretched hand. Grabbing the gun, Jean Pierre shoved it into the beast's chest and pulled both triggers.

The rougarou gave Jean Pierre an evil glance before sinking to his knees, and then toppling to the ground.

"Jomo, get the dogs."

It took all of them to raise Brother Dunwoody's body into the coffin. Brother Bruce nailed on the top and drilled an air hole.

"I know you need me to lead you to Father Domenic and Brother Bruno, but I have to prepare the pod and make sure the exhaust pumps are working."

"I'll take them," Lilly said.

"No way," Jean Pierre said. "You go with him."

"You're a sexist pig. You don't want me because I'm a woman."

"A woman with no weapon," he said.

"I won't get in the way, I promise."

"You pretty damn hard-headed, you know that?"

"Please?"

"Hell, why not? I don't have a weapon no more either, come to think of it."

"Thanks," she said.

Turning his attention back to Brother Bruce, he asked, "What do you gotta do to prepare the pod?"

"We have auxiliary generators to power the monastery, and the pod needs power to operate. The generators also power the pumps that will keep this side of the berm from flooding."

"How long you think it'll take to get the power going?" Jean Pierre asked.

"Not more than a half hour, once I get started."

"Then take Jomo and the dogs with you, just in case. Miss Lilly can show us the way to Father Domenic's."

Brother Bruno, Jomo, and the two black mouth curs were barely out of sight when a disturbing howl splintered the silence.

Chapter Thirty Four

The howls were coming from one of the bungalows behind the swimming pool. Jean Pierre gave Lucky a pat on the head, and a nod to Landry and Lilly.

"Showtime," he said. "Let's get it on."

"Take my gun," Landry said.

"One of us is gonna be without a weapon. Might as well be me."

"I got another weapon," he said, pulling a dagger from his belt. "Mama dipped it in her poison. It'll stop him a minute or so, till you can shoot him."

"Now you making me feel guilty," Jean Pierre said as he took the shotgun and bag of shells."

"I already seen you can use a shotgun about as good as me. Ain' nobody can throw a knife as good."

"Hope you don't have to," Jean Pierre said. "Maybe we'll surprise him. Get him without a fight."

Landry grinned. "Yeah, and hell might freeze over tomorrow."

They soon reached the bungalow from where the howls had come.

"That's Wyatt's," Lilly said.

"No need goin' round back. I'll go in first. If he's in there, I'll shoot him. Lilly, you hold on to Lucky's collar."

Lighted by the ephemeral glow coming from the giant cloud, Jean Pierre entered the bungalow, Landry behind him. Once inside, he made his way slowly through the rubble on the floor. Just when he thought there was nothing there, something screeched behind him. He and Landry wheeled around as Lucky came bounding through the door.

"It's Wyatt's cat," Lilly said, following Lucky.

"I damn near had a heart attack," Jean Pierre said.

Lilly grabbed Kisses, cradling the cat to her bosom. "Poor baby."

"Better leave her," Jean Pierre said.

"No way," Lilly said. "She's shaking like a leaf."

"Well you can't take her with us. We huntin' rougarous here."

"Quit trying to be so macho," she said.

Lucky stuck his nose to the cat, his tail wagging in a slow moving arc. When they rubbed noses, Jean Pierre knew he'd lost another argument.

"Okay then, but if you see me and Landry start runnin', you better drop that cat and do the same."

"Fine. What now?"

"Take us to the rectory. We ain't got much time left."

They found the cypress and cut glass doors leading into the administrative offices of the monastery open.

"Kinda dark in here. Too bad we ain't got the flashlight," Landry said.

"I got this," Jean Pierre said, pulling something from his pocket. "My old Zippo I got while I was in the Army. Still works good as new."

"Father Domenic's rectory is the first door at the top of the stairs," Lilly said.

"Give me the Zippo and I'll lead the way," Landry said.

Jean Pierre flipped him the lighter and fell in behind him as they climbed the winding stairway. Halfway up, the cat screeched. Bounding from Lilly's grasp, it took off down the stairs. Lilly followed her.

"Just as well," Jean Pierre said. "They'll be waitin' for us when we get done."

"You ready?" Landry said, his hand on the rectory

door.

"As I'll ever be. Lead on, bro."

Lucky remained at Jean Pierre's side as they climbed the stairs, but wanted to be in the lead. Like the front doors, they found Father Domenic's also open. Before Landry or Jean Pierre saw anything, Lucky began to growl.

Eerie, outside light shined through the picture window. Staring into darkness, Father Domenic stood with his back to them. He was totally naked and spoke without turning around.

"I've been waiting."

Lucky was crouched, his voice a continuous growl.

"Stay, boy," Jean Pierre said.

Jean Pierre advanced in Father Domenic's direction, motioning Landry to stay in place. Father Domenic began closing the blackout curtains and transforming as he did. Jean Pierre halted. It was already too late.

Father Domenic was large, the rougarou he'd quickly transformed into something even larger. Jean Pierre only had time to see his fangs and the red glint in the creature's eyes when it ripped the shotgun from his hands. Then it was on the floor, on top of him.

Lucky rushed into the fray as Landry flicked the Zippo, its flame casting a strobe-like light on the scene of growls, grunts, and mayhem. Jean Pierre was trying desperately to get the pistol out of the bag, the creature smashing it before he had a chance. With the dagger in his other hand, Landry searched for something flammable, finding it in a brandy bottle by the door.

Ripping his tee shirt, he removed the top of the liquor bottle and stuffed the strip of cloth into it. Lighting it, he tossed it at the curtain behind the rougarou. It exploded in a tremendous flash of light and fire. When it did, the creature raised up and glared at him with eyes red as the pits of hell.

"Jean Pierre," he shouted. "Grab Lucky."

Jean Pierre knew in an instant what Landry was about to do. Grabbing Lucky's collar, he yanked him to the floor, just as Landry tossed the dagger.

Landry's aim was true, Mama's poisoned dagger burying itself deep into the rougarou's chest. Grabbing the dagger with both hands, the creature bounded to its feet, turned once before crashing through the picture window, dragging the burning curtain with it.

"Shut, mon. You and Lucky done saved me twice tonight. The pistol's broke, so we better get the hell outa here."

"Don' matter none now. He dead."

"Thought you said you can't kill a rougarou."

"Got him through the heart. He dead."

"You sure about that?"

"Come see."

Jean Pierre and Lucky followed Landry down the stairway, and then outside to where the creature had fallen. Father Domenic was lying there, broken glass and the remnants of the burned curtain still smoldering around him, his eyes open, staring at the strange cloud, both of his hands clutching the dagger buried in his heart.

"Rougarou flambé," Landry said.

Landry laughed when Jean Pierre said, "One French dish I never wanna try."

As Lucky sniffed the body, rain and wind began whipping up, the noise level becoming again intense.

"We comin' outa the eye. Ain't got much time left," Landry said.

"Lilly," Jean Pierre yelled. "Where the hell are you?"

"Maybe she went back to where we foun' the cat," Landry said.

They returned to Wyatt's bungalow. Not finding her, they did a quick recon of the area, continuing to shout her name.

"Now what?"

"She probably already in the pod," Landry said. "Come on. We got no more time."

Putting their faces into the wind, they headed toward the pod, Brother Bruce and Jomo waiting outside for them.

"Did you get them?" Brother Bruce asked.

"We got Father Domenic, but Brother Bruno's still out there somewhere."

When they went inside the pod, they were surprised to see Sierra and Mama Malaika.

"How did you get here?" Landry asked after hugging them both.

"Professor Quinn came in the airboat and rescued us."

"What about Wyatt?" Jean Pierre asked.

"Mama gave him a dagger coated with poison. He stabbed the rougarou but missed his heart. He helped us hide and then lured the beast away when the poison started wearing off."

"Brother Bruno," Jean Pierre said.

"We passed them on our way to the berm. Professor Quinn ran over the monster with the boat. We couldn't stop for Wyatt. He went back to get him after helping us over the berm."

"Shut!" Jean Pierre said.

Landry grabbed Sierra's arm when she said, "I'm going back out there. They need help."

Jean Pierre glanced around the interior of the pod. The little chef and the others were there. He didn't see Lilly.

"Where's Lilly?" he asked.

"We haven't seen her."

"Then open the door," he said.

"You can't go out there," Brother Bruce said.

"Yes I can. Open it."

When Brother Bruce reopened the pod door, Jean Pierre, and Lucky rushed off, into the wind and rain, back toward the monastery. Sierra followed him out the door, standing in the rain, staring at the berm.

"I have to go see," she said.

Landry grabbed her arm. "No amie. No use."

"I can't handle this," she said, hugging Landry.

"I'll go," Brother Bruce said.

"No way. You the only one can control the pod,"

Landry said.

"There's a touch screen on the wall by the door. It will tell you what to do."

"The storm gonna kill you too," Landry said.

"Keep the door open until you see the surge coming over the berm. If we're not back by then, close it without us."

⁌⸜⸝⸌

I was a hundred yards away when I heard the rougarou howl, signaling it had recovered from the stab wound I'd inflicted. I was already tired. Trying to slog through six inches of water didn't help. My only consolation was to understand the creature hadn't stuck around the village long enough to find Sierra and Mama Malaika.

The wind and driving rain was at my back, making running a little easier. It didn't matter because it was also at the creature's back. The eye of the storm had been over the village when I'd reached it. Now, it had returned with a vengeance. It wouldn't be long before the surge began racing in from the Gulf, covering the island with ten to fifteen feet of water. If the rougarou caught up to me before I made it to the pod, it wouldn't matter anyway.

Standing beside the creature in the doorway of Mama Malaika's cabin marked the first time I'd seen a fully-transformed rougarou. Though Father Domenic, Brothers Bruno, and Dunwoody were big, this beast was bigger, not just weight wise, but taller and thicker in width. It made the transformation seem even more supernatural to me.

Out of shape from two drunken weeks at Chrissie's, my legs already ached. Moreover, my mind ached as I trudged forward, feeling as though my worst nightmare had come true. This time, when the creature caught me, I wouldn't awaken in a cold sweat.

As dull thoughts droned through my head, I heard something else in the distance. It wasn't the sound of the storm.

I sensed the creature was gaining on me with every

step. Though I'd purposely not thought of the consequences of having the beast catch me, my subconscious had, sending adrenaline rushing through my veins, numbing me from the exertion of running as fast as I could manage for the two and a half to three miles to the berm.

My head felt disembodied, disconnected from my suddenly senseless body, unable to feel my legs churning through the rising water. I realized I was experiencing what marathoners know as a runner's high. Hearing the rougarou howling behind me, I had no time to savor the experience.

My mind did remind me of the absurdity of the situation: racing in the brunt of a hurricane from a creature intent on ripping me to shreds. As oxygen depleted from my blood, thoughts became like a waking dream, racing from one highlight to the next: the wake of my recently deceased wife Mimsy, the loss of Desire, the one woman I'd thought I truly loved. My cat.

Something else. The depth of the water was increasing rapidly, already up to my knees. It only added to the crazy thoughts flying through my head. When the rougarou caught me, could I swim underwater long enough to get away? Despite fear and exhaustion, I had to smile at the thought of the rougarou trying to free-style like an Olympic swimmer.

The smile faded, replaced by something eating away at my gut and causing my heart to race out of control. It was fear, an emotion with various flavors: fear of failure, fear of rejection, fear of death. The third flavor played on my mind as I could almost feel the creature's hot breath on the back of my neck.

If the water continued rising, I wouldn't have to worry about the claws and fangs of the rougarou rending my flesh into bloody pieces. Water would take me under, and the power of the hurricane would keep me there until my lungs, screaming for oxygen, inhaled briny Gulf water into them. Which death would be worse? I wondered as rain and wind slowed my forward motion, returning me to my recurring nightmare of running, but barely moving as the monster behind me grew ever closer.

The roar of a super-charged engine interrupted my thoughts. Professor Quinn's airboat roared past me, not slowing as it raced ahead toward the berm. Was I dreaming, hallucinating, or was it actually Professor Quinn. I suddenly had the strange feeling the rougarou was no longer directly behind me. It didn't matter because I dared not turn and look.

Minutes passed when I heard the engine again. The hull of the boat appeared through the driving rain. When it reached me, it did a one-eighty, circling around, then bumping me.

"Hurry," Professor Quinn yelled. "And don't sink us."

I'd stopped running, but my legs were still churning, at least mentally as I climbed over the side of the boat, physically unable to pull myself aboard. It was then I saw the approaching rougarou, less than ten feet away. Quinn released the control, dragged me into the boat and then gunned the engine and raced head-on into the creature.

The resultant impact would have killed a human. The rougarou held onto the bow as the professor raced in ever-widening circles, trying to shake it loose. When he hit a submerged tree, he accomplished his mission, but stalled the engine as he did. Unable to move, I was powerless to help.

Professor Quinn apparently knew every wire and spark plug in the boat's engine on an intimate basis. After wriggling a wire, he cranked the engine, and it fired, sputtering in the rain before coming to life, though not fast enough to prevent the rougarou from grabbing the boat and managing to throw one leg over the side. Summoning strength I didn't know I possessed, I grabbed an oar and began beating the creature with it.

Professor Quinn raced off at full speed, scraping the rougarou loose against a tree. Free of the creature, he turned toward the berm.

"Look behind you," I yelled. A wall of water was coming up behind us though it hadn't yet overtaken the rougarou. "We'll never get over the wall before the wave reaches us."

"Then hold on to your hat," he said.

Quinn whipped the boat around, flying past the rougarou and heading straight for the approaching wave. Since I had no hat to hold, I grasped the support bars instead. Just when I thought we would be swamped, he turned the boat, feathering the throttle for just a bit until we crested the top of the wave like a giant surfboard. By now, I was sitting up in the boat, not believing what was happening. The airboat was fast, the wave faster, carrying us on a collision course toward the berm.

"Don't let go," he yelled.

He needn't have wasted his breath. I was hanging on with both hands and would gladly have used my toes if I'd possessed that particular talent. The rougarou was climbing the wall when the wave and our boat reached it.

My heart went into my throat as we sailed up and over the berm, sliding sideways when we hit the ground with a jaw-slamming thud. Professor Quinn somehow managed to hang on to the controls, quickly pointing the boat toward the pod. It was then I saw Brother Bruce standing almost directly in our path.

"One shot, Mr. Thomas," he yelled as he barreled toward the wide-eyed monk.

Turning at the last split second, he came close enough that I was able to grasp the little man, hold on for dear life, and then wrestle him into the boat. We looked up to see the open door of the pod, Sierra and Landry standing in the rain and wind, yelling and waving for all they were worth. Behind us, the wave had crested the berm. Though the wall had slowed it some, it was now barreling toward us at rifle speed.

"This boat doesn't have brakes," Quinn yelled. "When I turn this baby, bail out."

Brother Bruce was praying frantically, and I was trying to keep from covering my eyes.

"Tell us when," I yelled.

Killing the engine, he turned the controls, putting us

on an arcing slide in front of the pod.

"Now!" he yelled.

The three of us shot out of the boat, sliding across the wet ground. We stopped almost directly in front of the pod's open door. By now, half the occupants were in the doorway. Almost as one, they rushed out, grabbing us and pulling us bodily into the protective pod.

The steel door shut with a mechanical thud, seconds before the surge swept over us. I wanted only to close my eyes and wait until my heart slowed. I didn't have the opportunity as everyone in the pod, led by Sierra, piled onto us.

For the next few minutes, the noise level inside the pod continued, higher than it was outside.

Chapter Thirty Five

When Jean Pierre realized Lilly wasn't in the survival pod, he headed back to the monastery to look for her, Lucky on his heels. Water had started pooling on the monastery grounds, and they sloshed through it as they hurried toward the main complex. As they reached the old cathedral, Jean Pierre saw a swirling light emanating from its large, stained glass window.

"This way, boy," he said, shielding his eyes from the rain as he ran around the building.

Lucky didn't wait for him, bounding up the short flight of stairs. The wooden doors were ajar when Jean Pierre, wondering why his dog hadn't entered the building, reached them. When he stepped out of the rain, he realized why.

The center aisle led to an ornate altar. The spacious building was awash in an eerie blue light that almost seemed alive, moving as if electrically charged. Like the outside window, stained glass bordering the rows of wooden pews also emanated ghostly light.

Shadows of people were proceeding through stations of the cross. Somewhere near the altar an organ accompanied the sound of chanting. Seven monks, their heads covered by cowls, were kneeling in front of the altar. Jean Pierre glanced around when Lucky put his nose into the soft spot behind his knee. Putting his hand on the dog's head, he softly rubbed an ear to calm him.

"Hello," he said.

The chant, some ancient hymn Jean Pierre had never heard, continued. He wanted to step backward, but found himself unable to move, resigned to watching as the monks got off their knees, and began walking toward him. He was locked in place as they approached.

The wraiths had no color to their eyes or faces, the rest of their bodies hidden beneath ashen-colored robes. When they reached him, they continued walking as if he weren't there. He and Lucky waited as the monks passed through them, his skin reacting as if touched by a cold cloud. Lucky also felt it because he sat down and whimpered.

Once the wraiths had passed, they disappeared, though the organ continued to play and Jean Pierre could still hear the monks chanting. The blue light moved above them, dancing to the supernatural music. Grabbing Lucky's collar, he gave it a yank.

"Let's get the hell out of here!"

Lucky beat Jean Pierre to the door, but turned to make sure he was behind him before exiting the building and reentering the storm. As they raced down the stairs, Jean Pierre slipped and fell. When Lucky licked his face, he put an arm around his neck and leveraged himself out of the mud.

"I wish you could talk, big boy, cause no one's ever gonna believe me when I tell them what we just seen."

They weren't far from the administration building, the last place he'd seen Lilly. Father Domenic's body near the front door was a grim reminder of what had happened when he and Landry had confronted him in his room.

He'd long since lost his flashlight. Now, with rain falling in sheets, it would probably have done little good anyway. Between flashes of lightning, he saw something he recognized. One of Lilly's flip flops. Picking it up, he put it under Lucky's nose.

"I know you ain't no bloodhound. Can you take a whiff of this and tell me which way Lilly went?"

Labs are intelligent animals, and Jean Pierre often thought Lucky could understand every word he said. When the chocolate dog barked and started away from the administration building, he had to scramble to stay with him.

Water had begun rising rapidly, now well over Jean Pierre's ankles. With visibility almost nonexistent, he tried not to lose sight of the running dog. Though he wished he had his cowboy hat to shield his eyes from the rain, he realized he wouldn't have kept it long in the wind now blowing at gale force.

At least the tempest was at his back as Lucky stopped. In front of them was the faint outline of Celebration Fountain. Both he and Lucky also saw something else. Lilly was sitting on the ledge, under the overhang and out of the rain. Wyatt's cat was in her lap.

"Lilly, is that you?" he yelled.

He didn't wait for her answer, joining her beneath the shelter. Lilly hugged him as if grasping for a life jacket when he sat beside her. The wind was blowing so hard they had to shout to hear each other.

"Oh my God! We're going to die."

Lucky jumped up beside them, touching noses with Kisses.

"You probably right about that, Miss Lilly. This ledge ain't gonna be high enough out of the water when the surge comes up over the berm."

"How much longer?" she asked.

He touched her hand and said, "Any minute now. Don't cry, Miss Lilly."

"It's just not fair."

"Life ain't always fair. Usually just the opposite."

"You're not frightened?"

"No use being scared. Won't help us none now."

"Then we're going to die."

"Maybe not. Somethin' will come along."

She was shouting when she said, "How do you know?"

"Gotta have faith," he said.

They were clutching each other tightly when

302

something thudded against the fountain.

"What is it?" Lilly asked.

Jean Pierre pulled loose from her grasp and crawled to the other side of the fountain where a large object was banging against the wall in the wind.

"What is it?" she shouted.

"Our somethin'. Hurry before it blows away."

Jean Pierre and Lucky were already in Quinn's airboat when she crawled to the other side of the fountain, Kisses in her arms.

"Where did it come from?"

"Don't have a clue," he said, grabbing her hand.

"Does the motor work?"

"Don't matter. We got no place to go. We just need someplace to stay afloat, and this is it."

"It's half full of water."

"And gonna sink unless we do somethin' about it," he said, tossing her a bucket. "Now stop yapping and start bailin'."

※

The inside of the survival pod was an engineering marvel, bunk beds rimming the perimeter with enough room for thirty people. There was also running water, a bathroom, and even a kitchen with a well-stocked larder. After the celebration, I claimed one of the beds, laid back and almost closed my eyes.

Two guest chefs, keeping me from nodding off, got into a disagreement about who would prepare the first meal. Professor Quinn got things under control, proposing a contest to see which one could prepare the best dish from the ingredients available. The resultant game kept everyone occupied during the first few hours of our stay in the pod.

The fury of the storm was muted by the capsule's thick walls, though very much on everyone's mind. I'd already noticed at least two people were missing.

"Did Lilly decide to go home after all?" I asked Brother Bruce when he passed my bed.

He shook his head. "She insisted on coming with us.

She got separated from the others and never made it to the pod."

Landry was standing near. "We found your cat. Miss Lilly, she stay with her while Jean Pierre and me deal with Père abbé."

"You found Kisses? Where?"

"Votre chambre."

"My bungalow?"

"Yes. Miss Lilly she say we take it with us. They stay downstairs for Jean Pierre and me. When we come back, she gone, her."

"You couldn't find them?"

"We tink she come here. When Jean Pierre see she ain't, he leave and go lookin' to find her."

"Now I do feel guilty," I said.

"Sorry, mon," he said.

He'd already walked away when I realized I'd been so worried about Kisses, I'd forgotten to ask him about the rougarous. It didn't seem to matter. We were all stuck in the pod until the hurricane passed. I'd have plenty of opportunities then.

Professor Quinn finally finished helping the quarreling chefs in the kitchen. When he and Sierra joined me, I shook his hand.

"You saved my life, and I thank you."

Sierra was beaming when she hugged him. "He's my new knight in shining armor. I'm never going to call you an old fart again."

"Likely story," Professor Quinn said, shrugging off her affection.

"We thought you'd be in Mississippi. What possessed you to return?"

"I couldn't stop worrying about my hard-headed assistant. Once Chuckie and King Tut were safe with friends, I turned around. I had to launch the boat north of Delacroix. The conditions had grown so terrible, I didn't think I was going to make it."

"We're glad you did," I said.

Professor Quinn grew reflective, listening to the

muffled sounds of the storm.

"It feels safe and secure inside this pod even though it isn't totally soundproof. I think the hurricane has stalled again."

"How long will it last?" Sierra asked.

"Until it dumps two feet of rain on us. Could be twenty-four hours or more."

His prediction proved accurate. For the rest of the night and much of the next day, the storm continued with an intensity that would have frightened me to death, in some place other than the pod. Sometime during the night, Landry returned with Mama Malaika. When she stood beside the bed, I realized how tall she was, fully six feet, looking regal in her African-print dress.

"Let me see your back," she said, pulling up my shirt. "Landry, get me a damp rag."

After cleaning the wound imparted by the rougarou, she put iodine from a first aid kit on it.

"Thanks," I said. "I was trying to forget about it, though without much success."

"Your rougarou will plague you no longer. Agwe has sent him back to hell," she said.

"How do you know?"

"I know," she said.

"Your dagger bought me enough time to get a head start. Too bad I didn't kill him then."

"Thank you, mon for saving Mama and Sierra," Landry said.

I had to smile. "I'll probably see it in my nightmares the rest of my life. What about Dunwoody and the others?"

Landry gave me a thumbs up. "Jean Pierre and me put them to sleep and then packed them away in coffins, 'cept for Père abbé. He dead."

"Father Domenic is dead?"

Landry grinned. "Another one of Mama's daggers, but mine found his heart. Brother Bruce nail the others up in coffins. If the storm don't carry them into the Gulf, the boxes will be safe till it pass."

The beds were comfortable, but there was too much noise and light to get any sleep. Worried about Lilly, Jean Pierre, and Kisses, I probably wouldn't have slept well at any rate. What seemed like many hours later, Brother Bruce peered out the porthole in the front door. Hurricane Aquirre had passed, and he opened up the pod to blazing sun we hadn't seen in several days.

Unlike the past celebration, we went into the sunshine in sobered anticipation. Brother Bruce ran immediately to the monastery to see what was left. Sierra noticed the blue funk I was in and put her hand on my shoulder.

"Why are you so sad?"

"Three words. Lilly, Jean Pierre, and Kisses."

"That's four," she said.

"Whatever. You know what I mean."

Except for broken windows, damaged tile, ruined paint and stucco, the monastery had survived the hurricane. Not so the once-manicured grounds. When the surge breached the berm, it brought with it mounds of brush, broken trees, and seaweed. The speed of the incoming surge had also uprooted acres of grass and had left muddy bare spots on the expansive lawn.

The earth was spongy, but the auxiliary pumps had done their jobs. Most of the water on our side of the berm was gone. The other side wasn't so lucky, standing water still reaching almost to the top.

The waterfowl had somehow survived, hundreds, maybe thousands of ducks and geese feasting on the vegetation cut loose by the hurricane. Several pelicans were circling to land. Above, high in the clear blue sky, a pair of snowy egrets winged toward a row of trees protruding from the water.

Mention of Jean Pierre had returned me to my lousy mood, and it didn't change as Brother Bruce came running back from the monastery, a smile on his face.

"The coffins are safe," he said, out of breath.

"Did you see Lilly or Jean Pierre?"

"No," he said, shaking his head.

Professor Quinn joined us. "We need to look for them. We'll form several groups and cover every inch of the monastery grounds. Maybe they're still alive."

The Professor's take charge attitude quickly revived my spirits. Landry knocked them back down a bit.

"Jean Pierre, he a brave man, him," he said. "Mama and Jomo go to check on our people. I stay and help you look for him and Miss Lilly."

What stucco remained on the walls of the buildings was smeared with mud. There was also lots of water damage on the ground-floor buildings and bungalows. We found the body of Father Domenic near the main doorway of the monastery. Though his eyes were open, he looked at peace as he clutched the dagger in his heart. Brother Bruce threw a tarp over his body, crossed himself and said a prayer.

We'd soon checked out almost every office, storehouse, and bungalow without a trace of Lilly and Jean Pierre. When we opened the door of Lilly's bungalow, her Indian headdress floated across my shoes. Landry, Sierra, and Professor Quinn looked at me as if I were crazy when I started running toward the far end of the island.

"Wyatt," Sierra called. "Where are you going?"

I didn't stop to answer, not slowing until I was past Celebration Fountain and had reached the Indian mounds. Lucky was the first to see me, bolting off the edifice to jump on me and lick my face.

"Jean Pierre," I called. "Lilly. Are you up there?"

The ancient, man-made hill was too muddy to climb, so I ran around it, and then to the one with the culvert on top. It was then I saw Professor Quinn's airboat, overturned and stuck in the mud. Landry and Sierra came running up behind me, Sierra grabbing my shoulder when she saw the airboat.

"Oh my God, Wyatt, do you think. . . ?"

I'd already thought about the possibility, but didn't want to believe Jean Pierre and Lilly were beneath the boat.

"Jean Pierre," I called again. "Lilly."

Lilly and Jean Pierre were asleep beneath the culvert, opening their eyes when they heard me yell. Landry was the first to see them poke their heads out. We all started yelling when they came out of the culvert and slid down the hill.

"Wyatt, I got your cat," Lilly said.

She didn't have to give Kisses to me as the happy cat bounded into my arms. Grabbing Lilly, I gave her a grateful hug as Jean Pierre, Sierra, and Lucky joined in. They weren't the only occupants of the mound. The two peacocks, oblivious to the antics of the crazy humans, were preening their feathers in the sunlight.

Brother Bruce appeared, out of breath as Landry, and Jean Pierre embraced.

"How the hell you still alive?"

"Shut, you shoulda known your daddy was too ornery to let a little ol' hurricane get the best of him."

Chapter Thirty Six

Tony and Tommy had continued canvassing the neighborhoods, checking for people too feeble, or too stubborn to evacuate the area. As the night dragged on, weather conditions progressively worsened, the two finally forced to seek protection from the storm.

The city had created a temporary shelter at the Louis Armstrong Park on the outskirts of the French Quarter. Exhausted, Tony sat in a wooden chair, the dog he'd rescued in his lap. The wind, blowing in continuous gusts, kept threatening to topple the building. It was late when a young black woman tapped his shoulder, awakening him.

"Sorry to wake you, mister. Someone told me you were with the police. Can you talk to my son? Tell him everything's okay."

Tony glanced at the little boy, crying as he clutched his mother's leg. He put his hand on the boy's shoulder."

"Hey buddy, what's your name?"

"Demetrius," he said.

"You look a little scared, Demetrius." Demetrius didn't answer as he buried his face deeper against his mother's leg. "Why don't you climb in my lap with my dog and me and I'll tell you a story."

The boy glanced at his mother. When she nodded, he held up his hands for Tony to pick him up. He was soon sitting in Tony's lap, the dog sitting in his.

"This your dog?" he asked.

"Guess so. I found him out in the storm."

"What's his name?"

"I just been calling him Patch because of the black patch around his eye. He's a little scared of the storm too."

"He don't seem scared."

"That's cause he's up here with me. I'm an N.O.P.D. cop, and the N.O.P.D. takes care of dogs and kids. You stick with me, and I'll protect you from the storm."

"You serious?" Demetrius asked.

"I said I'm a cop didn't I? You got my word on it," Tony said, winking at Demetrius' mother. "Try to get some sleep. I'll take care of him."

The storm continued, sometimes so strong he wished he had his own safety lap to sit in. Sometime during the night he fell asleep. When he awoke, sun was beaming through the windows. Patch and Demetrius were asleep in his arms, his legs numb.

The boy's mother appeared, smiling at Tony. "Thank you. I been so scared myself, I couldn't calm Demetrius."

Tony handed her the boy, and she walked away, her handful still asleep. He put the dog on the floor, stood up and stretched. After a glance around the building to make sure everyone was okay, he exited the front door and started walking down N. Rampart.

There were still clouds in the sky, but the storm had passed. Shingles, limbs, siding, and trash littered the neighborhood. Overhead power lines were down, draping all the way to the sidewalk in places. Windows were blown out, abandoned cars and standing water in the streets. Halfway to Bourbon Street, he heard someone calling him.

"Tony wait up. It's me."

It was Tommy, chasing after him down the street. When he turned around, he realized Patch was also following him. When he kneeled, the dog jumped into his arms.

"What up?" he said, waiting for Tommy to catch him.

"I was looking all over the place for you. Where you going in such a hurry?"

"Don't have a clue," he said. "I just felt like taking a walk."

"Where's your cell phone?"

Tony pulled the phone from his pocket and gave it a look.

"Batteries dead. Why?"

"The Chief called. He wants to talk to you."

"About what?"

"Don't know. He told me to ring him when I found you."

A person peddled past them on a bicycle, the rear wheel throwing up a rooster tail behind it. Tommy dialed a number on his phone. When someone answered, he handed it to Tony.

"Tony, it's Chief Wexler." When Tony didn't immediately respond, he said. "You there?"

"I'm here."

"Tony, thanks for helping out."

"You knew I would," Tony said.

"I still need you. We're so short-handed right now we can't even provide the most basic police services."

"Are you offering me my job back?"

"Didn't say that. When it comes to your old job, the Feds are in charge."

"Well then where are they?"

"What do you mean?"

"If the Feds are in control, why aren't they here?"

"Federal assistance doesn't happen that quickly."

"Your ass and you know it," Tony said. "If they're in charge, they should be here now, directing traffic, taking care of domestic disputes, and keeping the peace while they clean up this shit in the streets."

Chief Wexler didn't immediately answer. When he did, it was clear he didn't appreciate Tony's suggestion.

"The Feds don't work for the city. You know that."

"I'm torn here, Chief."

"About what?"

"More things than I can even consider right now. Where are you?"

"Houston. Why?"

"Why aren't you here? Why are you calling from Houston, asking me to do something you apparently think you're too good for? Why didn't you stay and help?"

"I don't think I like the tone of your voice."

"I don't give a damn what you like."

"Watch it, Tony. You're bordering on insubordination here."

"Good because I don't give a rat's ass. I'm done mopping up shit for your sorry ass. Don't ever call me again, for any reason."

Tony handed the phone back to Tommy who stared at him with disbelieving eyes.

"Geez!" was all Tommy could say.

"I haven't felt this good in years. I should have quit five years ago."

"What are you gonna do?" Tommy asked.

Tony reached down and rubbed Patch's ears. The door to a bar was ajar. He went inside, opened the refrigerator behind the counter and fished out two cans of Dixie. Tossing one to Tommy, he popped the top on the other for himself.

"You know, Tommy, sometimes you want something your whole life and never get it. Then when you least expect it, it appears out of nowhere and jumps into your arms."

"You talking about the dog?"

"Not just the dog, though he's part of it. I got someplace I want to go. Can you take me?"

Tommy saluted him. "I'd go with you to hell and back if you ask me, Lieutenant."

Tony smiled and slapped his shoulder. "Just across town," he said.

❦

Tony had Tommy take him down St. Charles Avenue, and then into the Garden District. Several of the centuries-old live oaks bordering the street were uprooted, laying across the streetcar tracks. They passed a bag lady pushing a shopping cart, seemingly oblivious to the effects of the hurricane. A brindle cat ran across the road in front of them as they turned onto Frenette's street. Tony didn't know what to expect when they reached his house.

What he didn't expect was what he saw when Tommy parked the patrol car by the side of the street. Frenette was sitting on the porch in his antique wheelchair. Latrice was in the front yard, cleaning storm debris. A man he didn't recognize was helping her.

"Mister Nicosia," Frenette said with a smile when he saw him approach. "You survived."

"Looks as though you did too. This is my partner Tommy."

"Pleased to meet you, Tommy," Frenette said. "Pull up a rocking chair and sit a spell. Latrice, it's Mister Nicosia."

Latrice smiled and waved, but continued raking leaves, limbs, shingles, and assorted rubbish.

Unlike before, Frenette had a can of Dixie in his hand instead of brandy, a beer cooler on the porch beside him.

"You run out of brandy?" Tony asked.

Frenette reached into the cooler, retrieved a couple of Dixies and tossed them to Tony and Tommy.

"Calvin likes beer better."

"Calvin?"

"He had fangs and claws the last time you saw him."

"That's Calvin?"

"It's him, and he's cured."

Tony took a long pull on the Dixie.

"Where'd you get the beer?"

"Calvin cleaned out a convenience store up the road. Have another," he said, tossing Tony a second can.

"Well congratulations. Sounds like your serum works just the way you thought it would."

"It works. Calvin, can you come here a minute?"

The man quickly joined them on the porch. He was tall, probably mid-forties with dark, thinning hair and a whopping Cajun smile. Patch had followed them to the porch, and was lying beside Tony. Calvin petted him.

"I'm Calvin," he said, shaking Tony and Tommy's hand. "Doc Frenette here saved my life."

"That's wonderful," Tony said.

"Not really. I'm eighty something, and look and feel about forty. I'm sure my wife's long dead and my kids probably don't even remember me."

"You might be surprised. At least you're alive and not some. . ."

"Monster?"

"You ain't no monster, Mr. Couvillion. I appreciate your feelings about losing your wife. Sometimes that's the way things happen."

Latrice stopped raking and joined them on the porch. Tapping Calvin's shoulder, she pointed to the front door.

"You have way too much information to handle all at once, Calvin. You'll have plenty of time to sort this mess out later. Lets go get those cookies out of the oven."

"Was the rougarou hunt on the island successful?" Frenette asked.

"Don't know yet. The battery on my cell phone needs a charge."

They laughed when he said, "Don't we all."

"Like Latrice said, no use worrying about it until tomorrow or the next day. Maybe even next week, from the looks of the water and wind damage."

"If they captured any, have them send them to me. Latrice and I had to work through a few rough spots with Calvin, but we know how to do it now."

"Goose Island must have taken a direct hit. If anyone's alive it'll be a miracle," Tony said.

Latrice and Calvin had returned from the kitchen with a pan of freshly baked cookies. Tommy didn't have to be asked if he wanted one.

"Miracles happen," Latrice said.

"Yes ma'am they do," Tony said as a passing tugboat on the river blew its whistle.

An hour later, Tommy pulled into Tony's driveway, broken limbs, and assorted debris littering the yard, his stockade fence lying on the ground.

"That was about the strangest meeting I think I ever attended," Tommy said.

"How so?"

"For a while there I thought you and the doc were serious about rougarous. You weren't, were you?"

"Hell, Tommy, I don't know what's real and what's not anymore. You gonna be okay?"

"Don't know. After hearing what you told the Chief it got me thinking."

"About what?"

"Maybe I need to quit too. Wexler did sort of sell us down the river."

"That he did. Don't matter none though. There's no such thing as a perfect boss. You keep your job. The city needs you."

"What about Ernie and Doc?"

"What about them?" Tony asked.

"You said you'd help them get a lawyer."

"I didn't forget. I been asking around. I located the meanest lawyer in the Big Easy, and he wants to file a class action lawsuit. You think the gang will go for it?"

"They'll go for anything you tell them to," Tommy said. "If you win the suit will you take your job back?"

"I'll keep that option open if you quit looking so down in the mouth."

"Can't help it. It just won't be the same without seeing your homely face every morning. The Chief told me who my new partner will be."

"That's great," Tony said.

"Maybe not, especially after all those nasty things you said about Marlon, and all."

"Marlon's your new partner?"

"Unless you come back."

"Ain't gonna happen," Tony said. "At least not anytime soon."

"Then what are you gonna do in the meantime?"

"Clean up this mess in the yard. Check for holes in my roof. After that, if my car's not totalled, me and Patch are gonna drive to Shreveport and join Lil."

"Then what?"

Tony strolled away, the dog at his heels. "For the first time in twenty-five years I don't have an answer. And you know what? I'm feeling pretty good about it."

Before he'd gone ten steps, Tommy said, "Betcha Miss Lil makes you get rid of that dog."

"Not this time. I'm keeping him."

There was a tear in the burly cop's eye when Tony walked back and gave him a hug.

"This just ain't right."

"Quit your blubbering. You know you'll be here next week for Lil's meatloaf. We're family, and that's never gonna change."

Epilog

Two months had elapsed since the hurricane struck New Orleans, tourists already beginning to return to the French Quarter. It wasn't quite dark yet, Bertram's regulars and various French Quarter crazies yet to make their nightly appearance.

"What you got?" Bertram said.

"A letter, Mr. Nosy Butt."

"From one of your girlfriends?"

"I've sworn off women."

"My ass! Ol' Bertram knows better than that. Who's it from?"

"Here," I said, handing him the letter. "You want to see it? Go ahead."

He waved it off, indignation in his voice when he spoke.

"No way, but you could read it out loud. Then we'd both know what it says, and you won't have to make up a lie about it."

I had to shake my head. "It's from Sierra, the young woman I met while working on the monastery case. She says she's loving her job with Professor Quinn, though they're having to commute from Chalmette since the hurricane destroyed their house."

"That ain't good," Bertram said.

"No, but the state is rebuilding it for them, bigger and

better than before. She says it's almost ready to move into."

"What else?"

"She broke up with her boyfriend Landry because of his roving eyes."

"Coonass, huh? Smart girl."

"She also filled me in on the torrid but short romance between my friends Lilly Bliss and Jean Pierre Saucier. They've both gone their separate ways."

"You mean Tony's friend, the cop down in Chalmette?"

"Yep."

"What's the deal with Tony? He get his job back?"

"Word on the street is he's done with the N.O.P.D. and never going back. He and Lil are together again, though I heard through the grapevine his new dog almost came between them."

"I didn't know Tony liked dogs," Bertram said.

"He does now and apparently, they're inseparable."

"What's Lil think about it?"

"She's coming around to the idea."

"What's the deal with the N.O.P.D.?"

"I'm surprised you didn't hear about his last conversation with Chief Wexler. Everyone else in town has."

"I heard about it all right. Sounds like Chief Wexler may soon be looking for a new job."

"Sometimes when you're rolling heads, it's hard to keep your own off the chopping block."

"Amen to that, bro," he said. "Now what's Tony gonna do?"

"Work with me, at least every now and then. I heard he helped a bounty hunter during the hurricane, and the man sent him a check for ten grand. Before you know it, he'll be wondering why he didn't quit the force years ago."

A five-man marching band passed on the street outside the door, the sound of their brass instruments shaking the antique mirror behind the bar, and bottles of liquor on the shelves. Bertram was looking at something behind me.

"I think you got someone here to see you," he said.

At the tap on my shoulder, I turned to see the movie producer Quinlan Moore.

"Hope I'm not disturbing anything important." he said.

"Nothing but a slow summer evening in Bertram's bar. Mr. Moore, this is Bertram Picou"

Moore smiled when he shook Bertram's hand. "Ah yes. There are talent agencies in L.A. and New York that could learn a thing or two from you."

"Cajun 101," Bertram said.

"Can I buy you a drink?" I asked.

"Are you drinking again?"

"Just lemonade. What'll you have?"

"Vodka, with a little water and ice."

"You look good. Guess Dr. Frenette's cure worked."

"He saved my life, and Wyatt, so did you. I'm eternally grateful."

"I didn't exactly do it for free. You paid me handsomely."

"And worth every penny of it. The final report you sent me was informative and professional."

"I couldn't have done it without a lot of help."

"It's unconscionable the medical community shunned Dr. Frenette all those years. I wish there was some way to repay him."

He smiled when I said, "A biopic of his life maybe?"

"Not a bad idea."

After pulling up a stool, he became thoughtful as he sipped his vodka. When two tourists walked in off the street, Bertram hurried to their table to wait on them.

"You okay?" I asked.

"You relieved my fears about the monastery. I still have unanswered questions. Maybe you can help."

"Like Bertram would say, axe me."

He smiled for the first time. "I've heard several versions. What's the real story on Father Domenic and Brother Bruno."

"The Father Domenic we knew was actually someone else, his real name Byron Perkins. He was doing time in the New Orleans' jail when Katrina struck."

"He escaped during Katrina?"

"He didn't have to. The jailers opened the doors and let everyone out."

"How in the world did he find his way to the monastery?"

"He was the nephew of the real Father Domenic. They'd apparently corresponded."

"You think he killed his uncle?"

"All the monks were old and had scattered to wherever they'd originally come from. Father Domenic was the last of the order that had decided to disband. Byron Perkins might have killed him, or he could have perished in the hurricane. We're never going to know."

"So Byron Perkins assumed his identity."

"And apparently recruited monks and workers from people he'd known in jail. Not so different than the Tracists' earliest beginnings."

"Is that where Brother Bruno came from?"

"We could find nothing about Brother Bruno. He just appeared from thin air, as they say."

"Interesting," Moore said.

"Another drink?" I said.

"I'd rather take a walk. Join me?"

"Why not?"

"Let's go to Jackson Square," he said.

"Is your movie still filming there?"

"Put it in the can a month ago. Hopefully, everything's back to normal."

Early evening in New Orleans was sultry, and Moore wiped his forehead with a handkerchief. Knowledgeable tourists tend to avoid the Big Easy, along with its oppressive heat and humidity, during July and August. Throngs of tourists watching a white-faced mime juggling three red balls beneath a street light didn't seem to care.

"What about Stormie?" I asked.

"Cured, like me. Still ornery as ever. She's helping me

raise money to restore the monastery, though it doesn't need much. Brother Bruce is the new Abbott. They talked Brother Degas into returning to the island and retiring there. Who knows? Maybe even Brother Italo will return."

"The place was gorgeous," I said. "But. . ."

"But what?"

"The entire time I was there I thought I was in southern California."

Moore laughed. "Then our architects were doing their job. What's your suggestion?"

"Make it look like Louisiana this time."

Moore nodded. "Perhaps you're right. I'll think about it."

"You aren't here to talk about the monastery, are you?" I asked.

"Not actually. You know Lilly Bloom."

"How is she?"

"I hired her to write a French Quarter, werewolf spec script based on my book *Blood Horror.*"

"I didn't know it takes place in New Orleans."

"It doesn't, but Miss Bliss modified it to make it work."

"She's already written the screenplay?"

"Yes and it's good, though it needs a little something to make it great."

"Like what?"

"You wouldn't happen to know anything about voodoo, would you?"

"It was my turn to grin when I said, "I know an authentic voodoo mambo that does, but she's not cheap."

"Neither am I," he said, patting my shoulder. "I originally hired you because of your knowledge of ghosts and the paranormal. You haven't proven me wrong. Will you come aboard as a consultant? I'll pay you handsomely."

"I know nothing about making movies."

"You didn't know anything about being a lawyer until you passed the bar and defended your first client. You didn't know anything about being a private investigator before you became one. What's the difference?"

"Nothing, I guess."

He grinned. "If Bertram negotiates your fee, you'll probably make more than you've made in your last ten cases. You game?"

"Sure," I said.

"Good. I'll give Bertram a call and settle your fee. There's a part in the movie for him."

"That I can't wait to see," I said.

"He's not the only one. I'm casting Stormy, though she may have to play second fiddle to a younger actress. I might even have a small part for you."

"Save it for a hungry actor," I said. "I'm not interested."

Quinlan grinned again. "You'll come around. Meantime, Lilly Bliss will contact you. I want you to introduce her to your voodoo mambo and then work directly with her in bringing the script to perfection. Can you handle it?"

"I'll do my best," I said.

Quinlan Moore tapped my shoulder and smiled. "Happy to have you on board. Now I must return to L.A. See you soon," he said, raising a hand to hail a taxi.

After watching the cab disappear up Decatur, I walked down the hill to the river. The Moonwalk was deserted, too late for older tourists and too early for the influx of late-night party people.

Unlike the Moonwalk, the river was alive with activity, running lights of boats and barges creating a spectral portrait painted on a watery canvas. The dying whistle of a passing oiler sounded more melancholy than rain dripping from a French Quarter balcony as I stared over the water.

With the sound of a jazz band wafting from the French Quarter behind me, I sat on the bank of the river, watching the sunset, listening to ship's horns, and letting the moment engulf me.

End

About the Author

ERIC WILDER is the author of *Big Easy*, as well as *City of Spirits*, *Ghost of a Chance*, *A Gathering of Diamonds*, *Murder Etouffee*, *Morning Mist of Blood*, and *Prairie Sunset—of Love and Magic*, among other books and short stories. He lives in Oklahoma, about a mile from historical Route 66, with his wife Marilyn, four dogs and two cats.

CPSIA information can be obtained at www.ICGtesting.com
Printed in the USA
LVOW11s2000190216

475863LV00001B/314/P